24: **ROGUE**

Also available from Titan Books:

24: Deadline by James Swallow

ROGUE

David Mack

TITAN BOOKS

Print edition ISBN: 9781783296453
E-book edition ISBN: 9781783296460

Published by Titan Books
A division of Titan Publishing Group Ltd.
144 Southwark Street, London SE1 0UP

First edition September 2015
10 9 8 7 6 5 4 3 2 1

A CIP catalogue record for this title is available from the British Library.

Printed and bound by CPI Group (UK) Ltd, Croydon, CR0 4YY.

For Marco, who put my name in the hat

CHRONOLOGICAL NOTE

The following events occur one year, seven months, and twenty-three days after Jack Bauer was forced into exile and left the United States (*24: Deadline*). All times are East Africa Time.

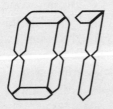

08:00 P.M. - 09:00 P.M.

The Gulf of Aden — 11°01'23.8" N, 44°57'04.4" E
Approximately 40 Miles North of Berbera, Somalia

The skiff's prow cleaved through black waves. Salt water sprayed Osman Xasan Muhamad's face as the narrow boat slammed into a trench between crests, kicking cold froth over its gunwales. At his back were two more skiffs loaded with armed and desperate men. Behind them hovered the waxing half disk of the moon, low and languid in its descent toward the western shore. Far ahead, lightning danced between the sea and the edge of a storm cloud.

He looked back toward Sadiq Khalif Fárah, his second-in-command, who manned the lead skiff's outboard engine. "Faster! We're going to miss them!"

"This is as fast as it goes." Sadiq held the boat's rudder in one hand and a digital compass in the other. He hollered back over the spluttering of the engine, "We should be close!"

As Osman peered into a darkness with no horizon, the fear

of a missed deadline set his guts churning. "I don't see them. They must be running dark." Another spurt of water doused his face and left him spitting brine. "If we miss the rendezvous—"

"We won't."

Osman wondered if Sadiq would be so calm if he were the one who would have to answer for their failure should the freighter slip away. He tightened his grip on his AK-47 and strained to pierce the deepening gloom of night ahead of the speeding skiff.

Nothing but shadows pitching and rolling against other shadows.

All that Osman had, and all he hoped to have, depended on this mission. Raiding the freighter was a once-in-a-lifetime opportunity. Beyond the outrageous ransom he and his men had been promised for delivering its most valuable cargo, they each stood to earn a fortune from selling the rest of the ship's freight on the black market—not to mention the vast sums the ship itself would command from the right buyers. This score would free Osman from his life of piracy and fund his escape from Somalia—a journey for which he had longed his entire life.

Unfortunately, Sadiq appeared not to care about any of that. A sadist, he seemed born to live under the black flag. He needed money as badly as Osman and all the rest of their tribesmen, but that wasn't what drove him. Osman knew from the predatory gleam in Sadiq's eyes that he enjoyed being a pirate. An outlaw. A killer.

By tomorrow we'll be done, Osman promised himself. *After that, I will never have to see him again. He will be free to walk his path, and I will walk mine—far from here.*

He squinted against a stinging spray over the prow, wiped his eyes, and struggled to see anything ahead except darkness. Then he found what he sought—a pale red dot of light. Staccato blinks in Morse code, the prearranged signal from their contact on the freighter.

"I see them! Shift heading, north-northeast."

The skiff rolled and bobbed with nauseating swiftness as Sadiq adjusted its course toward the signal light. Osman fought back the urge to retch—he had always hated water travel—and watched the blinking crimson dot until he was sure he had seen the entire message.

"Their course is steady. Speed, ten knots. We're clear for an aft approach."

"Got it." Sadiq plowed the skiff through another frothy crest of water, right on target. Osman relayed the information to the other skiffs with his own red signal light. Then he tucked the miniature beacon back into a deep pocket on the leg of his cargo pants and faced the rest of the men in his and Sadiq's skiff. "As soon as we reach the main deck, you all know what to do?"

"I lead the search belowdecks," said Ashkir.

Osman pointed at another man. "Dubad? Where do you go?"

"My men and I help you secure the pilothouse and radio room."

"Good." Osman trained his keen eyes on the group's hothead, Feysal. "You?"

Sullen and brimming with half-muzzled violence, the youth muttered, "I hold the prisoners on the forecastle."

"*Prisoners,* Feysal. *Not* corpses. Remember that." He looked at his last henchman, Yusuf. "You need to clear the engine room as fast as possible."

Yusuf ejected the magazine of his AK-47, blew a speck of beach sand off it, then slapped it back into his rifle. "I know what to do."

"Everyone remember the plan, and by dawn we'll all be rich men." It was not an empty promise. Osman had every reason to believe that this mission would prove as lucrative for his men as it would for him and Sadiq. That had been a key factor in his decision to accept such a dangerous operation against so infamous an adversary. He had come to pay the ransom on his freedom and take back control of his own life.

Another series of red flashes from the target. The way was ready, the approach clear. Despite the cover of night, Osman began to discern the shape of the freighter slicing across the gulf ahead of him and his men. He swallowed his fears, mustered a brave smile, and looked back at Sadiq. "It's time. Take us in, and stay out of their wake."

• • •

Unarmed, his back to the *Barataria*'s forecastle bulwark, Jack Bauer suppressed years of well-honed combat reflexes and let Callum Trent seize the collar of his shirt, when all he wanted to do was break the man's neck and dump his limp body overboard.

"I can't figure you out, Conway," the gunrunner said. Trent knew Jack only by his alias, Tom Conway, a name Jack had dredged up from an old mission profile and adopted as his own.

It took all of Jack's vast experience at deception to project an air of innocent alarm, and even more concentration to fake a Belfast accent. "What do you mean, Mr. Trent?"

"I mean, I don't get what you're doing here. You had a good thing going as a fixer for the IRA. So what're you doing on this rust bucket, pushing lead from port to port?"

Jack knew enough about the real Conway's troubles to pass them off as his own. "Times change. So do the people in charge. When my friends dropped out, I knew it was time to go."

"The way I hear it, McPherson didn't give you much choice."

"As I said—it was time to go."

It seemed Trent's misgivings had been set to rest. He let go of Jack's shirt and stroked his bushy horseshoe mustache. Then he shook his head. "Here's what bothers me, Conway. You were Belfast's bogeyman for years. Nobody agreed what you looked like. There were no photos of you, no arrest records, no fingerprints. You were a ghost. Now you're swabbing decks for Karl Rask. Why come out of the shadows for scut work?"

"You really need me to say it? I lost everything when things went bad in Paris."

Trent nodded. "Yes, the death of Seamus must have been quite a setback."

"You can't imagine." Jack was gambling his life on the fact that only a handful of people in the entire world knew the real Tom Conway had been assassinated after an undercover agent took out one of the Irish Republican Army's senior leaders, a merciless terrorist named Seamus O'Rourke. Both killings had been part of a clandestine mission Jack secretly set in motion several months earlier. As far as he could tell, no one yet realized he had been the source of the intelligence that led to O'Rourke's and Conway's respective downfalls. Fortunately, there were enough similarities between Conway's story and Jack's that he found it easy to steal.

"I can't go home. Not for a while, at any rate. For now, I need to make new friends."

"You want friends, you've come to the wrong place."

Jack sensed Trent would never respect anyone who didn't come at him from a position of strength. He changed his rhetorical tactics to keep the man off balance. "You're right. I never had much use for friends, either. What I need are new business relationships. New connections."

"A fixer without connections isn't much use to anyone."

"Seamus wasn't my only ally. I'm lying low—not down for the count."

"Meaning what? You think you have something I want?"

"You? I couldn't say. But your employer? Aye. Maybe I do."

Trent's eyes narrowed. "I doubt you have anything Mr. Rask needs."

"Maybe that should be for him to decide."

Derision put a smug smile on Trent's face. "You don't talk to Rask unless I say so. If you think you have something he wants, you have to convince *me* first."

There it was—the opportunity for which Jack had wrangled his way aboard this massive ark of arms and ammunition. The chance to put himself within striking distance of the inner circle of Karl Rask, one of the world's most elusive and notorious smugglers and dealers of arms great and small. The man could procure seemingly anything for anyone, anywhere. He had his hands in everything from small arms to field artillery, from fighter jets to cluster bombs.

"What if I told you I could get my hands on undocumented MIRV warheads?"

"Rask already has half a dozen waiting for buyers."

Jack masked his frustration with a grin. "Or the new MI6 ciphers?"

"We get weekly updates from our own source at Vauxhall Cross."

It was like trying to bluff someone holding four aces. "How about six vials of Russian smallpox virus, weaponized and ready for deployment?"

That cocked Trent's eyebrow. "Interesting. Where, when, and how much?"

"Odessa, four weeks from now. Twenty million, American."

"Tempting. Tell me again—why would we need *you*?"

"Introductions. And directions—Odessa's a big city."

Trent seemed almost amenable to the idea. Then his stare hardened. "I guess what really bothers me is that I've heard more than one person tell me Conway's dead." He shot an accusatory look at Jack. "Got his brains painted across the back of an elevator in Madrid."

Jack chuckled, as if at an old joke. "Good. That means the money I spent spreading that rumor wasn't wasted." A faux-humble shrug. "As the saying goes, 'The greatest trick the devil ever pulled was convincing the world he didn't exist.'"

"You have an answer for everything, don't you?"

"No. You just keep asking questions I can answer with the truth."

Trent relaxed his guard—not by much, just enough that Jack sensed his interrogation was either over or at least on hold. The lean, thirtyish gunrunner looked out over the bulwark into the darkness ahead of the freighter, which plowed on a steady course toward its next port of call in Mumbai, India. "I don't want you to think your experience and your connections aren't valued or respected, Conway. But we have to be cautious."

"I understand. Hell, that's what led to Seamus's undoing. He let himself get too close to what was happening on the ground. It got him a bullet in the head."

"Precisely." The ghost of a sly notion animated Trent's weathered features. "Think you can talk your Odessa contact down to fifteen million for the smallpox?"

"Maybe. But they'll need to know I have the cash on hand when I arrive."

"That can be arranged, but I'll have to go with you to the meeting."

"Naturally."

Trent took a pack of Gauloises from his pants pocket, shook one cigarette loose, tucked it into his mouth, and lit it with a stainless steel Zippo. After a long drag that flared the tip of the cancer stick cherry red, he extended the pack toward Jack, who refused with a casual wave. Shrugging, Trent tucked the blue box of pungent French lung darts back into his pocket. "I thought Gauloises were your favorites."

"I quit after I went underground. Changed my habits to stay off the radar."

"Very smart." Trent put away his lighter—and came up with a loaded Beretta, which he pointed at Jack's face. "Conway *never* smoked. He was born with asthma." He backed up a few steps to keep his pistol out of Jack's reach. "Now, then. Why don't you put your hands on your head, kneel on the deck, and tell me who you really are?"

With his lie unraveled, Jack folded his hands atop his head and sank to his knees. "It's a long story."

Trent leaned against the forecastle bulwark and steadied his aim. "That's all right. We have plenty of time to sort out the details. So let's start with your name."

What did he have left to lose? He dropped the accent. "My name is Jack Bauer."

• • •

A mouthful of harsh chemical aftertaste told Simon Dedrick, the ship's third mate, that he had smoked his cigarette down to the filter. He tapped its last crown of ash over the aft bulwark, then flicked the smoldering filter into the night, condemning it to oblivion in the sea.

Two quick, dim red flashes from astern. The pirates were close and ready to board.

He released the accommodation ladder on the *Barataria*'s aft starboard quarter. It fell with a shriek of rusted metal, loud and piercing enough to rouse the dead. Dedrick cursed under his breath and fought to ease the ladder toward the froth surging against the freighter's waterline.

It had been hard enough getting out of the pilothouse and off the superstructure without drawing attention. Then he'd had to risk being spotted by anyone who might be on deck, in order to signal the pirates in the skiffs. He still couldn't see them, but he had glimpsed their Morse code response, and whether he was ready or not, it was time to do what needed to be done.

Another red flash from below. The pirates were approaching the ladder.

Dedrick lifted the radio from his belt and pressed the talk button. "Conn, this is Dedrick! Man overboard, port side! Cut the engines! All stop!"

The second mate, Johan Schupp, answered without delay. *"All stop!"*

Alarms sounded throughout the freighter, on the main deck and through the labyrinth of compartments below. The great thrumming of its engines slowed and went quiet.

Another barked order into the radio: "Give me lights and a rescue party at the port bow."

Members of the crew scrambled up from belowdecks and sprinted forward. From high atop the superstructure, the *Barataria*'s spotlights snapped on. Blinding beams sliced through the darkness and swept the water ahead of the ship and along its port side.

Dedrick leaned over the aft starboard bulwark and looked down the accommodation ladder. The men of the first skiff were already piling out and climbing toward him, assault rifles in hand. As the last man left their skiff, he set it adrift to make way for the next one.

Osman was the first to reach the main deck. He greeted Dedrick with a condescending light slap on his face. "Good boy. Just like we told you."

The other pirates skulked past them, stooped like old men as they hurried in different directions—some forward, some toward the superstructure's aft staircase. Dedrick struggled to keep his attention on Osman. "I did what you wanted. Now let my family go."

"They go free when we control the ship." He pointed a Glock semiautomatic pistol at Dedrick's gut. "Take us up to the radio room."

"Not until I know my family is safe." It had been forty-eight hours since accomplices of Osman's broke into Dedrick's home in Pretoria, South Africa, and taken hostage his wife, Elaine, and his daughter, Karla. At the time, he'd known he had no leverage for bargaining. Now that the last group of pirates was climbing the ladder and their skiff was floating away, they were committed—which meant they needed his cooperation or else they were all going to die. "Let them go now, and show me proof, or you won't get anywhere near the radio room."

Osman's eyes burned with resentment. He summoned one of his men with a whistle. "Sadiq. Show him his women."

It surprised Dedrick to see the young Somali thug pull a large smartphone from inside his vest. He couldn't imagine how impoverished Somalis could acquire such a device, much less get a service plan for it, but he put aside his questions when Elaine and Karla's faces appeared on the screen. They looked haggard, with eyes red from weeping, but they were undeniably alive.

"Simon? Is that you?"

"It's me, *liefling*. Don't worry, everything's going to be all right."

Osman covered the screen with his palm. "Enough."

"They walk. *Now*. Or we all die."

An angry sigh. Osman took the smartphone from his man and grumbled into its microphone, "Bassar, we're done with them. Let them go."

He turned the screen toward Dedrick, who watched, unable to breathe, as a masked man cut Elaine and Karla's bonds, then shooed them out their house's back door. Osman switched off the phone and tucked it into his pocket. "My man can still chase them down. Take us to the radio room, and he won't have to."

"This way."

Dedrick led Osman and six bedraggled pirates up the superstructure's rear stairs, to the aft entrance of the command suite. Below them, a dozen of their compatriots split into teams of three and prowled forward on the starboard side, all but unnoticed by the *Barataria*'s crew, who were gathered on the port side searching for a nonexistent man overboard.

Standing at the keypad beside the aft door, a small inner voice of courage urged Dedrick to enter the alarm code, to make at least an attempt at stopping the pirates. Then he pictured the pirates putting a bullet in his head, and he clung to the irrational hope that he might live through this calamity if only he cooperated. He entered the access code and unlocked the door.

"Thank you, Mr. Dedrick." Osman shouldered past him and pulled the door open. He flashed him a grin of stained, crooked teeth. "You've been most helpful."

Behind his ear, Dedrick heard the hammer of a pistol being cocked, and he knew his hopes of survival had been in vain. The crack of a gunshot was the last thing he heard as his world went black and washed away, just another flick of ash in the sea.

• • •

"You're making a mistake," Jack said.

Callum Trent was certain he held every advantage. He had the Beretta. He was standing, and Jack Bauer was on his knees, hands clasped on top of his head. So why was Bauer acting as if he were still the one in charge?

"Give me one good reason not to put a bullet in your brain."

"Because I'm not bluffing about being able to hook you up with Russian smallpox."

Suspicion gnawed at Trent. "Why would you do that? You're CTU."

"Ex-CTU. If you know my name, you know I'm a wanted man." He moved his hands from his head, then froze as Trent cocked the hammer on his pistol. "Living on the run takes money. I can't hold a regular job with half the world hunting me. This is all I have left."

Trent lined up his sights on the space between Bauer's eyebrows. "A minute ago, you tried to pass yourself off as Tom Conway. You're a bit short on credibility."

"My credibility will be the money I can help you earn. I *had* to lie about my name. I can't walk around telling people who I really am. I have too many bounties on my head."

What he was saying was plausible, but Trent's doubts ran too deep to be overcome so easily. "Maybe we should just put you up for auction, see who makes the highest bid."

"Advertising you have me would just get you killed."

Bauer was right, and Trent knew it. Neither the Russians nor the Americans took kindly to being extorted. Trying to pick their pockets for a bounty would only put Trent, his men, and the rest of Karl Rask's operation in the crosshairs of competing special forces operators.

He lowered his weapon just enough to signal that he was reconsidering his options. "All right. What am I supposed to do with you?"

"Hire me."

"I'll give you credit for audacity if nothing else. And how will I—?"

Alarms whooped from loudspeakers mounted on the superstructure and the cargo derrick in the middle of the main deck. The steady rumbling of the engines ground to a sudden halt. Searchlights mounted above the pilothouse snapped on and swept down the port side of the ship as members of the crew scrambled up from belowdecks and hurried forward, toward Trent and Bauer. Careful not to let Bauer use the distraction against him, Trent stole furtive looks at the unfolding chaos. "What the hell is going on?"

The captain's voice blared from one of the loudspeakers: *"Man overboard, port side!"*

Bauer looked as confused as Trent. "What're they talking about? Who's overboard?"

"Maybe they spotted someone adrift."

"I don't like it." Bauer tried to stand, then dropped back to his knees as Trent refreshed his aim. "It feels off. Who the hell would be adrift here?"

"Stranger things have happened." Trent was torn between curiosity about what was happening on the other side of the ship, and the nagging concern that Bauer might be right. "Let's just stay put and let the crew do their job. If it turns out to be—"

A faint crack of gunfire from the aft end of the ship turned both their heads.

Trent took his aim off Bauer and dropped to a crouch. "Did you hear that?"

Bauer nodded. "I need to check something." He motioned for Trent to follow him to the bulwark. Moving in tandem, they leaned over the side and looked aft. Bauer pointed toward the waterline. "Damn it! The ladder's down. We've been boarded."

Out of the shadows, Trent saw the dark shapes of men carrying assault weapons, a dozen of them, moving single file up the port side of the main deck. He and Bauer were outnumbered and outgunned. "Fall back," he whispered. They darted to cover on the forecastle, behind the gearboxes for the ship's anchors. Trent lifted his radio. "Shattuck! We're being boarded! Send a team to protect the shipment and get the rest of our men out of their racks, now!"

"Roger," replied his right-hand man. *"On our way."*

Bauer peeked through a gap in the gear assembly. "They'll be here any second. Do you have a backup piece?"

"You don't really think I'm handing you a loaded weapon?"

Frustration sharpened Bauer's whisper. "There's no time to argue! When they come up that ladder, it's gonna take *both* of us to hold them off."

"Then I regret to inform you that, no, I don't have a backup weapon."

"Tell me you at least have a spare magazine."

Trent bit down on his growing anger with Bauer. "I didn't expect to need it."

Bauer shook his head. "Great. Could this *get* any worse?"

Bursts of automatic gunfire ripped through the air. Fiery flashes from the muzzles of rifles lit up the shadows in the center of the main deck, revealing a second team of pirates, who had sneaked into position behind the ship's crew on the port side.

Trent frowned. "The number of hostiles just doubled. I'd say that qualifies as *worse*."

Six pirates moved toward the forecastle ladder. Bauer eyed the deck between himself and ship's bow; then he turned to Trent. "Do you trust me?"

"Not one bit."

"Too bad. On the count of three, make *them* duck for cover."

"Why? What are you going to do?"

"Everything I can to save your ass and your shipment." He

crouched and tensed. "One. Two. Three!"

Bauer leaped into motion. Trent sprang to his feet and emptied his Beretta at the squad of pirates. When his weapon clacked empty, Trent dropped back to cover behind the gear assembly. He caught a fleeting glimpse of Bauer's feet as they disappeared over the starboard bow.

I'm sure as hell not taking that way out, Trent decided. He cast aside his empty pistol and reached for his phone. He keyed the speed-dial code for Rask, who answered on the second ring.

"What is it, Cal?"

"We've been boarded. Somalis, I think. Don't know how many. We—"

A rifle's warm muzzle nudged his temple. Callused hands plucked his phone from his grasp. A pirate whose facial scars looked like Hell's highway map flung the phone overboard. He and five of his cohorts surrounded Trent.

The man spoke in thickly accented English. "On your knees. Hands on your head."

Forced to adopt the stance he had imposed on Jack Bauer only minutes earlier, Trent couldn't help but admire the cruel whimsy of life's little ironies.

• • •

Several short bursts from Sadiq's assault rifle reduced the *Barataria*'s radio room to sparking junk. White-hot phosphors spit from mangled banks of electronics, stinging Osman's face as he marched past the smoking mess. He keyed in the access code he had seen Dedrick use on the outer door. The magnetic bolt lock on the door to the pilothouse released with a buzz. He pulled the door open and stood aside to let Sadiq and his men charge inside, rifles braced.

Sadiq blasted out a side window with a single burst. "Nobody move! On the deck!"

The ship's officers did as they were told. Within seconds, the captain and his two senior officers were on their bellies, hands on their heads. The pirates searched their pockets and relieved the men of radios, keys, and cell phones. Sadiq took a .45-caliber

Colt semiautomatic from the captain and tucked the bulky pistol under his belt.

Osman was bewildered by the consoles covered in gauges and levers. Dials and knobs were crowded together, and despite his facility with spoken English, he found it difficult to make sense of the controls on large ships such as the *Barataria*.

Sadiq seemed to sense Osman's quiet dismay. "What's wrong?"

"Nothing. I just—" Gunfire from the main deck cut him off. He rushed forward and looked out the window. Half a dozen men armed with sophisticated assault weapons and body armor had emerged from belowdecks and were engaging the teams Osman had sent to secure the crew. He turned toward Sadiq and pointed aft, toward the door. "Make sure they don't come in behind us! And dump them overboard when you're done."

Moving in fast strides, Sadiq snapped orders on his way out the door. "Khaled! Samir! Stay here with Osman! Everyone else, with me!" He led the other gunmen from the lead skiff out of the pilothouse, out onto the superstructure.

Alone with the ship's senior officers and only two of his men, Osman decided not to take any chances. "Samir, bind them. Khaled, cover them while Samir ties their hands and feet."

His men worked quickly, trussing the white officers as if they were goats primed for the fire. As soon as Osman was sure the situation was under control, he returned to the window and crouched to look over its edge, careful not to make himself a target for any stray bursts that might come toward the superstructure.

Muzzle flashes blazed in the darkness as Sadiq and the rest of the first team rained bullets down on the gunrunners. Blood spattered across the main deck as the mercenaries fell. The metal decks and bulkheads of the superstructure rang with bright ricochets from the mercenaries' wild attempts to return fire at opponents they couldn't see.

From his vantage point in the pilothouse, Osman watched the mercs group themselves into a tight huddle between a ventilator block and the heavy-lift crane. It wasn't a bad position for a defensive stand, at least in the short term. It would protect them from getting snared in a cross fire, and it would bottleneck any incoming assaults.

But only if the people attacking them don't know any better.

Osman fished the radio from his pocket and thumbed the talk switch. "Ahmed? It's Osman. Do you hear me?"

The starboard-side team leader answered in a hoarse whisper. *"What do you want?"*

"Listen to me. The gunmen on the main deck. They took cover ahead of you, between the crane and the ventilator block. Do you still carry that stun grenade you found?"

"I understand. Hang on."

A few seconds later, Osman watched Ahmed lean around a corner and lob the grenade toward the crane. Next came a blinding flash and a deep boom. In the seconds of smoky confusion that followed, Ahmed and his team charged from cover and descended on the cornered mercenaries, firing on full automatic until they were sure the last of the gunrunners was dead.

"Good job, Ahmed. Main deck looks secure. Round up the prisoners as planned."

"Okay, Osman."

He turned toward Samir and Khaled and pointed at the captain. "Get him up." His men lifted the gaunt middle-aged white man off the deck and propped him up in front of Osman, who studied him with contempt. "What is your name?"

His accent was unmistakably German. "Captain Markus Rohde."

Osman aimed his pistol at the head of one of the junior officers lying on the deck. "And who is in command of this ship, Mr. Rohde?"

The older man conceded Osman's point without argument. "You are."

"I am glad we understand each other." He kept his pistol trained on Rohde as he barked at his men, "Take them down to the main deck and put them with the others!"

Samir and Khaled ushered the ship's three officers out of the pilothouse at gunpoint and marched them down the outer stairs of the superstructure. Once they were gone, Osman looked out the windows and shuddered with anticipation of how rich he was going to be come daybreak.

By the time anyone knows this ship has been taken, I will be on the other side of the world, with a new name, a new life, and more money than I can ever spend.

• • •

Tightly wound bare copper wire bit into Trent's wrists. He resisted the urge to struggle against his bonds; doing so only forced the wire deeper into his flesh, and his palms were already sticky with his own half-dried blood. He and the crew of the *Barataria* sat in a tight cluster atop the forecastle, their backs to the bulwark. They all had been searched and stripped of weapons, radios, and phones. The pirates kept the weapons; the rest they'd pitched into the sea.

None of Trent's men, who had been separate from the ship's crew, survived the initial attack. Two pairs of pirates busied themselves heaving corpses overboard. Trent took a small measure of satisfaction from the fact that a few of the bodies being dumped were part of the pirates' contingent. *At least my men didn't go down without a fight.*

A lone pirate with an AK-47 slung behind his back climbed the port-side stairs from the main deck and joined the rest of his men. He shouted in Arabic at one of his comrades, who yelled curt answers in reply. Trent's Arabic was rusty, but he understood enough to realize the first man had asked whether the prisoners were secure, and the second man, the one with the dramatic facial scars, had assured him they were.

The one in command put himself in front of the ship's captain. "The ship is drifting."

Captain Rohde turned his weary gaze up at the pirate. "So?"

"Tell me which of your crew are qualified to drop the anchor."

Rohde let slip a derisive snort. "Are you stupid? You can't drop anchor here."

The second, scarred pirate reached for a pistol tucked into his waistband. "Why not?"

"Because anchors are meant to be used in water less than a hundred meters deep. We're in open ocean, you fools." He looked at the two pirates, who didn't seem to comprehend the simple words he was telling them. "There's nearly *fourteen hundred* meters of water beneath us. Drop an anchor here, and you'll just lose it to the sea."

They received his bad news with pained grimaces and rolling eyes. The pirate in charge struggled to rein in his temper. "How do we stop the boat from drifting?"

"Put me and my crew back at our posts. We can run the engines dead slow and set the rudder to hold our position against the current."

The leader refused with an adamant shake of his head. "No. You tell us how."

"I can't teach you twenty years of nautical experience in one chat at gunpoint."

Scarface pulled the pirate leader aside. The two Somalis traded angry whispers that Trent strained to hear. The leader didn't want to back down, but his second-in-command urged him to forget about the ship's drift. Scarface tapped the face of his battered wristwatch, the universal sign for *We're on a schedule.*

The leader frowned and breathed an angry sigh. He turned back toward Rohde. "These men around you. They are all of your crew, yes? Anyone missing?"

"No. All my men are accounted for."

An accusatory finger pointed at Trent. "Any more of *his* men?"

Rohde tried to play dumb. "What do you mean?"

"Rask's men."

Scarface tilted his head at the last of the bodies going over the side. "The gunrunners."

Sickening dread snaked through Trent's gut. There was no reason mere pirates should know Mr. Rask's name—and if they did, and knew who he was, they shouldn't have been brash enough to risk killing his employees or stealing his property. What was going on?

Scarface waved his gun at Trent as he told the leader, "We should kill this one, Osman."

"Not yet. We still need him." Osman squatted in front of Trent, drew the .45 from his belt, and pointed it between Trent's legs. "Now I ask you: Any more of *your* men aboard?"

"No. You just sent the last one down to Davy Jones's locker." Osman fixed his stare on Trent's eyes, as if searching for a glimmer of untruth. Trent kept his poker face slack and steady. *Technically, I told him the truth. Bauer's not one of my men—he only pretended to be.*

Apparently satisfied, Osman smirked and put away his pistol. "Tomorrow, I will be a rich man. Do what I tell you, and you will live to see my words come true. Cross me, and you will join the rest of your men."

Osman stood and issued a fast string of orders in Arabic. Trent caught that Scarface's name was Sadiq, and that he was to leave a team of six men to guard the prisoners and lead the rest of their team below to arm up from the ship's inventory. As soon as Osman finished giving orders, he descended the port stairs and stalked aft with a troop of four men close behind him.

Captain Rohde leaned a few inches closer to Trent and muttered while trying not to move his lips, "What are we going to do now?"

"Stay still, and be quiet," Trent whispered back, "until I tell you otherwise."

There was no reason for Trent to think that Bauer was his friend, but the renegade American agent was now the only hope he and the *Barataria*'s crew had of living through the night. Because regardless of Osman's promises, if these men conducted themselves the way most Somali pirates did, neither Trent nor the ship's crew could expect to see another dawn.

• • •

Jack swam below the surface, following the waterline of the *Barataria*. Every few strokes, he came up just enough to exhale and draw another breath, then submerged again and kept swimming. The ship had come to a near total halt in the water, but the current was pushing it backwards at a fraction of a knot. That had added some time and distance to the hundred-meter swim back to the accommodation ladder, which had been left down by the pirates.

He climbed onto the ladder's bottom platform, taking care

to move as quietly as he could. There was a lot of commotion up on deck, more than enough noise to muffle the drizzling of water running off his clothes, but he knew not to take unnecessary risks. He squeezed the excess water from his hair, then took off his linen shirt and wrung it until it ceased to give water. Pressing his palms against his legs, he forced most of the moisture from his pants.

His first step up the ladder produced a squishing noise from his sneaker.

Damn it.

He knew of no way to wring out Nikes. Mumbling profanities, he kicked off his low-tops and set them adrift. He regretted the loss of foot protection, but he couldn't risk the damage the waterlogged shoes would have done to his ability to move stealthily with speed. He peeled off his socks and cast them into the gulf, then started back up the ladder.

Barefoot, unarmed, and soaking wet, Jack padded up the steel steps. He dropped to a crouch as he neared the top. Pirates moved about the main deck in pairs or groups of three. Most of them were armed with AK-47 assault rifles, but several also carried semiautomatic pistols, and a few wore bandoliers festooned with grenades.

To his relief, they had posted no guards near the accommodation ladder. He guessed they hadn't considered the possibility that anyone other than them might use it to reach the main deck. He watched the nearest pair of pirates until they turned away and moved forward. Then he slipped onto the main deck and darted into the shadows along the superstructure. He checked the starboard side hatch. It was unlocked. He nudged it open and listened.

From below came echoing footsteps, shouting voices, bursts of rifle fire.

The pirates must be rounding up the engine room crew, Jack realized. *I can't risk moving belowdecks until they bring the engineers topside.*

He slipped through the door and eased it shut at his back. Taking the stairs with slow, exaggerated care, he climbed to Level 01, where his shared cabin was located. He paused at the door and checked through its window to make sure no one was lurking on the other side. Confident the corridor was clear, he turned the door's latch by slow degrees, then opened it just wide enough to slip inside and guide it to a soft close behind him.

Now it was time to move quickly. He jogged to his cabin and went directly for his rack. He lifted the mattress and its platform to get at his clean clothes, making sure to pull the darkest items he could find—black jeans, a dark gray T-shirt, black socks and underwear. He tossed them on the bunk beneath his, then stripped off his wet clothes and hid them under his mattress. *Can't have one of the pirates finding my wet clothes and sounding an alarm.*

In less than a minute, he was dressed in dry clothes. Recalling that his cabinmate, an Israeli engineer named Yiram, wore the same size shoes that he did, Jack checked under the man's mattress platform and found a spare pair of rubber-soled black work boots. He sat down and put them on, knotting the laces as quickly as he could.

There were just a few more things Jack needed.

He went back to the space beneath his own mattress, shoved aside his dirty laundry, and uncovered what had been his best friend for the last nineteen months: a nine-millimeter SIG Sauer P229. He kept a full 13-round magazine in the weapon and three spares loaded and ready. He pulled back the slide, chambered a round, then tucked the SIG in its holster and secured it on his right hip. He took his shoulder duffel from atop the bed and loaded it with the spare magazines, four boxes of jacketed subsonic hollow-point rounds designed to inflict maximum damage on soft targets, and the pistol's suppressor.

For good measure, he grabbed a leather fold packed with lock-picking tools—torsion wrenches, rakes, hooks, and assorted other tools of the trade—and tucked it into his back pocket. Last but not least, he retrieved a flat-black KA-BAR knife with a partially serrated edge and secured it, in its sheath, on his left hip.

That would be enough, he hoped, to get him belowdecks, where more serious armaments were stored in shipping containers bound for Karl Rask's various international clients. He slung his duffel behind his back, drew his SIG, and slipped into the corridor. The pirates had rounded up the ship's entire crew on the main deck.

Time to call in the cavalry. He crept upstairs toward the command level.

Jack suspected it was no accident the pirates had targeted this ship for hijacking, but he was determined to make sure it proved to be a mistake—one they wouldn't live to regret.

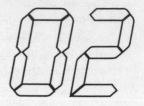

09:00 P.M. - 10:00 P.M.

Patience had never been one of Sadiq's virtues. Countless times he had heard Osman promise they would be rich men after they delivered the target to the client, and sold off the rest of the ship's cargo to the black market. Sadiq didn't want to wait that long. He wanted a fortune in his hand now, and he had a plan for how to get it.

His three most reliable men were behind him as he climbed back atop the forecastle to confront the last of the gunrunners. "You! What is your name?"

"None of your business."

Sadiq slammed the butt of his rifle onto the man's knee. He took great pleasure in hearing the arrogant Westerner howl in pain. "Your name."

A growl through gritted teeth. "Go to hell."

"You like to suffer?" Energized, Sadiq kicked the smug bastard in the gut, then in the ribs and the back. The toe of his boot slammed home, and he was sure he felt a few of the man's smaller ribs crack.

He was about to shift his target to the man's head when the ship's captain blurted out, "Trent! His name is Trent! Now, stop, before you kill him!"

So, the captain is the weak link. Good to know.

It annoyed Sadiq to be interrupted, but he knew there would be time for more such amusements later. He kneeled beside the gunrunner. "Where is the money, Mr. Trent?"

Trent gasped for breath and winced when he found it. "What money?"

"You think I am stupid, Mr. Trent? You sell weapons. Lots of them."

Disbelief scrunched Trent's features. "I just *deliver* weapons. My boss sells them, and he gets paid by wire transfers. There's no cash on board."

"You are lying! Gun merchants always carry cash!"

"Maybe in your dust heap of a country. In the modern world, orders and payments are made online. Money isn't my problem."

"It will be if I do not get paid."

Trent answered Sadiq's threat with a glum chortle. "You want cash, tough guy? I've got sixty-three dollars in my wallet. And you can take my credit cards if you want, but I gotta warn you, they're all maxed out."

Sadiq was tired of playing games. "If you never see money, explain Beirut." The immediate change of Trent's expression, from glib to grave, told Sadiq he had scored a hit. "Three men from Hamas boarded this ship, each carrying a briefcase. Each left empty-handed. What did they bring you, Mr. Trent? Love letters?"

"I don't know what you're talking about."

"Two weeks earlier. Izmir, Turkey. You welcomed a man from the Chechen rebellion. He, too, left your ship missing a briefcase he had carried aboard. Was he just forgetful?" Silence and a murderous stare from Trent. "Where is the money?"

"I sent it ashore at Suez."

"You did not make port at Suez. And no cargo has left your ship since Port Fuad."

A sneer. "If you know so much, why don't you know where the money is?" He studied Sadiq, sized him up. "You had someone spy on the ship. Or someone did. Maybe not you. But whoever it is, they don't have a man on board. Am I getting close, hotshot?"

"You do not ask questions. Tell me where the money is. Now."

"I don't feel like it."

Sadiq summoned his men with a snap of his fingers. He pointed at Trent. "Stand him up." As soon as his men had Trent on his feet, Sadiq punched the man in the groin. Trent doubled over. An upward jab of Sadiq's knee struck Trent's nose, releasing a spill of bright red blood. The other pirates pulled him upright just in time for Sadiq to backhand him. Sadiq drew his knife from its sheath and held its tip in front of Trent's left eye. "Do not make me do this."

"I'm not making you do anything. You're digging your own grave all by yourself."

Now Sadiq understood: Trent was a man who genuinely did not care for his own well being or survival. It had been either trained or beaten out of him. However it had been done, it had left him impervious to traditional means of persuasion. It became clear to Sadiq that if he wanted to find the gunrunners' money, he would have to exploit a softer target.

"Put him down."

His men pushed Trent back to the deck; then they followed Sadiq as he paced in front of the ship's crew, taking each man's measure with a steady eye. As he walked back the way he had come, he made his decision and pointed at the youngest-looking member of the crew, a Filipino who he guessed wasn't much older than eighteen or nineteen. "Him. Get him up. Put him over there, away from the others."

His men stood the youth by the starboard bulwark, near the anchor chain and hawsepipe. Sadiq waved his men to retreat behind him; then he stood facing the young man. "Your name?"

"Miguel. Miguel Blancaflor."

"What is your job on the ship, Miguel?"

"Cargo hand."

"And do you know where Mr. Trent keeps his money?"

"No."

"Then what good are you?" Sadiq hefted his rifle and fired a burst that blew young Miguel's head off, spattering the bulwark and the deck with blood, bone, and brain matter. The half-decapitated body slumped to the deck like a marionette severed from its strings.

Sadiq looked back at the rest of the crew. "Who is next?"

Captain Rohde lifted his hands. "Stop! Don't hurt my crew!"

Fed up with delays and excuses, Sadiq advanced on Rohde, jammed the barrel of his AK-47 against the captain's chest, and shouted, "Tell me where the money is!"

"Trent's stateroom. In a hidden safe, behind the painting of the Yankee clipper."

Now he was making progress. "Which cabin is his?"

"Level Three," Rohde said. "Forward port corner. It's the largest suite on the ship."

Sadiq pulled his radio from a pocket on his cargo pants and thumbed the transmitter button. "Hamal, this is Sadiq. Are you still on Level Three?"

"Yes."

"Go to the forward port stateroom. Is there a painting of a ship on the wall?"

"I will check." Several seconds passed before Hamal added, *"Yes."*

"Look behind it. Is there a safe?"

Another brief pause. *"Yes."*

"Good." Sadiq looked at Rohde. "What is the combination?"

"Only Mr. Trent knows."

Trent smiled. "Kill all the deckhands you want. I'm not giving you the combination."

"I won't need it." Sadiq walked away, heading aft.

From behind Sadiq, his trusted accomplice Samir asked, "What now?"

"First, we find this ship's machine room and raid it for tools. Then, we rip that safe out of the wall and cut its damn door off."

• • •

Footsteps thumped through the overhead, bringing Jack to a halt. He listened to the movements of the pirates. Running steps in the superstructure's interior stairwell overlapped into a manic beat. Jack retreated into an empty crew compartment and put his back to the wall.

Voices followed the patter of running feet. Jack caught snippets of broken English and Arabic, in between bits of what he guessed was Somali. Listening carefully with both hands tight on the grip of his SIG, he did his best to parse the non-English phrases he overheard.

"Need tools," a hoarse voice said. "Keep looking."

Random items clattered against the floor of the compartment across the corridor. Jack braced himself for a showdown while he listened to the pirates tossing the crew's living space. If they didn't find what they were looking for there, their next stop was likely to be the cabin where he was hiding. This wasn't where or when he had intended to face his enemy, but he knew from hard experience that a soldier had to deal with facts on the ground and fight the battle he was in, not the one he wanted to have. He drew a long, slow breath and concentrated on slowing his pulse. He became utterly still—ready to act, however and whenever necessary.

Static squalled from a radio in the corridor. A tinny voice broke through the noise. *"We found the machine shop,"* a nasal voice said in Arabic. *"Just off the engine room."*

"Good work," the hoarse-voiced man answered in Arabic. Then he barked some orders in Somali, and the hurried storm of running men raced back to the stairwell.

Jack kept the SIG raised and ready until the last footsteps faded away.

Since when do Somali pirates use military-grade radios?

He recalled various incidences of Somali piracy he had read about over the years. Most had seemed like low-tech, slapdash operations. If there was a signature feature to the majority of attacks by Somali pirates, it was amateurism. By contrast, these men were organized and well equipped. They had radios and solid firepower, and their tactics were decisive. *Almost like they've been coached.* He corrected himself: *No,* exactly *as if they were coached.*

Jack poked his head around the corner and scouted the corridor. It was clear. The pirates had used the starboard interior stairs, so he circled around to the port stairwell. He pressed his ear to the door. All sounded quiet on the other side. With care he turned the door's handle and eased it open. Without the thrumming of the ship's engines, the stairwell was so quiet that

Jack discerned the subtle buzz of the wall-mounted emergency floodlights recharging. He guided the door to a silent close behind him, then climbed the stairs with practiced stealth.

He turned the corner at the switchback with his SIG leading the way. Seeing no one on the next landing, he kept climbing. He checked the next corner and continued upward, always assuming the next turn might be a trap. In less than a minute he reached the top of the stairs, and he closed in on the door to the command suite. It was locked, but he had hacked its access codes weeks earlier, as a matter of routine tactical preparation. He hoped the pirates hadn't been savvy enough to change them.

As he entered the code, the keypad's feedback tones sounded disconcertingly loud in the tomblike quiet of the stairwell. The door's magnetic lock released with a final beep. Jack pulled the door open, but paused to listen for any signs of reaction from the suite beyond or the stairwell below. Both were quiet. He ducked through the door and shut it by hand to prevent its bolt from clacking as it passed over the lock plate.

To his left, at the end of a narrow passage, was the aft port door to the pilothouse. Directly ahead of him was the door to the radio room. Between them, halfway down the short corridor, was the door to the chart room.

Jack padded down the corridor and looked through the window of the pilothouse's door. There were three pirates inside, each armed with an AK-47 assault rifle. In addition, each man carried a different kind of pistol, and one of them wore a bandolier of grenades. Storming the pilothouse might be possible, but the odds of success would be slim.

He edged back down the passage to the radio room. Sending an SOS was his top priority. Bringing in reinforcements from Rask's organization would improve his odds against the pirates—and if Jack happened to be the one to summon that help and save Rask's shipment, it would go a long way toward establishing his bona fides with Rask, and facilitating his infiltration of the arms dealer's international empire of industrialized murder.

There was no window on the radio room's door. Jack pressed his ear against it. Hearing no activity on the other side, he nudged the door open as softly as he could. He saw no movement through the sliver, so he opened the door wider. There was no one in the radio room, and the reason why was immediately clear: The ship's communications suite had been destroyed.

Racks of sophisticated electronics had been reduced to splintered, bent metal, scorched plastic, and smoking circuits. An acrid stench of burnt metal filled the small compartment. Jack inspected each of the room's many pieces of gear, and he found they all had been riddled with bullets. So much damage had been done, he couldn't hope to cobble together enough working parts to make a new radio.

So much for calling in the cavalry.

He needed to keep moving and change his plan. Unless he could create enough of a ruckus to draw attention from other ships in the gulf, he would be on his own against the pirates.

It was fortunate, then, that he happened to be on a ship loaded from bow to stern with tons of the deadliest cargo known to man. Cargo he meant to put to good use.

He withdrew in careful steps from the radio room and returned to the port stairwell. As before, it was deathly quiet.

Jack braced his SIG with both hands and proceeded down the stairs, one flight and corner-check at a time. His next destination was Hold 3, the farthest-aft of the ship's cargo areas. From there, he could assess how thoroughly the pirates had already infested the cargo decks, while at the same time make his way forward to the hostages being held on the forecastle.

Putting stronger firepower in his own hands might be helpful—but arming the ship's hostage crew and unleashing them on the pirates would be far more effective.

• • •

"Faster! Just pull it out of the wall!" Sadiq stood at the back of the sprawling suite. Four of his men attacked the wall with a power saw, a hammer, a blowtorch, and a crowbar. Chunks of the bulkhead fell away or bent back as they dismantled the structural supports around the wall safe hidden inside Trent's stateroom.

The safe had been installed by professionals. A new structure had been welded to the stateroom's original starboard bulkhead to support and conceal the safe, since it would not have been possible to carve any usable space from the ship's sardine-packed superstructure. Industrial-strength welds held the safe in place. Even now, with five of its six sides exposed, the box looked impregnable.

A high-pitched shriek of stressed metal became a mournful groan. The safe fell free of the wall, and the four pirates tasked with its retrieval scrambled out of its way as it slammed to floor, filling the stateroom with a resounding boom. It tumbled like a heavy-metal die for a couple of feet, and then it rolled to a stop, door-side up in front of Sadiq.

"What are you waiting for? Get it open!"

He stood back and gave his men room. The safe was strong enough to thwart ordinary thieves using the kinds of portable gear commonly employed in clandestine heists on land. Like most safes, however, it was just a steel box, and the kinds of tools that were carried aboard most working merchant marine ships were more than enough to reduce it to scrap in under an hour—especially when there was no need to fear capture or interference.

Sparks flew and smoke choked the stateroom. Sadiq moved to a porthole along the forward bulkhead and cracked it open to let in some fresh air. The roar of the acetylene torch and the whine of the saw made it impossible to concentrate on anything other than enduring the onslaught of piercing noise that surrounded him. Then, after several minutes that had felt like forever, the cacophony subsided. Samir called out, "It's open, Sadiq!"

Sadiq hurried over to the safe and pushed past his men. The thick steel door had been melted and sliced off. A pool of molten metal had burned through the carpet, all the way down to the metal deck plate underneath. Taking care where he touched the floor, Sadiq kneeled in front of the open safe. Its interior was packed with riches.

He emptied the safe one greedy armful at a time and made a mental inventory of its contents as he went. There were stacks of American dollars and European euros, divided into thick bundles of large-denomination notes. Beneath them was a sheaf of negotiable bearer bonds, each one worth more than half a million dollars on the open market. The middle shelf of the safe was jammed with bricks of gold bullion and velvet pouches packed with uncut gemstones. It was more wealth than Sadiq had ever imagined laying hands on in his entire life.

But all he could see was what was missing. What was supposed to be there but wasn't.

I thought it would be here. He wanted to revel in his new riches, but all he could think about was having to confront Osman's criticism. *Now we have to do this the hard way.*

"Pack it up. We'll divide it when we get back to land." He headed for the door.

Samir stood next to the safe with a confused look on his face. "Where are you going?"

"I need to have a talk with Mr. Trent."

• • •

Slipping past the pirates on the third level of the superstructure, right below the command suite, proved easier than Jack had expected, thanks to the unholy ruckus they were raising in Trent's stateroom. The buzz, roar, and whine of power tools mingled with the chorus of shouting voices, which made it somewhat more difficult for him to figure out what they were saying, but he quickly determined they were focused on breaking into Trent's hidden safe.

Jack continued down the stairs, to the *Barataria*'s lower decks. The engine room and shaft alley were situated beneath the superstructure, but with the vessel adrift, a surreal hush had fallen over the cavernous spaces. Jack had grown accustomed to the engines' clamor masking his footfalls when he traversed the metal stairs. Now he had to concentrate to land on each step without making a sound. He kept his SIG steady and poised for action as he descended to the aft upper 'tween deck, which extended forward just past the superstructure.

As he expected, the pirates had left open the doors that led from the engine room to Hold 3's upper 'tween deck. The aft and center holds of the *Barataria* each had been fitted with two peripheral 'tween decks for carrying smaller containers and shrink-wrapped cargo pallets. The forward hold was subdivided into two full 'tween decks jammed with palletized cargo, and a lower hold reserved for military-grade jet fuel and bulk storage of mortar rounds and RPGs. Jack had a good idea what he would find, having scouted the ship's cargo days earlier to gauge the scope of Rask's business. He just hoped the pirates hadn't already taken the things he needed most.

Service lights cast limited pools of dim orange light and threw long shadows across the narrow 'tween decks, while the centers of the holds were crowded with steel shipping containers. The red, gray, orange, and blue boxes reached from the hold's pitch-dark bottom deck almost to the cover plates on the main deck, with barely any clearance above them. Stealing forward, Jack moved with care while he let his eyes adjust to the gloom.

Many of the cargo pallets had already been cut open and pilfered by the pirates, just as he had feared. A few of the larger crates also had been forced open, including one that he knew had been loaded with fragmentation grenades. He glanced inside the crate as he passed it. Only three of the dozen boxes had been taken, but he was certain more pirates would soon come to help themselves to the rest. He used his knife to break the seal on a new box, then stuffed two grenades into his shoulder bag.

Knife sheathed, he advanced behind his SIG, his eyes penetrating the shadows, keen for any sign of movement. He slipped behind a pallet loaded with upright tanks of acetylene and found a massive wooden crate tucked into a corner, covered with a gray tarp. He pulled off the heavy sheet of oiled canvas and cast it aside, then holstered his SIG and pulled out his lock-picking tools. It took him only a few seconds to open the crate's padlock. He lifted the lid and inspected the crate's contents.

Boxes within boxes, all nestled in dry straw. Logos and model numbers printed on the boxes' lids indicated they were packed with Heckler & Koch hardware. On the top were smaller boxes; some contained spare magazines. Others were boxes of accessories, such as cleaning kits, scopes, and straps. Jack pulled out the top layers of boxes to get a look at what was under them. The next layer was semiautomatic pistols. He began to fear this detour was a waste of time—until he saw the model numbers stenciled on the bottom stratum of boxes.

They were loaded with MP5SD-N submachine guns.

He moved the boxes of pistols out of the way, then lifted out one of the military-grade submachine guns. Its barrel was fitted with an integral stainless steel sound and flash suppressor. It was just what Jack needed—significant firepower coupled with a moderate degree of stealth. Best of all, it used the same 9 mm ammunition as his SIG.

He kneeled beside the crate, ejected the HK's 30-round magazine, and loaded it with standard rounds. He slapped the full magazine into the weapon, then raided the accessory boxes for three spare 30-round magazines and an adjustable strap. In less than a minute he had the magazines stowed and the submachine gun slung across his back.

Now to get guns to the hostages.

Watertight doors through the transverse bulkheads were located on the starboard and port sides of the upper 'tween decks, but the only way to the lower 'tween deck and the main hold was via ladders built into the center of each compartment's forward bulkhead. The ladders also led up to covered hatches on the main deck.

Jack could tell at a glance where the pirates had been belowdecks. They had left watertight doors open everywhere they went. Normal operations required all such hatches and weather doors to be closed at all times when the ship was at sea—a protocol of which the pirates seemed to be either oblivious or contemptuous. He resisted the reflexes honed during his military training and left the doors open as he stepped through the doorways, his HK braced against his shoulder, his eyes and ears alert to the faintest signs of danger.

There was movement beyond the next open hatchway.

Jack sidestepped behind a row of shrink-wrapped pallets and crouched for cover. He heard hushed voices and heavy footsteps moving closer to him. There were three men, all speaking a language Jack couldn't translate, but whose cadences and sounds he recognized as Somali. He waited until they had passed his position and continued through the doorway behind him, to the aft hold's upper 'tween deck, before he resumed his push toward the bow.

More pirates roamed the lower decks. He evaded them by treading lightly and keeping to the shadows. It helped that they weren't engaged in an active search. They seemed to think they had already captured everyone who was on board, and now they were occupied with their inventory of the ship's cargo, and with their fantasies of how they were going to spend their share of the wealth it was going to bring them. All the same, it slowed his progress, making a dash that should have taken minutes last for what felt like an eternity.

He passed through the last cargo hold doorway. Moving in a slight crouch with the HK firmly braced and balanced at eye level, he advanced to the forecastle bulkhead, an unbroken barrier that ran from the ship's keel up to its main deck. It was designed to protect the rest of the ship from flooding in the event of a collision that breached the hull anywhere in its bow. There were numerous compartments on the other side, but the only way to reach them was through a topside hatch on the forecastle.

From his position, Jack had only one viable path up to the main deck: the ladder built into the bulkhead. He slung his HK behind his back to free his hands and climbed quickly, aware that the pirates raiding the holds could come back at any moment. In under twenty seconds he had disappeared into the darkness of the ladderway above the hold. Effectively blind, Jack proceeded by touch alone until he reached the hatch.

He knew the crew kept the gears and dogs of the ship's hatches well oiled, so he had no fear the hatch cover would betray him with a shrill squeak when he pushed it open. His chief concern was that if the pirates had posted guards on the topside hatches, he was about to find himself in a very hairy situation.

He turned the wheel, released the lock on the hatch, and nudged it upward a fraction of an inch. Wind rushed in and spilled down the ladderway.

Jack peeked through the narrow opening. There was no one

forward of the hatch, or on either side. He knew the hatch cover opened up and tilted aft. If someone was behind it, they would see it open before he saw them. He took that chance.

The hatch lifted open, its motion smooth and silent. As it tilted back, Jack looked over his shoulder. There was no one between him and the Hold 1 hatch covers. He climbed out, careful to stay crouched, and shut the hatch gently.

Though the ship was adrift, strong winds and the irregular slap of waves against the hull bled together into a curtain of gray noise ideal for covering the sound of his movements. Jack unslung his HK submachine gun and prowled forward, toward the forecastle. He paused beside the starboard stairs and looked over the edge at the forecastle's topside.

The hostages sat crowded into the bow's peak with their backs to the bulwarks. Most of them did not seem to have been bound, which was a good sign. Less encouraging was the trio of anxious, wild-eyed gunmen posted to guard them.

Won't take much to set them off, Jack realized. *I'll need a diversion if I want to slip weapons to the crew.*

Movement on the edge of his vision—two figures were approaching up the port side of the ship. Jack ducked out of sight beside the cargo hold cover.

Two pirates. The one in front had a scarred face. His cohort was slim to the point of being gaunt, and he had the dead eyes of a hardened killer. Both men were lean and rough hewn by adversity. They climbed the port ladder to the forecastle and stalked toward the hostages.

The angry duo descended on Trent. Scarface lifted the gunrunning middleman from the deck by his shirt collar and roared, "Give us what we came for!"

"What? It's right where the captain said, behind the painting in—"

Crazy Eyes leaned in to add his measure of menace. "Not your safe! *That* we found!"

"Then what're you on about? You're rich men. You've made millions for a day's work."

Scarface pressed his pistol under Trent's jaw. "You *know* what we want!"

Trent played it cool. "What? Machine guns? Land mines? Just name it."

The next words from Crazy Eyes sent a chill down Jack's spine.

"We want the missiles!"

10:00 P.M. - 11:00 P.M.

Missiles? Jack's mind reeled at the thought of the mayhem pirates could unleash with that kind of armament. *I knew this ship was moving heavy ordnance, but I didn't think it held that kind of firepower.* He strained to tune out the roar of the wind and the hiss of seawater breaking against the hull so he could continue to eavesdrop on the pirates' confrontation with Trent.

The gunrunner made no effort to infuse his denial with the sound of sincerity. "I don't know what you're talking about." It was clear to Jack the man was just delaying the inevitable.

Scarface cocked the hammer of his pistol, which remained steady beneath Trent's chin. "I do not believe you. You are Rask's man on this ship. You know where the missiles are."

"Maybe you're confused. Did you really think I could fit a missile in my *safe*?"

The pirate rewarded Trent's defiance by pistol-whipping the older man and knocking him to the deck. "I was looking for the *container* number! Tell me what it is!"

Trent palmed bright red blood from the side of his scalp. "I don't remember." He glared at his tormentors. "Guess all these hits to the head gave me *amnesia*."

The scarred pirate aimed his weapon at Trent's head, but his partner pushed his hand off target. He castigated Scarface in Arabic. "Sadiq, stop. We can find it without him."

"Then let me kill him, Osman. If he won't help us, he's useless."

"No, he might still be worth a ransom. If Rask won't pay for him, *then* we kill him."

Sadiq lowered his pistol. "If you say so."

"Come with me. The manifest will be in the cargo control room. We can use that to find the missiles, wherever they are in the hold." Osman coaxed Sadiq to follow him with a sideways nod. "The hostages aren't going anywhere. Come. We have work to do."

An angry, resigned sigh. "Fine." Sadiq eased the hammer of his pistol back down to its normal position, then tucked the weapon under his belt. He turned and followed Osman off the forecastle and back up the port side, toward the ship's towering rust-red superstructure.

Jack wondered how the pirates knew about Rask, much less the missiles. *Who's feeding these guys their intel? These aren't ordinary pirates. So what the hell's going on?* Those were mysteries to solve later, he decided. Stopping them was all that mattered now. *Give them a crate full of Stingers and they could take out ships, passenger jets, embassies—anything they want. It'll be Mogadishu in '93 all over again, except this time the Somalis will be able to do even more damage. And no one will see it coming till it's too late.*

The new Somali government was far from perfect, but it was struggling to restore stability and order to a country riven by competing warlords, plagued by militant Islamic radicalism, and hampered by rampant poverty, disease, and famine. If a criminal faction captured the *Barataria,* it might end up better armed than Somalia's overtaxed military and police forces. That would be a recipe for a new Somali civil war and countless more civilian deaths.

Even worse, al-Qaeda was everywhere in Somalia. If the pirates captured the ship's trove of weapons, it was all but certain a good portion of them would end up in the hands of terrorists.

He slung the HK behind his back and returned to the ladderway hatch. A final look around verified no one was facing his way, not that there was much risk of anyone seeing him in the dark. He opened the hatch, climbed inside, and pulled it to a soft close over his head.

Halfway down the ladder to Hold 1, he paused to confirm the upper 'tween deck was clear. He finished his descent and headed for the port side. In the weeks he had been aboard, he'd had time to steal looks at only a small fraction of the *Barataria*'s illicit cargo, but he recalled enough to help himself now. He knew which containers held Claymore antipersonnel mines, which pallets were packed with detcord, which crates had detonators and timers.

It had been a while since Jack had enjoyed a chance to unleash complete and utter mayhem with a clean conscience. He planned to make the most of it.

• • •

High above the main deck, looking down from the lofty vantage of the *Barataria*'s pilothouse, Osman watched a few members of the ship's crew use its deck-mounted cranes and derricks to begin the tedious process of removing and stacking the hatch covers from the cargo holds. It would be a few minutes before the first cover was lifted out of the way, but already the slow pivoting dance of the titanic steel arms and their myriad cables impressed him.

The phone on the control board rang. He picked it up. "What?"

Sadiq snapped from the other end, *"There is no manifest."*

"There has to be."

"There isn't!" Staticky noise and banging sounds muffled his grumbled curses. *"Just a few clipboards, with nothing on them but cleaning schedules."*

Osman pressed his hand to his aching forehead. Sadiq could be useful when the task at hand involved hurting someone or destroying something, but the subtleties of the modern world eluded him. "It would not be on paper. It will be on the computer."

The silence from the other end of the call was scathing.

After a few seconds, Osman added, "Do you need me to come down there?"

"If you can make the machine work, yes."

"I am on my way." He hung up the phone and picked up his

rifle on his way out the door. *At least the walk down the stairs is easier than the climb up.*

He descended to the cargo control room, a narrow compartment on the forward side of Level 02 of the superstructure. There he found Sadiq staring at a blank computer monitor.

"Did it do something?"

"Not yet," Sadiq said.

"Good. Don't touch anything." He stepped past his bloodthirsty second-in-command and sat down at the keyboard in front of the small screen. Unsure what to do, he feigned confidence and tapped a random key. To his relief, the screen blinked on, and from under the countertop he heard the hum of a computer purring back to life.

Like most Somalis, Osman could speak a fair amount of English. Reading the language, however, was harder. As he had feared, the ship's computer system had been set for English as its default language. *If only we had been sent to hijack an Arabic ship.*

Looming over his shoulder, Sadiq brimmed with impatience. "Well?"

"I'm working on it."

The interface seemed simple enough. This was a dedicated machine, with a limited number of functions. Osman guided the cursor from one part of the screen to the next, and he noted which spots seemed to change color, indicating a function waiting to be triggered. At the same time, he did his best to make sense of the words and symbols on the monitor.

"You don't know what you're doing, do you?"

"I have not used this machine before. I need a second."

It had always been this way between him and Sadiq. No matter how many times Osman had proved himself, no matter how many of his schemes had paid off for them both, Sadiq was always looking for some new way to undermine him. It was a sickness, in Osman's opinion. Sadiq was the kind of person who could never accept his own limitations; he could never be content to take orders, even if they were for his own good. He was the kind of man who couldn't feel good about himself unless he was tearing someone else down.

And tonight he is my problem, once again.

Osman felt confident he had parsed the interface's commands. "This should bring up the manifest." He used the mouse to position the cursor on the screen, and then he clicked its button, the way a Peace Corps instructor had shown him and scores of other youths during a failed attempt at schooling several years earlier. His gambit succeeded, and the menu on the screen was replaced by a grid of numbers and letters corresponding to the ship's loaded cargo. "There."

"What does all of that mean?"

"It is a list of what is on the ship, and where it is."

"And it will tell us where to find the missiles?"

"It should."

Sadiq crossed his arms and struck a haughty pose. "Show me."

Pretending would no longer be good enough. They had everything they needed to finish their mission except the coordinates of the one container they needed to find—and the expertise to coax that information from the ship's computerized cargo logs.

Osman reclined his chair. "We need one of the crew to work the computer."

"Too bad we killed Dedrick."

Osman scowled at his accomplice. "You mean too bad *you* killed Dedrick."

"I thought that was what you wanted."

"It wasn't."

"You should have been more clear."

There was no point arguing with Sadiq. He wasn't one to admit mistakes or make apologies. All he understood was strength, money, and results. Osman pointed him toward the door. "Go get one of the officers. *Not* the captain. Ask for the cargo chief."

"Am I your errand boy?"

"I was not aware I needed to say please when giving orders."

Sadiq bristled, but he obeyed.

Osman watched him leave, and then he breathed easier.

It is going to be a very *long night.*

• • •

In addition to arms and ammunition, the ship's hold contained a fair amount of general military surplus gear. There were boots, canteens, MREs, everything a guerrilla fighting force might need to sustain itself and keep moving—including old-fashioned U.S. Navy seabags. Jack had snagged one of the tube-like canvas sacks from a pallet of miscellaneous gear in the forward hold's upper 'tween deck, and now he was in the center hold compartment, loading the seabag with bricks of Semtex. A little of the plastic explosive would go a long way in the confined spaces belowdecks, but it was light enough that it wouldn't hurt to bring an extra block or two.

Semtex would be good for tucking into hidden spaces, but Jack planned to turn the entirety of the *Barataria*'s lower decks into kill zones. For that, however, he would need Claymores, and those were all the way aft, in Hold 3's lower 'tween deck.

He hefted the quarter-full seabag by both its padded straps and toted it over his left shoulder. With one hand occupied supporting the bag, he had switched back to the SIG as his primary defensive weapon. For the sake of stealth, he had fitted its suppressor into place.

Passing through an open doorway, his left foot was in Hold 2, but his right foot was still in Hold 1. That was when he saw two pirates on his right, chatting in muffled Somali while leaning against a long pallet of double-stacked wooden crates.

Damn it. He knew no good would come of trying to reverse his motion in midstride, so he continued forward and ducked for cover between two pallets along the starboard bulkhead. *If I'm lucky, they didn't notice me. Or thought I was just one of their own men passing by.*

He listened. Everything was dead quiet. Then the two men exchanged words in confused tones of voice, and Jack imagined he could guess what they were saying.

Did you see that?

Yes. What was it?

No idea. Maybe we should check it out.

Footsteps drew near. They were moving toward him.

He set down the seabag with care. The last thing he wanted to do was draw more pirates into the fray with a firefight.

Moving with practiced slowness, Jack raised his SIG and waited for a target to appear.

The muzzle of an AK-47 poked into view. Jack knew the man would be close behind. He held the SIG at eye level, his finger poised in front of the trigger.

A shift in the angle of the rifle's barrel warned Jack the man was turning toward him. The pirate was in mid-pivot when Jack fired. Even with the suppressor, the bang resounded off the multitude of hard surfaces in the hold. There was a bright *ping* of brass on steel as the ejected casing ricocheted off the pallet to Jack's right, then bounced across the deck.

As the first pirate collapsed, Jack leaned forward just enough to get his SIG around the corner and glimpse the second man. The pirate clumsily struggled to lift his rifle from his hip so he could aim. He fell with a bullet in his chest before he got the chance.

The slap of the second man's body hitting the deck was accompanied by the plink of another ejected cartridge skipping away and falling into the lower hold. Sulfuric smoke snaked from the SIG's barrel. Jack froze, wondering if more pirates were coming. Even muffled by a suppressor, no firearm was ever truly silent, especially not in a tight space such as this. Still, the suppressor had turned the crack of the SIG into a muted bang, like that of something heavy being dropped, and the thick bulkheads would serve to contain most of the sound.

From where Jack stood, all seemed quiet in the belly of the *Barataria.*

He holstered the SIG. One at a time, he dragged the two dead Somalis into the gap between two pallets, and covered the corpses with a blue polyester tarp he took from atop a pile of lashed-together crates.

The path ahead to Hold 3 was clear. Jack picked up his seabag and moved aft, reminding himself each step of the way to remember to check his corners next time.

• • •

None of the four pirates sent to drag Trent and Captain Rohde back to the superstructure could tell them what was going on, but Trent felt reasonably certain he wasn't going to like it.

At least they untied our hands so we could use the ladders.

He and the white-haired merchant marine commander were ushered up the port stairs at gunpoint. When they reached Level 02 they were shoved into the corridor and marched together into the cargo control room. Waiting there were the ship's cargo chief, Dieter Stutzman, and the motley boarding team's two leaders, Osman the bug eyed and his half-trained attack dog Sadiq. Stutzman was on his knees with his hands behind his head. Sadiq aimed his stolen .45 semiautomatic with both hands at the back of Stutzman's head.

Trent's head still ached from his last encounter with Sadiq, but he had learned the hard way never to show weakness to an enemy. "What now, boys? Can't figure out how the stove works in the galley? Want us to make you a midnight snack?"

Osman nodded at his men standing behind Trent. One of them kicked the back of his knee, buckling it under him. He dropped to the deck and landed facedown. Someone grabbed a handful of hair on the back of his head and pulled him up onto his knees.

There was no mania in Osman's manner. With aplomb he pulled out a rolling chair from Stutzman's desk, set it in front of Trent, and sat. He leaned close and spoke softly. "The missiles are not listed in the manifest."

"Maybe that's because there *are* no missiles, genius."

A frown and a shake of the head. "No. They are here." He pointed at the small monitor on the desk behind him. "So are many other things not on your computer."

Trent refused to show the slightest surprise or alarm. "So what?"

Sadiq stepped forward and stood behind Osman. "Your manifest does not match your cargo. Any of it. What it says should be there, is not. What is there, it does not list."

There was no mirth in Osman's ugly grin of stained teeth. "Your manifest is a fake." He shifted his narrowed gaze to the captain. "Where is the real one?"

Rohde broke like an egg under a hammer. "I don't have it." He deflected the pirates' accusatory glares with a tilt of his head toward Trent. "He controls the manifest."

"From where?" Osman pointed at Rohde. "Be precise."

"He works from here, but he uses his own laptop." Seeing that he had confused Osman, he clarified. "He uses a small portable computer that he plugs into our system."

Trent fumed. *If we live through this, I'm giving Rohde a ride on the anchor.*

Osman got up and pulled the chair back to the desk. Sadiq stepped toward Trent and took over the questioning. "Where is this portable computer?"

"I don't remember."

Sadiq smacked Trent in the jaw with his pistol. "Think harder."

"What if I don't?"

"Then you will be sorry." Sadiq backed up his threat with a swift kick in Trent's groin. The pain left Trent doubled over and pawing at the deck like a wounded animal. Then the pirate stepped on his wrist, pinning it to the deck. "Tell me."

"Go to hell." It was pure bravado, but it sounded good.

A loud gunshot filled the small compartment. A blaze of white heat and searing agony shot up Trent's arm. When the red haze cleared from his vision, he saw the huge smoking wound Sadiq had blasted through the back of his hand. His cool, sarcastic pretensions abandoned him. All he had left now were burning pain and panic.

"No one can resist forever, Mr. Trent. You still have another hand and both feet. Wouldn't you like to keep them?" He planted his foot on Trent's back and flattened him onto the deck. The next thing Trent felt was the still-warm muzzle of the .45 on the back of his head. "Give me the computer. Or the missiles, if you like. Either one will save your life. For now."

Trent tried to dredge a few more moments of defiance from some deep pit of his soul, but all he could see was the blood oozing from his smoking, ruined hand. His courage disintegrated.

"It's in my stateroom. Under a false bottom in the storage space beneath my bunk. Lift the mattress and look for the release lever in a groove under the front edge."

Osman nodded to his men waiting in the doorway. One of them hurried away to confirm Trent's confession. To the three who remained he said, "Put them back with the others."

The pirates dragged Trent and Stutzman to their feet. Rifle barrels against their and Rohde's backs propelled them into the corridor, down the stairs to the main deck, and back to the bow. They climbed the ladder to the forecastle—a task Trent now found much more difficult without the use of his right hand— and slumped back into the huddle with the rest of the crew.

Rohde was a portrait of dejection. "Maybe now they'll leave us be."

Trent tore off part of his shirt and wrapped it around his wounded hand. "Why? Because you sold me out so they could make me give up my laptop? I've always thought you were an idiot, Rohde, but now I have proof."

His vitriol churned the captain's bitter stew of resentments. "To hell with you, and to hell with Mr. Rask. All I care about is the safety of my crew. If saving them means handing over you and every last bit of cargo on this tub, so be it. That's a choice I can live with."

"Not for long, you won't. If you surrender this vessel's cargo, you'd better hope the pirates kill you. 'Cause if they don't, Rask will—and he'll make sure it takes you a good, long time to die." He finished knotting his makeshift bandage. The pressure made his hand sting as if it had been skewered by a million burning needles, but it stanched the bleeding.

The captain sighed. "So what now? You've given them the laptop. It's over, isn't it?"

Imagining his next face-off with the pirates put a grim smirk on Trent's face.

"Hardly, Captain. In fact, I'd say this game's only just begun."

• • •

It was pitch dark at the bottom of the ship's aft hold, and that suited Jack just fine. He had helped himself to a lightweight headset on which was mounted a pair of night-vision goggles that rendered his surroundings in a spectral pale green monochrome. The lack of color didn't bother him; it wasn't as if he were trying to defuse a bomb based on the color of its wires. All he needed was to see what he was doing as he filled his seabag with antipersonnel mines.

They weren't authentic Claymores but Chinese-made knockoffs. The slightly curved gray-green boxes had all the necessary parts—clacker triggers and plenty of detcord for daisy-chaining the mines to make larger kill zones—but where their convex surfaces would normally bear the iconic instruction FRONT TOWARD ENEMY, these had four Chinese pictograms.

Good thing I already know which way they go.

Though the Claymores were compact, they were heavier than they looked. Ten of them in his seabag, on top of the plastic explosives and other gear he had already tactically acquired on his trip through the cargo holds, had brought the canvas duffel's loaded weight to nearly fifty pounds. He had hauled that much weight over far greater distances during his Delta Force selection phase, when he was nearly twenty years younger—but his chief concerns now were stealth and speed, neither of which benefited from carrying a heavy pack.

Call it motivation, he told himself. *The faster I work, the sooner I lighten my load.*

He was about to close up the top flaps of the seabag when he noticed movement from the corner of the hold. Acting by reflex, he ducked for cover in a narrow space between pallets.

A lone Somali walked beside the towering stacks of shipping containers. He swept a flashlight beam back and forth as he eyed the mountain of metal. As he moved closer, Jack heard a faint scratch of electronic noise, like random interference crackling through a radio.

With an upward glance, Jack confirmed there were at least two more pirates above him, rooting through crates on Hold 3's lower 'tween deck. Drawing their attention would be a disaster. If he were above them, on the upper 'tween deck, he would have options, places to go. But he was in the lower hold, and from here there was only one way out—the ladder on the forward bulkhead. He couldn't risk using his SIG, not even with the suppressor.

He drew his KA-BAR with his right hand and brought it up

to his left shoulder, with the blade pointed outward. Listening to the pirate's shuffling footsteps, Jack put his back to the pallet. And then he waited.

The pirate stepped into view, his eyes still turned upward at the shipping containers. Jack noted the AK-47 across the man's back, but he couldn't see what he was carrying. It was small but required the use of both of his hands. A faint glow emanated from the device, and the pirate looked back and forth between it and the containers.

He looked in Jack's direction for only a fraction of a second, but that was enough to seal his fate. Jack struck a lightning-fast stab into the man's larynx, preventing him from crying out in fear or pain. As Jack pulled the blade free, he cut the pirate's carotid artery with his exit stroke. A long spurt of blood jetted from the wound as the man fell forward. Jack let the dying man stagger and fall, but he made sure to catch the device tumbling from the pirate's hand.

The body struck the deck face-first with a weighty *thump*.

Jack stared at the device in his bloodstained hands.

It was a Geiger counter.

All at once, Jack understood what was really going on. The pirates weren't looking for conventional missiles. They had come aboard looking for nukes. In the hands of terrorists, such weapons could kill millions of innocent people.

Damn it, Rask. What the hell have you done?

• • •

Every problem Osman solved revealed a new dilemma; every hurdle he cleared led to a new obstacle. He was starting to regret having accepted this job. It was proving more troublesome than the client had led him to expect, and he suspected matters would only worsen as the night dragged on.

He led Sadiq down the port side of the ship and up the ladder onto the forecastle. It was important to him that he be the one in front. He needed to reinforce for his men that he was the one in charge, not Sadiq, no matter how volatile and overbearing his right-hand man might be.

They came to a halt in front of the prisoners huddled at the bow. Osman did his best to project authority and menace. "Mr. Trent! The password for your computer. Now."

"Found the encryption, eh?" A self-satisfied chortle. "I wondered how long that would take. I'll give you credit, I didn't expect to see you again so soon."

Sadiq's temper frayed. "Give us the code."

"Or else what?"

The taunt lingered between Trent and Sadiq for half a second, and then Sadiq snapped. He charged with an inchoate yell, hefting the butt of his rifle to cave in the gunrunner's skull.

Trent sprang to his feet and lunged at Sadiq. He caught him off guard and tackled him backwards onto the deck.

The fight was one-sided—Trent had only one good hand— but the thrill of it brought the rest of the ship's crew to their feet, and they all pushed forward to see it. Sadiq forced Trent onto his back, seizing the advantage—until Trent hit him in the groin. They went in opposite directions—Sadiq fell left, Trent rolled right. As Trent found his feet, Osman saw the knife the gunrunner had plucked from Sadiq's belt. Trent lifted his arm to throw the blade—

Two bursts from Sadiq's AK-47 cut him down in a spray of blood.

Trent's bullet-savaged corpse slid down the bulwark, marking it with a dark smear of blood, then tumbled headfirst over the ladder to land with a wet slap on the main deck.

Osman lost his last shred of control and grabbed Sadiq's collar. "Are you mad?"

"I should have let him kill me?"

"You could have wounded him! We needed that code!"

Sadiq swatted Osman's hand away. "We can find the missiles ourselves."

"How?" Osman pointed toward the hatch covers for the cargo holds. "There are more than a hundred containers on this ship! You want to open them one by one?"

"If we have to!"

"We need to find the missiles now! We promised to deliver them by midnight!"

"What difference does it—?" He spun and fired another burst from his rifle at one of the crewmen, who had made a diving grab for the knife Trent dropped. The scrawny Thai man jerked like a puppet controlled by an epileptic as the hail of bullets ripped through him.

Then the rest of the crew leaped to their feet and charged.

Sadiq emptied the last few rounds from his rifle in Captain Rohde. Osman and the two guards he'd posted on the hostages, Feysal and Abiid, reflexively laid down narrow arcs of suppressing fire into the surging wall of bodies. Within moments, all was still, and a stiff ocean breeze swept aside the ragged pall of acrid gun smoke to reveal the piled dead.

Osman threw his empty rifle to the deck and let rip a slew of curses in his native tongue. The burden of failure overwhelmed him, and he fell to his knees and pounded the deck with the sides of his fists. "This is not happening!" Cruel laughter answered his laments. He shot a bitter look up at Sadiq. "You think this is funny?"

"What good were they? No one would have paid their ransoms. Good riddance."

"We needed them to sail this ship to Berbera Port!"

Sadiq loaded a fresh magazine into his rifle. "Why bother? Too many questions at the port. Too many bribes to pay. We'll just run the ship aground and put her cargo on the beach."

Now it was clear to Osman why Sadiq was doomed to die poor. He was a wastrel. "The ship itself is *half* our reward. Run it aground and she's worthless."

"There will be other boats." A dismissive laugh as he walked back to the ladder. "Really, my friend. You worry too much."

Osman watched him descend the ladder and head back toward the superstructure. With the crew dead, Osman realized he now had only two enemies left on the *Barataria:* his second-in-command and the unstoppable hands of the clock.

There was only one way left for him to finish this job. He had to swallow his pride and contact the one person who had just as much interest in this mission's success as he did.

It was time to call the client and ask for help.

11:00 P.M. – 12:00 A.M.

Jack worked fast and kept things simple. In the bottom of Hold 3, he had set a sizable charge of C-4 at the base of the ladder on the forward bulkhead, and another at the base of the aft bulkhead. He had shaped the charges to direct the bulk of their explosive force downward, through the ship's hull. Only once had he paused in his efforts, when he heard a crane removing the hold's cover hatch up on the ship's main deck.

Now he was back in Hold 3's upper 'tween deck, creeping from one corner to the next to secure a Claymore under the raised coaming of each watertight door. Three of the mines were in place, tilted upward at a slight angle, held fast by duct tape and linked by detcord.

Jack lurked behind the mountain of twenty-foot-long shipping containers in the hold's open center, waiting for a pair of pirates to move away on the far side of the compartment. As soon as they were behind the far corner, he checked over his shoulder to make sure there was no one behind him, and then he hurried forward in a crouch to the last door, his munitions-filled seabag on his back and his shoulder duffel at his side, feeding out detcord behind him as he went.

Speed was his chief concern. He took a mine from the seabag and set it below the door. Using a roll of duct tape one of the crew had left on top of a cargo pallet, he fixed the Claymore into position. Then he retraced his steps and tucked the detcord out of sight against the port bulkhead, behind the pallets. A final check confirmed all the blasting caps were secure, and that the trigger device had been paired to Jack's remote detonator.

He took a few seconds to decide what part of the ship to rig next, the engineering decks or the superstructure. The engine compartments would take longer to prepare, but he was less likely to meet roving patrols of pirates down there.

He moved aft and descended toward the machinery spaces in the bowels of the ship. He needed to deprive the pirates of the ability to maneuver the ship under its own power, and to sink it or set it ablaze, if necessary, to deny them control over its deadly contents.

The seabag and the duffel were cumbersome and left him slow and off balance, but he had to move hands-free down the ladderways so that he could have his SIG drawn and ready in case he met resistance. He didn't expect there to be any pirates in the engineering section of the ship, but he wasn't going to risk his life on that assumption.

Residual heat greeted Jack as he descended into the lower decks of the engine room. Odors of machine oil and diesel fuel filled the air, but they weren't strong enough to mask the pervasive reek of stale sweat infused into the space over decades of operation. It was clean and well maintained, and there was a strong stink of bleach and fumes from the fresh layers of mint green paint that covered nearly every square inch of the decks, ladders, railings, and machinery. The whole section shone with a sickly glow from its pervasive fluorescent lighting.

With all the engines shut down, it was quiet enough for Jack to tell he was alone in the compartment. Confident he could move without being detected, he hurried to the lowest deck and made his way to the port fuel tank, where he set his next charge. He hid his next two demolition-strength wads of plastique under the main engine assembly and the auxiliary diesel generators. His fourth charge he placed against the starboard fuel tank, and then he found the deck hatch that led down into "shaft alley"—the narrow tunnel housing the drive shaft that linked the engines to the ship's propeller. He jogged to the end of the narrow passage and placed a generous wad of C-4 with a radio-controlled detonator against its aft bulkhead.

That ought to do some damage.

He gathered up his duffel and seabag for the climb up the ladders, back to the main deck.

On the upper engineering 'tween deck, he stopped to take two charges and detonators from the seabag, and then he hid the bag and his duffel behind a cluster of large pipes. Placing charges at key points on the superstructure was going to require speed and stealth, which meant leaving behind any nonessential gear. He took off his submachine gun, tucked in his T-shirt, and wedged the two pliable half bricks between his waistband and the small of his back. Then he returned the HK to its place across his back, drew his SIG, and climbed the stairs.

He paused at the topside weather door. It was dark out on the main deck; any spill of light would draw attention. He unscrewed by hand the wire-mesh cage around the light mounted on the inner bulkhead next to the weather door, then broke the hot bulb with the grip of his SIG.

With a pass of his hand he lowered the lenses of his night-vision goggles into place. He turned the door's handle and nudged it open. There was no one on the other side. He checked through its window as he pushed it open, to make sure there wasn't a pirate hiding behind it. All clear. He shut the door behind him, its metallic *clonk* muffled by the roars of wind and sea.

The stairs above him looked clear, so he took them two steps at a time. His destinations were all the way at the top, and he had to reach them and return as quickly as he could. He still had charges to rig belowdecks in Holds 1 and 2, and it was dangerous being exposed for any length of time.

A door opened ahead of him. There was nowhere to hide if the pirates turned toward him. He swung his legs over the railing and climbed down until he dangled by his fingertips from the edge of the superstructure deck. Above him, two pirates passed by, oblivious of his presence at their feet. As they walked down the next flight of stairs, Jack pulled himself back up and out of their field of view with barely a second to spare.

He listened for any indication that they'd spotted him, but

the pair went on chatting in Somali as they continued down the next flight of stairs.

Jack pushed on, still moving in fast strides but exercising more caution as he reached each new level. He passed the command suite and climbed the last flight of stairs up to the "monkey deck," a bulwarked platform located above the *Barataria*'s bridge. The ship's twin searchlights were operated from there, and it provided ladder access for the signal mast and radar assembly. He set one of his charges at the base of the signal mast, and he placed the other directly above the ship's pilothouse.

Satisfied with his handiwork, he was about to head back down the stairs to continue his labors belowdecks when activity on the ship's bow caught his attention. He crouched behind the bulwark and adjusted his night-vision goggles until he had a clear view of the forecastle.

The few pirates not working with the cranes were busy dumping the crew's bloodied bodies overboard. The last corpse to go over the bulwark was that of Captain Rohde. Jack looked to port and starboard, and he noticed the faint outlines of dead crewmen bobbing on the waves as they drifted away. He was alone now in a battle to the death against however many pirates were still alive on the *Barataria*.

Jack frowned and withdrew to the stairs.

If they aren't taking prisoners, neither am I.

• • •

There was no mistaking the irritation in the client's voice, even when it was flattened by the portable radio. *"You assured me you could do this job, Osman. I trusted you."*

"I can, Colonel." Osman had met Colonel Newbold only once, but the American's keen stare, bone-white crew cut, and tanned, battle-scarred scalp still haunted his memory. "My men control the ship. We can get you the missiles."

"But not on time." A disgruntled grumble. *"You were supposed to be calling for the chopper by now, not for technical support."*

Osman was desperate not to let this contract go awry. He had heard hushed rumors of what happened to those who bungled their promises to Newbold and his private military company, Firethorn. "Colonel, my men are opening the last of the cargo hold covers now. We are ready to retrieve the missiles. All we need is the container's position in the hold—but to find that, we need help cracking the gunrunner's computer."

"Maybe you should have thought of that before you killed him."

"It was not I who pulled the trigger."

"You were in command, Mr. Muhamad. That makes it your responsibility."

"Yes, *my* responsibility—but *your* problem. You want the missiles? I need your help."

His point seemed to hit home with Newbold, who blunted the edge in his voice. *"Do you still have the smartphones my men gave you?"*

"Yes."

A note of condescension crept into Newbold's tone. *"If I tell you to turn on its Bluetooth and pair it to Trent's laptop, do you know what that means?"*

It pained Osman to admit his ignorance, but he knew better than to pretend he understood modern technology. "No, but my man Jibríl would."

"Then put him on. I'll have my engineer walk him through it."

"Yes, sir." Osman snapped his fingers at Jibríl, who stood in the open doorway of the cargo control room, and beckoned him with a frantic wave. The hunger-thin youth hurried to his side and listened with intense focus as Osman handed him a smartphone and the radio, then gestured for him to take his seat at the computer. "Do what they tell you. Our lives depend on it." He pointed at the radio. "Hold this button down to talk, let it go to listen."

Jibríl nodded, then pressed the button and muttered into the radio. "Hello?"

A woman's voice answered. *"Is this Jibríl?"*

"Yes."

"My name is Pilar Sánchez. Do as I tell you. We'll go one step at a time. Okay?"

"Okay."

"Turn on the laptop."

"It's on."

"What operating system is it using?"

Jibríl checked the laptop's technical specs. "OS X ten eight."

"Mountain Lion? Okay, good. Turn on the smartphone."

He woke the small device from its standby state. "It's on."

"Open the phone's settings menu. Find the control labeled 'Bluetooth.' Turn it on."

Some fiddling and tapping. "Done."

"Now open the system preferences on the laptop. Find the section marked 'network.'"

"Done."

"Open it and turn on the Bluetooth function."

Clicking and tapping, slower this time. "Done."

"Okay, now the fun part. We're going to pair the devices so that I can use the smartphone to access the laptop's hard drive. Ready?"

A mumbled affirmation from Jibríl was enough to cue the woman into unleashing a stream of technobabble gibberish that meant absolutely nothing to Osman. Jibríl was quiet as he worked, but to Osman's relief, the youth seemed able to follow the mercenary woman's directions. A few minutes later, windows began to open and close on the laptop's screen without Jibríl touching the trackpad or the keyboard. Osman wasn't sure what had been done or how it worked; all he cared about was that something useful seemed to be happening.

Newbold's voice crackled over the radio. *"Mr. Muhamad?"*

Osman grabbed the radio from Jibríl's hand. "Yes, sir?"

"Don't let anyone or anything interrupt our connection to that laptop. Make sure the laptop has a steady power supply. Don't let the smartphone go to standby. And unless you want me to strangle you to death with your own intestines, do not let that phone's battery go dead. Do I make myself clear, Mr. Muhamad?"

"Very clear, sir."

"Good. As soon as we hack the laptop's encryption and find the container's coordinates, we'll let you know. Until then, no more mistakes. And no more delays. Or else. Newbold out."

Osman put down the radio and realized only then that his hands were shaking. He looked back at his man Samir. "Pull everyone out of the holds. I want them up here, guarding the superstructure. Now!" Samir nodded and stepped out of the cargo control room to the corridor to relay Osman's orders to the rest of their team via radio. Osman palmed the sweat from his forehead, wiped his hand dry on his pants, then gave Jibríl a reassuring clamp on the shoulder. "Good work. Keep an eye on it. Tell me if anything changes."

"I will."

Stricken with a sick stomach from anxiety, Osman stood by the room's only window, which looked out on the *Barataria*'s opened cargo hatches. Through the openings in the main deck he saw the multicolored tiers of stacked intermodal shipping containers.

Each hold contained six rows of containers, stacked two deep and five tall. Hold 2 held the forty-foot-long containers. All the twenty-foot-long containers were in Hold 3. Osman had no idea which container in that mountain of steel was loaded with Newbold's precious missiles, but he knew that unless he found it within the next two hours, the rest of the ship's cargo would no longer be worth stealing—because then nothing on Earth would save him from Newbold's wrath.

**Radisson Blu Iveria Hotel
Tbilisi, Georgia**

The knock at the door echoed through the executive suite and turned Karl Rask away from his unparalleled view of the glittering urban nightscape outside his floor-to-ceiling windows. He looked over his shoulder at his lanky, fair-haired Norwegian associate. "Nils, get the door."

This was not a meeting Karl Rask wanted to have. He preferred to spend his time meeting new clients and initiating new business, not delivering bad news. Placating the irate and the dissatisfied was a delicate matter under the best of circumstances, which the present situation most decidedly was not. Especially not when his organization needed to take responsibility for an error that was both predictable and, in theory, preventable.

Unfortunately, as the one in charge, it fell to Rask to atone for his subordinates' failures.

Nils opened the suite's door and ushered in Rask's guest, Hakeem el-Jamal. The bodyguard stopped the middle-aged Saudi businessman to wave a metal-detector wand over his limbs and torso. Another of Rask's sentinels, a swarthy bruiser named Arturo, scanned the lanky visitor with a radio and digital signals monitor, to make sure al-Qaeda's envoy wasn't wearing a surveillance device under his Armani suit. After a few moments of noninvasive inspection, the two guards stepped aside and let el-Jamal continue across the suite's main room.

Rask met el-Jamal and shook his hand. "Mr. El-Jamal. Thank you for coming so quickly."

"You said it was urgent."

"I did. Please, sit down." He waited until el-Jamal relaxed onto one of the room's two sofas, and then he sat down opposite him. "There's been an incident related to your shipment."

El-Jamal's brows knit with alarm. "What kind of incident?"

"Somali pirates attacked my ship in the Gulf of Aden about three hours ago."

The Saudi leaned forward. "Did they take my shipment?"

"So far as I know, they've taken the entire ship."

A pained wince, then el-Jamal clenched his fist. "What are you doing about it?"

"First, I want to assure you, the security of your shipment is my chief concern. I've activated the tracking devices inside your container. Wherever they go, we'll find them."

It was clear his efforts to placate el-Jamal were not succeeding. "And then?"

"I'm assembling a strike team to recover your shipment first, and then the ship and the rest of its cargo."

Narrowed eyes hinted at el-Jamal's distrust. "Where is this strike team of yours?"

"Here in Tbilisi. They'll be on my jet and headed to Somalia in an hour."

El-Jamal shook his head and dismissed the idea with a wave of his hand. "No. Your people lost the missiles. Mine will get them back."

"With all respect, Mr. El-Jamal, my men can—"

"Mine are closer. And smart enough not to be ambushed by Somali scum."

Not wanting to give el-Jamal any more ammunition against him than he already had, Rask kept to himself his suspicions that the Somalis had been aided by someone on the ship, which suggested that there was a leak in his organization, someone who had tipped off the Somalis—or whoever had put the Somalis in play—about the ship and its priceless nuclear cargo. "I can understand why you'd want to take matters into your own hands, sir, and I—"

"That's not all I want to take into my hands," el-Jamal said. "I want our money back."

"Excuse me?"

"We paid you a princely sum for those missiles. And not just for their nuclear warheads, but for the rarity of their origins. That's not a prize that can be easily replaced, not even by you. And since you seem to have lost them, we want a refund."

The meeting had taken a bad turn and was only getting worse. Rask did his best to present a calm face. "I'm not in the habit of giving refunds."

"Do you know what a 'fatwa' is, Mr. Rask?"

"I've heard the term, yes."

"Unless you wire every last euro of our payment back to our account in Geneva by the start of business, our network will make it its mission to burn your operation to the ground."

Salvaging the contract seemed hopeless, but Rask had to try.

"Let's not be hasty, Mr. El-Jamal. My men can recover the shipment. It will be delayed, but it's not as if the delivery were time-sensitive to begin with."

El-Jamal folded his hands on his lap. "It's no longer about promptness of delivery. It's about our ability to trust that you can deliver the shipment at all."

"Give my people twelve hours. That's all I ask."

"There are no second chances in our line of work. Only success, and failure. And you have failed us, Mr. Rask. My organization will recover the shipment without your help."

It would be bad for business for Rask to tell his men to kill el-Jamal, but it might be even more disastrous if word got out that he was issuing refunds for shipments gone astray. "You want to do the recovery? Fine. And you want compensation. I understand. But I can't refund *all* of your money. Expenditures were incurred. Payoffs were made to get the shipment through customs. I can rebate a quarter of your down payment."

"Half."

"One-third, and a million dollars in credit toward your next order."

"Done." El-Jamal stood, so Rask did the same. They shook hands. "My people will find the missiles. Tell yours to stay out of our way."

"I'll pass that along."

El-Jamal left without bothering to engage in the tedium of polite valedictions. Nils opened the door for el-Jamal, watched him depart, then shut it behind him.

Enervated, Rask palmed the sweat from his bald pate and stroked the rough whiskers of his graying Vandyke. *Some days I hate this business.*

"Nils, tell Quin and his men to stand down." Rask plodded back to the sofa and sank onto it, his limbs leaden. "Arturo? Someone told the pirates about our shipment. Find out who it was."

• • •

Nothing happening in the *Barataria*'s cargo control room made any sense to Sadiq. He didn't know why Osman had recalled all their men from the holds to defend the superstructure when they were the only ones on the ship, or what was meant by any of the gibberish passing back and forth between Jibríl and the woman speaking over the radio. All that Sadiq knew for certain was that someone was wasting his time, and he didn't like it.

"What is going on?" His demand was met by shushes and frantic waves of dismissal.

Osman left Jibríl's side and confronted Sadiq in the doorway. "Quiet! We're working!"

"And I am standing here. Doing *nothing*."

"You are guarding Jibríl and the laptop."

"From whom?" Sadiq made a show of looking around in mock bewilderment. "There is no one else here, Osman. Who are we keeping out? Sea monsters? Ghosts?"

Poking at Sadiq's chest, Osman said in a whisper pitched with anxious fury, "*This* is what the client wants. You don't *need* to understand. Just do as you're told." His edict delivered, Osman returned to other side of the small compartment to hover above Jibríl, who remained occupied poking at the keys of the portable computer, based on a woman's directions.

This is ridiculous. Fed up with standing idle, Sadiq retreated from the doorway and nodded at three of his men to follow him down the corridor toward the starboard stairs. Once they were far enough from the cargo control room that he was confident they would not be overheard, he spoke to his comrades in a confidential hush. "We need to continue the inventory of the cargo holds. To see what this ship's freight will be worth once we get her ashore."

His proposition unsettled Samir. "Osman told us to stay up here."

"To hell with him. Listen to me. We have work to do, and it's not getting done." Nervous looks were exchanged, but none of his men protested, so he continued. "I have to stay up here. Osman will notice if I go missing. But you three can finish the inventory without me."

Feysal asked, "You want us to help Caadil, Yasir, and Faaruq?"

Sadiq shot a puzzled look at the younger man. Until then, he hadn't registered the three pirates' absence. "I thought they were with the crane and derrick crew."

Ashkir shook his head. "No. Dubad and his brothers are running those."

Something felt off to Sadiq. He and Osman had come aboard with seventeen men. After the execution of the *Barataria*'s crew, he had thought his men accounted for. He looked at Samir. "Did they check in when Osman called us back to the superstructure?"

Confused expressions traveled back and forth among Samir, Feysal, and Ashkir. After a few seconds, Samir shrugged. "I don't remember."

He dug his radio out of his pocket and thumbed the talk switch. "Sadiq to Caadil, Yasir, and Faaruq. Do you hear me? Respond." He waited for several seconds, but no answer came. He tried again, but the result remained the same: stubborn silence. The sick feeling in his gut worsened, and he knew something was wrong. "Someone lied to us. Maybe the captain, maybe that devil Trent. But there is someone else aboard. Someone we missed."

His claim shocked Ashkir. "Where? We searched the entire ship!"

"Not well enough, apparently. Our missing men were on inventory detail. Which means the last place any of our people saw them was in the holds." He pointed at Samir. "Get three more men and lead a search team into the cargo decks. Go all the way forward and down, then work your way back from there, closing the doors as you go. If there's someone other than us on this ship, I want you to flush him out. And then I want you to kill him."

· · ·

Whatever had made the pirates abandon the hold in a hurry, Jack was grateful for it. Knowing they had all gone topside had given him a free pass to finish rigging the holds with booby traps. He made quick work of Hold 2, despite the fact that it was the largest of the ship's holds, and it had taken him only a few minutes to set the Claymores on the upper 'tween deck of Hold 1, since there were only two, with a single length of det-cord between them.

He had set a C-4 charge under the ladder by the collision bulkhead at the forward end of the hold, and he was fixing the last charge into place in the middle of the aft bulkhead when he heard voices filter down through the ladderway. He looked over his shoulder and saw harsh, blue-white flashlight beams slice through the darkness and dance against the edges of the deck that framed the ladderway.

The pirates were back, and they were descending into the bottom of Hold 1.

Damn it. That's the last thing I need.

Jack armed the last charge and paired its detonator to his triggering device. He cast aside the empty seabag, tucked his shoulder bag behind his back, and swung his HK submachine gun into position, with its metal stock braced against his shoulder. With one eye on the men descending the ladder at the forward end of the hold, he crab-walked down the center of the fully enclosed lower hold, dodging around the keel-welded center beams that provided structural support for the 'tween decks and the main deck. He took cover behind the last beam, kneeled, and aimed the HK.

He expected the advantage of having night-vision goggles would give him a few seconds of tactical superiority, and the lack of muzzle flash thanks to the HK's suppressor would conceal his position until the pirates scattered for cover. Even still, he had no idea how many men were coming, but from the voices he heard, it sounded as if there were several of them, and he didn't want to get boxed in down in the lower hold, from which the only escape was the ladder. He needed either to slip past them and gain the advantage of high ground, or to eliminate them with prejudice and head back to the upper 'tween deck, where he would at least have mobility forward and aft.

As the first pirate stepped off the ladder into the lower hold, Jack counted three men on the ladder above him, and he heard at least two more on the lower 'tween deck, awaiting their turns on the ladder.

Training and experience told Jack to hold his fire, to wait until his limited engagement area achieved its most target-rich state.

Then the first pirate off the ladder turned and shone his flashlight into Jack's face.

Jack's finger squeezed the trigger. The weapon kicked hard into his shoulder.

A short burst ripped through the Somali man's center mass. He dropped his flashlight and his AK-47 as he collapsed.

Directing controlled bursts up the ladder, Jack picked off the next three pirates. He caught the last of them just as he tried to clamber out of the ladderway onto the lower 'tween deck.

The man dropped from the ladder and slammed to the deck on top of his accomplices.

Panicked shouts in Somali echoed from the 'tween deck above.

Jack swung his HK to his side and reached into his shoulder bag. He had snagged a grenade launcher on his last pass through Hold 1. He opened its barrel with a flick of his wrist, loaded a tear gas shell, and closed it with a jerk of his arm. It shut with a solid *clack,* and he braced its stock against his shoulder. He charged forward, aimed at a slight angle up the ladder, and fired.

The shell rocketed up through the ladderway, rebounded off the next deck's overhead, and detonated with a loud *pop* somewhere on the lower 'tween deck. Heavy, billowing waves of gas overhead obscured Jack's view. Hacking coughs wafted down from above—the pirates were caught in the thick of the cloud.

Gunfire ripped down through the ladderway. Bullets pinged off the lower hold's deck and peppered the bulkheads with wild ricochets. Jack ducked between two pallets until the barrage ceased, and then he returned fire up the ladderway, shooting just as blindly as his foes—but with better luck. A pained grunt told him his shots had found their mark, and he dodged another falling body just before it crashed in a limp heap atop the other dead men at his feet.

Jack slung his HK behind his back and started climbing. As he passed through the ladderway on his climb past the gas-filled lower 'tween deck, he held his breath and squeezed his eyes shut against the stinging fumes. *If only I'd thought to grab a mask.*

He was three rungs shy of the upper 'tween deck when he froze. What if the escaping Somali pirate was waiting for him, lying in ambush? Fresh air spilling down from above cleared away some of the gas around Jack's head, so he risked half-opening his eyes. He drew his SIG and pulled himself over the edge, pointing the pistol to his right: clear. He twisted to his left: clear. He holstered the SIG, climbed onto the upper 'tween deck, and moved to cover between the pallets clustered in the middle of the compartment.

I can't stay here.

He glanced up the starboard side, through the open

watertight doors that linked the holds' upper 'tween decks. That was the direction from which the pirates would come, but on what side? He couldn't defend both at the same time; they were too far apart. He would have to choose one side to protect, and one to surrender. And he needed to make his choice quickly, because in a matter of minutes, his enemies would arrive in force.

He loaded a fresh magazine into his HK.

Here's where the fun begins.

12:00 A.M. - 01:00 A.M.

The hollered message over the radio bordered on unintelligible. At the first break in Samir's panicked flood of gibberish, Osman replied, "Say again? Samir! Repeat your message! Slowly!"

More garbled noise stuttered over the channel. It sounded to Osman as if Samir was trying to talk while running. He handed the radio to Sadiq. "Do you know what he's saying?"

Sadiq listened for several seconds, then shook his head. "No clue."

"He's shouting like he just saw the devil himself." Osman shot a suspicious look at Sadiq. "Why isn't he up here? And who else is missing?"

"Three of our men never answered your call to regroup. I sent Samir and a few others to look for them." He lobbed the radio back to Osman. "Sounds like they found something."

"Why did you not tell me of this?"

The question seemed to offend Sadiq. "I have it under control."

"Do you?" Osman waved the radio at him. "It does not sound that way to me."

Before their argument could escalate, Jibríl swiveled his chair away from the desk. "Osman! Pilar has broken the cipher on the laptop!"

He abandoned the confrontation with Sadiq and moved to Jibríl's side. More remotely triggered actions transpired on the computer's screen. "What about the manifest? Is it there?"

Pilar responded via the smartphone's speaker, *"I'm looking for it."* Sadiq pushed in close behind Osman as they awaited her next words. *"Found it. And . . . we have a new problem."*

That was not what Osman had wanted to hear. "What problem?"

"Trent didn't list the containers' contents or recipients in plain language. He used some kind of simple code. I'll search the hard drive to see if it can tell us what's what and who's who. But it's a good bet the individual files are encrypted, so this might take a few minutes."

Sadiq turned away with an exasperated growl and wandered back out to the corridor. Osman stifled his own mounting frustration and feigned calm. "Keep working. My man Jibril will stay on the line. Let him know when you find something." He gave the young man a reassuring double slap on the back, then followed Sadiq into the corridor—just in time to see Samir stumble off the stairs and careen off a bulkhead as he raced toward him and Sadiq. Osman caught Samir by his shoulders. "What happened?" All the youth could do was gasp and cough. "Look into my eyes!" A hard shake by Osman muted Samir's panic. "Breathe! Then talk!"

"Gunman. Hold One. Bottom deck. Tear gas." He swallowed once and slowed his breathing. "All dead. Feysal, Ashkir, Abiid—"

"Quiet!" Osman let go of Samir and faced Sadiq. "Get a head count. I want to know who's left, and who's missing."

"A head count?" Sadiq hooked his thumb at Samir, Khaled, Yusuf, and Hamal. "There's just these five, the two of us, Jibril, and the crane team."

Osman grumbled curses. "We need Jibril and the crane team where they are." He frowned at Sadiq and the others. "That means it's up to us. Samir, Khaled, you're with me. Yusuf, Hamal, with Sadiq. Saleem, stay with Jibril. We need to go belowdecks, find the straggler, and kill him."

• • •

The counterattack came sooner than Jack had expected.

He had set himself up at the forward end of Hold 2, behind the starboard corner of the stacked shipping containers. From there, he had a clear view aft on the starboard side of the upper 'tween deck, through two open doorways into the engineering section. The port side of the deck was obstructed from his view, but he had reasoned the pirates would likely split their attack between port and starboard. When he saw them coming on one side, he assumed they were advancing on the other, as well.

Muzzle flash—the angry buzz of AK-47 ripped around the corner, through the farthest aft doorway. Shots screamed past Jack's head, forcing him to duck behind the corner. More rounds caromed off the bulkheads behind him. The pirates were attacking on both sides, as he had expected.

He poked his head out and glimpsed a silhouette dashing to cover on the aft transverse of Hold 3. Jack jogged behind the shipping containers to the port side and looked aft, just in time to dodge another wild salvo from an AK-47. The shooting ceased, so he checked again. The port side was clear. No one lingered on the long straightaways.

They're smarter than they look.

By his count, the pirates had moved two men through each door, roughly twenty seconds apart. He hurried back to starboard, counted off the last few seconds of an imaginary countdown in his head, then pivoted around the corner firing short bursts from his HK. Most of his shots struck the deck and bulkheads, but a few came close enough to the pirate charging through the aft doorway to make the man duck as he ran to cover.

Retaliatory fire forced Jack back behind the corner. Shipping containers pealed like bells as one salvo after another deflected off their sides.

Six guys. They've already divided themselves. Now all I need to do is conquer.

He lay down on his back and rolled to starboard, ending in a prone position, ready to fire. As soon as his eye found the targeting sight of his HK, a pirate pulled shut the watertight door to the engineering section, plunging the hold into near total darkness. A heavy metallic clanking from the other side of the ship alerted Jack that the other aft door had also been shut.

It was a good tactical decision by the pirates. They were smart not to let themselves be silhouetted as they pushed forward, and it was reasonable for them to think the cover of darkness would work to their advantage.

It was also a mistake Jack intended to capitalize on, with a vengeance.

He got up on one knee and lowered his night-vision goggles into position. Then he traded the HK for the grenade launcher. This time he opened the launcher with slow, steady pressure, so as not to telegraph his attack. He loaded another irritant gas shell, eased the weapon closed, then braced it against his shoulder. *Fire in the hole, you bastards.*

The shell launched with a resonant *foomp*, flew through the open doorway between Hold 2 and Hold 3, bounced off the closed watertight door at the far end, then detonated, filling the rear quarter of the aft hold with choking gas. Rather than wait for the pirates to regroup, Jack loaded another gas shell and fired it through the doorway, this time aiming short to bounce it off the shipping containers so it would detonate along the starboard gangway.

That left the pirates only one clear path out of the smoke.

Jack tucked the still-warm launcher back into his shoulder bag, hefted the HK, and scrambled to the port side, where he dropped to one knee and took aim into the roiling curtain of noxious vapors expanding to fill Hold 3. It took a few seconds, but then he saw a trio of men stagger forward through the cloud, flailing their arms and weaving like drunks.

He switched the HK from semiautomatic to single-fire. A deep breath, a slow exhalation. His pulse slowed, and his aim steadied. He waited until he felt the perfect stillness that dwelled between heartbeats—then he fired.

A perfect head shot took off the top of one pirate's skull.

Another breath in, another out. He put a round clean through the next pirate's throat. Their gas-blinded comrades didn't seem to realize two of their number had been picked off.

Running footsteps resounded on the other side of Hold 2. Someone had made it out of the gas—more than one person by the overlapping of their footfalls. Jack retrieved the detonator from his bag and dashed back onto the transverse for protection as he triggered one set of mines.

A deafening explosion rocked the ship as the Claymores in Hold 3 detonated. The brimstone stench of cordite and the chemical tang of spent C-4 filled the air as orange flames and black smoke belched through the open doorways. Jack jogged back to the starboard corner of the shipping container stacks and looked aft. The dense smoke in the aft hold was aglow with the weltering light of isolated small fires.

There was no sign of the pirates—until an AK-47 was thrust blindly around the far end of the shipping container stack, to loose another barrage down the starboard side of Hold 2. Bullets danced off the bulkheads. Jack hit the deck—but not quickly enough. He winced at a hot sting of metal ripping into his left flank, just above his belt. He clutched the wound by reflex, only to jerk his hand away when the slightest contact sent hideous jabs of pain through his gut.

Son of a bitch.

Warm blood soaked the front of his shirt as he reached back to feel for an exit wound. To his dismay, he didn't find one. *Whatever hit me is still inside.*

More bullets rang out against the bulkheads on either side of him.

Can't hold my ground on two fronts, and I can't risk setting off the Claymores in this hold till I reach the next one.

He tried to stand. The heat in his side almost dropped him back to his knees. His hand pressed on the wound, and dark blood spilled over and between his fingers. He winced and swallowed his pain.

Don't go into shock. You go into shock, you die.

Taking out the pirates was no longer Jack's top priority. He had to stanch his bleeding before he lost consciousness. To do that, he had to find a first aid kit before it was too late.

With his left hand on his wound, he forced himself to stand. He drew his SIG and steeled himself for what had to be done.

He let the pistol lead the way as he stepped out from cover on the starboard side. Despite the searing pain in his torso and the lightness in his head, he kept the weapon steady as he laid down a steady barrage of covering fire, all while backing through the doorway behind him. As soon as the SIG clacked empty, he holstered it, then pulled the door shut in front of him and spun the wheel in its center to lock it down. Then he reached into his bag, found the detonator, and triggered another set of mines, filling Hold 2 with fire, smoke, and shrapnel.

Bleeding and in ever-worsening agony, Jack lurched toward Hold 1's forward bulkhead, fully aware he was heading into a dead end—and that all the pirates who were still alive would soon be coming in after him.

• • •

Scoured by shrapnel and peppered with splinters, Osman shook his head and fought to regain his balance. He, Sadiq, and Yusuf had been out of the direct line of fire when the mines exploded around them in Hold 2. Only Hamal, who recklessly charged ahead when the straggler ceased firing, had been in the killing zone when the charges went off. Through the ragged, lingering curtain of smoke, Osman saw Hamal's ravaged corpse lying facedown on the deck.

Despite being on the transverse gangway, Osman, Yusuf, and Sadiq had weathered a storm of ricochets and debris. Most of the wounds they suffered were minor, consisting of cuts and bits of embedded wood, plastic, and metal. Not enough to stop them, but enough to slow them down. The greater wound had been losing Khaled and Samir early in the fight. With them and Hamal now gone, Osman's tactical options were far more limited. Worst of all, as far as he had been able to tell, they had yet to strike a decisive blow against their lone enemy.

Sadiq sleeved blood from his face. "He had traps in Holds Two and Three. He might have more waiting for us."

"Agreed." Osman leaned and looked around the shipping containers. "He closed the starboard hatch. He wants to make us attack on the port side."

Yusuf loaded a fresh magazine into his rifle. "Then we should stay to starboard."

That sounded like a bad idea to Osman. "What if he trapped the door?"

"All his traps have been command initiated," Sadiq said.

"So far." Osman imagined the worst. "Maybe he *wants* us to open the door."

A voice on their radios interrupted the debate. *"Jibril to Osman."*

He thumbed the talk switch. "Go ahead."

"Pilar found the container! Bay four, row two, tier four!"

Finally, some good news. "Tell Dubad. Have him pull it up immediately."

"He and his brothers are already working on it."

Sadiq lifted his own radio and joined the conversation. "Dubad! This is Sadiq. How many containers do you have to move to retrieve the one for Newbold?"

There was a slight delay before the crane operator responded. *"Three."*

"Keep those containers safe. Whatever is inside them belongs to us."

Jibril's voice quavered. *"Colonel Newbold told us to dump them overboard."*

Rage distorted Sadiq's already fearsome mien. "What? Why?"

It was Dubad who answered. *"The only place I can put the containers after I pull them up is on top of other containers. Stacking them means locking them down, one corner at a time, to make sure they don't fall off the deck or roll on top of my brothers every time the ship rides a wave. Doing it that way takes time."*

Sadiq fumed as Jibril added, *"That is why Colonel Newbold told us to dump the other containers. His chopper is on its way, and he wants his container ready to go when it arrives."*

"I don't care what he—"

"Do as Newbold says," Osman cut in. He lifted a hand to quell Sadiq's protest. "There are over a hundred containers on this ship. We can lose three and still be rich men."

"If they were filled with money, would you be so quick to throw them away?" Sadiq continued, into the radio, "Dubad, any cargo you throw overboard comes out of *your* share!"

Osman grabbed Sadiq's sleeve. "Don't be a fool! Newbold is

paying us a fortune for the missiles! We can't afford to make an enemy of him!"

"Maybe *you* cannot. I do not fear him, or his toy soldiers."

That was the end of Osman's patience. He drew his pistol and thrust it up against Sadiq's jaw. "Then fear *me*." He talked into the radio. "Dubad, this is Osman. For every container I see stacked on the main deck, I will put one bullet in your brain. Do you understand?"

The crane operator sounded shaken. *"Yes, Osman."*

"Good. Jibril, you and Saleem get to the main deck and help defend the crane." Now he only needed to bring Sadiq under control. "Most of our men are dead. We have gone from splitting these riches between nineteen to sharing them among eight. We could dump a *dozen* containers and it wouldn't matter. You will be rich enough."

"No one is *ever* rich enough." Sadiq pulled free of Osman's grasp. "And right now, the only thing between me and my money is the man in the next hold. I am going in there to kill him. Are you coming? Or would you like to give *him* some of my money, too?"

Osman considered letting Sadiq face the straggler alone. Then he imagined his hotheaded subordinate emerging victorious and branding him a coward.

I have not come this far just to give up now.

He slapped a fresh magazine into his AK-47. "Let us finish it."

• • •

Jack was three-quarters of the way up the ladder to the main deck when he heard voices in the hold beneath him. *Here they come.*

He looked down. The starboard door was still closed, which meant the pirates had come in the port side, as he'd hoped. The wound in his side raged as he lifted his left hand to the remote detonator he had clipped to his duffel's strap, which was stretched diagonally across his chest. *Hope you boys like it hot.* He keyed the trigger.

Only the Claymore on the starboard side detonated, spewing smoke and scattering hot metal projectiles down the empty side of the hold. Jack grimaced, as much from disappointment as from discomfort. *They must have cut the linking detcord. I was afraid they'd figure that out.*

Dangling off a ladder was no vantage from which to engage hostiles. As much as Jack wanted to reach for his SIG or fish a grenade from his duffel, he gritted his teeth and climbed as quietly as he was able. In a few seconds he would be in the ladderway, between the hold's overhead and the topside hatch to the main deck. All he had to do was get out of sight before—

A pirate shouted a single word in Somali, and bullets tore across the bulkhead to Jack's left, and wild shots raked the steel plates that covered the hold from above.

Damn it.

White-hot jolts of pain shot through his abdomen as he forced himself to climb faster, scrambling to stay ahead of the fusillade from below. A flurry of shots narrowly missed his feet as he clambered into the ladderway. There was a small landing between the hold's ladder and the upper ladder that led to the deck. He stopped there to pull his duffel to his side and fish out one of the grenades he'd acquired a few hours earlier.

He waited until he heard running footsteps; then he pulled the grenade's pin and let it drop. Then he resumed climbing, growling through the burning sensation knifing into his side.

Below him, the grenade struck the deck with a *clang*. Panicked whoops. Cries of alarm. Then a bone-rattling blast, and a stinging rush of heat surging up the ladderway. A whiff of spent explosives put a smile of grim satisfaction on Jack's face.

He pushed open the topside hatch half an inch and peeked outside. There was no one on the forecastle, and the main deck was awash in the noise generated by the crane's motors and hydraulics. Jack drew his SIG and pushed the topside hatch all the way open, expecting a fight. Instead, he saw that the pirates had stacked the cargo hold covers from Holds 2 and 3 atop the covers for Hold 1, creating a barrier high enough to let him stand upright and remain hidden.

If only I could stand up without doubling over. He clutched at his wound. It was wet with fresh blood; climbing the ladder had only made it worse. *Hold it together.*

He closed the hatch to the hold, then drew his SIG and limped aft with one hand pressed to his side. Every step provoked new waves of pain in his gut, making the ship seem far longer than it had just a few hours earlier. *Just make it to the infirmary,* he told himself. The ship's medical bay was well equipped; serious injuries were a common occurrence aboard cargo ships of all kinds, and the *Barataria* was no different. Everything he would need to patch himself up would be there. All he had to do was get to it.

As he moved past the stacked hold covers, the stretch of the main deck between him and the superstructure suddenly looked very empty. Illumination from the crane's work lights spilled past the holds and washed away the shadows with vast pools of dim light.

The crane's gears turned, and as Jack got a clear look at it, he saw that it was lifting a forty-foot-long shipping container out of Hold 2. He expected to see it moved aside and restacked. Instead, the man in the crane cab swung the blue steel box over the port side of the ship—and then the taut wires holding the box level went slack and unwound, and the container plunged into the gulf. Its impact kicked up a wall of water that showered the deck.

I guess they know where the missiles are.

There was one man operating the crane, and two more moving around and between the stacked containers, hooking up cables and removing the connectors that linked the metal boxes. The man standing on the deck had an AK-47 strapped across his back, but his friend doing the monkey work of unlatching the containers down in the hold had shed his weapons to make it possible for him to fit in the tight spaces between the stacks.

If they're busy enough, I can wait until they turn away, then make a break for—

Even from across the deck, Jack heard the pirates' radios spit static, followed by a stream of high-volume Somali invective. All at once, the two men on the deck and the one inside the crane's cab started looking every which way around the deck.

Within moments, the men on deck spotted him. Jack winced as the crane operator trained his work lights on him. In less than a second, Jack had to choose between attack and retreat.

He put three shots into the man with the AK-47.

Monkey Man ducked into the gap in the container stack. The guy in the crane threw open the cab's door and climbed out while lifting his own AK-47 into position.

Moving back toward the cover offered by the stacked hold covers, Jack laid down suppressing fire on the crane cab. Three solid hits turned its shatterproof glass white with cracks and forced its operator back inside.

Automatic fire peppered the deck and the forecastle bulkhead. Jack looked for the source of the incoming rounds and spotted muzzle flashes from aft. Two of the men he'd battled below had come back up through the superstructure and were advancing on the starboard side. Two others charged up the port side.

The crane's work light tracked Jack as he retreated to the narrow space between the stacked hold covers and the forecastle bulkhead—just in time to see a scorched, bloodied Somali climb out of the same topside hatch he had used moments earlier.

Three snap shots from Jack's SIG scattered the climbing pirate's brains across the deck and took down the pair of pirates running up the port side before the pistol clacked empty with its slide locked open. He forced it shut and holstered it, then took a fast peek over the top of the stacked covers.

Starboard: The two men had reached the middle of the main deck and were closing in. Port: Monkey Man grabbed his fallen comrade's rifle and moved up behind the crane operator.

Making a stand where I am would be suicide—but moving would be just as bad. Jack dug out the grenade launcher and his last hand grenade. *Time to improvise.*

He loaded a tear gas shell into the launcher. Facing aft, he lifted the grenade in his right hand, pulled its pin with his teeth, and hurled it over the stacked covers.

It rebounded off the blocky base of the forward crane and detonated. Jack moved left and fired the tear gas aft down the starboard side. The fat shell hit one of the pirates square in the gut and knocked him on his back, just before it erupted and engulfed him and his companion in toxic smoke.

Knowing his cover would last for only a few seconds, Jack bit down on his pain and climbed the steps to the forecastle deck, then pivoted into position behind its bulwark.

On the main deck, the starboard pirates ran forward to escape the smoke. The two on the port side looked scuffed but otherwise unharmed.

Jack pulled the submachine gun off his back, loaded its last full magazine, and set the weapon for single-fire. He aimed over the bulwark and put his first shot in the crane's working light, which exploded and rained shattered glass and dying sparks on the pirates below. When the phosphors faded, the deck disappeared into near total darkness.

This, he decided, was a good time to negotiate. "Hey! On the deck! Can you hear me?"

A momentary delay, then a wary reply. "We can hear you."

"Lay down your weapons and abandon ship in one of the life rafts, and I'll let you live."

His ultimatum was met by laughter. A burst of automatic fire stuttered against the other side of the bulwark. Then a different, more arrogant voice called out, "This ship is ours! Throw down *your* weapons, and maybe we will let *you* live!"

Jack felt blood seeping from his wound. He didn't have time for a standoff.

I gave them a chance. He loaded a fresh magazine into his SIG. *No mercy. No prisoners.*

• • •

Huddled behind the stacked hold covers, Osman strained to see Sadiq right in front of him. The half moon hung low and red in the western sky; it threw a ruddy streak of light across the gulf but did little to illuminate the deck of the *Barataria*. The silence was disturbed only by the groans of shifting metal, the clanks of swinging chains, and the slapping of waves against the hull.

From the other side of the main deck, a sudden patter of

running footsteps was followed by the flash-crack of AK-47s spraying the forecastle bulwark in full auto. Lit up by the glow of their own weapons, Dubad and his brother Luqmaan made a run for the port forecastle ladder.

In the strobed light of their barrage, Osman watched both men jerk back and collapse in stuttered slow motion. Their weapons clicked empty as they collapsed a yard shy of the ladder.

He heard Sadiq whisper, "I have a grenade. When I give the signal, give me cover."

"How can you throw a grenade? We can't even see the forecastle."

"I'll have the light from your rifle." Sadiq shuffled past him, stirring the sultry air. "Stay here. I want to move closer to the crane to get a better angle for the throw."

"Wait! The signal?"

"I'll hit the deck three times with the butt of my rifle."

Osman listened until he lost track of Sadiq in the gray noise of wind and water coursing against the drifting ship. Alone with his thoughts, he was ashamed to find himself contemplating retreat. Then he imagined Sadiq returning home with the ship as its sole survivor and telling the world of Osman's cowardice. He tightened his grip on his rifle. *This will work. It has to work.*

Two muffled thumps from his left. Was that the signal? Had he missed it? He strained to hear Sadiq's signal to fire, but all he found was the wind. Then a scrape of motion behind him—

He saw no flash in the dark and barely heard the *pop* of a suppressed pistol—and then all he knew was the final, silent darkness of oblivion.

• • •

Smoke snaked from the muzzle of the SIG's suppressor. The pirates were dead, and the weapon grew heavy in Jack's hand. He holstered it and slumped sideways against the stacked hold covers.

The bleeding from his injury was worse. Through the monochromatic filter of his night-vision goggles, he couldn't see the stain spreading across his black shirt, but he felt it. He put pressure on the wound and grimaced. The piercing, acute pain became deep and pervasive. His balance betrayed him, sending his steps astray as he staggered aft. He used the starboard bulwark to hold himself upright.

Keep moving, he told his body. *One step after another.*

His head swam. He couldn't feel his feet, but he watched them move. His only points of reference were the smattering of lights left on in various compartments of the superstructure. As long as he kept them in sight, he knew he was headed in the right direction.

His vision blurred, and the hiss of the ocean breeze faded to a surreal droning.

Losing focus. Keep it together. Just reach the infirmary and patch yourself up.

Time became fluid. One moment the superstructure wavered in the distance, the next it loomed above him, monolithic and daunting. By memory he turned his feet toward the stairs. It was only three flights up from the main deck to the infirmary.

On hands and knees, he pulled himself up the first flight, growling like an animal. He dragged himself across the poop deck to the next flight of stairs. Halfway to Level 02, he collapsed. The impact sent blinding pain through his side, leaving his stomach sick but his head clear. Sprawled on his belly, he gasped for breath.

The infirmary was only one and a half flights of stairs away, but his strength was gone. Jack knew he couldn't fight his way up the remaining steps—just as he knew that if he didn't, he would be as good as dead in less than an hour.

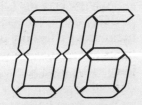

01:00 A.M. - 02:00 A.M.

Everything was spinning. Consciousness returned with a shudder and a sickening flood of nausea. Jack sucked air through gritted teeth and forced himself to remember where he was and what was happening. He was lying on a waffle-grate deck, between the stairs to the main deck and the next flight up, to the officers' quarters and mess in the superstructure.

His hand found the wound in his left side. *You've been shot. You're bleeding.* A deep breath, in through his nose, out through his mouth. *You need to stop the bleeding. Don't pass out again. Stay awake. Keep moving.*

Standing was too difficult. Climbing the stairs was out of the question. Then he saw it, lit by the faint spillage of light from a rear window of the superstructure. An enclosed orange pod mounted on downward-sloped steel rails: an emergency lifeboat. The *Barataria* carried two of them, one on each side of the aft poop deck. Jack and the rest of the ship's crew had been repeatedly drilled in the protocols for boarding and launching the escape craft in the event of an emergency. The ship's infirmary was out of his reach, but he knew from the training drills that there was a generously stocked emergency medical kit inside the lifeboat.

That'll do.

He crawled toward the lifeboat, pulling himself across the steel deck, suddenly thankful his palms had become tacky with half-dried blood. Across the narrow gangplank to the orange escape craft. It was agony to stretch his hand up to the handle of its door, but he pushed through the swimming sensation and locked his hand around it. His weight pulled the lever down, and the door swung toward him. He pushed it open just enough to slither in on his belly, taking care to keep his wounded side up, to reduce blood loss and avoid leaving too obvious a trail on the deck. As soon as his feet slipped past the heavy watertight hatch, it thumped closed behind him.

Jack navigated by memory, moving to the stern of the lifeboat. That was where the medical kit was located, under a panel in the deck. It wasn't locked, a precaution for which he was grateful. He probed inside it with his hands and found a small LED flashlight and the waterproof bag that contained the emergency surgical kit. This kind of gear was typical on vessels that operated in the open seas. After all, one never knew where a ship might go down, or what injuries might need to be treated in the aftermath of an evacuation.

He unzipped the waterproof bag and made a fast inventory of its contents, all of which were hermetically sealed. Nothing appeared to have been disturbed. Inside he found the medicine case, the suture kit, and the bandage kit. He unwrapped a thermal blanket, knowing it would be the closest thing to a sanitary bedsheet as he was likely to find in the lifeboat. Taking care to touch it only on the side that would be in contact with the lifeboat's deck, he unfolded it and laid it flat, to provide himself with a relatively sterile operating environment.

There was no point to trying to remove the bullet. He knew from his emergency field medicine training as a Delta Force operator that in a situation such as this, he would do more harm than good by attempting to extract the projectile. Most bullets and shrapnel entered the body hot enough not to pose a serious risk of infection. That usually occurred later, as the wounds were allowed to remain open and festering. If he went digging around for the bullet, all he would do was push more bacteria into the wound and increase his risk of sepsis.

I have to sanitize my hands before I touch the wound again.

He lay down on the clean sheet and took a small steel mirror from the surgical kit. With a roll of white medical adhesive, he taped the mirror to the side of a seat inside the lifeboat, at an angle that would let him observe his work. Then he used the same adhesive to fix his flashlight's beam on his wound.

Next, he tore open several packets of alcohol wipes and cleaned his hands until there was no more sign of blood or contamination. Then he put on sterile latex gloves, opened packets of presoaked alcohol swabs, and used them to clean his wound, whose edges he now saw were ragged and irregular, just as he would have expected from a ricocheted 7.62 mm rifle round. He placed dry, sterile gauze pads around the wound to isolate it and hone his focus.

Now to suppress any infection.

He swabbed the edges of the wound with an iodine solution, then poured a small amount into the wound. It frothed. He used some gauze to soak up the mess. *Not much reaction to the iodine. That's good.* He checked his shirt, to see if the bullet had taken any of the fabric inside the wound. When he pushed all the ripped edges back together, he didn't see any of the cotton missing. *Lucky.*

Had the bullet carried part of his shirt with it inside him, he would have had no choice but to risk cutting himself open to remove the potential infector. But seeing that the bullet had gone in alone meant he was free to move on to the next step of his self-assessment.

He selected a disposable needle from the surgical kit, loaded it with a measured dose of 2 percent buffered lidocaine solution, and injected it into the dermis at three points around his wound. Knowing it would need a few minutes to take effect, he gathered his surgical tools. Most of the key suturing implements were stored individually sealed and ready for use. Lastly, he inspected the wound in as gingerly a manner as he was able. In less than a minute he determined that despite the bleeding, there hadn't been any damage to any major veins or arteries. If he could stop the bleeding and close the wound, he might be all right.

With his left hand, he held the wound open a couple of centimeters. He held a packet of sterile, hemostatic gauze in his teeth and ripped it open with his right hand. Taking the gauze between his thumb and forefinger, he rolled it into a tube and guided it inside the ragged tear in his flesh. The mineral-infused gauze packed in without resistance, filling the cavity created by the bullet. Horrendous jolts of pain from inside his flank told Jack the lidocaine hadn't fully taken effect yet, but he couldn't afford to wait. The wound had to be closed now.

The edges of his torn skin finally went numb. He threaded some silk into the curved suturing needle and began working it through edges on either side of the wound, leaving enough slack to let himself work until he had the first few passes in place. Then he gently tugged them together and took up the slack, until he had knitted the wound shut. He snipped off the excess thread and discarded the needle.

Almost done, he told himself.

He opened a tube of topical antibiotic, squeezed out a pea-sized dollop on his fingertip, and spread it over his crude, crooked sutures. Next he laid a transparent surgical dressing over the stitches and secured it with four carefully overlapped strips of medical tape. Then he put another sterile gauze bandage over the whole mess, as a precaution.

Exhausted and shaking from adrenaline overload, Jack switched off the flashlight and let himself slip into the dark, silent bliss of unconsciousness.

• • •

"Where the hell is everybody?" From high overhead, in a circling CH-47 Chinook helicopter, Colonel Maxwell Newbold found it difficult to discern the details of the carnage on the deck of the cargo ship below. He nudged his command sergeant and shouted over the pounding clamor of the rotors. "Teej! Shine the spotlight over there. Near the forecastle."

Sergeant Major T. J. Andrzejczyk, or "Teej" as he was known to most of his comrades in Firethorn's elite command company, swung the searchlight toward the bow of the *Barataria*. The brawny noncommissioned officer never asked why, or what he was looking for. He just followed orders and got things done—a quality Newbold had always liked about the man.

The harsh white beam slashed across the deck and settled on a cluster of bodies. Newbold fought to steady his binoculars. "Looks like Muhamad and his men are out of the picture."

Teej sounded suspicious. "But who took them out?"

"No idea. Swing the light aft." Newbold followed the searchlight through his binoculars and assessed what he saw on the deck. "No sign of the ship's crew. Or anyone else."

"Maybe they got into a fight over money and clipped themselves."

"If that's the case, they just saved us a few bullets." Wind stung his face and made him squint as he pointed amidships. "Put the light back on the center cargo hold."

The sergeant major shifted the searchlight's beam onto the open hold and its exposed stacks of forty-foot-long shipping containers. He pointed at the one row whose top container was absent. "Looks like they started clearing the way but didn't finish." He hooked a thumb over his shoulder, at the squad they had brought along for the retrieval. "Time to send in the clowns?"

Something about the scenario felt wrong to Newbold. He noted tendrils of smoke rising from the opened holds. Scorch marks on the main deck where munitions—probably grenades—had been detonated. And the fact that all the pirates were dead, when at least half a dozen of them, if not more, had been alive an hour earlier. The details weren't adding up to a narrative that made sense. The pirates had been fractious, yes, but enough to self-immolate like this?

Andrzejczyk snapped him back into the here-and-now. "Colonel? What're your orders?"

There was nothing more to be learned from the air. It was time to put boots on the deck. "Send them in. Tell First Squad to get that crane working and put towing cables on our container. Make sure they know time is a factor. Have Second Squad sweep the ship for survivors."

"And if they find any?"

"Shoot to kill."

"Roger that, sir." Teej cupped his helmet mic. "Hangdog, this Oxbow. Put us over the ship's main hold. Squads One and Two, stand by to deploy. First Squad, secure the package.

Second Squad, secure the ship with prejudice. On my mark. Three! Two! One! Go, go, go!"

On the other side of the Chinook, a pair of four-man teams leaped from the chopper's open side door with only their ropes and harnesses to guide and control their descent to the ship's deck. Newbold didn't waste time worrying after any of them. They all had been trained by the world's best militaries and knew how to do their jobs with lethal speed and precision.

Despite that, Newbold knew he would prefer to be on the ship with them, leading the way, rather than remaining aboard the chopper. But the privileges of command came bundled with certain sacrifices, the chief of which was that his employers and their clients expected him, as a leader, to remain separate from the fray as much as possible, to ensure a continuity of command and control during all phases of the operation. All the same, like most adrenaline junkies born of combat, he missed his days in the mix and yearned to return to the action.

Andrzejczyk lowered his binoculars. "All our boots are down and safe." He cupped his mic again. "Hangdog, Oxbow. Resume circling, but keep us close."

Newbold checked his watch. Its digital face displayed the time as 01:21 A.M. "Best guess, Sergeant Major: How long until we're homeward bound?"

"Assuming the ship is clear, we'll finish our sweep in twenty. We'll have the package wired for flight in thirty."

"And if the ship isn't clear?"

A rakish smirk. "Then we'll finish our sweep in twenty-five and be good to fly in thirty."

"Hooah, Sergeant Major."

"Hooah, Colonel."

• • •

Coaxed back from oblivion by a devil's drumbeat reverberating through the deck, Jack jolted awake inside the sepulchral darkness of the lifeboat. It took him a second to get his bearings and focus on the steady, thudding tempo that had roused him.

What is that? It's not the ship's engines.

He sat up, winced at the deep ache in his side, and glanced at his watch. It was 1:53 A.M. The steady thumping's pitch rose and fell while he gathered his gear. He put a fresh magazine in the SIG, then reloaded one of the empty HK magazines. As he slung his rifle behind his back and hefted his shoulder bag, he recognized the sound pummeling the *Barataria*. It was a helicopter, a big one.

He sidled over to the lifeboat's hatch and carefully looked in either direction through its oval window. There were several men moving in pairs—all attired in body armor and camouflage battle dress uniforms, and brandishing M4A1 carbine assault rifles—descending the exterior stairs of the superstructure. They carried themselves like trained professionals, every action swift and decisive.

Their uniforms bore no national insignia. If they were members of some country's armed forces, Jack figured they were likely to be special forces operators, or some other unit that functioned without identifying marks, for the sake of deniability.

Then, as they turned on the stair's switchback, he saw the logo stenciled on the right side of each troop's helmet: a black lick of flame encompassing the reverse silhouette of a narrow, downward-pointing sword—the emblem of Firethorn International, an Australian-owned private military company that operated out of South Africa with little to no regulation or oversight.

Jack had heard Firethorn called "the French Foreign Legion of PMCs." It was a riff on its recruiting practices, which culled the most brutal and amoral talent from the world's militaries. Though most of its personnel hailed from English-speaking nations, it counted a fair number of members from South and Central America, Southeast Asia, and Eastern Europe. In addition to conducting legally and morally questionable paramilitary operations in trouble spots around the world, Firethorn had also made a name for itself training other paramilitary groups.

Which explains who prepped and equipped the pirates.

The two mercs moved out of sight. Jack opened the lifeboat's door and slipped back onto the lower poop deck. He still felt light-headed from blood loss, but forty minutes of rest had given him back a small measure of his strength. A few deep breaths slowed his pulse and improved his blood oxygen levels, giving him the energy to climb the stairs two at a time with his HK braced against his shoulder.

Level 02 was clear and quiet, so he continued up to Level 03, which was also deserted. If the mercs had left anyone up here, he expected them to be in the pilothouse. He moved around the back of the upper poop deck and entered through the port side door, near the radio room.

The door was still open, and there was no sound or sign of activity from inside the command suite. There was no one in the radio room, chart room, or pilothouse. One look at the ship's master console confirmed the *Barataria* was still adrift. Jack moved forward to get a clear view out the forward windows of the activity transpiring below on the main deck.

A plume of water jetted upward alongside the port side amidships as a steel shipping container was released by the aft cargo crane and allowed to plunge into the sea. Meanwhile, the helicopter, which had stirred Jack out of his stupor, was lowering a three-point cargo cable into the *Barataria*'s center hold, on which it had trained its spotlight.

If they're hooking up the chopper's cables, that means they've found the missiles—and I'm out of time. He turned and jogged back the way he'd come, then dashed up the stairs onto the observation deck above the pilothouse. He lay down, took the extra magazines for the HK out of his bag and put them within easy reach, and then found his remote detonator.

I can't let them airlift those nukes.

He set the remote and pressed the trigger.

Catastrophic blasts boomed from deep inside the ship's holds. Towers of smoke poured from Hold 2 and Hold 3. Four men scrambled up out of Hold 2 as fire alarms blared throughout the ship. Their four comrades, whom Jack had watched leave the superstructure moments earlier, raced to help them onto the main deck.

Jack settled into position beneath the observation deck's

lowest railing, set his HK for single-fire, aimed, and pulled the trigger. The suppressed report was swallowed by the Chinook's rotor noise, but his shot struck one merc in the throat and knocked him back into the open hold.

Another shot, another kill—clean in the back of one man's neck. *Two down.*

The dead merc's comrades recoiled from the spray of blood on their faces. In the fleeting confusion, Jack landed another shot in one man's unarmored thigh. The profound spray of blood from the wound confirmed the shot had severed the man's femoral artery. *Three down.*

The mercs scattered for cover. Above, rotor noise from the Chinook increased in volume and pitch as its pilot put all its power into a pure vertical ascent—the only maneuver it could make until the container it was lifting cleared the top of the hold.

Suppressing fire from a couple of mercs disintegrated the windows on the forward side of the superstructure. Two men, one on either side of the ship, sprinted aft toward the stairs.

Jack put down the rifle and grabbed the grenade launcher. *Time for the rough stuff.* He loaded a high-explosive shell, slapped the breechloader shut, aimed over the edge, and fired. The grenade screamed downward, giving away his position, but the exposure was worth it when a blast engulfed the main deck in an orange fireball that fried three mercs at once. *Six down. Time to move.*

He threw the still-smoking launcher into his bag, slung his rifle, and jogged in a crouch toward the stairs. As he'd expected, a spray of bullets from a gunner inside the Chinook chased him across the monkey deck until he made it all the way down the first flight of stairs and had the command level for cover. He put his back to the wall, drew his SIG, and caught his breath.

There was nothing stealthy about the men coming up the stairs on either side of him. Their boots clanged on the steel treads as they ran, announcing their every step. The man on the port side was the faster of the two. His head popped into view, and Jack put a bullet in it. As the merc's body pitched face-first onto the deck, his buddy bounded up the starboard steps, firing wildly, as if he had expected Jack to be standing in the middle of the deck. Before the second merc had a chance to adjust his aim, Jack put him down with a snap shot into his groin.

For good measure, Jack finished off the groaning soldier of fortune with a coup de grâce head shot as he passed him on his way down the starboard stairs.

A massive blast rocked the bow of the ship and blew the topside covers off Hold 1, sending pillars of flame high into the air. Jack grinned. He had wondered how long it would take for the jet fuel and artillery rounds in the lower hold to explode.

He sprinted from the stairs onto the main deck. The top of the shipping container had just come level with the top of the hold, whose deep recesses were lit by spreading flames. It would be clear in a matter of seconds, freeing the Chinook to escape with rogue nuclear weapons.

Muzzle flash lit up the open interior of the Chinook as its ramp-mounted machine gunner raked the superstructure of the *Barataria* to keep Jack at bay. Jack ran forward to cover beneath one of the side-mounted lifeboats, then ducked out long enough to spray a full-auto burst from his HK at the Chinook's belly.

Another withering burst from the chopper's onboard gunner forced Jack back under cover, then back behind the superstructure as the fearsome barrage tore the old lifeboat to pieces, peppering him with ragged fiberglass splinters.

Jack pivoted around the corner and emptied his magazine at the Chinook. He scored a lucky shot on its cargo hook mount, and one of the cables linking it to the shipping container snapped. Recoiling under stress, the steel cable lashed the deck like a whip, sending up sparks. The container, now supported by only two cables instead of a three-point rig, drooped and slumped nearly sixty degrees from level—but it remained solidly in the Chinook's grip.

Damn it.

Even with the container dipped to a nearly vertical posture, the Chinook wasted no time starting its retreat from the *Barataria*. It turned about-face above the ship and pointed itself south, toward the Somalia coast.

Jack ran toward the shipping container, which bounced off

the aft crane and twisted precariously from the Chinook's deceptively slender cargo wires. The cable he had severed from the chopper was still attached to the container, and it was being dragged across the deck. The container bashed through the starboard bulwark, leaving a sizable gap in the protective barrier. Whipping with serpentine undulations, its trailing cable followed it through the rent bulwark—and Jack dived toward it. He hydroplaned across the wet steel deck and collided with the fast-moving braid of coiled steel, and did the only thing he had time to do: He forced his right arm under it, then around it, three times, as quickly as he could. Then he braced himself and hung on.

A brutal jerk of motion yanked him through the break in the bulwark and lifted him into the air. It felt as if a giant were trying to tear his arm from his body. Beneath him, the midnight-black sea sped by. Wind stung his face and forced him to squeeze his eyes closed as the chopper accelerated away from the burning wreck of the *Barataria*.

His rifle was slung across his back, his SIG was secure on his hip, and his shoulder bag was pinned between him and the steel cable on which he had hitched a ride. He worked his left arm around the cable to take some of the stress off his already sore right arm, and then he repeated the process with his legs. He cracked open one eye to look up at the Chinook. He couldn't see it; the container obstructed his view.

That means they can't see me, either. Now all I have to do is stay awake and hope I don't rip all my sutures open.

He wasn't sure how long this ride would last or where it was headed, but he knew that whenever and wherever the mercs finally touched down, he planned to be there with them.

02:00 A.M. - 03:00 A.M.

USS *Belleau Wood* (CG-76)
The Gulf of Aden — 12°16'38.5" N, 45°09'17.7" E

Groggy and grouchy, Commander Jackson Reichert navigated his ship's corridors by memory on his way up to the command and control center. Sleep was a precious commodity aboard any U.S. Navy vessel, but it had grown especially scarce aboard the guided missile cruiser USS *Belleau Wood* since she and her crew were assigned to the antipiracy mission of Combined Task Force 151 off the eastern coast of Africa. Attacks had started to wane since the previous year's record high, thanks in part to aggressive policing by the international fleet assembled to defend the Gulf of Aden, the Suez Canal, and the Indian Ocean from the scourge of Somali buccaneers. Regardless, incidents continued to proliferate, which meant the *Belleau Wood*'s commanding officer never knew when the next crisis was going to erupt.

He stepped through the doorway into the crisp, air-conditioned air of the command center, a well-armored compartment beneath the ship's superstructure from which Reichert and his senior officers could direct all the cruiser's personnel, supplemental craft, and armaments. The space was packed tight with computers, radar and sonar display screens, and transparent tactical grids, all arranged around the central plotting table, which was configured to represent the ship's current designated area of operations. Third Watch personnel noted his arrival with obvious anxiety. They were unaccustomed to seeing the ship's CO on deck at that hour.

Reichert stood beside the ship's second officer, Lieutenant McPhail, who was serving as the shift's officer of the watch. "Sitrep, Lieutenant."

"Guyet picked up a report of a cargo ship on fire roughly seventy-five nautical miles from here." McPhail pointed out a mark he'd made on the plotting table's map. "Eleven degrees, one and a half minutes north, forty-four degrees and fifty-eight minutes east."

The location stoked Reichert's suspicions. It was less than forty miles from the Somali coastline. "Who called it in?"

"A container ship. The *Maersk Stepnica,* out of Rotterdam." McPhail pivoted away, then turned back with a printed report in his hand, courtesy of a fast-moving petty officer. He read from it. "Her bow watchman reported seeing explosions at oh-one fifty-six. He also says he might have seen a helicopter in the immediate vicinity of the burning vessel."

Since when did Somali pirates use helicopters? "Any Maydays?"

"None yet, but I have Guyet monitoring all marine channels."

It had all the hallmarks of a Somali attack, save for the troubling detail of the helicopter. Reichert wasn't sure what to make of that, but he wanted to know what was happening inside his patrol grid. He pulled his hand over his beard—which, like his hair, was dark, close cropped, and turning gray before its time. "Order a new course for the ship in distress, flank speed. Then wake up Spagnola and tell him to put a boarding team together."

"Strike or rescue?"

"Won't know till we get there. Have him roust marines *and* medics, just to be safe."

Reichert picked up a straightedge and a grease pencil, to plot the course and time to the stricken vessel. "Looks like our ETA is just under two hours. Give engineering a kick in the pants and see if we can't cut some time off that, Lieutenant."

McPhail nodded as he moved toward the radio. "Aye, sir."

• • •

Every muscle in Jack's body hurt. Holding on to a steel cable in winds exceeding 150 miles per hour had proved excruciating. The pressure of the coiled steel against his bare arms had left him with bleeding welts, and he felt bruises forming on his thighs under his black jeans. His left side still ached from his rushed and amateur self-surgery in the lifeboat, but as far as he could tell, his sutures seemed to be holding, for which he was thankful.

The Chinook started its descent. Some time in the past hour, the moon had set, and now the overcast sky was pitch dark. Not even starlight gave Jack any sense of how close he might be to the ocean's surface, and the rotor noise made it impossible to hear the surf below him.

Along the horizon, distant lights hinted at the presence of inhabited structures. Whether they were buildings in a city or campfires on the beach, Jack couldn't tell. All he knew was that they were getting closer by the minute, which meant the chopper was close to shore.

Tension in the wire under his legs was his first clue that the chopper had descended to an altitude below a hundred feet. The slack end of the wire was dragging through the water under Jack's feet, arresting its loose whipping motions. The chopper's pilot seemed intent on avoiding as much radar contact as possible during the final phase of his approach to the Somali coast.

More lights snapped on ahead of the slowing Chinook, describing a landing area on a flat and sandy patch of ground. Illumination from the fenced-in camp spilled over the beach and stretched across the breaking waves crashing ashore. Jack followed the white flicker across the wave tops and realized he was half a dozen meters above the water and dropping fast.

Time to bail out.

Jack unwound his arms from the cable first, then held on with his hands as he freed his legs. Ahead of him, waves broke into white foam on the shore. He let go of the cable.

Free fall sent a fresh rush of adrenaline through his body—and then he splashed down.

The ocean swallowed him whole. His feet touched the

shallow bottom. He kicked and propelled himself back to the surface with broad, steady strokes. His head broke free and he gulped in a chestful of air. It took him thirty seconds to swim close enough to begin wading ashore, and he let the crashing waves carry him forward, to save his strength.

Fewer than a hundred yards up the beach, the Chinook circled the fenced compound. Its dangling shipping container was dented and scorched. The chopper struggled to maintain a steady position as it lowered the banged-up container onto a big rig's flatbed, with the help of half a platoon of men decked out in desert camouflage. As soon as the container was secure on the flatbed, the Chinook released its cable harness, which fell to earth and kicked up a sandy cloud that spread across the campsite.

Jack knew a chance when he saw one. He sprang from the surf and sprinted up the beach toward the fenced compound while its personnel were all blinded by the dust storm. Before the cloud dissipated, he took shelter behind a dense outcropping of desert scrub.

From his vantage, he saw the camp was encircled by a twelve-foot-tall fence. He didn't see anything to suggest it was electrified, nor did he see any signs of surveillance equipment. The top of the fence, however, was ringed with double coils of barbed wire. Irregular discolorations in the sand on the other side suggested the mercenaries had taken the precaution of lining their perimeter with mines.

Inside the fence, Jack counted a half dozen men moving or standing guard, and he saw temporary barracks large enough to house a platoon. *I'm up against about thirty men here.* The mercs had no visible aircraft other than the Chinook, which spewed smoke and filled the air with sickly noises as it wobbled to a hard landing away from the buildings. But they had the semi for hauling the container, and a small convoy of desert-camouflaged SUVs.

Three dozen men, a fleet of trucks, and a barbed wire fence. If I had wire cutters, this would be no problem. But with no gear? He drew a breath and cleared his mind. There was always a way in. Every problem had a solution. He just needed time to find it.

The floodlights inside the camp switched off, and darkness

settled once more over the beach and the barren landscape around its perimeter.

He checked his submachine gun and made sure its mechanisms were clear of sand or other contamination from his rude splashdown minutes earlier. Then he drew his SIG from its holster and inspected it. Both weapons were functional. For the time being, he decided to rely on the SIG because it was quieter and better suited to close-quarter combat, should he stumble into a perimeter sentry.

His shoulder bag wasn't fully waterproof, but it was water resistant, which gave him reason to hope his night-vision goggles had survived the water landing. To his dismay, he found them fractured and useless. From this point onward, he would have to rely on his other senses to guide him in the dark as he ventured away from the safety of natural cover. SIG in hand, he stalked across the sandy ground and began his slow circle of the Firethorn mercenaries' camp.

Every fence has a gate. There's a way inside this camp, and I will find it.

• • •

Newbold followed Andrzejczyk across the compound to the shipping container, which now rested atop the flatbed of their sole trailer rig. A team of four men busied themselves locking down the container while the company's chief engineer, Captain Sánchez, waited at its rear with a crowbar and a massive pair of bolt cutters.

"Open it," Newbold called out.

Sánchez set down the crowbar, hefted the cutter, and sheared through the bolts on the container's doors. Newbold and Andrzejczyk reached her as she tossed away the mangled steel bolts and pulled open the double doors. "What the hell happened to this thing, Colonel?"

"There were complications."

"I'll say. It looks like it's been through a demolition derby." Sánchez tossed the crowbar inside, planted her palms on the floor of the container, and vaulted her slender form up inside the steel box. She landed in a sitting position facing the men. "Teej, pass me your light."

The sergeant major handed her his flashlight. Sánchez snapped it on, stood, grabbed the crowbar, and made her way deeper inside the container. Andrzejczyk climbed up next, then gave Newbold a hand up. They followed Sánchez, who sidestepped between crates cocooned in plastic sheeting while sweeping the flashlight's beam in slow arcs—left to right, up and down.

Anxiety and impatience gnawed at Newbold. "How does it look?"

"Like someone put it all through a blender." She trained the beam on a snapped binding cable. "A lot of the support hardware shifted in transit."

That wasn't good, and Newbold knew it. "Are the secondary components damaged?"

A defensive shrug. "No way to know until I open it up and run some tests."

Her vague answer riled Andrzejczyk. "How long is *that* gonna take?"

"I'm an engineer, not a fortune-teller. As long as it takes." She ducked under a long, narrow crate mounted on a rolling dolly whose wheels were locked. "Time to see if we got what we paid for." She wedged the crowbar under the crate's lid and pried it open. Andrzejczyk helped her pull the lid up and off, revealing the sleek, matte black marvel inside: an intact, American-made AGM-129 cruise missile. Its lean core was strangely angular, and its wings and tail fins were retracted, making it look less aerodynamic than it would be once deployed.

The mere sight of it put a smile on Newbold's face. "Ain't that a beauty."

Sánchez restrained her enthusiasm. "Let me check it before you fall in love with it."

Andrzejczyk picked up her crowbar. "I'll open the other one while you do that." He moved toward the far end of the container, where another long, narrow crate stood tucked into the opposite corner from the first one, and started forcing its lid off.

The engineer opened a Velcro-secured flap on her tactical

carrier vest, revealing a set of precision tools tucked into snug pouches and loops. Working with both hands, she quickly removed a panel from the nose of the cruise missile. Then she retrieved a miniaturized Geiger counter from a thigh pocket of her fatigues, held it to the exposed innards of the missile, and switched it on. After a few seconds of loud, fast, crackling noise, she turned it off. "Looks good. A W80 variable-yield physics package. Should be good for about one hundred fifty kilotons."

"Good." Newbold turned toward Andrzejczyk. "How does the other one look?"

"Like brand-new, Colonel. Whadda ya say, Captain? Want to give this one a look?"

"On my way." Sánchez slipped past Newbold and shimmied back to stand beside Andrzejczyk. It took her a couple of minutes to open up the second missile and repeat her test. She allowed herself a satisfied nod as she put away her tools. "Physics package intact."

Newbold checked his watch. It was 2:24 A.M. "How long until they're ready to fly?"

"I'll need at least an hour to run a basic systems check on both birds. After that, I'll need at least another hour to extract the warhead from Bird One, and another hour after that to finish the modifications to their pylon connectors. Assuming, of course, neither bird suffered any internal damage while you and your men were busy using them for a battering ram."

A frown deepened the creases on Andrzejczyk's face. "We're gonna be late."

"We were already late," Newbold said. "Now we'll be even later." He resigned himself to the situation as it was, however far from ideal it might be. "Sánchez, start the top-level—"

"Colonel!" shouted a man standing outside the open end of the container.

The trio inside the box pivoted toward the interruption. Sánchez aimed the flashlight at their brother-in-arms, and Newbold squinted to discern the man's features. "Mergenthaler?"

The prematurely balding German snapped to attention with a salute. "Yes, sir!"

"What do you want, Corporal?"

He lowered his hand. "Major Sealander says we're picking up an unauthorized signal from inside the container."

Newbold shot an angry look at Sánchez. "Check it out."

The engineer squirmed past him and hurried back to the doorway. She checked each door's edges, and on one she found a wire, which she followed up and around its top edge, past its hinge, to a camouflaged panel on the side of the container. "Here's our culprit." She tore off its concealing patch, revealing a digital display hooked up to a compact battery. Sánchez used the bottom of her borrowed flashlight to smash the transmitter into scrap. "Signal terminated."

"But the damage is done. Someone knows where these missiles are." Newbold struggled to contain his frustration. *So much for radio silence.* He took charge of his anger and defused it. There was no undoing what was done. It was time to go forward. "We need to break camp and regroup at the backup site."

Sánchez fumed. "We can't move the missiles! I need them stable while I work."

"You'll have an hour to do the systems check while we pack up. The rest will have to wait till we're back on the ground in Yemen." He turned toward Andrzejczyk. "Get the rank and file outta their bunks and into the trucks, RFN."

Andrzejczyk was moving before Newbold finished the order. "Roger that, sir."

Newbold moved to follow the sergeant major, but paused at Sánchez's protest. "If we move to the backup site, we won't make the delivery window."

"Worry about your own job, Captain. I've got mine covered."

He hoped Sánchez couldn't read the genuine concern on his face as he climbed out of the truck and quick-stepped toward the camp's command tent. Moving his men and the cruise missiles into Yemen would present a number of logistical headaches—but none so daunting as the prospect of informing his client of yet another delay. He steeled himself for the inevitable.

I'll have to hope I catch Mr. Malenkov in a forgiving mood.

• • •

Outside the windows of his stretch limousine, Hakeem el-Jamal saw nothing but the blur of night. By day he would have admired the lush colors of the Georgian countryside. Speeding away from Tbilisi under the cover of darkness on the Kakheti Highway, however, left him nothing to look upon but his reflection in the window.

On the screen of the smartphone in his hand, a symbol spun in endless circles, a hollow assurance that it, or some other distant mechanism he didn't understand, was still working to connect him through a secure channel to his contact on the ground in Somalia. He had been watching the hypnotic turning of the multicolored circle for nearly fifteen minutes. His driver had advised him it would be a couple of hours before they reached his destination in Azerbaijan. El-Jamal wondered whether his call would connect before then.

The spinning icon froze, then changed to one that meant his call was going through.

Praise Allah.

It rang a few times, and then his screen snapped to a stuttering video feed of Bashir ⊠awil Hanad, his comrade in the fight against the corruption of the West. The gray-bearded African was the leader of an al-Shabaab cell of militant Islamic terrorists who had gone into hiding in north Somalia after being ousted from their Mogadishu stronghold by a rival clan's warlord.

Hanad put his hand over his heart. *"Salamu alaykum."*

"Alaykumu salam, brother. You're a hard man to reach."

"No harder than you are, my brother. How may I be of service?"

"Are you and your men still based near Berbera Port?"

A tilt of Hanad's head. *"About two hours away. In a village called Xagal."*

"Close enough." El-Jamal pasted a prepared string of digits into a text message and pressed Send. "I just sent you GPS coordinates. They were transmitted by one of our tracking devices, from a site just outside Berbera. How soon can you and your men get there?"

"Who says we're going?"

El-Jamal felt his blood pressure rise in response to Hanad's subtle blackmail. "There is something there that was taken from me. Something vital to the cause. I want you to get it back, for the good of the jihad."

Even across a jittery video feed, Hanad's suspicion was crystal clear. *"What is it?"*

"A metal shipping container. Inside it are many crates. Two of them contain missiles." Anticipating Hanad's demand, el-Jamal added, "Al Qaeda will pay you and your men ten million euros if you recover both missiles and the rest of the container's contents intact."

Avarice widened Hanad's eyes and heightened his attention. *"Who has them now?"*

"I don't know. Whoever they are, they had sufficient resources to attack a ship of armed men, steal the container, and bring it back to shore. Expect to meet strong resistance."

Hanad scratched his whiskered cheek. *"I must admit, ten million euros would help me and my men reclaim our place in Mogadishu. But even with cash, weapons are in short supply here."*

"I can provide your group with any weapons you need or want."

"How will you get them past the peacekeepers and the warlords?"

He imagined how far arms dealer Karl Rask would be willing to go to avoid tasting al-Qaeda's wrath. "Let's just say I have a well-equipped ally who is in my debt. Now, do we have a deal, Hanad? Or do I need to find someone else to strike this blow for the cause?"

A slow nod and a greedy smile. *"We will get your missiles back. Await my call."*

"Masha'Allah, my brother."

"Insha'Allah." The screen went black as Hanad ended the call from his end.

El-Jamal turned off his phone and set it on the seat beside him. Dawn was just two hours away. If all went well, by sundown the missiles would be back in al-Qaeda's hands, the infidel Rask would be in his pocket, and the vermin who had dared to interfere in the jihad would know the bitter sting of defeat—and the cold, eternal embrace of the grave.

• • •

The fence served as Jack's guide. He prowled through the dark, toward the end of the compound that faced away from the beach. From the far side of the fence he saw the shine of a flashlight within the shipping container, and he heard male and female voices, but he couldn't tell what they were saying. Running footsteps warned of frantic activity throughout the compound, so Jack ducked for cover into another patch of scrub near the fence's corner.

As he had expected, there was a broad gate in the fence. It was defended by a pair of guardhouses. He strained to see their exterior details in the dark, but each small hut's lone sentry was betrayed by a faint glow of bluish light, perhaps from some kind of electronic security system's monitor. Both men were armed with American-made M4A1 carbines, just like the mercs Jack had tangled with on the *Barataria*. The two guards didn't speak to each other despite being less than twenty feet apart, and no sound issued from their posts.

There was no good angle from which Jack could attack them both. Taking out one would be almost certain to alert the other, who would raise an alarm. Jack considered a frontal assault on the gate, then thought better of it when he noticed electrical cables running up the steel support posts on either side of the entrance. He followed the cables to the top of the fence and saw they were connected to a bank of floodlights—which were linked to motion detectors that he suspected would switch on the blinding lamps if anything larger than a fat mosquito came within twenty yards of them.

He tested his theory by hurling a small rock past the sentries' posts. Even before it hit the ground, the lights snapped on, brighter than the sun. Jack squinted and stayed flat in the dirt behind the brush while he observed the guards' reactions.

Neither man emerged from his post. One leaned his head out, took a bored gander at the landscape, then ducked back inside his wooden shell as the floodlights turned off. "Bloody rats," he muttered, betraying his Scottish origins. "Cannae stand 'em."

The lamps come on almost instantly, and they stay on for ten seconds after all motion stops, Jack noted. Any plan he concocted for breaching the gate would have to deal with the lights as well as with the sentries. *I could snipe the lights, but if I do, the guards will sound the alarm.* He looked back along the length of the fence. *If I had an entrenching tool, I could dig under it. But with just my hands, that might take a while.* He got up, retraced his steps for a few dozen yards, then cut toward the fence. *So it takes a while. It's not like I have anywhere to be.*

Jack kneeled in front of the electrified chain link barrier, set aside his bag and submachine gun, and pawed through the hard, rocky soil with both hands. As he cast aside his third handful of pebble-strewn dirt, he felt the cold kiss of metal on the back of his neck, and he knew from experience that it was the muzzle of a firearm.

"Don't move," said a woman with an Australian accent. "Hands up."

He did as he was told, and made no sudden movements. "I surrender."

"What are you doing here? Who are you working for?"

He turned his head to see who had gotten the drop on him. As the camp beyond the fence came alive with activity, there was just enough light spilling from its barracks and tents that Jack could tell the woman who held him at gunpoint was young, attractive, of African ancestry—and dressed all in black, not the desert camouflage favored by the mercenaries. Her weapon was also not the same as the mercs' typical armament. She was carrying a 5.56 mm F88C Austeyr carbine—Australian military standard issue.

"You're not with Firethorn."

"Neither are you." She pressed the carbine's muzzle harder against his neck. "Hands behind your back. Now."

Not wanting to get shot or force a confrontation with a potential ally, he did as she said. She pressed handcuffs onto his wrists and tightened them until they felt as if they were biting into bone. Once he was restrained, she relieved him of his SIG and confiscated his HK and his shoulder bag. She tugged his collar. "On your feet."

"You don't have to do this. I can explain."

She marched him away from the compound, toward a

cluster of ramshackle buildings a short distance down the beach. "Sure you can, mate. But first you're coming with me."

"And you are—?"

"Agent Abigail Harper, Australian Secret Intelligence Service."

03:00 A.M. - 04:00 A.M.

Most of what was important in Newbold's office was already on his smartphone. He had busied himself not with packing up files for transport but with shoveling them into burn bags that he would order his men to torch before he boarded the Chinook. It was standard procedure when there was a risk that operational security had been breached: destroy everything incriminating and abandon anything that could be replaced.

Not all his men would be coming with him. Once he and his senior personnel were airborne with the cruise missiles, the remainder of his command platoon would make its way by truck to a rendezvous point just over the border in nearby Djibouti. Outside the lawless environs of Somalia, he had little need of so many shooters. When he and the missiles were safe at the backup site in Yemen, they would have all the protection they could possibly need.

Newbold filled the empty pockets of his tactical carrier vest with spare magazines for his M4A1 and his Glock 10 mm sidearm. Major James Sealander, the company's second-in-command, leaned through the office's open doorway. He was tall and broad, with rust-hued hair and a matching beard. In a bygone age, Newbold thought, the man would have made a great Viking. Concern knit Sealander's reddish eyebrows. "We have a problem."

The colonel waved Sealander inside. "Quickly, Jim. We need to be wheels-up in ten."

"That's the problem. The chopper's toast. Holes in the fuel tank we could fix. But slugs and shrapnel severed the fly-by-wire connections, and Hangdog's rough landing banged up the rear stabilizer."

Newbold wasn't ready to accept defeat. "ETA for repair?"

"Can't say. We don't have the parts we need to fix her. Till we do, she's grounded." He seemed compelled to put a silver lining on his dark cloud of bad news. "Maybe the client has a cargo chopper that can come get us and the package."

"No, just a launch vehicle. Delivery was up to us." Newbold pulled his chair back and slumped into it. "Have you talked to Pilar? How are the nukes?"

As if he had summoned the devil by speaking her name, Sánchez walked into his office, wiping her hands clean with a rag. "The missiles are fine. At least, as far as I can tell with only a basic systems diagnostic. What's this I hear about the evac being scrubbed?"

"Chopper's grounded," Sealander said.

Sánchez pocketed the rag. "That puts the Yemen site out of reach. Now what?"

Newbold stood. "Now we go to Plan C." He pointed at Sealander. "Booby-trap the chopper, then get everyone into the trucks with all the firepower and ammo they can carry."

"Where are we headed?"

"The old safe house in Berbera. We'll hole up there while we wait for the launch vehicle to arrive." A nod at Sánchez. "Once we're under cover, you'll finish modifying the missiles." He turned back toward Sealander. "How long till we can get everyone out of Dodge?"

"About an hour."

Newbold shook his head. "No, that's too long." He checked his watch. "You've got forty minutes. I want us all packed and on the road by oh-four-hundred. You copy?"

"Five by five, sir."

"Get it done." A nod toward the door. "Get out."

Sealander made his exit in long strides, moving like a man with a purpose. Sánchez lingered in Newbold's office wearing a mask of quiet concern. "Removing the warheads anywhere other than my lab could put us all at risk for radiation exposure."

"Don't you have field equipment?"

A nervous frown. "I do. But we're talking about a physics package loaded with weapons-grade plutonium. Extracting it would be dangerous even here, where I have a clean room set up for the operation. Separating it from the missile while we're taking cover in the old safe house? We might as well take up Russian roulette as a hobby."

Amused by her choice of metaphor, he savored a morbid chuckle. "We already did—when we made a deal with Arkady Malenkov."

• • •

Jack's forced march ended at a decrepit, empty concrete shell whose seaward side had collapsed into rubble. Harper nudged him inside with her carbine. "Into the corner."

"You're making a mistake. I'm not your enemy."

"Maybe not, but you're still my problem." She stopped him short of colliding with the wall, which he could barely see in the dark. "On your knees."

He kneeled. The hours-old wound in his side was as raw as ever, and his head felt light from all the blood he'd lost on the *Barataria*. His combined handicaps left him uncertain he could disarm Harper before she gunned him down. If he was going to find any way out of this predicament, it would have to come in the form of negotiation. "You don't have to do this."

"Really?" Her steps crunched on the sandy concrete floor as she backed away. "What do you think I'm about to do? Give you one in the head and two in the back?"

"The thought had crossed my mind."

Dull red light, almost imperceptible at first, gained in strength and made it possible for Jack to note the texture of the cracked and crumbling plaster on the walls before him.

"You can turn around now."

Jack looked over his shoulder. Harper sat on a couple of stacked cinder blocks. Beside her, an electric lantern with dark red film wrapped around its LED panels bathed the gutted structure in crimson light. Her carbine was laid across her knees like a bridge. She wore the ghost of a smile, but lit from below, it looked mischievous if not downright diabolical.

He turned toward her, sat on the floor, and splayed his legs as he leaned against the wall. "So, Agent Harper, what do you plan to do with me?"

"Depends who you are. Let's start with your name."

"I'd rather not."

"And I'd rather not shoot you, but I will if you don't start talking."

If he gave her his full name and she reported it to her superiors, it would likely take the United States, China, and Russia less than half a day to all send kill teams after him. He thought about giving her an alias, then decided it wasn't worth the trouble.

"You can call me Jack."

She conveyed her skepticism with one elegantly arched eyebrow. "No last name?"

"Not right now, no." Hoping to change the subject with some conversational judo, he nodded at her carbine. "I thought ASIS agents were banned from carrying weapons."

"So my handler keeps telling me. Why no last name? You on the lam?" She met his poker stare with one of her own. "Who's after you?"

"It would take less time to tell you who isn't. What's your interest in Firethorn?"

His persistence seemed to amuse her. "What's yours?"

"They orchestrated a Somali pirate attack on a cargo ship I was traveling on."

She leaned forward. "Is that where they got the container?"

"Yes. But if we don't move fast, they're gonna get away. We can't let that happen."

"Why? What's in the container?"

He had her on the hook. Now to reel her in. "First, tell me what you're doing here."

Her eyes narrowed. She didn't like being played; that was obvious. "My government thinks Firethorn might be training terrorists—and maybe even working for them directly."

"Then you and your government ought to know that container holds nuclear missiles. I don't know what kind, but it doesn't really matter. They need to be stopped, now."

She studied him warily. "What kind of cargo ship carries nuclear missiles?"

"One owned and operated by international arms dealer Karl Rask."

Her finger inched a hair closer to her carbine's trigger. "And you work for Rask."

"No. I'm trying to infiltrate his organization. So I can kill it from within."

Harper muffled an incredulous laugh. "You're a fugitive *and* a secret agent?"

"I don't expect you to believe me. But if you care about preventing terrorists from getting nuclear weapons, you'll call in backup to take these guys out and recover those missiles."

She stopped chortling. "You're serious? That's your only interest here?"

"Yes."

"How do I know you're not shining me on? That you aren't just trying to boost a load of gold or conflict diamonds or who knows what from that container?"

What was he supposed to say? "Contact your handlers. See what they say."

She shook her head. "I don't think so, mate. I'm not calling in a report of loose nukes till I've seen 'em with my own eyes."

"Then we'll have to get a look inside the shipping container," Jack said.

Her face scrunched. "'We'? I don't think so. You're moving slower than a sotted koala, and you look like you've been through a blender."

"It's just dehydration." Noting her look of gentle reproach, he added, "And blood loss."

"How much?"

"More than I'd have liked."

She got up. "Stay here. I'll be back in a few seconds."

"Where are you going?"

"To get something from my car." She slipped through a

broad fissure in the east wall of the building and vanished into the darkness.

Jack heard nothing from outside. He gave Harper credit for her stealth; she had been skilled enough to ambush him in the open. Someone at ASIS had trained her well.

He took another look around, noting possible escape routes, until Harper poked her head back through the gap in the wall. "Oi." She beckoned him with one hand. "C'mere, mate."

Getting up with his hands cuffed behind him was awkward, but nothing he hadn't done a hundred times before. He stood and plodded around the rubble on the floor to the wedge-shaped fissure. Harper guided him through it and led him into the dark. He heard a car door open ahead of him.

She placed a hand on his shoulder and nudged him forward, through what he deduced was the front passenger door. "Mind your head."

Despite her caution, he bumped his forehead on the edge of car's roof as he got in the car. He swallowed his curses and sat forward as she closed the door after him. He heard her walk around the car, and then she got in on the driver's side and closed her door. Then she turned on one of the overhead lights above the rearview mirror.

He found the glare blinding after spending so long in the dark. After a few seconds, his eyes adjusted. A look around revealed the car was hidden under a heavy tarp.

Harper reached behind Jack. "Let's get those cuffs off." She paused before unlocking them. "Don't make me regret this."

"Depends what you have in mind. We going somewhere?"

"Not until you're fit to travel." She removed his cuffs and tucked them into a pouch on her belt. "Tilt your seat back."

"Why?"

"You always this big a pain in the ass when folks try to help you?" She reached into the backseat, pulled forward a field surgical kit, and opened it. "You're a few pints low. I reckon I've got a couple to spare." She pulled out a blood transfusion kit that contained alcohol wipes, gauze, medical tape, a pair of curved Kelly forceps, a Velcro tourniquet, surgical tubing, sterile gloves, needles, and a 450 ml collection bag pretreated with anticoagulant.

"You're not serious."

"Don't worry, I'm not going direct. I'll tap a pint into the bag, then set you up. When you're done, I'll top you off with a bag of saline, to get your blood volume up."

"Are you sure about this? My blood type—"

"Doesn't matter," Harper said. "I'm O negative, universal donor."

"That's pretty rare."

She grinned as she stuck a needle in her arm. "I'm a special gal."

Xagal, Somalia

Rousting the men was never easy on a hot night, but it was doubly hard at such small hours of the morning. Hanad moved from one grass-roofed hut to the next, ducked inside each one, and banged a wooden spoon inside a dented steel pot. "Wake up! We need to go!" His men grumbled under their breath but most stirred from their bedrolls. Those who buried their heads beneath their blankets, Hanad kicked until they quit their slumbers. "Up!"

The last man to rise, as always, was Marwan. A faithful soldier, but an undisciplined one. He squinted up at Hanad. "Come back when it's light."

In no mood for insubordination, Hanad gave Marwan a kick in the small of his back. "Damn you, Marwan! We've been called to jihad! On your feet!"

The invocation of jihad was enough to free Marwan from sleep's chains. "Who calls?"

"Muster in the village center with the others. All will be revealed."

Hanad left the hut and walked toward the middle of Xagal, a huddle of crude shelters that seemed unworthy of being called a camp, much less a village. All the same, Hanad was thankful for it, however remote and impoverished it was. This place had given him and his men shelter at a time when enemies were everywhere and friends were far between.

There were just forty-three of his men left, the last survivors of recent skirmishes with the warlords in the territories north of Mogadishu. Gathered into a sloppy rank and file, they were as ragtag a bunch as Hanad had ever seen. All of them, himself included, had been hungry for so long that none of them remembered what it felt like to be sated. The only resource they possessed in abundance was ammunition for their careworn, vintage AK-47 assault rifles.

Now he had to rally these hungry men. Give them courage, hope, and motivation.

"Our brothers in the cause need our help—and they are prepared to pay richly for it." Eyes widened, and the group's collective focus piqued at the promise of reward. "Money, weapons, and manpower will be ours if we succeed. If we fail, we will meet Allah as martyrs." He paced in front of them with his hands folded behind his back, doing his best to imitate the mannerisms of a true leader of men. "Our destination is the north coast, just east of Berbera Port. Our target is a steel shipping container that's been stolen from our allies in al-Qaeda. We don't know who has taken it, but we know it contains missiles. Our friends want them returned—and they want the infidels who took them to pay for their crime with their lives." He came to a halt in the middle of the front rank. "This is our mission. For al-Shabaab . . . for al-Qaeda . . . for Allah!" He pumped his fist as he spoke the name of the Almighty, and his men cheered. He pointed toward their vehicles, which lay hidden beneath veils of camouflage netting. "Everyone, into the trucks! We ride for Berbera Port!"

Energized, his men ran for the SUVs and troop trucks, freed them of their concealment, then clambered inside and jockeyed for the best seats. Hanad took his place in the front passenger seat of the lead Jeep. Marwan climbed into the driver's seat beside him. The gray-bearded leader shot a needling glance at his young comrade. "You know the way?"

"I know the way."

Marwan turned the key, and the engine thrummed to life. He switched on the headlights, then checked the rearview mirror to confirm the others were also ready to depart. Then he put the vehicle into gear and stepped on the accelerator. In less than a minute, the five-vehicle convoy was speeding northwest at a breakneck pace, hidden inside a self-made dust storm.

Hanad checked their position with his smartphone to make sure they stayed on the trail, which someone with a perverse sense of humor had labeled as a "road" on the GPS map.

Outside his window, there was nothing to see. Glare from the convoy's headlights made it impossible for him to see the heavens' delicate speckling of stars.

Soon the sun would crest the horizon, and the night sky would once more be just a memory—as would the infidels who had dared to steal from the soldiers of the jihad.

• • •

Deep blue light suffused the *Belleau Wood*'s command and control center, where Commander Reichert and his senior officers listened to reports coming in from their boarding teams on the derelict freighter, whose registry identified her as the MV *Barataria*.

A video monitor on the bulkhead provided an exterior view, from high atop the cruiser's signal mast, that showed the foundering cargo ship. Smoke belched in crooked towers from its two open holds; flames danced inside its crumbling superstructure. The crippled ship listed hard to starboard and was sinking rapidly.

The only people Reichert saw moving on the *Barataria*'s deck were his boarding team, which was being led by First Sergeant Chiang, a senior NCO from the ship's marine security detachment. He and two squads of leathernecks had gone aboard and fanned out across the ship in a search for survivors, and for evidence of who had left the ship adrift and aflame.

Hunched over the plotting table beside Reichert was his executive officer, Lieutenant Commander Spagnola. The sandy-haired, chisel-featured XO listened intently to the reports filtering in from the boarding team, all the while staring at the table as if he were gazing through it into some unknown abyss. Under his breath, he confided to Reichert, "Did you catch that?

Chiang's grunts are finding crates full of ammo, grenades, and small arms."

Reichert nodded. "I heard it. Sounds like the Somalis attacked the wrong ship."

"But it makes no sense. A crew this well armed should've been able to repel a bunch of underfed pirates. So how'd it turn into a battle of attrition on board the ship?"

That question nagged at Reichert, too. "Can any of Chiang's men give us a look at the freighter's starboard side?"

Spagnola grabbed the microphone from the radio above the plotting table and patched into the channel for the boarding team. "Sergeant Chiang, *Belleau Wood*. Can your man with the helmet cam take a peek down the freighter's starboard side?"

Chiang's reply scratched over the speaker. "*Copy that, Belleau Wood. Stand by.*"

Moments later, an enlisted man at one of the communications posts piped up. "I have Corporal Le Beau's video feed on Channel Two."

"Put it on the big screen," Spagnola said. He and Reichert turned toward the video monitor as it switched to show the helmet-camera perspective of one of the marines on board the *Barataria.* The angle tilted to show the aft quarter of the stricken vessel. Reichert and Spagnola nodded in unison, both having noted the same detail. The XO folded his arms. "There it is."

"The accommodation ladder," Reichert said. "One of the ship's crew must have lowered it for the pirates." He extended his hand. Spagnola passed him the microphone. He thumbed the transmit button. "Sergeant Chiang, *Belleau Wood* actual. Tell your man we got what we need."

"*Roger that, sir.*"

"Crewman," Spagnola said, "switch back to bird's-eye view."

The video monitor reverted to the high-angle shot of the *Barataria* as Reichert and Spagnola turned back toward the plotting table. The commander lowered his voice. "If the Somalis had a conspirator on the ship, they probably knew what its cargo was."

A nod from the XO. "That stands to reason."

"If so, they would've come with enough force to seize the

ship. But something went wrong. And that's not all that bothers me." He glanced at the monitor. "The open cargo holds. Those would've been sealed tight while the ship was at sea. It looks like at least four shipping containers are missing. Where'd they go?"

"The helicopter." Spagnola rapped his knuckles on the tabletop. "The watchman on the *Maersk Stepnica* said he saw a helicopter near the *Barataria* when it exploded."

"Okay, but unless it was a Skycrane, that would account for only one of the containers."

"True. But it—" He was cut off by the radio.

"*Belleau Wood! We're picking up radiation warnings from the ship's main hold!*"

Reichert pressed the transmit button on the mic. "Say again, Sergeant?"

Chiang answered with conviction. "*I repeat,* Belleau Wood: *We have radiation alarms in the cargo hold of the* Barataria. *Weapons-grade nuclear material has been inside this ship.*"

"Sergeant, *Belleau Wood* actual. Get your men off that ship and report to de-con, RFN."

"*Roger that,* Belleau Wood."

The commander hung the mic back on the radio and aimed a grim scowl at his XO. "Get me a secure line to the DOD, on the double. We have nukes in play."

• • •

Fortified by the blood transfusion and the saline supplement—both expertly administered by Agent Harper—Jack felt more like himself as they moved together, as quiet as leopards on the hunt, edging toward the Firethorn compound's perimeter fence. So far, she hadn't given him back his weapons, and she insisted on staying a few paces back while he walked point, but he didn't hold that against her. Had their circumstances been reversed, he would have taken the same precautions for all the same reasons.

They were within five yards of the fence when Jack signaled her to take cover. He hit the ground on his belly in a patch of tall weeds. She squatted behind a patch of scrub.

A flashlight beam from the other side of the fence swept back and forth across their position a few times, and then the lone guard walking the perimeter moved on. Jack waited thirty seconds, then motioned Harper to move up as he continued stalking toward the fence.

He took a knee at the chain-link barrier and scouted the frantic activity transpiring in the middle of the jerry-built encampment. Almost the entire company of men appeared to be on its feet and occupied with the task of loading weapons and ammunition into its fleet of trucks. Only a few people worked inside the shipping container, whose rear doors were still wide open, no doubt as a concession to the box's lack of ventilation and the stifling heat and humidity that smothered Somalia's northern seacoast even in late October.

Harper surveyed the scene with a digital camera whose telephoto lens had been treated with a matte coating to help prevent it from being noticed at a distance. She had silenced the camera's feedback, so it made no sound as she captured a rapid-fire series of images. "Looks like they're bugging out."

Jack pointed at the shipping container. "Can you see inside there?"

"Already on it." She adjusted the focus ring. "They've removed some of the crating from around your missiles. Looks like they're working on the flight systems." After a few shots, she lowered the camera, and her jaw dropped. "That can't be right."

The shock in her voice worried Jack. "What is it?"

She took another long peek through the viewfinder, then passed the camera to Jack. "Look for yourself. Tell me I'm not seeing what I think I am."

He balanced the camera and peered through the viewfinder. Within seconds he focused it on the inside of the shipping container. The camera's light-amplifying filters enhanced the image, bringing the details of the missiles and the technicians into focus. With one look at the distinctive configuration of the two cruise missiles inside the container, Harper's disbelief became Jack's. "What the hell?" He zoomed in as far as the telephoto lens would go, just to make sure he wasn't imagining things. "Those are AGM-129 cruise missiles."

"So I'm not crazy," she said. "Good to know."

He gave her back the camera. "They shouldn't be here. They were all decommissioned. The last of them were destroyed six months ago."

"Apparently not." She fiddled with the camera's controls. "But assuming they were *supposed* to be, how did two of them wind up on a cargo ship full of illegal weapons? And how did these jokers know they'd be on that ship?"

Frustration, confusion, and alarm left Jack shaking his head. "I don't know."

She turned off the camera and detached its long lens. "Okay, mate. Riddle me this: What would thcy want with them? I thought they were made so the only bird that could launch 'em was the bloody B-52."

"They were." He peered through the night at the technicians tampering with the missiles. "They must be trying to recover the physics packages, for the plutonium." He shot an imploring look at Harper. "We can't let them escape with those missiles."

"I agree." She tucked the lens and the camera into her satchel. "Which is why I just signaled ASIS for backup."

"How long before it gets here?"

"A few hours. Our job is to shadow the missiles until ASIS drones can reach us. Then we'll paint the mercs' convoy with a laser. Once the drones pick up the target, we'll back off and let special forces do the rest."

Jack nodded. "Sounds good."

"Glad you like it, but I wasn't asking your approval." She hefted her carbine and retreated from the fence. "C'mon, mate. We need to move my ride closer to the gate and get it camouflaged before they move out. I want to be ready to roll the second they hit the road."

04:00 A.M. - 05:00 A.M.

Astrakhan, Russian Federation

There was only one inescapable fact of life in Russia's new capitalist economy: Money could buy anything or anyone. The Klub Rybakov country club was no exception to that rule.

Sheltered by deep woods on the banks of the Volga, just a few miles from the shores of the Caspian Sea, the resort and fishing club served as a retreat for many of the country's richest citizens. No expense had been spared in stocking its enormous log-cabin-style main building with culinary delicacies and other luxuries to please all the senses, and its row of riverfront bungalows boasted all the modern conveniences the nouveau riche could think to demand.

When filled to capacity, the resort could accommodate several dozen guests. Tonight, however, it had been reserved as the private domain of one man and his two guests.

A modest blaze crackled inside the central fireplace of the main building's great hall. Self-made oil baron Arkady Malenkov sat alone in the middle of a long sofa upholstered in cocoa-colored suede, savoring the warmth of both the fire and the chilled vodka in his glass. He had been up most of the night, yet his bespoke dark gray Savile Row suit remained crisp, with not a crease out of true. His one concession to the lateness of the hour had been to free himself of his Joseph Abboud tie and undo the top button of his custom-made dress shirt.

He heard the door to the riverside deck open behind him. A cool breeze wafted in ahead of his guests, whose steps on the hardwood floor echoed from the high, vaulted ceiling.

Malenkov sipped his vodka and admired the dancing flames in the brick hearth.

His partners in MPN Energy stepped around the end of the sofa on his left and stood before him like schoolboys summoned to face a headmaster's discipline.

Yuri Puleshko had grown portly in his mid-sixties, and his lumpy, bald head reminded Malenkov of a crenshaw melon. Despite being almost as wealthy as Malenkov, Puleshko had never developed a comparable instinct for fashion. His off-the-rack mud-brown suit was too loose in the shoulders and too snug in the middle. Even his shoes betrayed his lack of flair. Scuffed and worn-down in the heels, they were the footwear of a salesman, not an executive.

At the other end of the sartorial spectrum was Grigor Nikunin. At fifty-one, he was a few years younger than Malenkov, and he had the same lean and hungry quality to his bearing. He sported the carriage and keen affect of a former soldier, from his close-cropped silver hair to his immaculately polished handmade Italian shoes. Tonight he wore a midnight blue suit, custom tailored in Milan by some famous designer whose name Malenkov never remembered. There were many slights Malenkov could level against his longtime associate—that he was vain, a schemer, too hasty to cut his losses in the face of risk—but he could never malign the man's taste in clothes.

Nikunin was the first to speak. "I presume you woke us because there's news."

"There is." He nodded at the bottle of Grey Goose, beside which stood two glasses of heavy cut crystal. "Pour yourselves a glass and sit."

The two men each poured a drink. Puleshko took his and sank into an armchair by the fire, facing Malenkov. Nikunin, however, looked askance at his half-filled tumbler. "French vodka, Arkady? On Russian soil? Sacrilege."

"We make do with what we have. Will you sit?"

"I'd rather stand."

A dismissive shrug. "As you prefer." Malenkov emptied his glass with a long tilt, swallowed, then poured himself another round. His colleagues waited in patient silence while he collected himself. "There have been complications in the plan."

The news drew a snort of cynical amusement from Nikunin. "You don't say."

Puleshko's hands trembled to the point that he nearly spilled his vodka in his lap. "What kind of complication? What happened? Do we need to abort?"

Malenkov wore a blank expression and concealed his disdain for the fat man. *How did someone so high strung ever wrangle his way to the top of the corporate ladder?*

"We are not going to abort. Not yet." Another slow sip, to project an air of calm. "I just wanted you to know that we're running a couple of hours behind schedule."

"We've heard that before," Nikunin said. "When Trepkos botched our plan to push America to war with Islam."

"It's nothing so serious, I assure you. It simply took a bit longer to extract the missiles from the ship than we expected."

An atmosphere of distrust filled the ensuing silence among the three men.

Nikunin set his glass on the granite mantel over the fireplace, reached inside his jacket, and pulled out a gold-plated cigarette case. He took out a short unfiltered cigarette, put away the case, then lit up. Twin plumes of thick white smoke jetted from his nostrils as he regarded Malenkov. "So, the launch vehicle is en route to the rendezvous?"

"Not yet. Our contractor needs to move to a backup position before the modifications to the missiles can be completed. As soon as both are ready to—"

"Why does the contractor need to change position?"

Another swig of vodka to postpone the inevitable revelation. "Because there's been a minor security breach. A tracking device on the missiles might lead hostiles to their camp."

A bright crash of shattering crystal as Puleshko's glass hit the floor. Rivulets of sweat traced paths down the back of his ugly pink head as he bolted from his chair and paced like an a newly caged wild animal. "Whose tracker was it? Rask's? Or al-Qaeda's?"

"What difference does it make? Newbold and his men are securing the missiles."

"No," Nikunin said, "they're *trying* to secure the missiles. Which implies the risk of failure." The tip of his cigarette crackled as he took a long drag. Smoke spilled from his mouth as he continued. "This might be a good time to reach out to our friends in Moscow for help."

His suggestion elicited overeager nods from Puleshko. "He's right! We can't trust the mercenaries to finish this. We should bring in professionals."

That was exactly the kind of short-sighted, knee-jerk reaction Malenkov had spent years circumventing in order to grow MPN Energy into the world's fourth-largest petroleum company, and its sixth-largest energy conglomerate. He had come too far to let his less cutthroat partners sabotage his efforts now. "Listen to me, both of you. If we bring in the Spetsnaz, we'll end up in their debt, and all the profits we hope to realize will end up in *their* pockets instead of *ours*. But if we manage this ourselves, and see it through to fruition, we'll be able to dictate terms to *them*—and make the Russian government serve us with the same fanatic loyalty that the American government shows to its oil companies. *Do you understand?*"

A reluctant nod from Puleshko, a grudging eye roll from Nikunin. It was far from a vote of confidence, but it would suffice.

Malenkov stood. "As I said before, this meeting was merely a courtesy, so that you didn't turn on the morning news and wonder why our grand scheme wasn't on it. But I assure you: By midday, the missiles will have been launched, the world will be forever changed, and we three will be very, very rich." He downed the rest of his vodka. "When there's more to report, I'll let you know. Until then, *do* nothing, and *say* nothing—" He hurled his empty glass into the fire. "—or the last thing each of you will see in this world will be my hands around your throat."

• • •

Seven minutes past the top of the hour, Jack and Harper sat crouched in the front seats of her beat-up Toyota Corolla. Through a narrow gap in the car's veil of camouflage they observed the exodus of the Firethorn mercenaries from their compound. The mercs had loaded men, weapons, and ammunition into every ground vehicle that could move under its own power.

She peered through her binoculars. "Looks like they aren't leaving anyone behind."

"Which means they're either regrouping or making a run for it." Jack watched the mercs' convoy turn right after they passed through the camp's open gate. The line of SUVs, canvas-covered troop trucks, and the semi hauling the shipping container on a flatbed bounced away down a dirt road. It was hard to see beyond the rising dust cloud the convoy kicked up, but something caught his eye. "That glow over the top of the hill—is that Berbera?"

She shifted her binoculars westward. "Yeah."

"There's an airfield with a long runway on the other side of the city. If those nukes go airborne, we'll lose them."

"One crisis at a time, mate." A keen squint. "Right, get ready. Last one's rolling out." The tail end of the convoy passed through the gate and followed the other vehicles. She put away her binoculars, grabbed the car door's handle, and tensed for action.

"What are we waiting for?"

"Till they've gone far enough not to notice us."

His patience waned. "They're two hundred yards away in the dark. If we wait much longer, we'll lose them."

"*Pfft.* Not likely. There's only one road from here to Berbera." Another glance out at the retreating convoy. "Okay, go." She opened her door and sprang out—his cue to do the same.

Together they gathered up the camouflage netting. She tossed the folded-and-rolled bundle onto the floor in the back of the car, then settled back into the driver's seat. Jack got back in as she turned over the engine, which sputtered to life. If it were possible for a car to have asthma, Jack thought, it would wheeze and shudder just like this.

She nudged him with her elbow. "Be a dear, open the glove

box." He tugged it open and eyed its contents. It was easy for him to guess what she wanted. He took out a pair of slim-profile night-vision goggles from on top of a folded map of Somalia and handed them to her. She smiled as she put them on. "Thanks." There was a faint whine as she activated them. Then she stepped on the clutch and shifted the car's manual transmission into gear. "Seat belt, mate."

"Are you serious?"

"I never ride with anyone unless they wear the seat belt. It's one of my rules."

He pulled the belt across his chest and locked it at his hip. "Happy?"

"Ecstatic."

"Great. Can I have my SIG back?"

"No."

The car rolled forward. Harper worked her way through the gears with smooth, expert shifts as the Corolla gained speed. Hanging on to the door's armrest, Jack lamented the damage to his own night-vision goggles. He couldn't see anything outside the windshield except featureless darkness, making every swerve, bump, and drop a disorienting assault on his senses of balance and direction. He tried to distract himself from his growing nausea with conversation.

"I really think you ought to give me back my SIG."

Pale green light from her goggles lit up her face. "Not gonna happen."

"What if we go head-to-head with the mercs?" A jarring bump slammed the top of his head against the car's roof. "How can I back you up if I'm unarmed?"

"You worry too much." A swerve pushed them to the right. "I'm not here to mix it up with a bunch of professional jarheads. My orders are observe and report. So that's"—a forward lurch as they hit a downward slope—"what we're gonna do."

The car fishtailed as it hit a patch of sand, making Jack grateful his stomach was empty. "How long have you been in the field, Agent Harper?"

"Long enough to know not to give weapons to men who won't tell me their full names."

He absorbed the verbal jab. "I'm just saying, things don't always go as planned."

"Don't I know it. But you're in my AO, so we do this my way. We follow the mercs, report their position, and let special forces take 'em out. Right?"

He grimaced and resigned himself to the situation. "If you say so." A violent bump rattled the car like a baby's toy. "So, once this is done, can I have my gear back?"

"Anything's possible." A teasing smirk. "Behave yourself and we'll see."

Jack had no idea what to make of Harper. She had saved his life twice in the past two hours—first by stopping him from making an ill-advised and poorly planned assault on the Firethorn compound, and then by donating a pint of her blood to bring him a few steps further back from death's door. On the other hand, she refused to listen to reason and was proving to be the most nerve-racking driver Jack had ever ridden with.

Despite himself, he was starting to like her. Her single-mindedness, sense of humor, and pragmatism all reminded him of Renee Walker—a thought that cast a pall over his mood as he remembered the day his beloved Renee died in his arms, cut down by a Russian sniper's bullet.

He turned his face away from Harper so she wouldn't see his stoic façade slip into sullen melancholy, but she spotted it just the same. "What's wrong, mate?"

"Nothing." He forced himself to muster a disarming smile. "Just do me a favor and—" Another impact banged his head off the roof. "Try to miss a few bumps if you can."

She answered his smile with one of her own. "No promises, mate."

• • •

Commander Reichert was the calm eye at the center of the verbal storm in the command and control center of the *Belleau Wood*. His crewmen and officers fed reports toward the plotting table from every station, while over the secure line he suffered a tempest of invective from Vice Admiral Auerbach, the caustic deputy commander of USCENTCOM.

"Hang on, sir," Reichert said, eager to interrupt the admiral for any reason he could find. "I'm getting new reports." He covered the mouthpiece of the handset and trained a hard stare at his XO. "Tell me anything, Spag. Anything at all."

"Dr. Myer just gave our boarding teams clean bills—no sign of radiation poisoning."

He nodded, then removed his hand from the phone. "Admiral, good news. My CMO says the boarding team came back without any signs of radiation poisoning. We dodged a bullet."

Auerbach was unimpressed. *"That bullet's still flying, Commander. Whoever boards that ship next might not be so lucky. Send that boat to the bottom, in as many pieces as possible."*

"Aye, sir." He covered the phone as he snapped at his XO, "Spagnola! Ready a pair of Harpoons, move us to firing range, and sink the *Barataria*—immediately."

"Sink the rust bucket RFN," Spagnola said, confirming the order. "Roger that." He turned and started barking orders at the weapons officers to have two of the *Belleau Wood*'s formidable Harpoon antiship missiles loaded and prepared to fire.

With reluctance, Reichert rejoined his conversation with the admiral. "Sir, we're moving into position to sink the *Barataria*. But before I give the order to fire, shouldn't we take her in tow for further investigation? She had nuclear weapons aboard, sir. Until we know what she—"

"We already know," Auerbach cut in. *"NRO intercepted comms between ASIS and the Australian Defence Force. An ASIS agent on the ground in Somalia sent in credible intelligence about a pair of loose AGM-129s near Berbera and requested an air strike."*

"Are we letting *them* handle this?"

"With American-made nukes in play? Of course not. We're coordinating with USAFRICOM. I've ordered Captain Young to put his SEALs on ready alert, and I've got SecDef holding on Line Two. As soon as we confirm that ASIS report, we're going in hot."

"Understood. Is there anything my crew and I can do to support the op, sir?"

"All I need you to do, Commander, is sink that ship."

"Copy that, sir. Stand by." He wrapped his palm over the handset and called over his shoulder to Spagnola. "Do we have a firing solution?"

"Working on it!" Spagnola leaned over the shoulder of a tactical officer and traded tense whispers with the young woman. Then the XO turned back toward Reichert. "Thirty seconds!"

Reichert knew the admiral wouldn't tolerate thirty seconds of dead air on the line. He removed his hand. "Sir, we're moving to minimum safe firing distance and resolving our firing solution now. We'll have a clean lock in twenty-five seconds."

"It takes your crew this long to target a derelict ship? Maybe I should have called in the air force. They'd be done by now."

"I'm sure they would be, sir. Of course, they'd sink *my* ship first." A desperate look at Spagnola was rewarded by two hands up with all fingers spread. "Ten seconds, Admiral."

"I like you, Reichert. You can take a joke."

"Thank you, sir. Five seconds."

Spagnola sounded off the final countdown, which ended with, "Fire!"

Feedback tones warned the command and control center that a pair of Harpoon missiles had been launched. The ordnance barely had time to register on the ship's radar displays before it struck the *Barataria*. The video monitor flared white as the twin missiles struck the cargo vessel amidships and exploded, breaking her in half.

"Two hits," the weapons officer said.

An orange fireball rose and dissipated into the black predawn sky. The estranged halves of the *Barataria* tilted away from one another. Within seconds they vanished under the waves.

"Admiral, the *Barataria* has been destroyed."

"Well done, Commander. Resume your regular patrol."

"Aye, sir. *Belleau Wood* out." Reichert hung up the secure line. "Commander Spagnola, set a course back to our assigned patrol route. Lieutenant McPhail, log the sinking of the *Barataria*." He headed for the hatchway. "If anyone needs me, I'll be in my rack."

Spagnola stopped him at the hatch. "Sir? Shouldn't we stay and help look for the nukes?"

Reichert sighed. "Not my call, Spag. Direct orders from CENTCOM."

"But, sir, we're already here."

"Spag, don't tell me you're looking for logic from the U.S. Navy."

A weary eye roll. "Sorry, Skip. I don't know *what* I was thinking."

． ． ．

Two dots converged on the screen of Hanad's smartphone. The one in motion represented his Jeep in the convoy of al-Shabaab jihadis; the stationary point was his target, the coordinates provided by el-Jamal. Marwan slowed as they crested a peak in the road. Their headlight beams lit up the corner of a fence around a large compound.

"That must be it," Hanad said.

"Looks deserted." Marwan studied the dark and desolate camp. "Could be a trap."

"Maybe. Maybe not." Hanad adjusted his grip on his AK-47. "Find a way in."

Marwan put the Jeep back in gear and followed the dirt road around a shallow curve. He pointed past Hanad, at the compound. "There. An open gate."

"Take us in, full speed." Hanad picked up his radio and pressed the talk switch. "We're going in. Once we're inside, spread out and put the trucks in a skirmish line by the buildings."

Acceleration pressed Hanad into his seat. The SUV picked up speed. Every bump and divot in the road rocked its chassis and pushed its shock absorbers that much closer to failure.

El-Jamal's warning returned to him: *Expect strong resistance.* Hanad tightened his grip on his rifle, and he braced himself to face a hail of suppressing fire as Marwan sped them through the open gate. No storm of bullets came. There was nothing to mark their arrival but a slow-spreading cloud of dust churned up by their tires.

Behind them, the rest of the convoy split off to either side, each vehicle alternating left and right, until all five vehicles were parallel with one another. Hanad lifted his radio again. "All trucks, halt on my mark. Three. Two. One. Halt!" Marwan hit the brakes and swung the front of the Jeep to the left. The other vehicles in the convoy did the same, and they all came to a stop nearly bumper to bumper, arranged in a defensive line.

They met nothing to defend against.

Wary of an ambush, Hanad nodded at Marwan. The young driver got out and left his door open for Hanad, who climbed over the gearshift and exited on the driver's side. The other men in their SUV also took care to get out on the protected side of the vehicle, but the men in the convoy's other trucks showed no such caution and spilled out of their vehicles every which way.

"Spread out!" Hanad's voice was harsh in the eerie quiet of the desert night. "Search for survivors, maps, messages, anything that can lead us to the missiles. And watch out for traps!"

His men split up into pairs and trios and charged headlong into the compound's darkened buildings. Several minutes passed as they searched one room after another. Every radioed check-in reported the same result: nothing of value. No weapons, no ammunition, no ordnance.

In the east, the sky betrayed the first indigo hints of the approaching dawn. Hanad feared this rushed jaunt would be a waste of time, yet another blow to his already wounded credibility. How many more failures could he endure before his men lost all faith in his ability to lead them to victory over the infidels? How long until the morning he awoke with a bullet in his head?

A roving flashlight beam captured his attention. He turned and saw Marwan scrutinizing a patch of ground a few dozen meters behind the line of trucks. The young man kneeled and brought his flashlight close to the hard-packed dirt.

Curious, Hanad walked up behind him. "Have you found something?"

A solemn nod. "I think so. Three types of tire tracks other than ours. Most are from other SUVs. A few are from larger three-axle trucks. Troop carriers. And these tracks"—he traced two sets of double-wide tracks with the flashlight beam—"came from a semi hauling a trailer. Judging from the depth of the tracks, the trailer is rolling heavy. Which means it—and the rest of its convoy—can't be moving very fast. Not on these roads."

"How old are the tracks?"

"They're fresh." Marwan pointed out crisp tread patterns in the sand. "The wind hasn't had time to erase them. I'd say these were made less than an hour ago."

The enemy was still close. Hanad rekindled his hopes for victory. He reached inside his jacket and pulled out a tattered old road map. He had to unfold it with slow care, lest it fall apart in his hands. He extended an open palm to Marwan. "Hand me your light."

Marwan passed him the flashlight. Hanad shone it on the map. "There's only one road leading away from this camp. If they'd turned southeast, we'd have met them on the road. Which means they've gone to Berbera. Luckily for us, we have allies there." He lobbed the flashlight back to Marwan and folded up the map. "Back in the truck. We need to catch the infidels." They walked together to their Jeep. On the move, Hanad pressed the talk switch on his radio. "Everyone, this is Hanad. Back in the trucks. We're moving out."

A scratch of static preceded the reply of a young jihadi named Cigaal. *"Hang on! We found a helicopter on the other side of the compound."*

"A helicopter?" Vague misgivings knit Hanad's brow. Why would the mercenaries abandon a helicopter when they seemed to have left nothing else of value?

"It's been damaged. Bullet holes in the tail section and underbelly . . . They left a .50-caliber machine gun mounted inside. Gutaale says he's taking it."

Hanad heard Cigaal's words, but it took him a few seconds to process what the man's partner was doing. He lifted his radio. "Cigaal! Stop!"

An explosion turned the other side of the compound brighter than the sun. The flash faded as a bloodred fireball rolled into the sky and a storm of metal debris pelted buildings and scattered across the sandy ground.

"Everyone, back to the trucks! Now!" Hanad snapped at Marwan, "Head count!"

The rest of their men came back, all of them running. Marwan met them, shouted them back into ranks, and made them sound off. Meanwhile, the conflagration raged on the far side of the camp, filling the twilight with the ruddy glow of spreading flames. After a couple of minutes, Marwan returned to Hanad's side. "All accounted for except Cigaal and Gutaale."

Hanad was torn between his hatred for the infidels and his disappointment in his dead soldiers. Only Marwan heard his muttered complaint. "I warned them to watch for traps."

"They died for the cause," Marwan said. "Call them martyrs and move on."

He couldn't bring himself to praise men too stupid not to see such an obvious danger. "Call them whatever you like. They belong to Allah now." He opened the passenger door of their Jeep. "Get in. I want to be in Berbera before the sun rises." He sat down and slammed his door. "Bad enough we need to miss morning prayers. Now we have infidels to kill."

• • •

Gray light defined the eastern horizon, but the darkness ahead remained impenetrable to Jack's unaided vision. "Can you still see the convoy?"

"No, they went over another hilltop. But they can't be that far ahead." Harper downshifted to improve the car's climbing power up what felt to Jack like a gradual incline.

He glanced at his satchel in the backseat. It rested beside hers, and his HK submachine gun and her Austeyr carbine lay across the backseat beneath them. "If we tail them into the city, we could end up in ambush situation. You might want to—"

"I'm not giving back your gear, so forget about it." A serious sidelong look. "And don't even think of reaching for your piece. I guarantee you won't make it."

"You sure? You're driving, and I'm pretty fast."

"And almost twenty years older than me, I'd guess. Which means your reflexes are ten years past their prime and getting worse every day. Trust me, mate—don't test me."

He was confident Harper overestimated her abilities, but he

saw no reason to provoke her. For now, at least, they were on the same side, and he preferred to save his strength for the enemy they had in common. "Watch your speed when you crest the hill."

"On it." Despite her assurance, she accelerated instead of slowing down.

"Ease off. Give yourself time to—"

A lurch as the car summited the rise and then angled downward. "I said I've—"

Words caught in her throat as muzzle flashes lit up the blackness in front of them. Bullet strikes peppered their windshield. Jack ducked below the dash. Harper swung the wheel hard to the left and pulled the hand brake. The Corolla fishtailed and whipped into a spin as the windows on the passenger side erupted inward, driven by a furious barrage of small arms fire.

As soon as the car stopped skidding, Harper released her seat belt and pushed open her door. She dived out as Jack undid his seat belt and writhed free without lifting his head into the line of fire. Another barrage ripped into the side of the Toyota compact as Jack slithered over the gearshift and out the open driver's-side door. More shots blasted through the windows over their heads, showering them with broken glass.

From the ground, she reached up and opened the rear door. Her first grab pulled out her bag and the submachine gun. Then she lurched back in and retrieved the Austeyr and Jack's satchel. Lying on the ground, she hugged the whole caboodle to her chest like a kid hoarding everyone else's presents on Christmas morning.

A break in the gunfire was punctuated by voices shouting in German. Jack listened long enough to get the gist, then took Harper by the shirtsleeve. "RPGs! Move!"

She didn't argue—she got up, stayed with him, and matched his pace as they ran back the way they'd come, then dodged left into some brush beside the dirt road.

They slid under cover as a pair of grenades punched into the Corolla and blasted it into junk. The detonation scattered the doors, hood, and tires, leaving only the gutted chassis and its burning interior in the middle of the road.

From the far side of the automotive inferno came the sound of barked orders, followed by the slamming of doors and the roar of truck engines. Jack and Harper lifted their heads in time to see a lone vehicle from the Firethorn convoy, a troop truck lit by the flames that engulfed her savaged car, speed away from its meager glow and vanish back into the arms of the night.

She stood and glared at the wreck. "Well, that's bloody great."

"It could've been worse. They could've *started* with the RPGs."

She rubbed the back of her neck. "It's a few miles to Berbera. They'll have time to dig in before we get there, but it ain't a big town. Not much room to hide a force that size."

"True. But they ambushed us once. They'll try again."

She rolled her eyes toward him. "Your point being?"

"Now can I have my gear back?"

"As long as you don't bloody say 'I told you so.'" She dropped his satchel at his feet and handed him his HK. "Behave yourself."

"I always do." He pulled his SIG from the satchel and holstered it, then sheathed his knife. Rearmed, he faced the smoldering heap of the Corolla and, beyond it, the distant glow of Berbera Port. "Let's move. The less time we give them to go to ground, the better."

"Hang on—you're not in charge here, mate."

He respected her spunk. "Sorry. What do *you* think we should do?"

A smirk betrayed her grudging admiration. "I say we get a move on. The less time we give 'em, the better the odds we'll kick their teeth in."

She walked up the road, and he fell in beside her. "Sounds like a plan."

05:00 A.M. - 06:00 A.M.

Camp Lemonnier, Djibouti

At 0413, when the urgent call came in from the DOD, Captain Bryan Young had already been awake, courtesy of his decade-long struggle with insomnia. He had tried to fight it as a younger man. Now he saw his sleepless nights as a gift, a competitive edge that kept him ready and alert, like the proverbial watcher on the wall, while the rest of the world wasted its precious hours in slumber.

Because Young hadn't showered since the previous day, his brush-cut brown hair felt heavy with natural oils as he pushed his fingers through it, combing it back from his forehead. His uniform, however, was crisper than the first saltine out of a new box, and the shine on his shoes was so immaculate that his NCOs joked they set the standard for all mirrors on the base.

Young had spent the last forty-seven minutes collating new intel that was feeding into the command office from multiple sources. The NSA and the NRO both had been deluging him with foreign signals intercepts, most of them derived from taps on the Australian government and its national intelligence apparatus, concerning loose nukes on the ground in Somalia. USCENTCOM had relayed reports from the guided missile cruiser USS *Belleau Wood* regarding the detection of nuclear signatures aboard a derelict cargo ship. And the secretary of defense had just relayed presidential orders to initiate covert action on the ground to locate and recover the missiles, which credible intel had pegged as being of American origin.

He drained the last dregs of coffee from his mug as he stood behind his desk and stared out his office window, admiring the brightening sky to the east. This promised to be a memorable day in the annals of Camp Lemonnier.

He heard the clack of footsteps behind him and recognized their cadence.

"Reporting as ordered, sir."

The base commander turned to face the leader of his SEAL Team Five platoon. Lieutenant Commander Robert Burnett was the epitome of what Young had come to expect of Navy SEALs—not the Hollywood illusion of a muscle-bound supersoldier, but a trim man of hard muscle and lean sinew, a human whipcord with a piercing stare and fearsome discipline.

The captain put down his mug, then picked up a mission folder and tossed it across his desk to Burnett. "We have broken arrows on the ground in Somalia."

Burnett picked up the folder and flipped through its sheaf of reports. "Confirmed?"

"Hard to say. NRO intercepted photos snapped by an Australian special operator a couple hours ago. Analysts at the NSA say they look like Raytheon's AGM-129s."

The SEAL officer finished skimming the pages in the folder. "Warheads?"

"Red-hot. Devil Dogs on the *Belleau Wood* picked up plutonium signatures on a cargo ship off the Somali coast, about forty miles from where the Aussie took those pics."

Burnett dropped the folder back on Young's desk. "Who else knows?"

"If local chatter's any indication, AQ is in the hunt. But last we heard, a Melbourne-based PMC called Firethorn has the missiles. Motives unknown." He picked up a loose sheet of paper from his desk's in-box. "These were the mercs' last known coordinates."

The platoon leader looked over the data. "Outside Berbera."

"Right. About fifteen miles east of the port, along the coast."

"Mission profile?"

"Your call. Work up protocols for insertion, recovery, and exfil, and have them on my desk by oh-six-hundred."

"Before I get my hopes up, what assets do we have on hand?"

Young waved toward his office's window. "Just what you see on the lot, Commander."

"Roger that, sir. I'll have full specs by the top of the hour, but I can tell you right now I'll need a Black Hawk, fueled and ready for close air support."

"Consider it done."

Burnett snapped to attention with a perfect salute. Young returned it quickly, then shifted his focus to the reports on his desk. The SEAL commander turned on his heel and left as smartly as he had arrived. As soon as Burnett was gone, Young's yeoman, Ensign Laura Cadan, leaned in through his office doorway. "Sir? Another cup of coffee?"

"Affirmative, Ensign—and keep 'em coming until I say stop." He breathed a tired sigh, and once more saw his sleeplessness for the curse it was. "We have a *long* day ahead of us."

• • •

The car was still burning in the middle of the road a mile back, and Berbera Port was little more than a stretch of orange smog far ahead. Jack kept his thoughts to himself as he walked beside Harper, who stewed while she waited for her satellite phone to establish an encrypted connection to her handlers.

She rolled her eyes. "I hate this thing. I use most of its battery waiting for secure lines."

Jack scanned the horizon for signs of another ambush, and twice each minute he checked to make sure no one was coming up the road behind them. They seemed to be alone in the predawn wasteland. The eastern sky had turned more blue than black; a glance at his watch confirmed that sunrise was less than half an hour away.

He heard a voice from the other end of Harper's call. Her head lifted and her eyes widened. "Birdcage Zero-One, this is

Redwing. Color of the day is yellow. Word of the day is 'wayfarer.'" There was a brief delay while she awaited authentication. Words that Jack couldn't discern prompted her to continue. "Put the strike team on hold. I've lost sight of the target. Hostiles have gone to ground with the prize in a populated section of Berbera." More chatter from the other side. "Affirmative. Present coordinates unknown, but there is an elevated risk of civilian casualties." A few seconds of silence, then more talkback. "Roger that, Birdcage. Redwing out." She ended the call, switched off her phone, and tucked it into one of the pockets of her utility vest. "My orders are to reacquire the target, then check in."

"You just spent twenty minutes on hold so they could tell you to do what you're already doing."

A soft chortle from Harper. "Government efficiency strikes again."

• • •

Newbold shut off his Land Rover's engine as the rest of the Firethorn convoy backed up slowly and parked inside the gutted industrial warehouse on the western outskirts of Berbera. Andrzejczyk got out of the truck and returned to the entrance to wave in the rest of the vehicles, directing them to either side to make room for the semi behind his SUV. The big rig backed in last and took its place in the center of the tight cluster of vehicles. As soon as it stopped, Sánchez opened the passenger door, climbed out, and headed to the rear of the trailer.

The upper levels of the building were little more than broad concrete ledges ringing the towering empty space. Boarded windows hid the old factory's interior from prying eyes, and barricaded doors had prevented derelicts and squatters from laying claim to the site, which Firethorn had cultivated as a backup site in which to regroup should a local operation go sour.

Troops poured out of the other vehicles and deployed with the kind of speed and efficiency that came only from practice and experience. Several duos of snipers and spotters climbed the rickety stairs to the building's top level, where they set up lookout posts. Riflemen spread out on the middle levels below them, keeping watch over the streets through narrow, ragged gaps in the concrete walls. On the ground level, three demolition specialists moved to defend the street-level doors with Claymores, while machine gun teams set up in a number of covered positions that would enable them to suppress any attempted breach of the building.

Despite the flurry of activity, the enclosed space was relatively quiet. The men had been trained to perform as clandestine operators in urban areas, to attract a minimum of attention and make as little unnecessary sound as possible. No one barked orders or shouted questions. In the few instances when directions were needed, they came in the form of gestures.

A growl of suppressed hunger twisted in Newbold's gut as he walked to the back of the semi's flatbed. The doors of the shipping container were open, and Sánchez was inside, hooking battery-powered work lights through eyes on the support struts of the steel box's prefabricated roof. Her two senior mechanics, Corporal Guzmán and Private Kerwin, removed the safety harnesses that had secured the two cruise missiles in transit.

Sánchez noticed Newbold looking in. "Something else go wrong, Colonel?"

"Not yet, but the day is young. How long to get these birds ready?"

She wiped her hands on her shirt. "A couple hours. I need to turn this box into a clean room before I risk recovering the physics package from Bird Two."

"What about the pylons?"

"An hour, give or take." She poked Guzmán. "What do you think?"

He looked at the missiles, then at Newbold. "Forty minutes if we're lucky."

"Can you swap out the pylons by yourself?"

Anxious glances passed between Guzmán and Sánchez. His manner was cagey as he replied, "*Sí*. But then it'll take about an hour and change."

"That's fine." Newbold looked at Sánchez. "Captain, you and Private Kerwin focus on recovering the spare physics package. We have big plans for it after we deliver the missiles."

"Understood." She faced her men. "You heard him. Guzmán, swap out the connection points on the pylons. Kerwin, help me tent the second bird for warhead removal."

Satisfied the situation was well in hand, Newbold left Sánchez and her technicians to their work. He sidestepped between the closely packed vehicles and made his way to Andrzejczyk. "What's the word, Sergeant Major?"

"All secure, sir. We have eyes on the streets, and they're quiet. No airborne activity, no comm chatter."

"What about that dustup on the drive in?"

"Whoever they were, they didn't shoot back. Hitch and his guys fragged 'em and caught up to us without a scratch. Might've been nothing, but better safe than sorry."

"Good. Tell me if anyone reports strange activity or hostile contact."

"Yes, sir."

Newbold walked back to his Land Rover. The perimeter was secure, the package was safe, and the client, though unhappy, was mollified. Despite the delays and complications caused by outsourcing the attack on the *Barataria,* the mission was trending toward success. He opened the front passenger door of the truck, climbed in, and shut it behind him, thankful for a moment of solitude amid the madness.

He pulled his cap's brim down over his eyes and hoped to steal more than a few minutes of sleep before Arkady Malenkov's next long-distance ass-chewing.

I should be so lucky, he brooded as he sank into a shallow, fitful sleep.

• • •

"What is that?" Hanad's hands tightened around his Kalashnikov. "Slow down." Marwan eased off the gas as Hanad thumbed the talk switch on his radio. "Everyone, hang back. There's something in the road." He watched the bright spot take shape against the violet predawn sky. It was the burning husk of a small car. "Marwan, do you see anyone inside?"

Marwan stopped the car about ten yards from the fiery wreck. "No." His eyes searched the brush along the side of the road. "It could be a trap."

He was right, and Hanad knew it. Another order into the radio. "Kulame, take your squad and scout the sides of the road. Watch for an ambush, and look out for mines."

"On our way." Kulame and his men got out of the Jeep behind Hanad's and split into two trios, each advancing along a different shoulder of the dirt road. Soon they were ahead of Hanad's truck and searching the brush for any sign of attack. Overhead, the sky brightened by slow degrees until the search team were silhouettes against the horizon. Hanad saw Kulame lift his radio before he heard the man's reply: *"No one here. No mines."*

Paranoid curiosity nagged at Hanad. "What happened to the car?"

"Looks like it got hit with grenades. Lots of bullet holes, too."

Hanad checked his watch. It was 5:41 A.M. They had lost precious time investigating the abandoned car. He pressed the talk switch. "Leave it. We need to keep moving."

"Heading back." Kulame rounded up his men with a shrill whistle. The six men jogged back up the road to their Jeep and piled inside.

Once they all were inside, Hanad pointed at the blazing wreck. "Ram it off the road."

Marwan put the Jeep in neutral. "With pleasure." He stomped one foot on the gas and one on the brake. The tires screamed as he built up spin but refused to give it purchase. Then he popped the clutch and slammed the SUV into gear. It leaped forward with a roar. The road became a blur, and in seconds the burning husk of the car in the road changed from an obstacle at a safe distance to a barrier that obstructed Hanad's view of everything in front of the Jeep.

Then came the impact. It slammed his jaw shut and launched him forward against the restraint of his seat belt. Sparks exploded like fireworks across the hood, and flames from the wreck licked at the windshield even as the car spun and tumbled away, landing upside down in the ditch beside the road. Then the path ahead was clear, and the ubiquitous bumps and jolts of the unpaved road were reduced to mere distractions.

In the cracked side mirror, Hanad saw the rest of the convoy following him, without any sign of interference. Ahead of them, the port city of Berbera shimmered like a mirage in the dawn. Soon it would blaze beneath the unforgiving glare of a desert sun.

Daylight would expose all the city's secrets—along with its infidel vermin.

The city will not hide them, Hanad vowed. *Not from Allah— and not from me.*

• • •

The bliss of dreamless oblivion was shattered when the phone on the Land Rover's dash rang.

Newbold groaned as he reached forward to grab the smartphone. He glanced at the screen before he accepted the call. Not to see who was calling—that much he was able to guess—but to see how little sleep he had managed before being disturbed. It was 5:49. Fewer than fifteen minutes.

He growled like a junkyard dog, then answered the call. "What do you want?"

"You know what I want, Colonel." Arkady Malenkov never raised his voice, but the gravity of his threat was implicit in his tone. *"Where are my missiles?"*

The mercenary rubbed the itch from his eyes. "We're working on them now."

"We were supposed to be launching them now. How long until they're ready?"

"I gave you an estimate an hour ago."

"And now I want an update. How long?"

Newbold straightened in the seat and steadied his voice. "Two hours. It takes time to pull out a physics package."

The Russian oil magnate sounded apprehensive. *"Are you sure this time?"*

"Yes, Mr. Malenkov. We're sure."

"If I arrange to have the launch vehicle touch down at Berbera Airport at eight a.m., can you guarantee that your men will be there to meet it and transfer the missiles?"

The timing would be tight, and Newbold hesitated to make such a vital promise without absolute certainty that he could deliver. Then he imagined how Malenkov might react if he tried to hedge against yet another failure, yet another postponement of their mission. That wasn't a conversation he wanted to have, under any circumstances.

"Yes, my men and I will be there at oh-eight-hundred. Both missiles will be ready."

"I'm glad to hear it. But mark my words: There had best not be any more delays. If my aircraft isn't wheels-up with those missiles in three hours' time, you and your entire band of soldiers-for-hire will be as good as dead. Do I make myself clear, Colonel?"

"Clear as crystal, sir."

"Good." On the other end of the call, Newbold heard the flick of a Zippo's flint and the crackle of a cigarette's ignition. *"You'll get the rest of your money after my pilot confirms delivery of the missiles. But if no one meets him within five minutes of his landing, he'll turn that plane around, and our deal will be terminated."*

"I understand."

"Pray that you do, Colonel. Pray that you do." The line went dead as he ended the call.

Newbold leaned his head back and sighed. *If we botch this delivery, all the sacrifices we've made will have been for nothing.* He pocketed the phone and got out of the Land Rover.

Harassing Sánchez and her engineers wouldn't get the missiles ready any sooner. And none of his men seemed to be doing anything that would merit being ripped a new one. All that Newbold could do was hope someone was dumb enough to attack them—because what he wanted more than anything else in the world right then was to shoot somebody.

• • •

Less than fifteen minutes after the sun came up, its heat beat like a hammer of fire on Somalia's northern desert. Perspiration streaked out of Jack's sweat-soaked hair, and his shirt clung to his back. His mouth was parched and tasted of dirt; it was the only part of him that felt dry.

Harper plodded beside him, her dark brown complexion aglow. "Don't say it."

"I didn't say anything."

"I hear you thinking it." She closed her eyes, as if denying the daybreak. "I grabbed so much gear from my car, but I forgot to take a bloody canteen."

He kept his eyes on the road. "I didn't say a word."

They were close to the outskirts of Berbera. Ahead on their right, a trio of buildings surrounded a dead end about a hundred feet off the main road, past a sparse stand of withered trees. After that there was nothing on either side for roughly half a mile, until the first few blocks of sun-bleached houses formed an open residential perimeter for the small port city.

His eyes roamed the bleak landscape. "Look for any house with a car."

"Already looking."

Jack suspected their search for a new vehicle would be fruitless. If the neighborhoods ahead of them shared a defining quality, it was abject poverty. He doubted anyone stuck living in these dusty ghettos had ever owned a car in their lives. The best he expected to find this far from the port and the city's center were mopeds or dirt bikes. Neither would be ideal, but riding either one would be better than walking, especially as the sun rose higher and the day grew hotter.

The morning air was motionless and thick with humidity from the nearby sea. Even the slightest breeze would have helped cut through its sultry weight, but no matter which way Jack turned, he found the same stifling heat. A sound like a far-off wind made him look back the way he and Harper had come—and that was when he saw the dust cloud rising from the road half a mile back, from behind a dense row of short trees.

He bolted toward the shoulder and pulled her with him. "Get down! We've got company!"

They sprinted off the road and into the middle of a stand of half-dead brush. He shook off his gear as he hit the dirt, and she did the same. Side by side they lay on their bellies, both holding their breath, neither of them moving. From the road above, the droning of engines and the white noise of tires crunching over the stony roadway grew louder. The pale cloud that heralded the convoy's approach filled the air and spilled over the shoulders of the road as it settled.

Jack shut his eyes and covered his face with one arm as the dust storm rushed over him and Harper. Fine particles pushed their way into his ears, nose, and mouth despite his best efforts to block them. He fought not to cough, then lost the battle, but it didn't matter. His choking and hacking were drowned out by the rumbling of the trucks.

After several seconds blinded by dust and thick diesel exhaust, Jack blinked through the discomfort and lifted his head to get a better look at the vehicles that had passed them.

Harper pushed herself to a sitting position and spat dust from her mouth. "I'm guessing those weren't friendlies."

"They look like Somali guerrillas. They might be al-Qaeda, or some other Islamic splinter group." He shook the sand off his HK and hoped the barrel hadn't been fouled by dust.

She took out her binoculars and trained them on the retreating convoy. "One thing's for sure: They're well armed. I don't think it's a coincidence they're heading into town."

He shook his head. "Damn it. Just what we didn't need."

"That's the price we pay for being popular: Everyone wants to take us to the dance." She put away her binoculars. "Ready for some good news?"

"Always. Do you have any?"

She pointed down the road. "Gray minivan by a house up ahead, on the left."

He got up and dusted himself off. "A minivan?"

She stood and led the way back to the road. "My dad used to say, 'I only need one thing from a car.'" Over her shoulder, a disarming smile. "'To get me where I'm going.'"

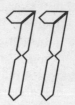

06:00 A.M. – 07:00 A.M.

The pair of men standing outside the Grand Executive Suite of the Al Pash Grand Hotel wore suits rather than uniforms, but Grigor Nikunin recognized them as Spetsnaz commandos. Their hunger-chiseled faces, ramrod postures, and soulless stares marked them as members of the Russian military's elite special forces contingent.

They stopped him at the double doors of the suite. One halted Nikunin with a raised hand. The other frisked him, his technique rougher than was necessary. Then the second guard picked up an electronic wand off a side table near the door and faced Nikunin. "Raise your arms."

Nikunin stood as if nailed to an invisible cross. The Spetsnaz commando traced the outline of his body with the wand, which let out whoops and oscillations of feedback, like a theremin in reverse. At last satisfied that Nikunin was neither armed nor wired for surveillance, the commando set aside the wand and nodded to his partner, who unlocked the suite's entrance with a key card and opened the door. Neither commando spoke as Nikunin passed them, so he refrained from thanking them and entered the sprawling suite.

Four stone-faced young men wearing dark suits and black sunglasses stood apart from one another around the main room's periphery. Nikunin faced the western wall's broad floor-to-ceiling window. It looked out on the Volga, which sparkled as the first rays of dawn touched its coursing waters, and on the lush greenery of the wooded isle that stood between downtown Astrakhan and its neighbor on the other bank of the river, the village of Trusovskiy.

To his left, two men sat at a long dining table. At one end, General Dmitry Markoff, a heavy man who wore a thick gray mustache and the uniform of the Russian Army. At the other, Vadim Zalesky, a slim man with thinning, light brown hair. He wore a suit so drab that Nikunin knew it must have been tailored to pass unremarked and be forgotten with ease. It was the attire of a man whose many names were nothing but lies, whose native tongue was silence, and whose remit was above the law and beyond appeal: a senior director from the GRU, Russia's military intelligence service, which had been operating in tandem with its civilian counterparts—first the KGB and then, after the end of the Cold War, the SVR—since World War II.

General Markoff motioned to the lone chair on the near side of the long table, halfway between himself and Zalesky. "Sit down, Mr. Nikunin."

It was vital in any business negotiation not to appear anxious; that was a cardinal truth Nikunin had taken as gospel for more than three decades. He mustered his bravest face as he sat down between the two government envoys, both of whom appeared to be about a decade older than him. Keeping his expression blank, he set his elbows on the tabletop and steepled his fingers. "Thank you for coming, gentlemen. Especially on such short notice."

Zalesky's voice was deceptively mild. "Our pleasure, Grigor. What troubles you?"

"I fear that Arkady Malenkov's ambitions have outgrown his abilities."

A sagacious nod from the spymaster. "This has been a long time coming."

Markoff pulled a cigar from an inside pocket of his jacket. "What has Arkady gotten us into this time?" He picked up a cutter and snipped off the end of the Cuban. "Not another fiasco like Los Angeles, I hope?" The general patted his pockets as if he had lost something.

"I'd be lying if I said there were no similarities between the two operations." Nikunin pushed his gold lighter across the table to Markoff, who snapped it up on the slide.

"Thank you." A pass of his hand flipped open the cover; another turned the flint. He lifted the tall but weltering flame to the end of his cigar and puffed it to life.

While the general lit his stogie, Zalesky folded his hands on the table. "If I might ask, Grigor, what are your specific concerns about Arkady's plans?"

There was no point being coy; having come to the threshold of betrayal, it was time to take the final step. "I think his decision to outsource several mission-critical operations was a mistake. He entrusted a foreign private military company with the job of securing a pair of American nuclear cruise missiles. They, in turn, subcontracted part of the work."

Between puffs, Markoff asked, "To what end?"

"It's not clear. Perhaps to reduce their own risk during the most dangerous phase. Maybe to give themselves plausible deniability should they find themselves implicated later."

Zalesky shrugged. "Nothing I wouldn't have done in their place."

"Maybe. But the best mercenaries are only as trustworthy as their paychecks. And I doubt these soldiers-of-misfortune deserve to be called the best at anything. They've already postponed delivery of the missiles twice in the last six hours. I think they might be in over their heads."

The general and the spymaster traded sly, knowing looks. Markoff blew a plume of smoke down the table. "And you want us to jump in and pull them out, is that it?"

"I would be—" He paused to consider his choice of words. "—*reassured* if I knew this matter was being overseen by soldiers loyal to Mother Russia."

A shift in Zalesky's body language signaled resistance. "A pity you didn't come to us sooner, Grigor. Had you sought our help before the operation was under way, there would be more we could do to help. But now . . ." He raised his upturned palms and rolled his shoulders.

"My esteemed colleague is too polite to say we don't want to inherit a botched op."

"I never said the operation had failed. Far from it. I just think it could be . . . better managed under my supervision, with direct assistance from your organizations."

Markoff raised one bushy eyebrow. "Do you, now?"

A glimmer of amusement informed Zalesky's reptilian stare. "Why do I get the feeling, Grigor, that this meeting is less about ensuring the success of the operation, and more about sidelining Arkady while you consolidate control over your company?"

"I have no idea what you're talking about, Vadim," Nikunin lied. "But if one day I should occupy the chairman's seat on the board, I would be certain to remember my debts of gratitude."

Markoff spoke around the cigar clenched in his yellowed teeth. "How magnanimous."

Zalesky did a better job of reining in his sarcasm. "The general and I understand that it's in Russia's national interest to protect important members of our energy industry. But you need to understand, Grigor, that if we step in and back you during a time of such *upheaval,* we will expect rewards commensurate with our risk." He got up and walked in slow, measured steps to Nikunin's side. Despite his unassuming façade and gentle voice, he projected a palpable aura of menace. "Just as important, if we allow you to drag us into your corporate escapade, and it goes sideways on us, our duty is to protect Mother Russia first, ourselves second, and you last." He leaned down and whispered with a diabolical rasp, "And if you try to cheat us or betray us, or if your incompetence puts us or this country in peril . . . you won't just disappear. All trace of your life will be erased. Your name will be expunged from history and never spoken again, in this life or the next." He straightened and put on a cold, aloof countenance that did little to mask his core of malice. "Now, bearing all that in mind, Grigor—do you still want our help?"

Nikunin swallowed his apprehension. *No one ever got rich by playing it safe,* he reminded himself. He was determined to push that blowhard Arkady out of the way, seize control over MPN Energy, and transform it within a decade into the largest and most profitable energy conglomerate in the world—no matter the risk or the cost. He turned his head and lifted his chin to face Zalesky with pride. "I want all the help you can give."

"Then it's yours."

The spymaster extended his hand. Nikunin stood and shook it. Then he turned and shook the hand of the general, whose grip felt like a vise. The die was cast. "How do we begin?"

"Simple," Zalesky said. He and Markoff leaned against the table's edge on either side of Nikunin. "Tell us everything you know about Arkady's plan. Then leave the rest to us."

• • •

Several blocks into the dense if decrepit sprawl of Berbera, al-Shabaab's convoy slowed to a crawl, then came to a halt. Golden sunlight lit up the dust stirred by the trucks' passage. Hanad's mouth tasted of dirt, and his eyes itched.

A voice rough with irritation squawked over his radio. *"Why are we stopped?"*

He lifted the radio, vexed that an underling expected him to explain himself. "Because we've lost the infidels' trail. If you see it, say something. Otherwise, maintain radio silence."

Marwan leaned against the steering wheel and yawned. Only after he was done did he note Hanad's toxic glare. "Sorry."

"I don't want apologies—I want answers." Hanad waved at the streets ahead of them. "Where could they have gone?"

"Almost anywhere. We don't know how many vehicles they used, or how long a head start they have. For all we know, they might have split up after they reached the city."

Hanad realized Marwan was right. They were missing too many crucial facts. Until he filled in some of the gaps in their knowledge of their enemy, finding them would be all but impossible. He opened the door of the Jeep and got out. "Stay here."

He pushed the door shut as he walked away to get a better look at their surroundings. They were on a narrow dirt road, less than a hundred feet from one of the city's paved main streets. To his left, squat buildings of off-white concrete and empty window frames covered by wooden shutters. To his right were the ruins of an ancient Ottoman building. Little was left of it but its war-torn façade. Through its shattered walls, Hanad saw there was no structure behind the building's face, just mounds of rubble heaped upon the former structure's footprint in the sand. Down the road, past the ruins, stood a long two-story yellow building whose upper floor was ringed by an outdoor terrace.

Sitting on the steps outside a street-level door of the yellow building was a young boy. His clothes were disheveled and dirty; he looked like a skeleton draped in ill-fitting leather. He stared at the ground with wide, dead eyes while scribbling in the sand with a short stick. There were thousands of youths like him throughout the city, all treated like ghosts: invisible and ignored. Which made him exactly who Hanad was looking for.

Hanad approached the boy in slow steps. When the urchin looked up at him, al-Shabaab's leader held up his empty hands to signal that he meant no harm. It seemed a good sign that the boy chose not to run away. Instead, he observed Hanad's approach with taut distrust.

"Relax, boy. I'm not here to do you harm." The boy said nothing, so Hanad continued as he took a few more steps in his direction. "Have you been sitting there long?"

A hesitant nod.

Encouraged, Hanad inched closer. "Have you seen a line of trucks go by today? Other than the ones behind me, I mean." Another nod. "Do you remember how many you saw?"

The boy froze, then bolted down the road. He was yards away by the time Hanad shouted, "Stop!" The pitch and volume of his voice arrested the kid in mid-stride. The boy looked back over his shoulder with petrified eyes. Hanad kept one empty palm up and out, and with his other hand he pulled a wad of local paper currency from his pocket. "Are you hungry? I can give you money. All I need are answers."

His request was answered by a terrified shaking of the boy's head.

A man's voice snapped at Hanad from behind him. "Get away from him!"

He turned to see a skinny, barefoot young Somali man in tattered pants and a stained short-sleeve shirt leaning out of a doorway and pointing a pistol at him. Almost as soon as the man's warning had turned Hanad to face him, the rest of Hanad's men had leaped from their vehicles and aimed their rifles at the stranger.

Hanad raised a hand toward his men. "Hold your fire! Weapons down!" His men obeyed, but only reluctantly. Meanwhile, the stranger kept his Beretta aimed at Hanad, who did his best to speak in a nonthreatening manner. "Are you the boy's father?"

"Uncle. His father's dead."

"No one means you or the boy any harm. All we need is information." He showed the man the cash in his hand. "We're prepared to pay well for it."

Hope and distrust battled to dictate the stranger's reaction. "What information?"

"Your nephew saw another convoy go past here a short time ago. We want to know anything he can tell us about it. How many trucks he saw, how many men, where they went."

The stranger edged past Hanad, then backpedaled his way to the boy. His weapon remained fixed upon Hanad, even as he took his nephew's hand. "And if he tells you what you want to know? What then?"

"We pay you, and we leave."

It was easy to see temptation gnawing at the man. "Why do you want to know? Who are you looking for?"

"Outlanders. Mercenaries. Killers hired by the oil companies. Four of them raped a mother and her daughter in Qardho. Now their comrades are protecting them as they flee justice and try to leave the country. We need to stop them and make them answer for their crimes."

It was an utter lie, but one so similar to horrific past truths that Hanad knew his fellow Somalis would not hesitate to believe it.

As he'd hoped, his accusation against the infidels relieved the stranger of his mistrust. He ushered his nephew forward and kneeled beside him. "Tell them what they need to know." With a gentle nudge, the stranger sent the young boy walking back to stand before Hanad.

"There were short trucks and big trucks," the boy said, his

small voice hoarse and dry. "Many men. Lots of guns." He pointed west, down the road, then north, toward the sea. "They went that way until they reached the mosque, then they all turned right."

Hanad squatted in front of the boy to look him in the eye. "Thank you. You've been very helpful, and Allah will reward you. Can I just ask—how long ago did they pass by?"

"A little while before the sun came up."

"Thank you. May Allah bless and protect you and those you love." Hanad pushed the wad of cash into the boy's hand, then returned to his Jeep. The stranger hustled his young nephew back indoors to the illusion of safety, and Hanad's men got back in their trucks.

Marwan turned a sideways look at Hanad. "So?"

"Straight ahead to the mosque, then turn right."

The young jihadi put the Jeep in gear and resumed driving. "And after that?"

"We'll see what helpful clue Allah has left for us next." Looking up at the buildings they passed, Hanad saw countless anxious faces looking down from the windows at him and his parade of holy warriors. "And once we find the infidels, we'll summon our allies."

• • •

There was no air-conditioning in the minivan Jack and Harper had commandeered, so the heat of the morning enveloped them gradually during their short drive into the city. Jack did the driving, a proposition that suited Harper, who preferred to keep an eye on him while he kept his on the road. Within minutes, they caught up to the Somali convoy that had passed them on the road at the edge of Berbera, and Jack pulled off into a narrow alleyway. Harper threw him a questioning look. He turned off the minivan's engine. "I don't want them to see us tailing them."

He got out of the minivan, skulked to the end of the alley, and peeked around the corner at something transpiring on the road ahead of the convoy. Curious and impatient, Harper sidled up behind him. "What's going on?"

"One guy got out of the front Jeep to talk to a boy on the

side of the road. Now he's talking to a local who's pointing a gun at him."

"Sounds promising."

A cynical frown. "Don't count on it. The local's standing down." He squinted against the harsh light and the sting of windblown dust. "Now the kid's pointing west and north." A few seconds later he pulled back from the corner. "The convoy's moving out."

Harper started to get back in the minivan. She paused when she saw Jack wasn't doing the same. "What are you waiting for? Don't you want to follow them?"

"No, I want to get ahead of them." He walked to the front of the minivan, used its fender as step, and strode onto its hood. "They'll track the convoy by chatting up locals." Another step put him atop the minivan's roof, which bowed under his weight. "I've got a better idea."

Jack jumped toward a balcony that ringed the second floor of one of the buildings that bordered the alley. He caught two railings, then winced in pain as he pulled himself over the wrought-metal barrier.

Imagining the agony that would result if he tore his stitches, Harper grimaced in sympathy. "Go easy, mate."

"I'm fine," Jack said between grunts as he hauled himself onto the balcony. He looked down at her. "Toss me your binoculars."

She retrieved them from the minivan and lobbed them to Jack.

He caught them, then beckoned her with a tilt of his head. "C'mon."

She backed up a step, then sprang forward. In two strides she was on the minivan's roof. Her third step vaulted her to the railing, and she swung herself over it to join Jack on the balcony. "Now what?"

He nodded at a ladder nearby. "The roof."

She followed him up and emulated his hunched-over jog across the rooftop. At the edge, they hunkered down side by side. Jack peered through the binoculars at the city.

"What are you looking for?"

"Places where the mercs could hide a convoy and not draw

attention from the locals." He lowered the binoculars and took in the big picture of the port city. "The jihadis will find them sooner or later. I'm betting they know these people a lot better than the mercs do. But they're tracking them the hard way." Another look through the binoculars. "And judging by the people they're talking to, I'd say they're asking the wrong questions."

"And you know the right ones?"

"Maybe." He handed her the field glasses and pointed north. "Check it out."

She squinted as she focused the binoculars on an endless grid of rooftops. "What am I looking for?"

"How many buildings could hold the mercs' convoy?"

"At least half a dozen I can see from here."

"And are they in any of them?"

Shifting her view from one structure to the next, all she saw were gutted spaces speared by shafts of daylight stabbing through their crumbling roofs and floors. "Not that I—" Then she saw it, and she understood what Jack had meant for her to find. A multistory industrial building whose interior had been rendered a mystery by the plywood panels that covered all its windows and doorways. It was in a deserted quarter of the city, one ravaged during the civil strife of the past decade. She lowered the binoculars. "The plywood palace."

"That's where I'd be. Of course, I'd have camouflaged it better." He retreated toward the ladder. "Let's go. We need to get there before the jihadis tip off the mercs they've been found."

• • •

Despite having been warned of the risks—including radiation poisoning—that came with being inside the shipping container during the procedure, Newbold had insisted he bear witness while Sánchez performed a miracle of nuclear surgery that would secure Firethorn's financial and professional futures well into the next century. They and her assistants were cocooned in tentlike protective gear with full head coverings, and Newbold was sweating like a whore in church.

Sánchez watched her engineers' hands while she worked exclusively by touch and memory. "Mind the ground wire." Guzmán froze and awaited Sánchez's next instruction. Her manner was calm and methodical, without a hint of anxiety, despite the deadly nature of the cruise missile's plutonium-fueled physics package. "Cut the white lead wire only."

The Colombian munitions expert followed Sánchez's directions. "Lead wire cut."

"Nice work. Remove the screws from the right side of the warhead harness. And don't lose any of them. We'll need them all when we put in the dummy warhead."

"Got it." The technician continued working while Sánchez reached into a blind spot on the underside of the missile's warhead. "I'm decoupling the trigger." She winced, though Newbold wasn't sure if her reaction was one of concentration or discomfort. Then her face relaxed, and a small smile of satisfaction appeared. "Trigger decoupled. Warhead's locked." She extracted her arm and stood back. "How're we doing with those screws?"

"Almost done." Guzmán pulled a few more screws, then stepped back. "Clear."

Sánchez waved forward her junior assistant, Kerwin. "Help him lift the physics package out of the frame."

Kerwin and Guzmán stood on opposite sides of the missile. They took a few seconds to adjust their grips on the warhead's payload. As the one with rank, Guzmán called the shots. "Lift on my mark. Three. Two. One. *Mark.*" They grunted with effort as they hoisted the cumbersome physics package out of the missile's nose cone. They struggled to heft it above the missile and shift it forward, clear of the flat-black rocket, toward a waiting receptacle.

Newbold hunched forward to watch the enlisted men lower the warhead's nuclear material into a special lead-walled transport container with a slab of compressed industrial felt custom-cut to hold the plutonium core and its surrounding mechanisms. As soon as they settled the core into place, Guzmán retreated and let Kerwin lock down the container's leaden lid.

Sánchez peeled off the beekeeper-style hood of her yellow NBC suit. "We're clear."

"Finally." Newbold unfastened his suit's headpiece and pulled it off. The air inside the shipping container, as stuffy as it was, felt fresh compared to being trapped with his own body heat for the better part of half an hour. "So, is that it? Are we good to go?"

"I think so." Sánchez pointed at the lead-lined box on the floor. "I swapped the physics package from Bird Two with a dud, and I've armed Bird One."

"Good." Newbold pointed at the midsection of the missile. "What about the pylons?"

"All set. I've modified the connectors with the new hardware, as planned."

"And you're sure it'll fit the launch vehicle?"

The engineer shrugged. "It should. But I might need to make some last-second tweaks after we get them together." Forestalling his next question with a lift of her palm, she added, "Shouldn't take more than a few minutes at most."

There had been too many surprises today for Newbold to risk leaving anything more to chance. He looked Sánchez in the eye. "Anything else I need to know before we proceed?"

"No. We're set, sir."

"You'd better be right, Pilar." Newbold walked to the back of the shipping container, opened its rear doors, and climbed out into the atrium of their Berbera hideout. His men remained on alert, spread around the gutted building's perimeter on several levels, all watching the outside world for the slightest signs of danger. He found his satellite phone and keyed in the speed-dial code for Arkady Malenkov.

Malenkov answered on the fourth ring. *"This had better be good news, Colonel."*

Wary of the risk that their conversation might be intercepted, Newbold made sure to stick to their prearranged euphemisms. "It is. The shipment is ready for delivery."

"You're certain?"

"Positive. Both have been prepped for pickup."

"Has one been modified as I asked?"

"It has. I observed the process myself. Everything is ready."

"Then it's time to initiate Phase Two. Proceed to the alternate rendezvous point."

Newbold remained mindful of the potential for a double cross. "Your pilot will bring the rest of our payment, yes?"

"Of course."

"See that he does. Because if you try to screw us on this, we'll frag him and sell this shipment to someone who'd love to see it land in your backyard."

"There's no reason for us to threaten each other. We're partners, remember?"

"Just make sure your men don't forget." Newbold terminated the call and checked his watch. It was one minute to the top of the hour.

If all went as planned, in sixty-one minutes he would be a multimillionaire.

07:00 A.M. - 08:00 A.M.

Burnett squinted into the morning sun as he led his SEAL squad across the tarmac of Djibouti's Ambouli International Airport, to their waiting UH-60 Black Hawk. The insectoid-looking helicopter was warming up, filling the sultry air with the deep rhythm of rotor noise and wreathing itself in a subtle veil of golden dust.

He shouted through the din at his commanding officer, who was escorting them to the Black Hawk. "Do we really need to make this drop in broad daylight?"

"No choice!" Captain Young hollered back. "Executive orders." He handed the SEAL leader an annotated map of Somalia's northern coast. "You'll make a saltwater drop five miles off the coast and swim ashore fifteen miles east of Berbera Port." Despite being the only man jogging across the runway without the burden of battle gear, Young struggled to keep pace with the SEALs. "Confidence is high, Commander. You and your team are to scout those coordinates for any sign of nukes, American-made or otherwise."

"And if we find them?"

"Recover at all costs. If you meet resistance, respond with deadly force."

"Copy that, sir." Burnett sprinted ahead to make sure he reached the chopper before his men. He hustled them aboard in single file. "Let's go!" As soon as the last man was on board,

Burnett climbed in behind him. Out of force of habit, he made a head count, to ensure they were all still inside before he cleared the bird for liftoff. All four of his SEALs were in their assigned combat positions. Burnett put on a headset with a link to the cockpit. "Valkyrie, this is Bugbear. All boots are up, ready for dust-off."

"Roger that, Bugbear," replied the Black Hawk's female pilot.

The rotor noise grew louder and pitched upward as the chopper lifted off. Down on the landing pad, Captain Young backed away and shielded his eyes from the sun. As soon as the Black Hawk had enough altitude to clear the base's perimeter fence, its nose dipped and it began its headlong flight southeast, toward Somalia.

Or Somaliland. Or Puntland. Or whatever the disputed regions were being called that week. The ambiguity of national borders and controlling authorities in eastern Africa made Burnett shake his head. It was all too easy to start an international incident here. There was no way to be certain whom one needed to placate, no firm answer on where any of the lines were drawn in the region's ever-shifting sands of civil war and social unrest.

Legally, Somaliland had no standing; it wasn't recognized by the United Nations, and the official government of Somalia claimed these lands along the northern coast as its own. On the other hand, Somaliland had its own currency and visa stamps, though they were rarely used anywhere except along its border with Ethiopia.

As long as Burnett and his team got in and out of the region without complications, none of that would matter. But if shots had to be fired, if lives needed to be taken, or if—heaven forbid—one of his men died on foreign soil, there would be no end of angry blowhards back home, spouting hot air on Capitol Hill while looking for someone to blame.

Not my circus, not my monkeys, Burnett reminded himself.

His only concern was getting his men and himself in and out of hostile territory in one piece, preferably with their mission objective achieved. He waved to get his team's attention. Once he had it, he cupped his hands over his ears to signal that they all should don the headsets that hung between them, on mounts secured to the chopper's bulkheads. He waited until they all had their ears on; then he used the panel beside his head to put them all on an isolated channel.

"Here's the lowdown, gentlemen. We're making a saltwater splash and swimming in east of Berbera Port. We're hunting loose nukes on the ground in Somalia. We might be up against mercenaries, shooters with real experience, so look sharp." He reached over his shoulder and patched in the cockpit channel. "Valkyrie, Bugbear. What's our ETA to the drop zone?"

"Bugbear, ETA is sixty-five minutes. Recommend you grab some shut-eye."

"Copy that. Bugbear out." He disconnected the cockpit link and looked at his men. "Any questions?"

Just as he'd expected, his corpsman, Pearson, was the first to raise his hand. "How many hostiles do we think we're looking at?"

"Not sure. Current intel suggests we might be looking at a full company of mercs."

None of the other SEALs reacted to the news; they had been trained to hold poker faces no matter what came their way. But the grave silence that followed Burnett's answer told him his men knew they might all be in for a very bad day. The only thing he could do was try to bolster their spirits with a bit of sarcasm. "Cheer up, gents. This is what the navy promised us— not just a job, an adventure."

A cocked eyebrow from Yant, the sniper. "Adventure? More like a cluster—"

"Secure that, mister." Burnett propped his M4A1 between his knees and leaned his head back against the bulkhead. "Now, grab some shut-eye. Might be the last we get for a while."

• • •

There were few sounds Newbold found as satisfying as the angry bark of his sergeant major hectoring the men into action. He listened from the passenger seat of the semi as Andrzejczyk unleashed a torrent of invective on the troops who were failing to live up to his expectations.

"Move it, Detmer! You got lead in your ass or what?" A pivot and a fresh rant. "Royce! What's the holdup? Get that truck loaded! We're rolling out of here in five! Bakutis, get—"

A shrill whistle from above ended Andrzejczyk's spiel. He held up a fist, and all the men who had been busy packing up gear, weapons, and ordnance stopped what they were doing. The sergeant major looked up, so Newbold stepped out of the semi's cab and did the same.

From the building's upper level, one of the company's sniper–spotter pairs, Beyer and Permenter, hand-signaled a warning: *Someone's coming.*

There was no more yelling inside the hideout. Andrzejczyk acknowledged the snipers' report, then directed the rest of the men back into position along the perimeter. Ordnance techs who had unwired the Claymores near the boarded-up street-level entrances hurried to reconnect them. Riflemen on the narrow tiers above the sardine-packed convoy aimed toward the street.

Newbold watched the gestures passing back and forth between Andrzejczyk on the ground floor and the sniper–spotter team high above. No one had to translate the signals for the colonel; he had spent his time in the mix, just like all Firethorn personnel. Within moments, he knew what his sentries did: Six vehicles carrying armed Somalis were approaching. They were traveling in a single column from the south, and following the same route he and his men had used when they came to this safe house a couple of hours earlier.

We're being tracked.

He beckoned Andrzejczyk to his side and lowered his voice. "Teej, we don't have time to go defensive. If we get pinned down in here, we'll miss the rendezvous."

Another short whistle from above. Beyer signaled that the incoming convoy had split up, three trucks on one side of the building, two on the other.

"Whoever they are," Andrzejczyk said, "they're flanking us to divide our fire."

"Maybe. But if all they have is five trucks, we have superior numbers."

The next sound to interrupt them was Permenter snapping his fingers twice. He directed the other sniper–spotter teams to check the perimeter. Within half a minute, the grim reality of the situation became clear. Silent warnings filtered down of more armed Somalis advancing on foot from other parts of the city and gathering on nearby rooftops. Andrzejczyk hid his concern from the men but grumbled to Newbold, "Looks like they called in some friends." He frowned at the distant shouts of angry words in Arabic. "So much for having the advantage in numbers."

"Stay calm, Sergeant Major. We still have superior weapons and a fortified position."

Andrzejczyk took a breath. "So, how do we play this?"

"Same way we did in Angola." Newbold picked up his rifle. "Head-on."

• • •

Despite being nearly three blocks from the boarded-up old warehouse, Jack and Harper had a prime vantage on the roof of a half-deserted residential building. They had found the front door open and the stairwell empty, both of which enabled them to reach the roof unseen.

Perched now at its edge, they looked out on the growing mass of Somalis surrounding the barricaded warehouse. Dismay infused Harper's voice. "I'm guessing that's not a coincidence."

"Probably not." Jack scoped the scene through Harper's binoculars. "I count sixty, maybe seventy jihadis. I'd guess about half are local."

"How can you tell?"

"The ones controlling the trucks are toting AKs. The ones who came in on foot are using a mishmash of whatever they scrounged off a battlefield—shotguns, revolvers, old carbines." He handed her the binoculars. "Also, the ones with the trucks stay in formation and cover each other like soldiers. The rest of them move like a mob."

She surveyed the blocks adjacent to the fortified building.

"I've got a dozen more jihadis on the rooftops around the target." She lowered the binoculars and shook her head. "Idiots. Don't they know the mercs have the high ground? They'll be sitting ducks."

"Good." Jack pulled the magazine from his submachine gun and blew on it to shake loose a few grains of sand that had sneaked in. "Right now, our best-case scenario is they slaughter each other so we don't have to get involved."

Harper squinted at the warehouse. "Are we sure the nukes are in there?"

"Pretty sure."

"Then why not paint it with a laser and let an air strike take it out?"

He skewered her with a look. "An air strike on two nuclear warheads? It'd be an instant dirty bomb. I know this isn't New York or Sydney, but there are still innocent civilians who live here. They don't deserve to die like that. There's got to be a better way to end this."

She nodded, struck by his earnest intensity. Whoever he was, he was the most principled fugitive she had ever met. "You're right. How do you rate the jihadis' chances?"

"They don't have any. The mercs are gonna eat 'em for breakfast."

She found his assessment less than encouraging. "So what's our play?"

"Stay clear and let them hurt each other as much as possible. If we're lucky, the jihadis might get a few lucky shots in—maybe even immobilize the semi before it can roll out of here."

"And if we're not lucky?"

The look on his face suggested he knew of hundreds of ways to answer her question. "Depends on the mercs. If they've got discipline, they might come out of this untouched. If they're green, they might panic and set off the nukes."

"Sorry I asked."

He squinted against the glare of sunlight off white rooftops, then pressed himself flat, behind the roof's shin-high parapet. "Get down—it's starting."

Harper laid herself flat on the roof at Jack's side. Seconds later she heard the buzz of automatic gunfire rip through the quiet morning air. As the battle erupted just a few hundred feet away, there was nothing more she and Jack could do but pray.

• • •

Newbold answered his phone after its first buzz. "What's the word?"

"*Launch vehicle inbound from Sana'a,*" Malenkov said. "*ETA, twenty-five minutes.*"

"We'll be there." There was nothing else to be said, so Newbold and Malenkov both ended the call at the same time. Newbold pushed the phone back into his jacket's inside pocket and walked to the semi, where Sánchez and Andrzejczyk conferred in hushed tones. They looked up and straightened when they noted his approach. "The clock's ticking. Where do we stand?"

Sánchez nodded toward the shipping container. "Secure for transport. We've got armor on the birds and the extracted warhead."

Andrzejczyk was less confident. "We're surrounded and outnumbered two to one."

"I know the odds. Are we ready to move?"

"Ready as we'll ever be, sir."

"Then give the order, Sergeant Major. It's time to roll."

"Roger that."

Andrzejczyk stepped past him and issued silent orders to the rest of the platoon. Sánchez, meanwhile, was a portrait in anxiety. "I hope you know what you're doing, sir."

"That makes two of us. Get in the truck and armor up. I'll need you at the rendezvous."

She confirmed the order with a nod and hurried to the back of the shipping container, where Corporal Guzmán stood, waiting to help Sánchez don her body armor.

Newbold pulled on his own body armor, adjusted the strap on his helmet, then grabbed his rifle and made his way toward the stairs to the first tier. Before he started climbing, Andrzejczyk blocked his path. "Sir, what're you doing?"

"Finding a place to set up."

A resolute shake of his head. "Bad idea, sir. You should stay with the convoy."

"And miss all the fun?" He made a deliberate intrusion into Andrzejczyk's personal space. "Stand aside, Sergeant Major. That's an order."

Overruled but still reluctant, Andrzejczyk pivoted out of Newbold's path. "Hooah, sir."

"Wait for my order to fire." Newbold took the stairs two at a time, then shimmied and sidestepped along the narrow concrete tier, behind several of his deployed shooters, until he found an unmanned window barricade from which he could assess the situation outside the building with his own eyes. It looked just as bad as Andrzejczyk had described.

Jihadis occupied the rooftops across the street from the old warehouse, and they had been spotted on the adjacent—but thankfully lower—roofs of the structures flanking the Firethorn stronghold. The enemy also had men inside those other buildings, as well as in the streets on all sides of the warehouse, and they had used a variety of vehicles, ranging from SUVs to minivans and compact cars, to block the streets.

I hope this part of town is deserted, or we're about to cause major collateral damage.

Newbold had no compunctions about risking innocents in the cross fire; he tried to avoid it for the same reason he avoided any unplanned action: he didn't like drawing attention to himself or his company. It was better for everyone concerned if Firethorn went about its business without anyone ever knowing it had done so. Gunfights in populated areas were exactly the kind of publicity they didn't need. To Newbold's chagrin, he was at a loss for better options.

Outside, four jihadis, all carrying AK-47s, advanced on the front of the warehouse. Clicks and whistles from the spotters on the top tiers warned that more attackers were moving on the other sides of the building, as well.

No more point being coy. They know we're here. Newbold snapped his fingers to get his troops' attention. "I want mortars and grenades on the cars at the west intersection until they're gone. Shooters, target their flanks and funnel them toward the doors. On my mark." He braced his rifle and aimed through a jagged break in the uneven pine planks that covered the window. He trained his sights on a half-concealed jihadi who appeared to have an RPG launcher.

"Three. Two. One. Fire!"

Earsplitting gunfire shattered the tense pre-battle silence and resounded inside the concrete shell of the gutted warehouse. Odors of sulfur and hot metal filled the air and put a sick grin on Newbold's face—he loved the smell of freshly fired rounds. Beneath the rattle of automatic weapons rang the bright noise of ejected brass casings bouncing off concrete and collecting in shimmering clusters on the ground floor. Then came the heavy *foomp* of an RPG being fired, and a smoky trail streaked from the upper tier of the warehouse into the knot of cars blocking the intersection along the convoy's escape route.

On the street, jihadis fell in sprays of rosy mist, shredded in midstep as they charged. The cars in the intersection exploded as the RPG hit its mark. Fire, shrapnel, and a gut-shaking shock wave flattened the jihadis unlucky enough to find themselves near the blast. Scorched bodies flew from the fireball, limp as rag dolls, and landed lifeless in the dust. Their less fortunate comrades ran from the point of detonation, their clothes and hair aflame, human torches cloaked in fire and spewing greasy black smoke.

Wild sprays of automatic fire peppered the warehouse's façade. As the jihadis adjusted their aim, concentrated bursts tore apart the wooden planks covering the windows and doors.

Andrzejczyk was on the ground floor, defending the front entrance. "Stay under cover!" He squeezed off another burst to empty his magazine, ejected it, and slammed in a fresh one. "Keep hitting their flanks! Give them a clear path to the doors!"

It was hard for Newbold to gauge the enemy's progress. Every time he tried to look out the window, more incoming bullets forced him back to cover. Through a crack in the wall, he saw that his snipers had done a superb job of wiping out the jihadis on the nearby rooftops. Then one of the spotters shouted, "They're almost at the doors!"

The men on the ground level ran for shelter in the center of the parked convoy. As the last of Newbold's men ducked to cover under the semi's trailer, the jihadis breached all the entrances in unison—triggering the Claymores.

In the confined space, the roar of the blasts was shocking. Great plumes of gray smoke rolled upward from the discharged munitions, and their scattershot shrapnel cloud left very little standing in the streets outside. Everything seemed to go quiet, until Newbold's hearing struggled to return through a roar of noise followed by a painful ringing of tinnitus.

They had dealt the jihadis a serious blow, but now all their stronghold's entrances were wide open. The position had just become far less defensible.

He got up and barked orders on his way back to the stairs. "Everybody up! We gotta move before they do! In the trucks! Now! We're buggin' out!"

The rest of the platoon scrambled into motion. Andrzejczyk, Mergenthaler, and Hitchens took up covering positions at the now-exposed doorways while the rest of the team raced single file down the narrow staircases and into the vehicles, all of which had been backed into the warehouse precisely to facilitate a fast exit such as this. Newbold counted heads as the platoon regrouped for evac, then called to Andrzejczyk, "All in! Pop the gas and fall back!"

Andrzejczyk and the other rear guard troops ducked behind cover. Each launched two tear gas canisters out his doorway, fired a few bursts into the stinging clouds for good measure, then ran back to the convoy. Everyone clambered into his ride except Andrzejczyk, who slung his rifle, sprinted to the rear of the warehouse, retracted the steel crossbar that had kept the broad garage-access doors shut, then windmilled his arms to cue the convoy to move out.

Despite the risk of damage to the warheads, the semi was the first vehicle through the doors. It bashed them open with Andrzejczyk running next to it, and he hitched a ride on the rig's passenger-side running board. Holding on to the door mirror's frame with his left hand, he drew his .45 Glock in his right and laid down suppressing fire at any jihadis foolhardy enough to show themselves in the street. Those he didn't cap, the rest of the platoon harassed with gunfire as they sped past. A flurry of shots rained down from one rooftop, but two bursts from a .50-caliber machine gun mounted atop one of the Land Rovers put a stop to it.

The rig rammed through the twisted wreckage of the blasted cars in the west intersection, sending the blackened, empty frames caroming off the fronts of buildings. Less than five minutes after the attack had started, the Firethorn convoy was clear of the fight and speeding through the narrow streets of downtown Berbera on its way back to the main road.

Newbold picked up his radio. "Rainmaker, this is Broadside. Do you copy?"

Sánchez answered. *"Roger, Broadside. Go ahead."*

"How's our package holding up?"

"Five by five, Broadside. Good to go for delivery."

"Copy that. Prep for handoff as soon as we make the rendezvous. Broadside out."

The end of the mission was in sight, but far from feeling relief, Newbold found his sense of peril keener than ever. For him, an op was never over until the last objectives were accomplished and all his people were clear of danger. As close as the rendezvous point was, home was still a long way away—and he didn't plan to let his guard down until he and his men had reached it.

· · ·

"They're on the move," Jack said. He sprang to his feet, grabbed his satchel, and made a run for the stairs. After a few seconds' delay, he heard Harper's running steps behind him. He didn't slow as he descended the stairs. She was quick on her feet; he trusted her to catch up.

Nervous eyes peeked at them through cracked-open doors as they hurried past. Jack had no doubt everyone in Berbera had heard the rifle fire and explosions of the mercs' brief battle against the jihadis. It wouldn't be long before the authorities, despite being undermanned and outgunned, came to investigate.

He knew not to be here when they arrived. More important, he knew not to let the Firethorn convoy out of his sight.

He shouldered the front door open ahead of him and dashed into the glare of daylight. As his hand closed on the handle of the minivan's driver's door, Harper's hand closed on top of his. "What do you think you're doing?"

"I'm driving."

"You think so?"

"You drove us into an ambush."

"You're still chafed about that?"

"Still? It was three hours ago!"

She refused to relent. "I know these streets. Do you?"

"Fine." He let go of the door handle and circled around to the passenger side. "Just try not to get us spotted this time." They avoided eye contact with each other as they got in.

Harper fastened her seat belt, started the engine, then stared daggers at Jack in the passenger seat until he took the hint and fastened his. "Thank you."

"Can we go now?"

"Who peed in your corn flakes?" She shifted the two-decade-old minivan into gear and stepped on the gas.

Through a hole in the floor between Jack's feet, he watched the ground blur past. He clutched the armrest as Harper whipped through a fast turn. "Stay off the main roads."

"I *have* done this before." She yanked the wheel left. They fishtailed through the turn and scraped the walls of a narrow alleyway, shearing off the side mirrors and filling the minivan's interior with a grinding screech of brick on metal that reminded Jack how long it had been since he'd seen a dentist. Seconds later they raced out of the alley and hooked right down an uneven road hidden behind two long rows of tenements with walled-in backyards.

"Let me guess: This is a short cut?"

"S'right. The alleys are too narrow for the Land Rovers the mercs are driving, never mind the semi." A high bump and a steep drop in the dirt road left them airborne for half a second. They landed hard enough to break off another small piece of the floor under Jack's feet.

Harper shot him a sheepish smile. "Sorry."

Somalia doesn't need food, Jack decided. *It needs pavement.*

Ahead, the hidden road dipped and became a drainage channel that passed under the main road on the south edge of the city. Filthy muck splashed through the gap in the floor as they raced through the underpass. On the other side, Harper made a hard right turn and steered up a shallow grade to put them on the main road.

A few kilometers ahead of them, heading east away from Berbera, was the Firethorn convoy. "The good news," Harper said, "is that these roads are too rough to move a rig that heavy more than fifty klicks per. Which means we might catch them at the end of the road."

Jack squinted at the retreating line of Land Rovers. "What's the bad news?"

She frowned. "That's the road to the airport."

• • •

For a facility that had the audacity to call itself Berbera International Airport, there wasn't much to the place, at least not that Newbold could see. It consisted of three buildings: a cramped terminal with almost no modern infrastructure or information services; a small motor pool and maintenance garage; and a tiny outbuilding for the security detachment. Separate from these was the squat control tower, which his scouts' earlier reconnaissance had confirmed was almost never locked. It was quite possibly the least secure airport on the face of the earth.

His convoy swung into the terminal's traffic circle, scattering the sparse crowd of civilians who seemed always to be milling about to no apparent purpose. A few of them gawked at the semi rig, but most had the good sense to disperse with haste when they saw the machine gun mounted on the back of the last Land Rover in the formation.

Newbold was out the door and on the ground as soon as his ride stopped moving. He waited until he saw his men pile out of the other trucks, and then he started giving orders.

"Teej, lock down that security barracks. Major, take first squad and clear the terminal. Mergenthaler, take second squad and secure the runway. Beyer, hang back with Squads Three and Four to defend the shipment and protect Captain Sánchez. Fifth squad, with me."

He led a team of four shooters across the dusty access road that branched off from the traffic loop while the rest of his platoon split up to carry out their assignments.

Less than a minute later, muffled gunshots from inside the security building signaled the airport's police had been neutralized, and high-pitched shrieks of panic announced the exodus of the innocent bystanders inside the terminal. More chattering of assault weapons echoed off nearby structures as the squads defending the convoy motivated the fleeing civilians not to slow down until the airport was well out of view behind them.

All of which was Newbold's cue to breach the control tower.

His scouts' advance reports proved correct: the ground-level door was unlocked. He and his riflemen bounded up the stairs and charged into the cramped, octagonal control room at the top. Its only occupants were four unarmed civilian men, all of whom raised their hands at the first sight of the mercs' assault weapons. Only one of them wore a tie. Newbold pointed at him. "You speak English?" The terrified stick of a man nodded. "Are you the one in charge?" Another nod. "Do you or any of your men have cell phones?"

His voice trembled. "Yes."

"Give them to me—now." He held out his hand. The four Somalis surrendered their antiquated flip phones. Newbold dropped them on the floor and stomped them into shards. "Get out, start running, and keep running. Go!"

No one argued; no one needed to be told twice. All four men leaped from their seats and darted past Newbold and his men. Their running steps echoed in the stairway.

Seconds later, Newbold looked out one of the angled windows of the control tower and saw the four men fleeing as swiftly as they could, all retreating without a backward glance.

He picked up his radio. "Broadside to all units. Tower secure. Stand by for rendezvous." He directed his shooters into the chairs vacated by the tower crew. "Get on the radio. Warn off all traffic except ours. Then find our guy and clear him to land."

His men went to work. They had all rehearsed this operation countless times, and they knew their parts down to the letter. It took only a few minutes before Corporal Sutton, the lean and wiry Brazilian squad leader, swiveled his chair to report, "Traffic cleared, and our bird is on approach. She'll touch down in ninety seconds."

"Good work, gentlemen. Hold down the fort." Newbold headed for the stairs. "I have to go meet our guest—and get us paid."

• • •

Bellies in the dirt, Jack and Harper crawled on knees and elbows through the scrub that lined the edge of Berbera Airport's runway. Out on the dusty tarmac, a squad of Firethorn mercenaries in desert camouflage forced a small commercial jet's pilot, copilot, and dozen passengers off their aircraft and condemned them to a headlong retreat through the unforgiving Somali desert.

Those weren't the first panicked civilians the duo had seen. A parade of frightened faces had coursed up the road toward them as they had neared the airport. Realizing the mercs must have taken control of the airfield, they had ditched their stolen minivan along the road's shoulder and finished their approach to the airport on all fours, making use of whatever sparse cover the desert granted them. Now they were close enough to spy all the activity around the small airfield.

A nod from Jack. "Five men watching the runway." He pointed right. "Looks like they've cleared the terminal and seized the tower."

"They must be meeting an aircraft." She searched the horizon through her binoculars, but the morning sky was so bright that all she saw was a white mist above the sea. "What do you think? Is it just a handoff, or part of their exit strategy?"

"Hard to say. Depends on—" He flattened himself on the ground. "Here it comes!"

Harper heard the whine of jet engines approaching. She did

her best to stay down and keep still, but she also tried to point the binoculars toward the incoming aircraft.

It was barely visible, a ghost hidden behind a veil of heat distortion rising off the runway. The gray shimmer was smaller than she had expected, and faster. It broke through the rippling mirage, its nose up as its rear wheels touched down, and its engines roared as the pilot fired them in reverse as part of its braking for landing.

It was a sleek aircraft with an aggressive needle nose, backswept wings, and double rear tail fins above its twin afterburners. Painted in gray-and-white aerial camouflage, its only concessions to convention were the distinctive red stars of the Russian military painted on its tail fins and wings, and the block stencil numerals 71 on its fuselage below the cockpit canopy.

Eyes wide, she looked at Jack. "What the hell is that?"

"A Russian Su-34 fighter-bomber."

"I don't get it. Why would they be meeting that?"

The rumbling of a truck's engine turned their heads. A Land Rover led the semi and its trailer toward the runway. There was a hard certainty in Jack's eyes as he squinted at the Firethorn vehicles. "It's not part of their exit strategy. And if they were just selling the missiles, they'd have met a cargo plane." His jaw tensed as he watched the Su-34 taxi to a halt in front of the trucks. "They aren't handing off the nukes. They're *deploying* them—*right now.*"

08:00 A.M. - 09:00 A.M.

There would be no room for error. Jack scuttled across the hot sand, grateful for every tiny bit of concealment the desert scrub gave him. If not for the whining shriek of the Su-34's idling turbofans, he suspected the merc in front of him would have long since heard his approach. As it was, he lurked now quite literally in the man's elongated morning shadow.

The sentry was alone, standing guard beside the runway. He seemed to have been posted there almost as an afterthought, as if by someone who had no better idea what to do with him. It struck Jack as a waste. The man knew how to hold his weapon, and his stance was solid. His only flaw as a sentinel was his tendency to remain faced in the same direction, leaving him with a significant gap in his situational awareness—one that Jack meant to exploit.

A few yards behind him, Harper kept watch on the mercs in the tower, while Jack gauged the alertness of the sentry's nearest comrades. The closest was more than a dozen yards away. All of them seemed preoccupied with the just-arrived fighter-bomber.

Jack tensed to strike. *I just need a few seconds with no one looking.*

Out of the corner of his eye, he saw Harper signal all clear.

He sprang, snaked an arm around the merc's throat, and twisted the man's jaw backwards. The guard's cervical vertebrae broke with a wet crunch, and his body went limp in Jack's embrace. Jack dragged the corpse down into the brush, then pulled him away from the runway.

A few steps later Harper caught up to him. Together, they towed the dead merc behind a large red-and-green taxiway sign. Jack put aside the sentry's rifle and set to work stripping off the man's fatigues. "As soon as I suit up, I'll move toward the semi."

"That's it? That's your plan?"

He flipped the dead man over to remove his uniform jacket. "I'm making it up as I go."

"Encouraging." She reached into one of the pockets on her cargo pants and took out a pair of in-ear transceivers. She tucked one into her left ear and handed the other to Jack. "Here."

He pushed the small, rounded plastic nodule into his ear. "What's the range?"

"A couple klicks, at most. So don't wander off."

"Wouldn't dream of it." He unlaced the dead sentry's boots. "If you circle around that outbuilding, you could make a run at the control tower."

"Are you serious?"

He removed the man's boots. "It might be a shot to take out the leader."

She studied the scene with a skeptical eye. "Or a chance to get my head shot off."

"If you don't have a clear line of attack, forget it. But I'm gonna need a diversion to steal the semi before they unload those missiles." He finished his assault on the dead man's dignity by yanking off his pants. "Whatever we do, it has to happen now. We're running out of time."

He pulled on the camouflage fatigues over his tattered clothes while Harper took another look around the area with her binoculars. "You say you want a diversion?" She handed him the field glasses and pointed at the mercs' parked convoy. "How 'bout a Land Rover packed with explosives? Third back, in front of the troop truck."

Jack took the binoculars and aimed it where Harper pointed. The SUV in the middle of the mercs' convoy was loaded with small-arms ammunition, grenades, and antipersonnel mines. It brought a smile to his face. "Nice."

• • •

Headwinds and explicit orders to stay off local radar had added several minutes to the Black Hawk's projected flight time. It was eighteen minutes past the hour as the chopper swung about, came to a halt, and hovered ten meters above the rolling sea. To the southwest, ghosted behind a veil of industrial smoke, loomed the skeletal silhouettes of gigantic cranes at Berbera Port, and the profiles of the container ships they were servicing. Dead ahead was a barren, empty smear of beach where Somalia's northern desert was kissed by the Gulf of Aden.

Burnett's SEALs tugged at their wetsuits. They had checked and rechecked one another's gear three times in the last ten minutes, and now they were anxious to get underwater and out of sight. He didn't blame them; he felt exactly the same way.

The pilot's voice was flat and tinny through the passenger cabin's headphones. *"Bugbear, Valkyrie. We're in position. Deploy when ready."*

Burnett cupped his hand over the headset's mic. "Roger that, Valkyrie. Stand by." He moved the mic up, away from his mouth as he addressed his men. "Ready?" Four thumbs up told him all he needed to know. He pointed out the helicopter's open side door. "Go, go, go!"

The first man to make the ocean drop was Spitfire Pearson, the squad's corpsman. He tucked his scuba mouthpiece into place, stepped over the edge, and rode the rappelling cable until he vanished beneath the waves. Next out of the bird was Nightshade Yant, the squad's sniper, followed seconds later by its nuclear ordnance specialist, Hawkline Colberg. The last man out ahead of Burnett was the team's newest member, Pitchfork Oteri, who, like Burnett, was certified in advanced special operations.

As soon as his men were away, Burnett lowered his headset mic. "Valkyrie: Boots are in the water, I'll be out in ten. See you back at the shack."

"Good hunting, Bugbear. Valkyrie out."

He took off the headset and hung it on the bulkhead. He checked to make sure his tether to the rappelling line was secure, and then he put in his scuba mouthpiece, set one hand against his diving mask, and jumped out the door. It was unusual for him to see the water rushing up to meet him. Like most SEALs, Burnett had grown so accustomed to acting under the cover of darkness that making a daylight drop felt almost unnatural.

The sea enveloped him. As soon as his descent ceased, he reached over his shoulder, detached his flippers from his watertight backpack, and pulled them onto his feet. All around him, the rest of his team lingered just a few meters below the surface. Knowing that the disorientation of a fast drop could confuse even a seasoned diver, Burnett checked the compass attached to his wrist and verified the direction to shore before signaling his men into motion with a brisk thrust of his arm.

Within moments his men had fallen in alongside him so that they formed a five-man wedge, with him at its apex. It would take them more than half an hour to swim ashore against the tide, and from there they would have to risk moving about in broad daylight, in hostile territory where they could expect no air support, and from which they would receive no exfiltration unless they laid hands on the nukes alleged to be loose somewhere on the mainland.

The part of him that wanted to keep nuclear weapons out of the hands of terrorists hoped the reports turned out to be mistaken, and that there were no errant cruise missiles to be found.

The part of him that didn't feel like humping more than two hundred miles through the northern Somalia desert to get back to the naval base in Djibouti hoped there were.

• • •

Newbold escorted the Su-34's pilot and copilot into the shade inside the hangar at the end of the runway. He waited until his men pulled the towering hangar doors closed, affording him and the two aviators a measure of privacy; then he turned to face the two Russians. "Welcome, gentlemen. I'm Colonel Newbold."

The pilot shook his hand. "Captain Petrovich." A nod at his colleague. "My flight officer, Lieutenant Seshkov." His accent was dense almost to the point of being impenetrable.

"What do you know about the attack profile?"

A look passed between Petrovich and Seshkov before the pilot answered. "We were to understand you would provide the details."

"Good." Newbold pulled a map from inside his jacket and unfolded it. "You'll take off and maintain an altitude of less than three hundred feet, to evade coastal radar. You're to follow this north-northwesterly heading." His fingertip traced a line already marked on the map.

Petrovich took the map from him and studied it. "Toward Saudi Arabia."

"That's right. You have two targets. It's vital the correct package hits each one. The missile on your left wing has an armed nuclear warhead. That one's meant for Mecca. The other, on your right wing, is a dud. Make sure it hits those coordinates in Medina."

Silence followed his instructions. Petrovich looked him in the eye. "Today is the first day of the hajj. There are three million Muslim pilgrims in Mecca today."

"I'm aware of that, Captain. Is that going to be a problem?"

Another cryptic exchange of stares transpired between Seshkov and Petrovich before the pilot replied, "No. No problem. Why are we launching a dud at Medina?"

"To ensure it's found by the Saudis. An intact AGM-129 in Medina and a confirmed U.S. radiation signature for the fallout from Mecca will ensure America is blamed for this attack."

His explanation was answered by satisfied nods. "When do we launch?"

"As soon as we load and refuel your bird."

"How soon will that be?"

Newbold checked his watch. "If all goes to plan, in less than—"

He was cut off by a squelch of static from his radio. *"Sánchez to Newbold."*

That was a bad sign, and he could tell from the Russians' narrowed stares that they knew it as well as he did. He stepped away, lifted his radio, and turned down its volume before he pressed the switch to respond. "Go for Newbold."

"We have a problem. Whoever did the mods on the jet's pylons didn't follow directions. The connectors aren't aligned properly."

She didn't need to elaborate. He understood the problem. The AGM-129s had been made to be fired from only one ordnance system in the world, the U.S. Air Force's B-52H Common Strategic Rotary Launcher, or CSRL. To make these two hijacked missiles deployable, Sánchez and her Russian counterparts had needed to make many complex adjustments—some to the missiles, some to the connection points on the Su-34. Unless both modified systems meshed perfectly, the weapons not only couldn't be fired, they couldn't even be loaded.

He did all he could to mask his mounting irritation. "How long to fix it?"

"Barring any more complications? About an hour."

"Are all the fixes on their side?"

"So far. I followed directions. No idea what the Russians were doing."

Newbold sighed. "Work fast, and keep me posted. Newbold out." He tucked the radio back into a pocket on the leg of his pants, then put on a car salesman's smile and faced the pilots. "You men might want to find a place to sit. We're going to be here awhile."

• • •

Lurking beside one of the hangar's cracked-open windows, Jack pressed his hand over his ear and hoped the earbud comm transceiver Harper had given him would pick up his whisper. "Harper? Did you catch all that?"

Her voice was tense, like his. *"I heard it. Are they out of their minds? Don't they know what'll happen if they launch a nuclear attack on Mecca during the hajj?"*

"I think they know *exactly* what'll happen: Every Islamic nation on Earth will join the jihad." He lifted his head just enough to peek through the slightly ajar window at the meeting inside. "And they're working to make sure America takes the blame."

"How long did their tech say it would take to arm the jet?"

"About an hour. Something about needing to tweak the connection points on the wings."

"Should we hold off, cook up a better plan?"

Jack considered a direct assault, a charge inside the hangar to take out the pilots, but he couldn't be certain the mercs didn't have anyone else qualified to fly the Su-34. He moved back to the corner of the hangar and took another look at the runway. Blowing up the jet would keep the missiles on the ground, but the semi and its trailer were parked so close to the aircraft that any blast powerful enough to destroy the jet would scatter the missiles' nuclear material. He'd have a front-row seat to a dirty bomb.

"Let's stick to hijacking the missiles." He looked over his shoulder at the traffic loop and the mercs' parked convoy. "How's that distraction coming?"

"I'm setting a remote trigger now. Give me sixty seconds to get clear and find cover."

On the tarmac, the Firethorn technicians huddled beneath the wings of the plane, leaving the semi and its open trailer unattended. Jack felt a flash of dangerous inspiration. He pushed his satchel behind his back to cover his diagonally slung submachine gun and lifted his tactically acquired M4A1 assault rifle. Then he stepped around the corner and walked straight toward the semi.

"Harper, I'm on the move."

Her alarm came through loud and clear. *"To where?"*

"I'm taking the truck now." He did his best to mimic the mercenaries who milled about between the airport's single-story buildings and stubby tower. He emulated their unhurried pace and their brazen disregard for unit cohesion. As he had hoped and suspected, no one gave him more than a cursory glance. To the mercs, he was just another white man wearing their camouflage pattern. That was enough to make them assume he must be one of them.

His pulse raced as a pair of Firethorn sentries emerged from beyond the far side of the hangar. They, too, were heading toward the semi. It was too late for him to turn back or change direction without attracting suspicion. It would be only a matter of seconds before he and they converged. As effective as his ruse was from even a moderate distance, Jack knew that a platoon's members all would be likely to know one another, and to recognize an impostor. He had to avoid close-range scrutiny at all costs.

"Harper. Sit-rep."

"Good to go."

He pulled down the brim of his camouflage cap as far as he could without blinding himself. "After you blow the truck, fall back to the end of the traffic loop, where it meets the road. I'll pick you up there on the way out."

"Roger that."

Jack fixed his eyes on the semi and took a deep breath. "In three. Two. One. *Now.*"

Half a second later, the cry of the desert wind was buried by an explosion inside the mercs' ammunition-packed Land Rover. The detonation shattered the windshields and windows of the SUVs immediately in front of and behind the target vehicle. Its reddish-orange fireball gutted the vehicle from within and hurled its charred, mangled chassis into the air. It seemed to hover for a split second; then it crashed to the ground.

To a man, the mercs were all looking at the conflagration in the middle of their convoy. Which meant no one was looking at Jack.

He sprinted toward the semi, while at the same time he pointed at the two nearby sentries and shouted, "Close the trailer! Protect the missiles! Move!"

In the heat of battle, neither merc hesitated to obey Jack's order. They both ran for the back of the semi's trailer and pushed its doors shut, just as he had told them to do.

More barked orders from men on the tarmac overlapped staticky demands for updates coming in over the radios. Jack's window of opportunity was closing. He dashed toward the driver's door of the semi.

From underneath the jet, the Firethorn technical specialists stared at him. He hollered and waved them away without missing a step. "We're under attack! Take cover!"

There was nowhere better for them to go, but his order left them perplexed for the handful of seconds he needed to scramble up the rig's sideboard, pull open its door, and get in. As he'd hoped, the mercs had been thoughtful enough to leave the keys in the ignition.

He turned the key and felt the powerful vibrations from the semi's engine as it thrummed to life. His left foot pushed in the clutch. He shifted the rig into gear and stepped on the gas.

It took nearly ten seconds before the mercs realized he was stealing their truck and the missiles with it. Then they peppered its windshield with bullets.

Jack ducked his head and pushed the pedal to the floor.

There was now only one way out: straight through the enemy.

• • •

The explosion worked even better than Harper had hoped. Sneaking past the mercs and rigging their C-4 with their own detonators had proved easy; avoiding the storm of shrapnel unleashed when she triggered the detonator had been the hard part.

Shards of metal and ragged chunks of fiberglass blew past her, followed by long twists of smoke tracing black arcs through the sultry morning air. Atomized bits of debris stung the back of her neck as she turned away from the blast and hit the ground.

After seconds stretched by adrenaline and fear, she looked up to see the semi accelerate away from the jet. It sped down the runway and circled around the far side of the terminal building, harassed by automatic weapons fire every foot of the way.

Seeing how fast Jack was driving, Harper knew she wouldn't have much time to make it to the pickup point at the end of the traffic loop. Despite the risk, she broke from cover and ran, hoping the pandemonium following the explosion would keep the mercs occupied.

Halfway to the pickup site, someone shouted at her to halt. She spun in mid-stride, leveled her carbine, and squeezed off a short burst. Most of her shots impacted on the merc's body armor, but one lucky round tore into his throat. He clutched at his mangled Adam's apple and staggered. Blood coated his hand, and then he pitched face-first into the dirt.

Harper sprang back into motion, running for the only road away from the airport.

A squad of mercs scrambled out of the terminal building. One carried a tripod, another was draped with belt ammo, and a third hefted a .50-caliber machine gun. Moving with a speed and precision born of long experience, they set up near the corner of the terminal, facing the narrow road that Jack would be using to bring the semi to the exit.

At the far end of the building, the semi turned the corner, directly into the machine gunner's sights. The mercs fed the belt into the machine gun and primed it to fire. There was nowhere for Jack to swerve to avoid the incoming hail of large-caliber rounds.

Harper made a hard turn and charged the machine gunners from behind, laying down suppressing fire. Her first rounds went wide, her aim fouled by the jolts of firing while running. She corrected her aim as the gun team tried to swivel their weapon toward her. Crisscrossing bursts took out the ammunition handler and the spotter. She clipped the gunner just before he got the chance to fire back. He collapsed, dead, as her carbine clacked empty.

Incoming rounds from her left ripped chunks of asphalt from the road. A merc stood in the back of the last Land Rover in the convoy, aiming its .50 cal at her.

She ejected her empty magazine as she sprinted toward the terminal for cover. The machine gunner's storm of lead chased her every step of the way. On the edge of her vision she saw the semi race past the traffic loop and swing wide through the exit, tearing off part of the security gate as it went. Harried by the machine gunner, she dived through an open door into the terminal. An angry buzz of high-power automatic rounds shredded the doorframe as she slid on her belly across the tiled floor.

At the other end of the terminal, a merc spun and noted Harper's arrival with surprise.

He lifted his rifle as she drew her sidearm. He fired a single burst that screamed past her before she dropped him with a single shot between his eyes.

Jack's voice roared through her earbud. *"Harper! Where are you?"*

"The terminal. I got detoured." Voices outside got louder, closer. Mercs surrounded the building. She slammed a fresh magazine into her carbine, and then she ran in a crouch to the man she'd killed, to relieve him of his rifle and his body armor.

Too many ways in and out, she realized. *I can't defend them all.* She hurried behind one of the service counters. Its cheap plywood front wouldn't provide much protection, but it would at least give her a few seconds of concealment before her standoff came to its inevitable tragic ending. She checked the straps of her borrowed Kevlar vest. *Not how I'd hoped to meet my maker. But at least now Jack's got a shot of escaping with the nukes.*

The talking outside stopped; the crunching of boots on sandy ground ceased. The mercenaries' counterattack was imminent. Harper steeled herself to go down fighting.

In a flash, everything turned to mayhem—but none of it was directed at her.

She stood bewildered, not understanding what was happening.

Not until she heard the roar of an engine.

• • •

By the time Jack saw the machine gunners ahead of him, it was too late to stop. Breaking through the fence on his left would put the semi on loose sand, where it would end up stuck within moments. He didn't have enough momentum to smash through the terminal's brick outer wall. And he could never stop the truck and back out of firing range before the machine gun shredded the semi's cab and him with it. He did the only thing he could: he accelerated.

The gunner had him in his sights, and Jack realized he wasn't going to make it.

Then bullets tore across the machine gunner and his team, and they swiveled their weapon away from Jack and the semi. Seconds later, as Jack sped past them, the last of the gun team had fallen, and the entire traffic circle in front of the terminal was shrouded in oily plumes from the demolished Land Rover. Multiple bursts of automatic fire filled the air, but none seemed to be aimed at him or the eighteen-wheeler. He counted himself lucky and fought to keep all the rig's axles on the ground as he took the exit turn at full speed.

The road ahead was deserted, and he saw nothing in the rig's side mirrors but the chaos he'd left behind at the airport. He pressed his hand over his earbud. "Harper! Where are you?"

"The terminal. I got detoured."

He glanced at his side mirror. Through drifts of dark smoke he saw mercenaries converge on the terminal. Harper was a good operator; that much Jack had been able to tell. But even the best agent could do only so much when surrounded, outnumbered, and outgunned.

His sense of cold pragmatism told him to leave her behind, that every minute Firethorn wasted fighting Harper would mean another mile's head start for his escape with the missiles.

His sense of honor made him pull off the road into an empty parking area, force the truck through an awkward U-turn, and head back toward the airport with the pedal pressed to the floor.

A push of the clutch, a shift into higher gear. He leaned forward and punched the rig's spiderwebbed windshield free of its frame. The cracked-white sheet of safety glass slid off the hood. Hot wind blew sand and grit into Jack's eyes. He drew his SIG as he drove through the open gateway, barreling at full speed across the traffic loop until the rig mounted the curb, onto the sidewalk that ran along the front of the terminal.

Muzzle flashes lit up the dust and smoke. Near misses ripped past his head and tore holes in the cab's roof. Jack returned fire as he drove into the maelstrom. Then his attackers fell before his rig, their disappearance marked by *thump*s of collision and sudden bumps.

Several yards shy of the terminal's main doors, Jack put in the clutch and hit the brakes. The rig skidded to a whining halt, blocking the doors. He continued to fire at anyone who moved outside the terminal. "Harper! I'm at the main entrance! Fall back to me!"

"On my way!"

He emptied the last rounds from his SIG, dropped it on the seat, and hefted his borrowed M4A1. Its buzz saw roar reverberated inside the rig's cab as he laid down short bursts wherever he saw enemy muzzle flashes or hints of movement.

The passenger door opened, and he looked back just long enough to confirm it was Harper climbing in. He waited until she shut her door; then he pushed the rifle into her hands. "Half full. Suppressing fire, nine o'clock to twelve o'clock."

"On it." She braced the weapon and snapped off more controlled bursts.

She kept firing as Jack shifted the rig into gear and plowed forward, through the mercs, around the traffic loop and past their convoy. The Land Rover at the head of the line pulled across the road in a futile bid to stop the rig, which was several times its size. Jack downshifted as he hit the gas, and half a second later he rammed the oversized SUV off the road. It flew away in a bobbling spin and a shower of shattered glass.

A flurry of rifle fire pockmarked the trailer behind the rig, and a stray shot disintegrated Jack's side mirror, scouring the left side of his face with stinging shards.

"Oi! You all right, mate?"

He palmed blood from his cheek and temple. "It only hurts when I laugh."

"Oh. You'll be fine, then." She met his frown with a wan smile, followed by a quizzical look. "You were free and clear. Why'd you come back?"

He shrugged. "It'll take time to find a place to stash the missiles. Thought I could use some company for the drive."

A faux pout. "And here I thought you were starting to like me."

"One thing at a time." He upshifted for speed as the road straightened. "Help me get out of Somalia both alive and free. *Then* I'll start to like you."

A sly look. "It's hard to become your friend, isn't it, Mr. Jack?"

"If you knew how most of my friends end up, you'd realize I'm doing you a favor."

09:00 A.M. - 10:00 A.M.

Burnett lifted his head out of the water and reconnoitered the shoreline. A weak and slanted spire of smoke marred the great yawn of blue sky. Beneath it stretched the desert, still and silent.

He signaled his team back into motion. Yant and Oteri emerged from the waves and moved ahead of him. He followed them ashore as Pearson and Colberg surfaced beside him. The five SEALs moved in a loose formation, close enough to support each other should they come under fire, but far enough apart to prevent a single shooter from spraying them all with one burst.

They waded through the shallows, each man keeping a cautious watch on the terrain ahead. Moving with equal measures of speed and caution, they fanned out onto the beach.

At the first sight of a fenced compound several dozen meters inland, Burnett raised his fist, signaling his men to halt. Then he lowered his hand in a motion that set his palm level with the ground. He and the rest of the team dropped to the ground.

He listened for any indication that they might not be alone.

The only thing moving for miles around was the wind.

Using hand signals, Burnett ordered Yant to cover Colberg and Oteri, whom he sent ahead to the compound's perimeter. Yant unfolded his sniper rifle's barrel-mounted bipod and gazed through its targeting scope, his keen eye following his comrades as they jogged forward. Pearson rolled onto his back and monitored the beach behind the team.

They were far enough from the nearest civilian settlement that Burnett had no reason to expect they would encounter any noncombatants, but he preferred not to take unneeded risks. If the op resulted in any kind of collateral damage, that would only make their exfiltration more difficult. His squad had been deployed without official U.S. identification or insignia. If the mission went sideways, they all would be disavowed by the navy and the U.S. Department of State, and would need to extricate themselves from hostile territory.

Confirmation signals came back from Oteri and Colberg. The camp was clear.

Burnett stood. "Move up." Yant and Pearson gathered their gear and followed him to the fence, where they regrouped with their teammates. He looked to Oteri for information. "Report."

"Ghost town." He pointed toward the north side of the compound. "Someone fragged a Chinook on the ground. Based on the scorch pattern, I'd say it was booby-trapped."

"Who set it off?"

Colberg said, "Somalis, I think. Two bodies, flash-fried, next to the bird." He pointed south. "Front gate's wide open. Whatever happened here, I'd say we missed it."

"I wouldn't be so sure. Let's get inside and do a sweep for radiation."

Yant eyed the seemingly deserted buildings beyond the fence. "You want to go in the front? Or make our own door?"

"Play it safe. Cut through."

"Yes, sir." The sniper slung his weapon, pulled a pair of wire cutters from his gear bag, and made fast work of the chain-link barrier. In less than a minute he cut a two-meter-long curve through the fence. He stepped back and put away his cutters as Oteri moved ahead, pushed open the loose section of chain link, and held it open with his body. "Door's open, sir."

"Good work, Lieutenant."

Burnett ducked through the gap in the fence while Oteri kept watch for any sign of resistance from inside the compound. Yant was the next man through, followed by Colberg and Pearson. The team moved together to the wall of the largest structure.

"We need to confirm these buildings are empty. Yant, take

the motor pool. Pearson, Colberg, sweep the barracks. Oteri, we'll check the command hut. Move out." They split up and darted in different directions, all moving with their weapons braced for action.

After several minutes of fruitless room-by-room searching, Burnett spoke into his headset mic. "This is Bugbear. Command building is clear. Spitfire, anything in the barracks?"

Pearson replied, *"Negative, Bugbear. Nothing here but skid marks on the sheets."*

"Nightshade, anything moving in the motor pool?"

"Not even a mouse, Bugbear. Whole place is empty, not a wheel in sight."

"Copy that. Head for the roof. If we're gonna have company, I want to see them before they see us."

"Roger, Bugbear. Going topside."

"Everyone else, regroup outside. Hawkline, start your sweep."

"I'll fire up the clicker, sir."

Soon, everyone except Yant was back outside, in the square flanked on three sides by the compound's buildings. Colberg's attention was fixed on the Geiger counter in his hand, while Pearson, Oteri, and Burnett stood in a protective formation around him, each keeping watch over a different arc of the surrounding area. It didn't take more than a few minutes before Colberg frowned at his handheld radiation sensor. "I'm reading traces of radiation, but only out here in the square. I didn't pick up anything inside the barracks."

"Is the signal strong enough to be weapons-grade?"

"Oh, yeah. Score one for the Aussies. We're looking at a pair of broken arrows."

Noting the grim looks on his team's faces, Burnett resorted to gallows humor. "On the bright side, at least we didn't make this trip for nothing." He cast his eyes across the bleak expanse of the desert. "Now we just need some idea where to go next."

Yant's voice filtered through all their headsets. *"I might have a suggestion, sir. I'm seeing evidence of major detonations in the direction of Berbera and its airport."*

"Let's be optimists and assume that's not a coincidence."

Burnett unfolded his map of the area and noted the distance and direction of the airport from the compound.

Pearson leaned in for a look at the map. "How far is the airport from here?"

"Close enough for us to run there, and far enough that you won't be happy about it." Burnett tucked the map back into his pocket and keyed his radio. "Good work, Nightshade. Regroup at the gate. We're heading to the airport, and we ain't getting paid by the hour."

• • •

Sunlight blazed into Jack's eyes as he drove, making it hard for him to see the road. Everything ahead of him was a nearly featureless white blur. All he could do was squint against the glare, but the effort was exacerbating his already awful headache. The deafening roar of wind in his face and fumes from the rig's diesel engine weren't doing him any favors, either.

Harper busied herself reloading the magazines for her Austeyr. "You all right?"

"I'd kill for a cheap pair of sunglasses." He winced as his stomach growled, almost loud enough to be heard over the road noise. "Or something to eat."

She set down her carbine and opened the glove box. After digging through it for a few seconds, she came up with a granola bar, which she handed to Jack. "Sorry. No shades, mate."

"One problem at a time." He tore open the wrapper with his teeth and devoured the chewy, fruit-goop-filled snack bar in just four bites. "Now I'm thirsty."

"Oi! You're a needy bugger." She went back to work, loading his spare rounds into his emptied magazines. As she set aside the first refilled magazine, she squinted into the morning sun. "Hook a right up here."

He knew where that fork of the road went. "I'd rather not."

She paused her labors and shot a surprised look his way. "You said you want the missiles back in American hands. The closest American naval base—"

"Is at the airport in Djibouti. I know. But I can't go there."

Her surprise turned to suspicion. "Why not?"

He slowed the truck and brought it to a halt at the fork in the road. There was no good way for him to explain himself to Harper, no way that would make sense except the truth.

"My real name is Jack Bauer. I used to be a CTU field agent. Now I'm a fugitive from justice in the U.S., and I'm pretty sure the Russians and the Chinese both want me dead." He breathed a dejected sigh. "I told you the truth: I want to put these missiles back in American hands. But I'd rather not get myself captured in the process."

Harper processed that with admirable sangfroid. "Right. What's your plan?"

"Get them somewhere safe. Then call in the SEALs and fall back, to someplace I can keep an eye on the missiles until the SEALs arrive. Once they evac the missiles, I'll move on."

"Just like that?"

"Just like that."

It would have been charitable to call her reaction incredulous. "I'm guessing this must be your first time in Somalia, because one thing this country is short on is *safe places.*"

"I'm not talking about vault-at-the-Bellagio secure, just someplace out of sight. Somewhere to put the missiles where no one would think to look for them." He squinted at the road sign, a classic pair of opposite-direction arrows spiked to a wooden post. "Someplace that doesn't require me to drive onto a U.S. military base and surrender myself."

Harper shook her head. "I'm going to regret this, but . . . what the hell." She pointed left. "Follow the signs to Garowe. I know a bloke there who runs a trucking outfit. We can park this rig on his lot. No one'll look twice at it."

It wasn't a perfect plan, but it was better than any idea he'd had. "Sounds good."

She resumed loading spare magazines. "I must be bloody mental."

He put the truck back in gear and hit the gas. "Garowe, here we come."

• • •

One rude surprise that morning had put Arkady Malenkov in a sour mood. The second made it a struggle for him not to raise his voice. He glared at the shaky, stuttering, washed-out image of Max Newbold on his data tablet. "What do you mean you've lost the missiles?"

"An ambush." Newbold's voice cut in and out as static hashed his mobile transmission. *"Special operators. Don't know whose."*

It took all Malenkov's discipline to resist the urge to place blame. What mattered now was finding a way to salvage what was left of his operation. "Where are they now?"

"A few miles ahead of us, on the road to Burao."

"You have them in sight?"

A nod. *"For now."*

Malenkov felt the pressure of his colleagues' anxious stares. "Can you catch them?"

"Maybe. Taking them in transit raises the risk of damaging the missiles."

He shook his head. "That won't do, Colonel. We need them intact, and soon."

"As soon as they stop, we can make a play for the truck. Once it's back under our control, we can bring the missiles back to the airport and finish arming the jet."

From the other side of the coffee table in the Klub Rybakov's main room, out of view of the data tablet's camera, General Dmitry Markoff slid a note to Malenkov, who perused its contents: a simple question the general wanted him to ask Newbold.

"Colonel, did you capture any images or video of the operators who stole the missiles? If we can identify them, we might be able to help you."

His request put Newbold on the defensive. *"How would you be able to ID them?"*

Markoff plucked the tablet from Malenkov's hand and turned its built-in camera to face himself and Vadim Zalesky of the GRU. "Let it suffice to say, Colonel, that certain parties within the Russian military intelligence community have taken an interest in your mission—and are now invested in securing its success."

Standing behind the general and the spymaster were Malenkov's deceitful business partners, Nikunin and Puleshko. Both avoided Malenkov's reproachful stare.

Newbold's voice grew even more tremulous. *"The airport's security system might have recorded them, but we didn't think to retrieve it before we left."*

"Not a problem." Markoff looked at Zalesky, who turned and nodded at a GRU support technician manning a laptop from an armchair on the side of the room. The general returned his focus to Newbold. "When did their attack at the airport take place?"

"About half an hour ago."

"Good enough. Thank you for the report, Colonel."

He handed the tablet back to Malenkov, who noted Newbold's aggrieved expression. *"What's going on, Arkady? I thought this was a private contract."*

"My apologies, Colonel. There was a last-minute adjustment." Another accusatory glance at his partners. "Courtesy of our friends Grigor and Yuri."

The GRU technician hunched forward in the armchair. "Tapping into the Berbera Airport's security network. Accessing its video feeds now." A few clicks on his trackpad, a few taps on his keyboard. "I have footage from the attack—and a clear look at the operators. A white male and a black female. Running facial recognition analysis." He noted the keen attention of Markoff and Zalesky. "This might take a few moments."

On the tablet, Newbold simmered. *"This is not the mission we signed up for."*

"I know," Malenkov said. "But until you recover those missiles, I have no leverage—and no argument for refusing help from the government. Do you understand?"

"Perfectly."

The room's mood intensified as the technician jumped to his feet and almost fumbled his laptop. "We have a match on the male operator!" He hurried over to Markoff and Zalesky and handed them his computer.

The general and the spymaster studied its screen, then Markoff handed it back to the technician. Zalesky pulled his cell phone from inside his jacket and stepped outside, onto the deck overlooking the Volga, and the general pointed at Malenkov. "Tell your rented soldiers to stand down!"

Newbold's eyes widened; he had heard the general's command. *"What happened?"*

"I don't know. But keep your distance until we know more. Malenkov out." He ended the video conference and switched off the tablet. "General, what's going on?"

Markoff postponed his reply with a raised hand as Zalesky returned from the deck. The spymaster tucked away his cell phone as he met Markoff. "We'll have a Spetsnaz team in the air from Sana'a in forty-five minutes."

"Good." The general flashed a reptilian smile at Malenkov and his partners. "Gentlemen, it seems some small measure of victory might yet be salvaged from your failure. Your bungled operation in Somalia has flushed out one of Russia's most-wanted international fugitives: the renegade American assassin, Jack Bauer."

· · ·

Sickly sweet hookah smoke choked the basement redoubt of the warlord Osan Hadid Kamal. A languid atmosphere obtained in his fan-cooled sanctuary of shade and secrecy, a welcome relief from the unseasonably hot, late-autumn day that had broken over northern Somaliland.

Peace, as ever, proved elusive. The gentle swinging of his hammock kept lulling him toward sleep, but tickles of sweat traced irregular paths over his skin and prevented him from slipping off into dreams. All he could do was try to empty his mind and wait for the next wash of cooling air as the head of the fan rotated once more in his direction.

Bright light struck his eyes. He lifted his hand to block the glare. "Shut the door!"

The blinding wedge of sunlight shrank and vanished as a silhouetted figure closed the door to the street. A fearful apology came from the restored shadows: "Sorry, Lord Kamal."

He knew the owner of that groveling voice. It was the

weakling boy he had tasked with monitoring the shortwave radio for messages from their spies. "What is it, Qeyd?"

"I bring news, Lord Kamal. Valuable news."

Kamal draped his forearm over his eyes. "I doubt that."

"Nuclear missiles are being driven out of Berbera with almost no one to defend them."

He lowered his arm and looked at the scrawny youth. "You know this how?"

"Our spy from al-Shabaab's sect in Xagal was at a firefight on the north side. Hanad made his men attack a platoon of mercenaries."

"Who won?"

"The mercenaries. But our spy survived, and he followed them to the airport. He says two people hijacked a truck carrying two nuclear missiles. A man and a woman."

Kamal swung his legs off the hammock and sat up. "Just two people? He's sure?"

"He was very specific, my lord. They blew up the mercenaries' other trucks and stole the big one with the missiles."

Wheels turned in Kamal's imagination. "How big is this truck?"

"The kind that hauls trailers."

"Heavy and slow, then." He stood and scratched his stubbled chin. "Where is it now?"

Qeyd bowed his head as Kamal stepped toward him. "Our road men just spotted it driving south, past the Shiikh settlement, on Werdada Berbera."

"They're on their way *here*? They're on the road to Burao?"

"Yes, my lord."

It was too good an opportunity to ignore. Taking Westerners hostage had proved lucrative on a few occasions. But if rich Europeans would pay hundreds of thousands of euros to get their people back, how much more would they pay to recover nuclear weapons? And could they possibly pay more than al-Qaeda was almost certainly willing to offer? Military convoys had passed Burao in the past, but they had been too heavily defended to be worth the risk. After all, an army of preadolescent boys was easy to control, but it was rarely a match for a professional army of men. A man and a woman alone in a slow-moving semi, on the other hand . . .

"Wake up everyone," Kamal said to Qeyd. "I want them all in the trucks with their rifles loaded in ten minutes. We need to stop the rig before it reaches town."

Qeyd bowed. "Yes, my lord." He backed toward the door. "I'll rouse the others."

"Move!"

His shout spurred the boy into action. Qeyd turned, yanked open the door, and ran down the line of shanty huts, banging on doors and crying out for everyone to rise and assemble.

Kamal stretched his arms above his head, bent side to side until he heard satisfying cracks from his limber spine, and scratched his bare chest. Outside his door, a fortune was waiting to be had. He donned a sweat-stained, short-sleeved linen shirt, put on a pair of sunglasses, pulled on his sun-bleached cap, and picked up his AK-74 assault rifle.

I've waited my whole life for a chance to be rich. He slammed a fresh magazine into his Kalashnikov. *Time to bring my waiting to an end.*

• • •

Burnett and his men crawled toward Berbera Airport, moving low and slow so they would kick up as little dust as possible in the harsh morning light. They had fanned out, keeping at least two meters apart from one another. Now, at the edge of a gully that offered them a small measure of cover, they all peered through their targeting scopes and scouted the situation at the airport, where half a dozen mercenaries milled about the husks of their convoy, which lay smoldering and shattered along one side of the traffic loop in front of the terminal.

"Now we know what made all that smoke," Burnett said. "Land Rover flambé."

Pearson watched the other side of the traffic loop. "Someone shot the terminal to hell."

"Probably these guys," Oteri said. "They look pretty proud of themselves."

A mocking snort from Colberg. "For what? Losing their own convoy to an IED?"

Burnett smiled. "They're mercs. They're happy if they make it through the day with their butts still attached." A sidelong glance down the line. "Yant? What's that on the runway?"

"Looks like a Sukhoi 34." A squint and a scowl. "Pilot and navigator both sport Russian colors. Whatever they're up to, it looks like they're in no hurry."

Nothing Burnett saw made any sense. "Everybody take another look. Do we see anything that might be holding a pair of nukes?" After several seconds of reconnaissance, no one had anything new to report. "We have mercs twiddling their thumbs. A fragged convoy. An idling Russian fighter-bomber. And no nukes?" He looked up from his targeting sight. "Would anyone care to guess what the hell is going on?"

"We're about to have a problem," Yant said. "Roof, one o'clock."

A slight shift was all Burnett needed to turn his sights toward the hangar rooftop. As soon as he did, he understood his sniper's warning: there was another sniper looking back at them.

"Take him."

Yant fired. Burnett held his aim to confirm the enemy sniper was neutralized. Then he saw the merc's spotter make a run for it. "Fire." Another suppressed shot from Yant dropped the spotter, but as the second merc collapsed, Burnett saw a radio fall from the dead man's hand.

A handful of mercs turned toward the gully and opened up on full automatic. Bullets screamed past above the SEALs' heads, suggesting the mercs were firing blind.

"We're made. Light 'em up!"

The entire SEAL team returned fire together, single shots and controlled bursts, a patter of suppressed pops from their submachine guns. Half the mercs were on the ground before the other half realized what was happening. The remaining enemy personnel scattered, betraying their preference for individual survival over unit cohesion.

"Zoned fire," Burnett said.

A handful of wild shots by the enemy kicked up the dirt in

front of the SEAL team, but none came close to finding their mark. Burnett snapped off precision shots into his area of coverage, and each of his men diligently covered his own arc of the battlefield, picking off any merc unlucky enough to blunder into it. Within seconds, the firefight was over, and the last of the mercs was on the ground and out of commission.

The scream of a jet's engine split the air. Yant aimed his weapon at the Russian fighter-bomber, which taxied toward the runway. Burnett snapped, "Hold your fire! Let 'em go!"

"Sir?"

"The mercs were illegal combatants, no one's gonna make a stink over them. But one round in a Russian jet, and we're all looking at a court-martial."

Yant removed his finger from the trigger. "Roger that."

Half a minute later the Su-34 raced back down the runway, a silver blur that streaked into the pale blue sky and turned north, toward its homeland. As the roar of its engines faded, a deathly silence settled over the empty airport and its half-dozen dead, who lay sprawled in pools of blood beside their smoking convoy of shattered Land Rovers.

Burnett massaged his temples, which throbbed with a dull ache.

"Colberg, get CENTCOM on the horn."

"Sir? Are you sure? We don't have any lead on the missiles."

"That's *exactly* why we need to phone it in. Because we *don't* know where they are. But they're out there. And every minute we don't find them, we run the risk someone else *will*."

15

10:00 A.M. - 11:00 A.M.

Poor road maintenance combined with unsafe speed made the semi's cab shake as if it suffered from a palsy. Jack's hands were tense on the steering wheel, and he strained to pierce the desert's white glow. A few times every minute, a small pebble or a bit of grit bounced over the rig's hood and flew in through the empty windshield frame, forcing him and Harper to dodge to either side.

She studied him, her gaze intense but perplexed. "Explain something to me."

"If I can."

"You seem like a nice guy."

"I am a nice guy."

"Then why do so many people want you dead?"

Her query was so matter-of-fact that it made him laugh. "You just cut right to it, don't you?" Her unblinking stare made it clear she wasn't going to let her question be deflected. "You sure you want to know? Because everyone else who knows what I'm about to tell you is either dead or so far underground, they'll never see daylight again."

"I think I can handle it."

He ducked another incoming bit of road gravel. "Remember when the Russian–Kamistani peace talks fell apart in New York?"

"You mean the year before last? When President Taylor stepped down and President Logan ate a bullet?"

Jack said nothing in reply, knowing she would fill in the gaps on her own.

"You were involved in that? How deep?"

"All the way." He steered around a gaping pothole without missing a beat. "I was on the team that exposed the conspiracy between Logan and Suvarov."

Awkward silence followed his admission; then Harper's eyes went wide. "You were the one who attacked the Russian consulate in New York!" She didn't wait for him to confirm or deny her accusation. "Do you know what you did? You nearly started World War Three!"

"No, the Russians did that. I just made sure they paid for it."

"You're crazier than I thought." Despite her criticism, there was an almost grudging admiration in her eyes when she looked at him again. "And the Chinese?"

"Blame me for the death of Consul Koo Yin in Los Angeles." He hastened to add, "I didn't kill him. He was shot by his own men, and they blamed me to cover it up."

She shook her head. "And I thought I was bad at making friends."

He took the opportunity to steer the topic of discussion away from himself. "What's your story? How'd you end up on a solo posting in a Somali desert?"

A sour grimace and a shrug. "Same old story. Started off as my unit's hot new operator. The director who recruited me promised me my pick of assignments. Tokyo. Paris. Moscow."

"What happened?"

"Bean counters. One day we were fighting international terrorism. The next we had to defend ourselves from an internal audit. My boss got the sack, and the new top dog gave all the plum assignments to his cronies. I kicked up a fuss about it—and now I get to tell my sad story while riding in windowless trucks with American fugitives."

"So much for 'squeaky wheel gets the grease.'"

"You're telling me. More like the squeaky wheel gets replaced." A thoughtful look softened her features. "I still don't get it. Your own country threw you to the dingoes. Why spend your time drawing heat like this?"

"Why wouldn't I?"

"With your skills? You could go to ground, change your name, disappear."

"Did that already. Didn't care for it."

"I just don't get why you'd keep risking your neck for a country that disowned you."

He wondered if he could explain his rationale in terms she would understand. "I haven't devoted my life to serving my country because I expect a reward for it. If America needs to call me a criminal to keep its enemies at bay, then that's what I am. If it needs to cast me out to keep the peace, I'll live on the run."

"You're that loyal to a government what turned its back on you?"

"America doesn't owe me anything. And it never will."

She chewed on that, then nodded. "Now I feel like a heel for wanting a raise."

"Hey, patriots have to pay their bills, too."

Harper laughed, and Jack felt a true smile cross his face, the first in a long while. It felt good to enjoy a real connection with another person after spending so long hiding himself from everyone around him.

Then he spotted the first sign of an obstruction on the road ahead, and his good mood evaporated. "We've got company."

A pair of troop trucks, parked nose to nose, stood in the middle of the road. Arrayed to either side of the impromptu roadblock were two groups of Somali boys who appeared to range in age from ten to sixteen years old. All of them carried AK-47s or similar long rifles, and many of the older boys wore bandoliers across their famine-slimmed torsos. Standing in the middle of the formation, atop the trucks, with one foot on either hood, was an adult Somali man whose lean frame was garbed in a weathered khaki uniform. He held an assault rifle in a relaxed but ready stance.

It was a spectacle Jack had seen several years before, during his exile in the Central African country of Sangala: a warlord backed by an army of children, most of whom had likely entered his service against their will. Ugly memories assailed him, filling him with cold hatred.

The warlord fired a warning burst into the air, a clear signal for Jack to stop the truck.

He floored the gas and shifted up a gear. "Hang on!"

Harper was horrified. "You're not going to—?"

She forgot her question and ducked as the warlord leveled his weapon at the semi.

Jack ducked and kept his foot on the accelerator.

A spray of bullets tore past above him and Harper, adding holes to the back of the cab. Metal screeched and groaned as the rig bashed through the roadblock. The jolt slammed Jack's jaw shut and sent a hard shock up his feet, into his spine.

The next burst of gunfire he heard came from behind them. He lifted his head. They had broken through the roadblock, but he could barely see the road ahead through the plumes of steam from the rig's damaged radiator. "I don't think we're gonna make it to Garowe."

Harper craned her head out her window to look back at the failed roadblock; then she turned back toward him, suddenly manic. "Are you crazy? What were you thinking?"

"There's no way I'm getting into a firefight with a bunch of kids. But if we'd stopped, they'd have killed us. I guarantee it." He watched the temperature gauge climb steadily into the red. "We've got about ten minutes before the engine overheats. I need options."

"We should be able to make it to Burao, the next village." She threw another nervous look back out her window. "But I'm betting that's where our new friends came from—and odds are, they'll be right behind us."

"Then we're gonna need a place to hide, and fast. Do you know anyone in Burao?"

She pinched the bridge of her nose, as if she had just manifested the worst headache in human history. "I know one man in Burao."

"Is he a friend?"

"Sullah? He's the most vile bag of scum who's ever lived."

The steam belching from the engine turned to oily gray smoke.

Jack frowned. "Let's hope he's in a good mood, then."

Sana'a, Yemen

A casual observer could have been forgiven for thinking the four men crossing the tarmac were brothers. All had the same chiseled features, close-cropped hair, and lean physiques. The oldest was in his late thirties, the youngest in his mid-twenties. They all strode with confidence and moved single file, carrying their fully loaded black duffels toward a private jet whose engines idled with a steady, high-pitched whine.

What the naked eye couldn't see was that the four were closer than siblings; they were brothers-in-arms, Spetsnaz commandos, members of the Russian military's elite special forces, four of the best-trained soldiers on earth.

Their commander, Major Danko, walked point and led his team up the jet's short folding stairs and into its main cabin. Just as he had been told to expect, a GRU officer from the embassy was already on board. What he hadn't expected was that it would be Irina Corleeva, the woman with whom he'd enjoyed a fling months earlier, before learning who she really was.

The striking blond deputy consul swirled a cocktail of clear liquids in her right hand. With her left she thrust a sealed folder at Danko. "Your orders, Major."

He set down his duffel, took the folder from Corleeva, and ushered his men past him to their seats at the back of the cabin. "You remember my men, I trust?"

"How could I forget?" She recited each man's sins as he filed past her. "Captain Soltsin, your second-in-command. Twenty-six confirmed kills."

"Twenty-nine," Soltsin said. "But who's counting?"

An accusatory lift of her eyebrow. "Lieutenant Titov. Evaded capture in Paris by leading police on the longest car chase in French history."

"Not my fault. Bad signage."

She met the last man with contempt. "Sergeant Yakunin. Blown up any schools lately?"

He brushed off her disgust with aplomb. "Define 'lately.'"

Danko reviewed the mission file. "This is confirmed?"

"Less than two hours ago, at Berbera Airport. We're working

SIGINT to get a fix on his current location. As soon as we pinpoint his coordinates, we'll update you." She got up. Moved toward the exit, then turned back a step shy of its threshold. "Just to be clear, Major: Your orders are to take him alive. Our superiors want him to stand trial in Moscow for what he's done."

"Understood. Now, get off my plane."

She left without further ado, and as soon as she stepped off the stairs, the copilot pulled them up and sealed the hatch. "Strap in, gentlemen. We'll be wheels-up in ninety seconds."

Danko dismissed the man with a curt salute, then joined his men at the rear of the cabin. "We're going after a legend today, brothers: We're hunting Jack Bauer."

Their excitement was palpable. Then a grave look possessed Soltsin. "Did I hear the deputy consul say we need to take him alive?"

"Yes, she did." As the jet taxied toward the runway, Danko couldn't suppress a malicious smile. "Fortunately for us, 'alive' doesn't mean *unharmed*. We'll deliver Bauer to Moscow breathing and with a pulse. But beyond that . . . I don't recall making any promises."

• • •

The semi rig was a wheezing, lurching hunk of junk by the time Jack steered it down the narrow dirt roads of Burao, which to his eye resembled an uncovered landfill more than a town. A steady gray plume rolled from the rig's grille, over the hood, and into the cab, obscuring his view and stinging his eyes. Sleeving a greasy sheen from his brow, he missed the semi's windshield even more than he had when his only annoyances had been dust and sunlight.

He hoped the rig didn't stall as he slowed to get his bearings. "Which way?"

"Take a right here, then your first left." Harper palmed the oily patina of engine mist from her face. "I can't tell if we're laying down a smoke screen or sending up smoke signals."

"Both, I think." He steered through the two turns she had directed. "Where now?"

"Second right, then the fourth left."

Curious eyes watched them from inside every lean-to and shanty they passed. Emaciated Somalis in tattered desert robes noted their passage as if it were the most momentous thing they had seen in ages. For all Jack knew, it might have been. "So much for traveling under the radar."

"You have no idea. The entire city knows we're here by now."

Groans and rattles from the rig's damaged engine left Jack contemplating how to adjust his tactics if the truck died in the open. None of the scenarios he considered ended well. He clutched the steering wheel and projected his will through the dash into the truck's heart. *Don't you die on me, you hunk of junk. Not until we get to cover. Do you hear me? Don't die!*

They navigated around a large open square in the middle of the town. Its perimeter was ringed by ramshackle structures cobbled together from junk, debris, and salvaged materials. Halfway around the square, Harper pointed to his left. "There."

She didn't have to say more than that. There was only one open garage along the road large enough for him to pull the truck inside. He eased off the gas, tapped the brake, and downshifted as he guided the rig and its trailer to cover inside the shadowy warehouse of corrugated metal and scavenged wood. As soon as he brought the rig to a full stop, its engine perished with a shudder and a grinding of steel so horrendous, it made Jack wince.

He and Harper noted the shadowy figure reflected in her side's mirror. She implored Jack's patience with a look. "Let me handle this." She got out of the truck. Only after she was out the door did Jack notice that she had left behind her weapons.

Leaving her without cover went against his training, but they were on her turf. Even though years of experience told him to get out of the truck with his SIG at the ready, he put his trust in Harper's read of the situation and left his sidearm holstered as he got out and followed her to the back of the trailer, where an overweight and slovenly Somali stood waiting for them.

The fat man pointed a shotgun at Harper. "I told you never to come back here."

Harper approached him with her hands up and open. "I had

no choice, Sullah. We need your help. And we're prepared to pay well for it."

"How well?"

"Enough to get you out of this country once and for all."

Sullah lowered the shotgun. "You have that much on you?"

"I can get it."

He raised the shotgun's barrel toward her chest. "No more games, lady spy."

"There's a red house one mile east of Berbera Airport. Hidden in the brush next to the house is a gray minivan. In the back of the minivan there's a bag with more than sixty thousand euros, in cash."

"So you say. Get the bag, then come back. I will wait."

Jack wanted to reply, *You'll be dead,* but he kept his cool and let Harper handle it.

"How about diamonds, Sullah? You like diamonds?"

The Somali shrugged. "Who doesn't like diamonds?"

Harper smiled. "I'm going to lift my shirt with one hand, real slow." She maintained eye contact with Sullah as she raised the lower half of her shirt to reveal a wide band of tape wrapped around her midriff. Working with slow precision, and taking care to make sure Sullah saw all that she did, she unwound the long strip of adhesive, then held it up. Its sticky side glittered with hundreds of tiny points of light. "Half a million in uncut diamonds. Yours if you close the front and let us hide here until we come up with a way out."

He held out one hand but kept the shotgun ready.

"Toss me the diamonds, I close the front."

An underhand lob passed the strip of gray tape backed with precious stones from Harper to her doughy sweaty slimeball of a contact. He flashed a grin of yellowed teeth, then hurried to the chain that controlled the retractable door that covered the front of his spacious storage area. He unhooked it and let it fall shut. The heavy barrier dropped and hit the ground with a bang, plunging the interior of his hideout into near total darkness. Only slivers of light crept in through gaps in the walls and roof.

After a few seconds, Jack's eyes adjusted and he discerned

Harper and Sullah from the surrounding gloom. He said to Harper, "This'll buy us a little time, but not much. We need another rig to haul this trailer."

Sullah laughed. "Another rig like this one? In Burao? Not a chance."

Jack took Harper aside and lowered his voice. "If we don't move the missiles, we're dead. It won't take that thug and his boy soldiers long to find us."

"If Sullah says there aren't any more trucks in Burao, then there aren't. Like it or not, we'll have to make a stand here while we wait for someone to come retrieve the missiles." She took out her satellite phone and tapped at its keypad—then frowned as it refused to respond. "Damn it. Battery's dead." She called to Sullah. "I don't suppose you have electricity here?"

"Sure we do. Every other Tuesday, from six A.M. to eight A.M. Can you wait a week?"

"I'm starting to hate him," Jack said under his breath.

Harper shrugged. "Go ahead. Everyone else does." She left Jack and moved toward Sullah. "Still hoarding junk in all these boxes you keep lying around?"

"Never know what might be valuable one day."

"Mind if I scrounge around a bit?"

Sullah held up his tape strip of diamonds. "For this? Take whatever you want."

"Thank you."

Harper opened a box and rooted around in its depths. Noting Jack's watchful eye, she favored him with a reassuring smile. "Hang tight, mate. I once fixed a car with my old panty hose and blew up a Cessna with a yam. Pretty sure I can recharge a phone."

• • •

Someone had seen something; Kamal was certain of it. The interlopers and their crippled truck could not have reached Burao more than a few minutes ahead of him and his young company. Stiff winds from the south had dispersed the smoke trail from the rig's perforated engine, making it impossible to follow through Burao's myriad trash-strewn roads.

"Qeyd, stop the truck."

Kamal opened the passenger door and jumped to the ground as the troop truck slowed. Behind him, his truck and the one following it came to a halt. His troop of boys piled out of them, rifles in hand, and gathered to await his orders.

"Kick in every door. Bring everyone outside. If they resist, kill them."

The youths scattered and stormed inside the shelters of junk that lined the road. Pitiable cries of terror and pain followed as they herded the sheeplike residents out of their hiding places and corralled them at gunpoint into the harsh morning light. No one had to tell the weaklings to get on their knees. Kamal had ruled Burao as its resident warlord for most of the past year. His name alone was enough to cow the masses into submission. Those brave enough to have confessed their hatred of him had long since been put to death in the town's square. Only those fearful enough to hold their tongues still survived, and only so long as they remained of use to him.

He walked in front of the line of kneeling peons with a .45 semiautomatic in his hand. The men trembled behind blank stares. The women shed tears in silence. The children shut their eyes, bowed their heads, and no doubt prayed for an act of deliverance that would never come.

At random, he stopped in front of a bald man of advancing years and pressed the muzzle of his pistol to the bridge of the man's nose. "You saw the truck that came through here?"

"Yes, Lord Kamal."

"Where did it go?"

The skinny old man glanced to his left. "That way. They turned left at the red shack."

Kamal shifted his aim from the old man to the softly mewling little girl by his side, but he kept his eyes on the old man. "If I go down that street, will the people who live there say they've seen the truck? Or will I need to come back here and teach you a lesson?"

"I give you my word, before Allah: They turned left at the red shack."

He holstered his pistol and faced his boy soldiers. "Straight ahead, left at the red shack." They hurried back inside their transports, and Kamal returned to the passenger seat of the lead truck. It would be a short drive past the red shack, and soon after that, he and his fighters would need to play this scene again, with a new line of witnesses.

It was a tedious means to an end, but Burao was a small town.

Sooner or later, they would find the semi. Then its riches would be his—and the outsiders would pay with their lives for defying his authority in front of his people.

• • •

"They're going door-to-door. What are they? Salesmen?"

Newbold might have laughed at Andrzejczyk's cynical criticism if all their lives didn't depend on the outcome of this unexpected showdown in the desert. "I don't care if they are, Teej. This is their town. Let them search it their way."

A dozen personnel from the troop truck—the last one in the convoy left operational after the sneak attack by a pair of wily special operators—huddled behind him, all awaiting some word of what was happening in the hazy distance, past the shimmer of a mirage hovering above Burao. Private Hitchens and Corporal Mergenthaler flanked Major Sealander, all of them with their rifles at the ready. Sealander raised his chin and caught Newbold's eye. "Anything?"

"The Somali warlord and his preteen irregulars are going block by block."

"You've gotta be kidding me." The major pulled his hand over his dust-covered face. "We could be out here all day."

"I don't think so," Andrzejczyk said. "Whoever these guys are, the fact they haven't had to shoot anyone yet tells me they run this town. If our truck's down there, they'll find it."

Mergenthaler seemed less than encouraged. "That helps us how?"

Newbold fixed the man with a hard stare. "Never been hunting, have you, Corporal? When your game goes to ground, you don't find it by giving yourself away. You send in a big, noisy dog to flush it out. Then, when your prey's in the open . . . you take your shot."

The implications of his statement appeared to trouble Hitchens. "And if that platoon of kids gets in the way?"

A dismissive roll of his shoulders. "Not our problem. We didn't put them there." Newbold sensed resistance to his hard-hearted assessment. "I don't like it any more than you do, but we're running out of time. I want those missiles back before the Russians scuttle our deal."

Andrzejczyk lowered his binoculars and looked back at Newbold. "What if they do? If this takes longer than we think, and the Russians walk away . . . what then?"

It was a question Newbold had already considered during the drive from Berbera.

"If we make enemies of the Russians, we'll need the missiles more than ever." He peered across the desert at the slow-moving column of violence advancing through Burao's narrow streets. "Luckily for us, there will always be *someone* willing to pay for nuclear warheads."

11:00 A.M. - 12:00 P.M.

It was amazing what one could find if one were willing to dig deeply enough in old boxes. Most of what Harper had exhumed from the cardboard tombs of Sullah's garage proved useless, as she'd expected. However, she had found a string of old Christmas lights that suited her needs, along with a small pair of wire cutters.

She carried them to the semi, whose front end Jack had lifted and tilted forward to gain access to its engine. Using tools he had unearthed from beneath a pile of French pornographic magazines, Jack was doing his best to repair the engine's bullet-riddled core, over which he was hunched at an angle that Harper imagined must be profoundly uncomfortable.

"How goes it?"

He stood and sleeved sweat from his forehead with his forearm, being careful not to touch his grease-coated hands to his face. "They tore up the radiator and the main block." A disgruntled frown. "It's totaled."

"Then this is where we need to make our stand." She leaned past him and took a gander at the brutalized engine. "If you're sure it's toast, mind if I swipe the battery?"

"Go ahead. It's about the only thing they *didn't* shoot."

She reached in and detached the leads for the battery, then unfastened the clamps that held it in place. It was a leaden hunk of metal and acid, and she let slip a grunt of effort as she lifted it free of the engine. Jack followed her as she carried it to a nearby workbench.

"Charging the phone off the battery." He nodded. "Smart. I'm guessing you mean to use the Christmas lights as current regulators?"

"Hole in one, mate." She used the wire cutters to snip the male plug from the lights, then cut away the last section of wire before removing its female extension plug. Next she stripped the insulation from the ends of both sections of wire. The first length, which had the lights, she twisted around the positive lead on the battery. The other end, which was without lights, she attached to the negative lead. Then she retrieved her satellite phone and extracted its battery, which she laid on top of the truck's battery. She smirked at Jack. "Now for the magic."

She touched the end of the first wire to the metal node on the phone battery marked with a plus symbol, and the other wire to the adjacent surface, which bore a minus symbol. The lights on the string lit with a weak radiance. "Voilà," Harper said. "Current passes through the phone battery, but only after it's regulated by the lights."

"Good work," Jack said. "How long to charge the phone?" Her elation turned to mild embarrassment. "About an hour."

"That long?"

"I could cut the string to reduce the resistance, but I might fry the phone battery."

He shook his head. "We can't risk that."

He went to the truck and retrieved the few weapons they had left: his submachine gun and her carbine, and their pistols. The assault rifle was out of ammunition, and the only ammo they had left for the pistols, the submachine gun, and the carbine was what they were carrying on their persons. The rest of their ammo had been left behind in the minivan.

Jack handed her the Austeyr. "Keep this handy. I'll scout the area and look for choke points we can exploit for defense."

"Maybe look for an escape route if you've got a second?"

He replied as he walked away. "Count on it. I never walk into a place I don't know how to walk out of. And I don't plan on dying in Somalia."

• • •

Summoned like errant schoolboys, Malenkov, Puleshko, and Nikunin entered the upstairs dining room of the Al Pash Grand Hotel's restaurant, which had been closed for this private affair. The three men stood shoulder to shoulder at the end of a banquet table, where their hosts were seated and enjoying an early lunch next to windows that looked out on the lush countryside and the serpentine twists of the Volga. No one invited Malenkov and his colleagues to sit, so they remained standing, ostensibly ignored by General Markoff and Director Zalesky while the GRU agents and Spetsnaz troopers in plain clothes exited and blocked the stairs behind them.

Markoff ate a mouthful of caviar, set down his spoon, and dabbed his gray mustache with his napkin. "Thank you for coming, gentlemen. The director and I have important news."

Zalesky took a sip of his champagne, then continued Markoff's thought. "Your operation in Somalia has fallen apart. We would have supported a viable mission, but we're past that now."

Malenkov stepped forward. "What are you talking about? I haven't heard—"

"Most of your mercenaries are dead," Markoff cut in, "and our aircraft is on its way back—without the missiles. Your plan is now a failure in every respect."

"Save one," Zalesky said. "It had the unexpected benefit of exposing a fugitive from state justice. While there's no way this could have been part of your plan, you have our thanks for it."

"Too kind," Malenkov said.

Nikunin edged forward to stand at his side. "With all respect, sirs, I'm not prepared to abandon this operation, not yet. We have a considerable sum invested in this."

The spymaster regarded Nikunin with smug condescension. "We're well aware of the scope of your investment. I, for one, applaud your ingenuity. Not many men could have nested so many empty corporate shells within one another, all to buy up a controlling stake in an American nuclear munitions disposal company. If the rest of your scheme had been anywhere near so devious or so well executed, we might not be having this conversation now."

Puleshko palmed sweat from his expansive bald pate. "But what about our losses?"

It seemed to Malenkov that the general took real enjoyment from their predicament. Markoff grinned beneath his bushy mustache. "One should never gamble more than one is prepared to lose, Mr. Puleshko. A lesson I think you've just learned the hard way." He underscored his contempt by sucking the meat out of a cracked lobster claw.

Zalesky raised his glass, as if to toast the three executives. "You should thank your colleagues for seeking our help, Arkady. From what we've seen, your operation was doomed to fail. At least now, Dmitry and I have an incentive to help you clean up your mess." In a more ominous tone he added, "Provided you're smart enough to walk away while you still can."

Malenkov's pulse raced; his face burned with shame. "You expect me to thank you?"

"No," Markoff said through half-chewed lobster, "we expect you to leave."

The GRU director got up and walked over to stand with the trio. "My people will erase your digital trails. Communications, financial transfers, all of it. Within a few hours, it will be as if your operation never happened." He rested one hand on Malenkov's shoulder. "I'm not entirely unsympathetic with regard to your losses. If the team we've sent in is successful in bringing back the fugitive you exposed, we might be able to . . . *offset* some of your losses."

Nikunin said under his breath to Malenkov, "That sounds reasonable." On his other flank, Puleshko nodded in fearful concurrence.

There was nothing left for Malenkov to do but bow out with a modicum of grace. "A most generous offer, Director. I'm sure I speak for us all when I wish you the best of luck."

"Thank you, Arkady." He gestured toward the stairs. "I trust you know the way out." He turned and walked back toward the table, as if the three businessmen were already gone.

Malenkov led his colleagues down the stairs, out of the

restaurant to an elevator, and then through the lobby to the exit. They walked side by side down the steep and curving stairs in front of the hotel, their silence strained by unspoken resentments. At street level, a limousine stood waiting for them. The chauffeur opened the rear door as they approached.

"Destination, gentlemen?"

"Klub Rybakov," Malenkov said as he got into the limo.

As soon as the door was closed, Malenkov glowered at his compatriots. "If either of you says so much as one word to me before we get home to Saint Petersburg, I will kill you with my bare hands and pay the chauffeur to dump your bodies on a dirt road in Siberia."

• • •

All Danko's thoughts were focused on what he would do as soon as the Learjet landed. He would lead his Spetsnaz team off the plane into the Somali wasteland, find transport, and begin his hunt of the American expatriate Jack Bauer. If all went well, they would capture him and bring him back to the plane in under two hours, and be on their way homeward to Russia. To commendations, and good vodka, and maybe a decent night's sleep, for a change.

Then he noticed a shift in the plane's attitude. The nose had lifted. It was climbing.

"What the—?" He got up and made his way forward, past his team, to the cockpit door. It was ajar, so he pulled it open and leaned in between the pilot and the copilot. "What's going on? Why aren't we landing?"

"New orders," the pilot said. "We have reports of U.S. SEALs on the ground at Berbera. We're redirecting to Hargeisa."

Frustration welled up inside Danko. "No, that's too far out of the way."

"No choice," the copilot said. "Consular orders. 'Attempt no landing in Berbera,' they said." A humble one-shoulder shrug. "On the bright side, they'll have an SUV waiting for you when we touch down at Hargeisa."

There was nothing to be done. Orders were orders. Danko

took a breath and reminded himself to focus on the mission. "How much of a delay are we looking at?"

The pilot answered over his shoulder. "Twenty minutes, tops. We've got clear skies, so we should have you on the ground at HGA by five past the hour."

"Fine. Let me know if anything else changes."

Danko left the cockpit and returned to his men. "Who has the grid?"

Soltsin spread a map of northern Somalia across a foldout table between two facing seats. "What are we looking at?"

"Berbera's too hot. We're landing in Hargeisa." As he sat down in the empty seat on one side of the map, his smartphone chirped at him. He retrieved it from his coat pocket and checked the incoming message. "New intel puts Bauer somewhere in Burao. Find it."

Titov traced a road line almost due east from Hargeisa, through an empty stretch of desert, to a small town roughly eighty kilometers north of the Somalia–Ethiopia border. "There it is. At the other end of the Guleej Haji highway. It has an airport. Why not land there?"

"Its airport is closed for renovation. How long to drive there from Hargeisa?"

"For a civilian, driving safely? Three hours plus. I can get us there in less than two."

"You'd better," Danko said. "Because we need to get to Burao while Bauer's still there."

• • •

It was difficult for Jack to keep steady atop the stacked crates in the corner of Sullah's garage, but it was the best vantage point he had found from which to observe the inexorable approach of the warlord he and Harper had forced past on Werdada Berbera. Through a narrow gap in the corrugated metal walls, he tracked the slow-moving cloud of dust and exhaust. It moved through the streets and followed the same path they had taken to this hideout.

He kept his eyes on the target as he warned Harper, "They're getting closer."

"Mm-hm." She sat on a stool at the workbench and held the two stripped wires from the Christmas lights against the contact points on her satellite phone's battery. "Anybody shooting at us? Or kicking in our door?"

"Not yet, but it's only a matter of time."

"Everything's a matter of time, mate. Life, death, extinction, the sun burning out, the universe going cold. Give any situation enough time and it'll end badly."

Her predictions were so grim that he almost laughed. "Damn, Harper. You're a little ray of sunshine, aren't you?"

"Just trying to inject a little perspective."

"We've got enough people outside looking to put bullets in our heads. Let's not talk ourselves into doing it for them."

She was unfazed by his criticism. "If you think I'm depressing, that's on you, mate. When I think about how short life is, I look on it as a reason to love every second. We don't get enough time to waste any of it moping about."

In no mood to talk philosophy, Jack changed the subject. "How's that battery coming?"

"Almost there. Another minute should do it."

His patience evaporated faster than the sweat on his brow. "That's long enough. Try it."

Harper set aside the ends of the wire and inserted the battery back into her phone. She started the device. Its screen sprang to life, and she keyed in her access code. Then she waited.

She was too far away for Jack to hear the other side of the conversation. All he heard was her. "Birdcage Zero-One, this is Redwing. Color of the day is yellow. Word of the day is 'wayfarer.' This is a priority alpha communication." A pause. "Standing by." She rolled her eyes at Jack. Seconds passed before she resumed the call. "Package is in hand and under cover, but we're being tracked by local hostiles. We need immediate evac." She keyed a command into her phone, then continued talking. "Read my coordinates and send in a recovery team. *Now*." For several seconds, she listened intently. "Roger that, ASIS. Holding this position. Redwing out."

She switched off the phone and faced Jack. "ASIS says there's already a SEAL team on the ground in Somalia. They're handing off our request to USCENTCOM and sending the SEALs here." A thoughtful pause. "If the SEALs find you here, they might haul you away along with the missiles."

"That's my problem. Let me worry about that." He turned his attention back to the outside world, and to the plumes of smoke and dust rising over the streets of Burao. The enemy had just moved one step closer to finding them—and he had every reason to think they would reach him and Harper long before the SEALs would.

Harper intuited what was on his mind. "Not keen on shooting at kids, are you?"

"I won't do it."

"I doubt they'll show you the same mercy."

"Not the point." His finger yearned to close around the trigger of his HK. "I've dealt with thugs like this so-called warlord before. What I learned is that he's the cancer. Cut him out of the equation, and the rest of the disease goes with him."

"You think it's that simple? Shoot the top dog and the rest of the pack runs?"

Jack squinted into the sun-bleached urban hell outside their feeble shelter. "I hope so." Memories of moral compromises long past plagued him at moments such as this. "I've done . . . questionable things. Terrible things. Some I still regret. But one thing I've *never* done is pull the trigger on a child. I'll go to my grave before I cross that line."

Harper grabbed her carbine and took up a sentry post in the other corner facing the street. "Then I hope you have a brilliant plan hidden up your sleeve, mate. Because I'm betting that's a promise this cut-rate warlord will be happy to help you keep."

"The key is taking out the man in charge. I've seen his type before. He bullies the boys into doing whatever he wants. But fear isn't loyalty. Take him out and his militia's finished."

"Okay," Harper said. "Say you're right. If he acts like every other Somali warlord I've ever seen, he'll send his youth brigade to do the dying while he stays out of the mix. How do you plan to take him down? I mean, you won't get anywhere near him. No offense—you're skilled, I can see that. But in Somalia, you stick out something fierce."

"That's true. If only I had an ally who could blend in around here." He kept quiet while she inferred the meaning from his deadpan remark.

A few seconds later his patience was rewarded by Harper's heavy sigh of irritation mixed with resignation. "I hate you, Bauer."

"Good. That means you just doubled your chances of living through this. Now, hurry up and get changed. We've got about fifteen minutes before this whole situation goes to hell."

12:00 P.M. – 01:00 P.M.

High noon in Hargeisa. Everything outside the Learjet was too bright to see, and the air was too hot to breathe. Danko was reminded once again why he considered Somalia one of the worst places on earth. *The sooner we capture Bauer and get out of this dust bowl, the better.*

He descended the jet's stairs to the tarmac. His team followed him, in descending order of rank: Soltsin, Titov, and Yakunin. Each man, Danko included, carried a black duffel of arms, ammunition, and specialized equipment, and they all sported identical black sunglasses.

Awaiting them was a trim, tanned man in his forties. He had the close-cut hair of a GRU field agent operating under diplomatic cover. He wore light linen trousers, a white cotton shirt so thin, it looked like gauze, and mirrored sunglasses whose oversized lenses gave his face an insectile quality. Tucked under his left arm was a manila folder. Parked behind him was a tan Hummer H2, the purr of its idling engine all but imperceptible.

As the Spetsnaz commandos approached, the thin man stepped forward to meet them. "Major Danko? Welcome to Somaliland. I'm Ravil Lazarev, cultural attaché at the consulate." As he and Danko shook hands, he passed the folder to the major.

"Thank you, Mr. Lazarev." Danko nodded at the Humvee. "Unlock the rear hatch."

"It's open." Lazarev watched as Danko's men filed past

behind him. Yakunin took the major's duffel from him as he passed by, freeing him to open the folder Lazarev had given him.

Danko skimmed through the file. "Last we heard, Bauer was in Burao. Has he moved?"

"No. But we intercepted new signals a few minutes before you landed. We've narrowed his position to a two-block area in the middle of town."

Behind Lazarev, the other Spetsnaz soldiers loaded their duffels into the Hummer. Danko reviewed the transcript from the SIGINT office at the consulate. "This message was intercepted from an Australian operator. A woman, Abigail Harper."

"We have video of her and Bauer working together at the Berbera Airport."

The picture became clearer as Danko checked a few of the morning's earlier reports. "I see." He returned to the top page and noticed a troubling detail. "They've gone to ground with a pair of nuclear missiles and called in an American SEAL team."

"Yes, we don't have much time. The SEALs are already—"

"On the ground in Berbera. We know. It's why we got diverted here." He closed the folder. "How long until they reach Burao?"

"A Black Hawk's been sent from their base in Djibouti to pick them up. ETA to Berbera, one hour. From there, they could reach Burao in just over thirty minutes."

"Is there anyone else in the Hummer?"

"Just the driver."

"We don't need him. Tell him to get out." Sensing hesitation from Lazarev, Danko added in a harsher register, *"Now."*

The thin man turned toward the truck and made a rolling motion with his hand. The round-faced young man inside the vehicle lowered the passenger-side window. As soon as it was half-open, Lazarev said, "Give them the truck. Don't argue. Just get out."

Baby-Face did as told. As he blundered out of the vehicle, Titov climbed in and took his place. He checked the dash display, then looked over his shoulder before nodding at Danko. "Fully fueled, spare petrol cans in the back. Ready to go."

Danko opened the front passenger door and got in, while

Soltsin and Yakunin entered through the back doors and took their places behind him and Titov. As soon as they were settled, he favored Lazarev with a curt salute. "Thanks for the ride. We'll try to bring it back in one piece." Danko raised his window. Titov stepped on the gas, and they left behind the consular liaison and his hapless driver in a cloud of desert grit and gray exhaust.

"We're going to have competition," Danko told his men. "A SEAL team is going to reach Burao a few minutes ahead of us."

Soltsin's brow creased with concern. "What if they catch Bauer before we do?"

"Then we'll spend the rest of our days either guarding a gulag or living in one."

• • •

Of all the places Kamal could have chosen to be at noon in Somalia, none of them would have been the middle of a dusty street in Burao, baking in the sun, with not an inch of shade anywhere to be found. War, however, made intractable demands. As much as he would have preferred to pass the hottest part of the day sequestered in his hideout, basking beneath ceiling fans and counting the hours until sundown, there was work to be done.

There were priceless missiles to be found. There were outlanders to kill.

He leaned against the side of his truck and mopped sweat from his forehead with a rumpled cotton rag. His men moved door-to-door, rousing people from their naps and shouting at them to shock them awake. In other quarters of Burao, there was always activity at this hour—mostly, Muslims summoned by the lyrical calls of muezzins to midday prayers at one of the town's numerous mosques. But these few blocks of Burao were the province of heathens, a refuge for the lazy and the impious. This part of town belonged to the fixer known as Sullah.

Kamal blotted fat beads of sweat from his face. He considered lighting a cigarette, but thought better of it. *Too hot to smoke. I can barely breathe out here as it is. No point adding more heat.*

He wiped away more perspiration trickling through his stubble, only to feel the cotton fibers of his kerchief catch on his whiskers. He cursed under his breath, then tucked the rag back into his pocket, content to simply let his sweat fall where it would.

Movement on his right. His hand went for his rifle—he relaxed. It was only Qeyd, urging a hunger-lean young boy forward by holding his shirt collar and pushing him toward Kamal. As soon as they were within arm's length, Qeyd prompted the youth with a nudge. "Tell him."

Frightened eyes and a face taut from starvation. "I saw the truck."

The news brought Kamal to his feet. He loomed over the skeletal boy. "Where?"

"My family needs food and water."

"Tell me what I want to know, and you'll all have more than you can ever eat."

With effort, the boy lifted his trembling arm and pointed down the road. "Sullah."

I knew it! So many times over the past decade, Sullah had proved to be Kamal's only true rival for control over the people and economy of Burao. Their methods differed, of course. Kamal kept the masses in line through fear, but Sullah manipulated them through the barter of favors and the corruption of imported luxuries. He was the carrot to Kamal's stick.

This time, however, he had gone too far, and Kamal would make him pay for it.

"Get home, boy. When this is over, you'll be rewarded." He spooked the boy with a fearsome glare. "Go!"

The kid broke free of Qeyd's grip and ran for his life, wobbling on bony legs.

Kamal took a deep breath. It felt like inhaling from a furnace.

"Round up the troops, Qeyd. I have new orders." He smiled. "We're going to surround Sullah's junk-metal shack, smoke him out, and kill him. And then we're going to gut his visitors and drag their bodies through the streets—before we take possession of those missiles and make ourselves Somalia's richest men."

• • •

It was hard for Newbold not to feel vulnerable, squatting on a rooftop surrounded by Burao's sprawl of low-rise squalor. Sealander waited on one knee to his left, and Andrzejczyk was on his right, lying prone as much to save his energy as to reduce his visibility to anyone who might look their way—not that anyone or anything seemed to take any notice of their presence.

At the edge of the rooftop, Mergenthaler lay flat and kept a surreptitious watch over events on the street below. Without looking back at the other twelve Firethorn mercs, he beckoned them with one hand to join him. Newbold authorized the advance with a nod, then crawled forward with the others to flank the German-born shooter.

The mood in the street was deceptive. All seemed quiet. But as Newbold discerned its details, a different picture emerged. Young Somali boys crouched between parked cars and trucks along the side of the road beneath his position. Others crept down alleyways across the street, in a bid to sneak behind a building composed of scrap metal and reclaimed wood. No one was shooting yet, but all the youths toted long rifles, carbines, or pistols of various kinds.

Newbold queried Mergenthaler with silent signals: *Who's in command down there?*

His sharpshooter pointed up the road, toward the next intersection. A tall, long-limbed Somali man in khaki battle gear lurked beside a troop truck and perched a new AK-74 on his hip. Newbold was sure it was the same local warlord he had seen accost but fail to halt the semi on the Werdada Berbera. *Let's see if he fares any better against a stationary target.*

Sealander nudged Newbold. "How do we play it? Snipe, trap, or head-on?"

"Let's see how the junior terrorists' club does first."

On the street, the mood intensified. Frantic hand signals from the warlord moved more of the boys into striking position against the junk bunker. At the same time, a woman shrouded in a dark brown niqab scurried out of a building up the block and trotted in fast, nervous steps away from the impending point of attack. Several of the boys froze as she ran past them, and the warlord swung his arms in mad gyrations, to coax her out of harm's way in a hurry.

Everyone below tensed to strike.

Newbold felt his pulse quicken. *Here we go.*

Two soft pops turned his head in time to see the warlord slump against his truck and smear its passenger door with blood as he slid to the sidewalk. The woman in the niqab put another silenced shot into the back of the warlord's head as she walked back toward him. Then she reached under her full-body robe, pulled out a grenade, and lobbed it inside his truck.

As the female assassin sprinted to cover, staccato bursts of submachine gun fire peppered the parked cars below the mercs, cowing the handful of boy soldiers who had just seen their master assassinated. The front of the troop truck exploded, sending glass and metal shrapnel in all directions. A red fireball rolled skyward, chased by a mushroom of ink-black smoke.

By the time the other boys on the street realized what had happened, the smoke had cleared and the woman was nowhere to be seen. The shooting from the garbage palace ceased.

A man's hoarse voice called out from inside the building.

"We have no fight with you!" he shouted in his flat, middle-American accent. "You have no fight with us. The man who kept you as slaves is dead. Walk away now, and this is over."

On the far corner, another adult male Somali raced to the side of the fallen warlord, spent a few moments trying to revive him, then picked up the dead man's rifle. In Arabic, he shouted at the paralyzed brigade of boys. "Don't just stand there! Attack! Take your revenge!"

A teenaged boy swung his carbine toward the warlord's self-appointed successor and shot the man dead in a single burst. The teen's weapon clacked empty. He threw it aside and ran. Up and down the street, the rest of the boys scattered. A few left their weapons behind; most took their guns with them. In less than a minute, the street was once again deserted.

Sealander shot a disgruntled look at Newbold. "So much for letting the dog flush out the game. Do you have a Plan B, or should we just charge?"

"Neither." Newbold, who had kept his attention on the street, tapped Mergenthaler's shoulder to direct his aim at the female assassin, who was crossing the street on her way back toward the scrap-metal shelter where she and her accomplice had hidden the missiles. "We're gonna reduce our opposition by half. Corporal, take her out."

Mergenthaler peered through his targeting scope. "Yes, sir."

Newbold felt pleased with himself until a burst of automatic fire from across the street tore into the edge of the roof in front of him and Mergenthaler. Shards of broken concrete stung his forehead. He covered his face with his hands and scuttled backwards, away from the edge. The rest of his team retreated with him. When the smoke and dust cleared, he and the others all were clustered in the middle of the rooftop, curled up like seahorses.

Hitchens dusted himself off. "I think we've lost the element of surprise."

"We're not done yet." Newbold got up on one knee to recover some semblance of composure. "Mergenthaler, move over to the next rooftop and keep an eye on that building. The rest of us will head for street level and surround the structure until we find a way in."

Andrzejczyk was wary. "Do we have plan for how to breach?"

"Flashbangs only," Newbold said. "No high explosives. We can't risk damaging the missiles. And we'll need to check our fire in there, too."

Sealander cocked an eyebrow. "You want to launch an assault on a target whose interior is unmapped, against an enemy whose assets are unknown, using low-impact tactics."

"Yes, and I want it done in the next hour."

"Oh, we have *an hour*? Well, that's different." The major got up and moved to the back of the roof to climb back to the street. "I thought you wanted to do something *stupid*."

• • •

It's never felt so good to get undressed. Harper pulled the niqab over her head and hurled it away, thankful to be free of its weight, literally and figuratively. Under the full-body garment and its hood that had covered all but her eyes, she had stripped down to an olive tank top to keep cool and maximize her freedom of movement. It had worked, but it also made wearing a shoulder holster uncomfortable. She shrugged off the leather accessory, pulled out the silenced SIG she had borrowed from Bauer, and handed it back to him. "Thanks for the loaner."

"Anytime." He tucked the pistol back into his hip holster.

She pulled her black short-sleeved shirt back on. "I heard you snap off a few rounds when I crossed the street. Orphan squad fail to take the hint?"

"No, we've got a new problem. I think the mercs followed us from Berbera."

"Of course they did. I know I would've if I'd just lost a pair of nukes." Her joking mood faded. "How many, you think?"

"Not sure. About a dozen, maybe. Enough to make trouble."

She peered through a crack in the wall. "Especially since we're stuck in here."

"Exactly." He pointed to the sides of the garage. "I had Sullah block the alley doors."

"Think they'll hold?"

"They're solid. It'd take half a brick of C-4 to punch through. There's no way the mercs would use that much heat this close to the missiles." He pointed to the back of their cluttered redoubt. "What I'm worried about is the back door and the roof hatch."

"I've got a couple meters of detcord and a detonator hidden in the heels of my boots." She noted his surprise. "Standard ASIS field issue. For rainy days, right? Anyway, I could stuff 'em in a can with some nails and steel wool, maybe add a touch of gasoline. Whip up an IED to cook anybody who opens the roof hatch."

"I like it." He stared at the truck, and Harper could almost sense the gears turning in Jack's imagination. "The back door swings in. If we put the rig in neutral, uncouple it from the trailer, and use Sullah's forklift to push it, we can park it against the door. That'll leave the mercs no way in but the street door— and if we move some of this junk around, we can turn the whole front of the garage into a kill box."

It was a capital notion. "Outstanding, mate. Then all we'll need is a deck of cards."

"And a lot more ammo."

•••

Rotor wash blotted out the blue sky and the barren landscape with a dense golden haze of churned-up dust. Burnett and his team were crouched in a loose huddle, their heads bowed and the brims of their caps pulled down to protect their eyes as whips of wind and sand lashed at them. A final gust of compressed air passed between them as the Black Hawk touched down on the runway, less than a dozen yards from their position.

The chopper's side door slid open. Burnett sprinted forward, and his men followed. He stopped at the door and waved his team inside ahead of him. After the last man climbed aboard, he pulled himself up into the passenger cabin, took his seat, and put on the headset to talk to the cockpit. "Hangdog, this is Bugbear. All boots are on board. Let's go!"

"Copy that, Bugbear."

Burnett shut the side door. The droning of the engine pitched upward, and the rotors' tempo accelerated as the Black Hawk rose from the ground. A forward dip of the nose preceded a rapid acceleration. Within moments they leveled out. Through the windows, Somalia's northern desert was a cinnamon-colored blur less than a hundred feet below. Burnett activated his headset's mic. "Hangdog, what's our ETA to Burao?"

"By the book, thirty-five minutes. But we're looking to break some records if that's all right with you, Commander."

"Hooyah, Lieutenant. Blow the doors off this thing."

"Copy that. Hang on to your hats."

He switched off his mic and shouted over the cabin noise to his men. "Reload fast! Sounds like our pilot's bucking for a spot in the Guinness book."

Oteri grabbed a new, fully loaded magazine from the Black Hawk's onboard stash. "How much resistance do we expect on the ground?"

"No idea," Burnett said, "but we're going in hot. If anyone—and I mean *anyone*—gets between us and those missiles, shoot to kill."

01:00 P.M. – 02:00 P.M.

Corrugated steel plates on either side of Jack rang out like church bells as suppressing fire raked the front of Sullah's garage. Several rounds drilled through the scrap-metal sheets. Ricochets pinged off the trailer and other surfaces behind Jack, who watched through a narrow crack in the wall, alert for the first sign of movement from across the street.

A shift in the direction of incoming fire alerted Jack that something new was happening. He pivoted to change his angle of view. One of the mercs was advancing up the sidewalk parallel to the front of the garage, just out of Jack's field of fire. "Movement on the right," he said, just loud enough for Harper to hear him. "Check the left!"

At the other side of the garage's front wall, Harper adjusted her pose to look down the sidewalk in the other direction. "Company! One guy, moving into the alley!"

"So's mine. They're going for the side doors." He braced his HK against his shoulder and leveled the muzzle of its suppressor with a murder hole that faced the street. The half-meter-long ragged tear in the metal wall looked as if it had been gouged by a monster. His ammo was running out, so he set the submachine gun to single-fire mode. Every shot had to count.

Sweat ran down his neck. "They'll try to draw us away from the front. Stay put."

"But the side entrances—"

"They'll hold." He shot a nervous look at the mounds of junk in front of each door. Two old refrigerators, an upturned desk, and several taped-shut boxes of hardcover books blocked the north door. In front of the south door stood a sofa and a chest freezer, both turned up on one end and braced by the parked forklift. *They'd better hold.*

Half-blind and low on ammo, Jack was reminded how often he had taken for granted the tactical support once provided by his friend Chloe O'Brian. *If only I had Chloe on comms right now,* he brooded. *At least then I'd know how many hostiles I'm up against.* But those days were gone. The last Jack had heard, Chloe was a federal prisoner, her exact whereabouts unknown.

Harper steadied her carbine and kept her eyes on the street. She didn't look back at the side doors, not even a glance. Jack respected her discipline.

She tensed. "Here they come!"

Thundering booms shook the building from either side. The alley doors buckled inward. Fire and smoke rushed in around the improvised barricades, but failed to shift them.

At the same time, two mercs in body armor emerged from behind a truck, across the street from the front of the garage. They charged toward the garage's main entrance, aided by more suppressing fire from their comrades still under cover. Sparks flew from bullets caroming off the steel around Jack's murder hole. He winced at the barrage until his training overcame his body's natural reflexes; then he stared through the storm and took careful aim.

His finger closed around the trigger. A muted pop from the HK.

The merc's head snapped back in a spray of reddish mist; then he collapsed in the street.

Cracks from Harper's Austeyr echoed inside the garage as the second attacking merc retreated, chased by bullets every step of the way. Just before he reached cover, she put a shot through the back of his neck and dropped him to the pavement.

Another blast rocked the building, this time from the rear. After the smoke and fire dissipated, Jack saw that the back door was broken into several pieces, but they still hung loosely together. As he'd hoped, the semi's rig hadn't been budged, nor had the coils of razor wire Sullah had helpfully pushed under its front axle, to prevent any clever mercs from crawling in under the rig if the door should fail. "Back door's solid," he called to Harper, who continued to pepper the parked cars across the street with harassing fire. "They'll try the roof hatch next."

"Can you hold the front?"

He snapped a few shots through parked cars and rained broken glass on the far sidewalk. "Yeah, I've got this. Fall back and get ready to plug anybody who comes in from above."

Harper dropped back, away from the front, to take up a sniping position near the parked forklift. She rested her weapon on the crossbar of the forklift's roll cage and made ready to pick off anyone who dared to breach the roof hatch—assuming they survived the IED she'd set there.

Everything went still. No more incoming rounds from across the street. No one testing the strength of the doors' defenses. No signs of movement or sounds of enemy action.

The silence dragged on. Jack checked his watch. Minutes passed.

From across the garage, Harper asked in a stage whisper, "What's going on?"

"I don't know. But I don't like it." He looked up and listened for anything that might suggest the mercs were on the roof. Its loose panels of plastic and corrugated metal would be almost certain to betray anything as heavy as a grown man moving over them. But all was quiet.

"This is bad," Harper said. "If they've abandoned brute force, it means they're thinking."

"Agreed. We need to get eyes on—"

Cacophony and a blinding flood of daylight—a car crashed through the back wall of the garage and slammed to a halt when it hit one of the building's structural support pillars, which had been sunk into its concrete floor. Steam hissed in a great geyser from its broken engine block, and its horn wailed nonstop, like an air raid siren.

Jack put three shots through its windshield, just by reflex, before he realized the car was empty. "Kill that horn! And watch for snipers!"

Harper crouched and jogged to the front of the smashed-up old Ford. She popped up just long enough to fire one shot through a cable to the battery, silencing the jammed horn. Then she ducked back behind the wreck for cover while she looked through the break in the wall.

"I think we might have a gap in our defenses."

Jack admired her knack for understatement. "Cover the back. I've got the front."

"On it!"

Automatic fire ripped through the massive rent in the back wall. Jack and Harper hit the floor as ricochets filled the space and caromed off countless hard surfaces in search of a soft target. He heard her yell in pain and alarm, just before a stray shot slammed into his right shoulder. A blunt sensation of impact bloomed into white-hot pain within seconds, and warm blood coated his arm. He forced himself up to one knee so he could look out for danger coming from the street. "Harper! You okay?"

"As long as no one asks me to dance." She fired a few short bursts out the back of the garage to keep the mercs on their toes. "You?"

"A scratch." It was a lie, but morale demanded he not tell her the fingers in his right hand were starting to go numb, suggesting the bullet had damaged the axillary nerve in his deltoid. He shifted his grip on the HK to fire with his left hand and balance the barrel with his right, and adopted a bladed stance in front of the murder hole, determined to hold his ground.

More shots from behind screamed through the air over his head and pelted the wall above him, just as a fresh assault from across the street peppered the other side of the wall. All Jack's trained reflexes impelled him to dive for the ground, to find shelter, but he forced himself to remain still and keep watch through the rough-hewn cut.

Fast motion behind the parked cars. Through blasted-out windows, Jack saw a merc with a shaved head and a thick mustache pull the pin on a grenade and wind up to hurl it toward the garage. Jack aimed by instinct and fired as the man started his throw. Through the gutted car, his shot struck the merc under his armpit, just above his body armor. The merc stumbled backwards and dropped the grenade. Someone else, outside Jack's field of fire, scrambled past the shot merc and lunged for the live grenade—which detonated, hurling both men's burned and broken bodies through the air in a cloud of high-velocity shrapnel.

The next things thrown over the parked cars were smoke charges. They erupted and spewed thick curtains of green and red mist that mingled into a thick gray wall.

Jack remained in position until the obscuring fog started to clear. There was no sign of activity or assault from the other end of the street. He stayed low as he fell back to Harper's side behind the forklift. "They're regrouping behind us."

"You're sure?"

"They laid down smoke for almost five minutes, but didn't storm the front door."

"Why not?"

"I don't know. Maybe they're out of grenades. But my gut tells me they used smoke to cover a run down the alleys." He searched through the smoky veil outside the bashed-in wall.

"How many do you think are out there?"

"Based on what we've been hit with so far? Eight or nine. Hard to be sure."

Harper's mood brightened. "So, we've got a chance."

He didn't want to make promises he couldn't keep. "I didn't say that. All they need is one lucky shot and we're done." He steadied his HK on the rear engine block of the forklift to hide the fact that he was having trouble holding it steady with his increasingly paralytic right hand.

*Thump*s resounded from just beyond the breach. Dense plumes of green, yellow, and crimson smoke mingled to form an opaque screen between them and the world outside the garage. Fresh sweat trickled down the sides of Harper's face. "They're coming."

"Yup." Jack tensed for the attack he knew would come at any moment. He looked over his shoulder and caught Harper's eye.

"You can still make it out of here."

She sized him up with a stern gaze. "So can you."

"No, I can't. I won't hand these missiles over to terrorists. I'll die first."

A casual shrug. "Then they'll have to kill us *both*, mate."

He steadied his aim on the breach. "Glad I met you, Harper."

She braced her weapon and prepared for the onslaught. "Back atcha, Bauer."

Shoulder to shoulder, they waited for the silence to end and the dying to begin.

• • •

"Lay down some more smoke and wait for my signal." Newbold crouched amid a Stonehenge of empty oil drums as Sealander and Andrzejczyk lobbed another pair of smoke grenades toward the massive break in the garage's back wall. Plumes of violet- and mustard-colored gas erupted from the canisters and mingled into a blinding prismatic fog. Half a dozen Firethorn troopers, all champing at the bit to attack, flanked to either side of the command trio.

Confident he had a few moments to spare before pressing his attack, Newbold pulled out his satellite phone and dialed. Sealander shot an angry look his way. "What're you doing?"

"Calling the client."

"Now?"

Newbold silenced him with a raised hand as he heard the ringtone on the other end of the call. It repeated twice before Malenkov answered. *"What do you want?"*

"We're about to take back the missiles. We can still salvage the mission."

"The mission is over."

The news skewered Newbold. "What do you mean it's over?"

"Your men in Berbera are dead, and the Su-34 has been recalled. Russia is washing its hands of this operation, and of you."

"Mr. Malenkov, I'd urge you to reconsider. We can have—"

"There's an American SEAL team on the ground. If you're smart, you'll walk away."

He resisted the impulse to shout at the phone. "Walk away? With nothing?"

"With your life, *Colonel. Assuming you value it."* His sigh crackled into static over the long-distance call. *"The next time you call this number, it will have been disconnected. Don't contact us again. As of now . . . you're on your own."*

A faint *click* as Malenkov hung up. Newbold switched off the phone and tucked it inside a pocket on the leg of his pants. He swallowed his anger.

So what if the Russians are out? Once we have the warheads, we can sell the plutonium on the black market for a fortune. All we need to do is take them.

He looked at Sealander on his left, and Andrzejczyk on his right. "Gentlemen, the Russians are out. Which means if we can capture this building, those warheads, and all the profits we can squeeze out of them, belong to us. So . . . ready to get rich?"

If any of his men harbored doubts about proceeding with the attack, it was clear from the gleams of avarice in their eyes that they were willing to set them aside. Each man nodded his readiness, and they and the other troopers made a final check of their weapons.

Newbold drew a breath as a prelude to giving the order to attack.

That was when he heard the ominous and unmistakable sound of an inbound Black Hawk helicopter, and realized his time had run out.

• • •

A steep, banking turn by the Black Hawk made Burnett and his SEALs white-knuckle their seats' safety harnesses. Rising columns of multicolored smoke from the target coordinates had made it easy for the chopper's pilots to zero in on the action unfolding in the middle of Burao.

As the UH-60 pushed through the last degrees of the circling maneuver, Burnett got a clear look at the action on the ground. He didn't like what he saw.

On one side of a scrap-metal warehouse, a street was littered with bodies, smashed and burning cars, and wind-tattered curtains of violet and chartreuse gas.

On the other side of the building, nine men—all hefting American-made weapons, none wearing American colors—charged away from a cluster of rusted fifty-five-gallon barrels, toward the jerry-built structure, whose back half had been bashed in and looked ready to collapse.

Burnett keyed his headset mic. "Hangdog, Bugbear. Nine hostiles on the ground. Take us around a few times."

"Roger that, Bugbear."

The pilot pushed the chopper into another hard banking turn. Burnett nodded to Yant, who manned the cradle-mounted M134 minigun on the Black Hawk's left side. "Light 'em up!"

The minigun's furious, ripping buzz drowned out the rotor noise. Its high-velocity storm of lead dominated the battlefield, strafing the armed men on the ground and shredding them one by one, while its crimson tracers blazed like pure hellfire.

Reddish sprays of aerosolized blood and liquefied viscera painted the dusty ground, and old metal barrels erupted into flurries of metal shards, launched by the minigun's barrage.

Half a minute after the battle had begun, it was over. The minigun went quiet.

Below the chopper, nothing moved except trails of smoke twisting in the wind.

Burnett cupped his hand over his headset mic. "Hangdog, put us down."

"Copy that. Going in."

The Black Hawk swung back to an open patch of ground, beyond the wreckage of the empty oil drums Yant had obliterated with the minigun. As soon as its struts touched soil, Burnett and his men leaped out the side doors and charged toward the building.

With gestures, he directed Oteri and Pearson to the right. He led Yant and Colberg left. When they all had gathered on either side of the breach in the back wall of the sheet-metal bunker, Burnett leaned close to the edge of the opening and shouted inside.

"Attention! Inside the building! Identify yourself!"

A woman hollered back in a hoarse voice with an Australian accent. "Agent Abigail Harper, Australian Special Intelligence Service. Who are you?"

"Ma'am, I'm Lieutenant Commander Robert Burnett, United States Navy. Is the inside of the building secure?"

"Affirmative. All clear."

"We're coming in. Hold your fire."

"I will if you will."

Burnett ushered his men inside. They slipped around the corners and deployed around the building's interior perimeter, moving in pairs, always in covering poses. As one man checked corners, the other watched their flanks and guarded their rear. While his men secured the area, Burnett lowered his weapon and walked toward the sound of the woman's voice. "Ma'am, we were led to understand you've captured a pair of American-made nuclear weapons. Is that true?"

"That's right. I'm gonna stand up, behind the forklift. Hold your fire."

The first motion Burnett saw was the woman's empty hands. Then she stood, her movement slow and cautious. She was of African ancestry, in her late twenties or early thirties—it was hard for Burnett to tell her age through the tarnish of blood and dust that coated her face. Her hair was cropped short, and sweat made her fatigues cling to her athletic body. An Austeyr carbine hung from a strap across her chest. She pointed at the trailer of a semi whose rig had been used to obstruct the building's back entrance. "The missiles are in there."

"Copy that." He looked for his men and found them at the front of the building. All four gave him the all-clear. Burnett turned back toward Harper. "Ma'am, were you operating alone?"

A simple nod. "All by my lonesome. And *damn* am I glad to see you blokes."

He pondered the scope of the destruction he had seen on the street outside, and the odds against which she must have stood, then favored her with a smile. "Glad you're on our side." He turned back toward his men. "Colberg, secure the warheads for transport. Oteri, rig the missiles and everything else in that trailer for demolition. Yant, make sure the buildings around this one are empty before we light the fuse. Pearson, get over here. Agent Harper's been hurt."

"It's just a flesh wound."

"All the same, we owe you. Lieutenant Pearson's our corpsman. He'll fix you up."

A grateful, bashful smile. "Thanks, mate."

His men split up, each making haste to his assigned task. Burnett returned to the ragged gap in the rear wall and thumbed his radio's talk switch. "Hangdog, Bugbear. Stand by for hot evac and ask CENTCOM for a fighter escort. We're bringing home some arrowheads."

• • •

Harper winced as the SEAL corpsman tightened the gauze wrap he had put on her wounded left thigh. "Easy, mate. That a bandage or a tourniquet?"

"Tight is good," Pearson said. "You were lucky—the bullet passed through without hitting bone or an artery. You'll limp for a while, but you'll live."

"Small miracles. We done here?" Off his nod she stood and started to gather her things. "Tell your brother SEALs I need to defuse the IED I set by the roof hatch."

Pearson tried to stop her. "You really shouldn't be climbing on that leg."

"I'm fine. Just make sure your boys don't shoot me while I'm up there." She stuffed the last of her personal gear into her backpack and put it on. With her Austeyr slung by her side, she limped to one of the two ladders that led to the catwalk, which lay beneath the hatch. Just as the corpsman had warned her, the effort of climbing the ladder sent jolts from her thigh up through her hip and back. All she could do was grit her teeth and push through the pain.

The climb was slow and difficult, but she reached the top with her bandage and her pride both intact. She favored her good leg as she shuffled across the catwalk, and put her weight on it while she worked to unravel the deadly IED with which she had booby-trapped the hatch. In less than a minute, she had removed the detonator, rendering the bundle inert. She set it on the catwalk at her feet; then she opened the hatch and climbed the short ladder to the roof.

After having spent more than an hour in the shadowy interior of Sullah's garage-turned-fortress, Harper had to shield her eyes from the harsh afternoon light. She gave her vision time to adjust as she pivoted, a few degrees at a time, while scanning the surrounding roads.

In front of Sullah's place, Yant was on his way back, having finished his task of clearing the surrounding buildings. The alleys and most of the side streets were deserted and quiet, though a fair amount of activity was evident in distant, more prosperous quarters of the city.

There was much to see in every direction, but there was only one thing—one person—that Harper was looking for. And then she found him.

A man hunched under a Bedouin-style desert cloak emerged from a residential building and made his way up the street, a few blocks from Sullah's garage. When he turned his head to look up and back in Harper's direction, she knew his face at a glance. It was Jack.

He had made his retreat from the garage as soon as they heard the telltale rip of the Black Hawk's minigun. With the rear still obscured by smoke, and the street outside clear of hostiles, Jack had fallen back and exited through the front door. He hadn't asked Harper to lie for him to the SEALs. She suspected he'd known he didn't need to.

She waved to him once, a gesture of farewell.

He smiled and nodded, content to vanish without fanfare.

A beige Hummer H2 raced around the corner and mounted the curb in front of Jack. Its rear door swung open and slammed into him before he could dodge out of the way.

Jack collapsed onto the sidewalk as the H2 swerved and blocked Harper's view of the fray. Moments later, she saw Jack—he was up and running—and then he was tackled from behind. Three men, Caucasians with military-style crew cuts and sinewy builds, set upon him with fists and Tasers. Harper reached for her carbine, tried to bring it to firing position—

A black hood was pulled over Jack's head, and then he was dragged inside the truck, which sped away, turned another corner in a dusty cloud, and disappeared.

Just like that, Jack was gone.

There was no time to think, barely time to act. Harper's feet moved before her brain did. Seconds mattered now. She was back down the hatch, onto the catwalk.

No time for ladders. She ducked under the catwalk's railing and swung down onto the top of the trailer, wherein one of the SEALs was disarming the live missile. He looked up at her as she tumbled around the back edge of the open trailer and swung her legs to land inside. Before he could raise his voice in protest, she had hopped out to stumble-run across the garage, sparing her wounded leg as best she could. She grabbed her pack and hobbled toward the door.

Pearson called after her. "Hey! Where are you going?"

"Got a date!" She darted out the front door without waiting for a reply.

All the cars parked on Sullah's block had been destroyed. Windows and windshields shattered, tires shredded. Half of them were still on fire.

Every hurried step sent stabs of pain through Harper's thigh. She needed a car, *any* car, in running order. To find one, she had to get out of the battle's collateral-damage radius. It took her more than a minute to limp-jog two blocks to a row of undamaged vehicles. She ignored the closest one—it was a Chevette blanketed in dust, a sign that it hadn't been moved in a long time, perhaps because it had no fuel. She passed by a

Yugo with a flat rear tire. She stopped next to a white Citroën Xantia. It had to be at least fifteen years old, but it looked intact—and there were signs of fresh handprints around its fuel tank cover. *Bingo.*

Its door was unlocked. *We'll call that a sign.* She tossed her carbine and her backpack onto the passenger seat and climbed inside the car. Checks of the sun visors yielded no left-behind keys, so Harper unzipped her pack and pulled out her wire cutters. Then she reached under the steering column and yanked free the electrical bundle for the ignition. Using skills she'd learned during her ASIS training, she hot-wired the car in a matter of seconds.

The Citroën's engine purred to life. Harper made a cursory check of the dash readouts. As she'd hoped, a full tank of gas. *So far, so good.*

She put away the wire cutters and dug in her pack until she found the portable charging kit for her satellite phone. She plugged in the car-lighter attachment, then hooked the other end into the phone. It acknowledged the replenishing flow of electricity with an electronic chirp. She keyed in the speed dial for ASIS, activated the speaker, then set the phone on the passenger seat.

As the connection rang, she shifted the car into drive, hit the gas, and pulled away from the curb at breakneck speed. Its robust acceleration surprised her; she realized it must be a late-model Xantia with a three-liter V6 engine. She was racing down a straightaway when the command center answered. *"Taz Dee Business Solutions. How can I direct your call?"*

"Birdcage Zero-One, this is Redwing. Color of the day is yellow. Word of the day is 'wayfarer.' I need a secure line to Tiger Eye."

"Stand by to go secure, Redwing."

Three *click*s over the channel preceded the transfer of her call to her HQ-based tactical coordinator, her friend Jiro Chu. She heard the worry in his voice when he answered. *"Redwing, this is Tiger Eye. Are you all right?"*

"Affirmative. But I need your help, and I need to keep it off-book."

He clearly sensed she was up to no good. *"Harper? What're you doing?"*

She swung the hatchback through a hard right turn and swerved through a slalom course of confused pedestrians until they belatedly wised up and scattered. "I'm tracking a Hummer H2 on its way out of Burao. Tell me we still have a satellite on task for this sector."

"Hang on. Checking." She heard the patter of fingers on a computer's keyboard. *"Yeah, we're tapped into a milsat feed. I'll point it your way."*

The Citroën growled as Harper downshifted for power around a tight turn that put her on one of the main roads. There was light traffic ahead of her, forcing her to swing back and forth, in and out of the oncoming lane, as she struggled to pick up any sign of the fleeing Hummer.

Chu's voice pitched upward with excitement. *"Got something! Looks big enough to be your Hummer. Heading west, toward the Guleej Haji highway."*

"The Guleej? They must be headed to Hargeisa."

Harper made a hard left only to find her route obstructed by a herd of goats following their shepherd down the middle of the road. She detoured onto the sidewalk, honked her horn nonstop for thirty meters, and resisted the urge to plow through the bewildered pedestrians. As soon as she was clear of the goats and found a break in the line of parked minivans, she swung back into traffic. Behind her, a screeching of brakes, crunches of metal, and a torrent of Somali profanity confirmed her maneuver had not gone unnoticed.

Ahead of her, the road forked. She steered right, toward the highway. She wondered aloud, "Why are they going to Hargeisa?"

"If I knew who they were or why you were following them, I might be able to guess."

His plea reminded her how little she herself knew about what was happening. She was reluctant to tell Chu about Bauer. He would be duty-bound to report such an encounter, and after all she and Bauer had been through that day, she was loath to hand him over to anyone. On the other hand, if his abductors proved to be his own countrymen, there would be little she could do. She needed to play this smartly. One mistake could end her career—or Bauer's life.

"I don't know who's driving the Hummer," she told Chu. "But they grabbed one of my assets, someone important. I want him back alive." On the feeder road to the highway, she slowed down. Far ahead, beyond some twists in the uneven, unpaved so-called highway, she saw a white cloud rising into the sky. "I've got eyes on the Hummer. I'm gonna hang back so they don't spot me. But I need you to keep the satellite locked onto them."

"Already on it. I'm flagging it as 'suspected movement of terrorist supplies.'"

"Good man." She glanced at her phone's screen to check the distance between her and the H2: just under five kilometers. That felt right. Her eyes back on the road, she had an idea. "Jiro, can you run a signal intercept on the Hummer?"

"I might be able to push through a satellite intercept. Assuming none of the corner-office muckety-mucks start asking around."

"Get on it. We need to know who we're dealing with—before it's too late."

• • •

A limousine idled outside the Klub Rybakov. Arkady Malenkov looked down from his suite's window and noted the car's presence while he listened to his executive assistant, Mira, confirm his instructions over the cell phone he held to his ear.

"All files related to Project Gilgamesh have been deleted from the corporate servers," Mira said. *"Your interns are shredding the last of the hard copies now."*

"Thank you, Mira. Did you remember to check the archive backups?"

"Yes, sir. I had our friend in IT pull them up. All the encrypted backups have been erased, and I've been assured there were no offline copies, as per your instructions."

"Well done. Any word from Mr. Nikunin's and Mr. Puleshko's offices?"

"I've coordinated with their assistants at every step, sir. All data has been expunged."

"You have our gratitude, Mira. As soon as you're done, book a car to pick us up at Pulkovo this evening. We're heading back on the company jet as soon as we reach Narimanovo."

"The car's on standby, sir. I'll confirm your arrival time with operations."

"Thank you, Mira. You're a godsend. I'll see you when we get back."

"Safe travels, sir."

Mira hung up. Malenkov tucked his phone into his coat pocket. He turned away from the window. His rolling suitcase was packed, and his locked briefcase stood beside it. It had been a long time since he had needed to pack his own bags. Under normal conditions, he would have brought Mira with him to see to the mundane details of his travel, but the clandestine nature of his project with Nikunin and Puleshko had made her presence impractical.

It's for the best, he decided. If she had seen Zalesky or Markoff, she might have been eliminated as an unnecessary "loose end." He nodded at his rationalization. *It's better this way.*

He picked up his briefcase in his left hand and towed his suitcase with his right. The walk to the stairs from his suite was short, but the effort of lifting and toting his luggage down the steps by himself underscored for him just how old and out of shape he had allowed himself to become. *The years are catching up to me.*

At the bottom of the main staircase, his business partners stood waiting for him, their own luggage at their sides. Neither man spoke, but Nikunin, stylish bastard that he was, interrogated Malenkov with a subtle arching of his left eyebrow. They had known each other long enough that Malenkov understood his old friend's unspoken query.

"Yes, you can speak. What is it?"

"Are we in the clear?"

What else could he say? "Yes, I think so. All the files have been destroyed."

Puleshko remained as nervous as ever. "You're sure?"

"Mira says she saw to it personally. I trust her. It's done."

The overweight, balding Puleshko and the svelte, dapper Nikunin both breathed soft sighs of relief. Nikunin looked almost humbled by the experience.

"I guess we should be grateful, eh, Arkady?"

"That's one way of looking at it." He pulled his bags toward the door. "Let's go home."

The three of them left the Klub Rybakov, each man portering his own burden down the long front staircase to the limousine in the parking loop. Their freakishly tall chauffeur, Antek, helped them load their bags into the spacious trunk. "Destination, sirs?"

"Narimanovo Airport," Malenkov said. "The private entrance."

"Right away, sir."

Attentive and deferential, the chauffeur opened the rear doors for the three executives. They climbed inside the limo. Malenkov was the last one inside, and the door was eased shut behind him. Inside the stretch limousine's cavernous rear compartment, the complimentary bar had been stocked with a generous quantity of ice, premium vodka, and carved-crystal glasses.

Nikunin picked up a bottle of Stolichnaya. "I could use a drink. Anyone else?"

Puleshko and Malenkov nodded in agreement. Up front, the chauffeur got in and pulled away from the Klub Rybakov. As they rode away from the resort, Nikunin filled three glasses with chunks of ice and deep pours of vodka. He handed one each to his partners, then lifted his glass. "To future ventures, and future fortunes!"

Puleshko clinked his glass against Nikunin's. "To big women and bigger bank balances."

Malenkov ignored the toasts and drank, hoping to numb the sting of the day's failures.

Half a second later, his world turned white, and he felt nothing at all.

• • •

Mandy watched the fireball roll up from the broken chassis of the limousine. Some of her peers might have regretted the "collateral damage" of killing the chauffeur along with the three targets, but she had never harbored such sentimental notions regarding her work. Murder was her business. She saw no point to setting arbitrary limits on who did or did not deserve to die.

The diminutive brunette assassin sat in the woods and watched the limousine's twisted wreckage burn for five minutes. After that, she was confident no one would be crawling out of that conflagration. It was ironic—the dead executives inside the blaze had been part of the plot that had set her on a collision course with CTU many years earlier. To erase these men now felt like justice long overdue. She picked up her satellite phone and dialed the secure line that had been reserved for her one-time use. It rang only twice before her latest client picked up.

"Yes?"

"It's done. All loose threads clipped." She let that sink in before she added, "My money."

"Transferring now."

She lifted her personal smartphone and checked her numbered Cayman Islands account. In real time, its balance ticked upward by half a million dollars, the sum of what she was due.

"Pleasure doing business with you, Director Zalesky."

She hung up, dropped the phone, and put a bullet through it with her Glock G22.

Her work was done, and the shadows beckoned.

It was time to go home.

• • •

The Black Hawk's rotors drummed the air above Burnett as he counted heads. Pearson, Oteri, and Yant regrouped and piled inside the chopper. Colberg was behind him inside the Black Hawk, securing the second of two radiation-resistant cases in which he had stowed the physics packages recovered from the missiles inside the warehouse.

"Pack 'em in, gents! Time to go!" Burnett looked over his

shoulder at Colberg, who adjusted the straps on the warheads' containers. "Those ready to fly, Chief?"

"Hooyah, Commander."

"Just what I like to hear." The rest of the team filed past him on the way to their assigned seats. Burnett cupped his hand over the headset mic. "Hangdog, Bugbear. Boots aboard."

"Roger that, Bugbear. Stand by for dust-off."

Burnett and the others secured their safety harnesses as the tempo of the rotors picked up. Within half a minute, the chopper wobbled into the air, then soared on a shallow arc as it turned on a northwesterly heading, toward Camp Lemonnier at Djibouti International Airport.

"Oteri! Trigger the charges on my mark!"

"Ready!"

On the ground, huddles of earthen-colored buildings bled together as the chopper circled the rainbow-hued collage of corrugated steel and painted wood that had been cobbled into a garage. Burnett waited until the chopper was clear of the detonation radius, and he scouted the streets one last time to make sure no innocents had wandered into the blast zone. "Mark!"

Oteri flipped the switch on his radio detonator.

A white-hot flash consumed the junk bunker.

Wooden beams and ragged scraps of metal flew into the air, lifted on columns of orange fire and coal-black smoke. The blast caved in the walls of the brick buildings on either side of the former garage. On the street, the battered wrecks of cars tumbled away from the massive explosion. The last traces of the old structure collapsed into the smoldering crater, and then a mushroom cloud of smoke and dust ascended from the pit, hiding it from view.

The last glimpse Burnett got of the site through his binoculars showed no trace of the missiles, the truck, or anything else left intact. As far as he could tell, the entire site had been expertly vaporized with a minimum of extraneous damage.

A nod at Oteri. "We're good." He curled his hand around his headset mic. "Hangdog, target site is secure. Do we have an escort yet?"

"Roger that, Bugbear. Dogpatch has a pair of screaming eagles

ready to lead us home. They are inbound and supersonic. Give the word and we'll head to the rendezvous."

"The word is given. Take us home."

"Hooyah, Commander. Sit back and enjoy the ride."

Burnett relaxed as he felt a steady vibrato of acceleration animate the chopper's frame. Oteri and Yant pulled the side doors closed, reducing the wind noise in the passenger cabin. As the Black Hawk gained altitude and speed, everyone breathed a little easier, despite the presence of several kilograms of weapons-grade plutonium on the deck at their feet.

In the back of his mind, Burnett was bothered by the mystery of how the AGM-129s had found their way to Somalia. Worse, how had they been acquired by a team of mercenaries?

He pushed those questions aside. Those weren't his concerns. It would be up to intelligence analysts to sort out those details. All that mattered to Burnett was that the job was done, and he was bringing all his men home alive. That made today a good day.

In his line of work, that was all that really mattered.

• • •

The Guleej Haji's twists and curves cut a serpentine path through the desert. Harper was grateful for the Citroën's solid handling and reliable V6 engine. It hugged the turns even at the dangerous speeds she was forced to sustain in order not to fall farther behind the Hummer, which was traversing the rough road far more quickly than she would have thought possible.

A shrill ring from her phone cut through the rumbling of road noise and the growling of the engine. She tapped the touch screen to accept the incoming call. "Go for Harper!"

"Harper, it's Chu. We've picked up chatter from the Hummer."

"And?" She struggled to keep the car moving straight as it struck a deep gouge in the dirt road. "Talk to me, Jiro! What've we got?"

"No idea what they were yakkin' about, but we snagged enough of the signal to know they're using a Russian military cipher. Is that any help?"

"A bit, yeah." She recalled what Jack had told her about his run-ins with the Russians at their consulate in New York City, and how badly they wanted to make him pay for his actions. But she saw no reason to share any of that intel with ASIS—bringing them into the loop would only obligate them to inform the Americans, worsening Jack's predicament. "Let's assume these guys are Russian special ops. Why are they going to Hargeisa?"

Chu's frenzied typing came through as crisp clacks on the open line. *"According to SIGINT, a Learjet with Russian diplomatic credentials landed at Hargeisa International a few hours ago. It came in from Yemen, and its pilot just filed a flight plan for Moscow via Tbilisi."*

Harper dredged a random fact from her memory. "Of course! The Burao airport's closed! But why didn't they land in Berbera?"

"You mean aside from every intelligence service on the planet getting a heads-up that the SEALs just killed half a dozen Firethorn mercenaries on its runway?"

Though he couldn't see her, she nodded once. "Ah, well. That would do it." She swerved around a dead animal in the road, fishtailed through the gravel on the shoulder, then recovered control on the far side of an S-curve. "So, we know we're dealing with Russians, and they plan on leaving from Hargeisa. I need another favor, Jiro."

"We're already sending up red flags at HQ," Chu said. *"What else do you need?"*

"Keep that jet on the ground in Hargeisa. Break it, steal it, suck the gas out of the tank. Whatever it takes, Chu. Find an asset in Hargeisa, and ground that damn plane!"

More than ever, he sounded tired. *"You know what you're asking, don't you? This is a major breach of protocol. If we get caught, we could both end up on Black Stump patrol in the Outback for the rest of our lives."*

"I wouldn't ask if it wasn't important."

Tired became exhausted. *"I'll see what I can do."*

"You're a prince, Jiro. Ping me when it's done." She tapped the phone's touch screen and ended the call so she could focus on driving.

Harper had no idea if Chu would be able to find someone willing and able to sabotage their jet. Even if he did, and the Russians' departure was delayed, she had no plan for how to liberate Jack from their custody. All she could do was keep her car on the road, not lose track of the Hummer, and hope, by whatever miracle heaven might be willing to grant, that Jack would still be alive when she finally got to him.

Hang on, mate. You came back for me. I'm gonna be there for you.

03:00 P.M. - 04:00 P.M.

A wash of noise droned inside Jack's head. It felt as if he were trapped at the bottom of a murky sea, weighted down with chains of iron, barely able to tell which way was up. Harsh sounds broke through the sonic fog—voices speaking isolated words, all in Russian.

He tried to focus on the voices and the words. Only a few came clear.

Jet. Moscow. Tonight. Then he heard his name: *Bauer.*

Fragments of consciousness returned, each building upon the last. His thoughts reached backwards, in search of his last clear memory. Images of fire and smoke. Bursts of light and pools of shadow. Harsh African sunlight beating down on dusty streets.

He remembered escaping the garage in Burao. Nodding to Harper.

A stunning impact: a car door hit his chest. He'd landed hard on his back, out of breath. Three men set upon him, human attack dogs. Feet and fists, a steady rain of cruel blows, a brutal dance of motion and collision. He'd rolled free, tried to run. Someone tackled him.

Then had come a white jolt of electric pain—a Taser on the back of his neck.

Everything had gone black before he lost consciousness. He felt his labored breaths hot against his own face and realized he had been hooded.

One more jolt had pushed him over the edge, into the embrace of darkness.

Waves of nausea swirled in his gut. He felt light in his head but leaden from the neck down. It was a Herculean labor to force his eyelids open. They obeyed with fluttering reluctance.

It was hard to focus. Everything around him resembled muddy smears of color, splotches of light and darkness. He feared he was about to vomit. He forced himself to remain still and silent. The last thing he wanted was to draw his captors' attention.

Intestinal distress brought him a small measure of clarity. His hood had been removed. He trained his half-open eyes on the dashboard clock. Through his double vision, he saw that it read 3:07. He had been unconscious for over an hour.

Jack drank in the details around him—the style of the truck's interior, the features on its dash, the logo embossed on the top of its gearshift—and deduced he was in a Hummer H2. He saw that his wrists were cuffed in front of him, at his waist. A subtle shift of his left foot confirmed that he also had been bound at his ankles. Even if by some miracle he escaped the vehicle, he was in no position to make a run to safety.

Bumps and yaws to either side told him they were moving over rough road at considerable speed. It took effort to gauge the sun's position through the tinted windows, but after a few minutes he was certain they were heading west. The nearest major city in that direction was Hargeisa, at the other end of the Guleej Haji highway. He tried to steal a look out the windows at the landscape, but all he saw was a psychedelic blur.

His efforts were noted by the blond man seated to his left. "Look who's finally awake!" The man's Russian accent led Jack to suspect he was from the Volgograd region.

He tried to respond, but his mouth couldn't form words. The Russians snickered at him. The one in charge smirked. "Feeling out of focus? That's right—*you've been drugged*. If we dosed you correctly, you should be just strong enough to walk when we move you to the plane, but not strong enough to put up a fight. And you *do* like to fight, don't you?"

Before Jack could slur out a reply, the boss Russian punched him in the solar plexus.

Jack doubled over. Unable to breathe, he forced himself to relax his diaphragm.

The man on Jack's right grabbed the back of his shirt collar and pulled him to an upright position—then held him steady while the man in the passenger seat twisted around to jab Jack in the face. Jack's nose broke with a wet crack. Fresh, warm blood sheeted over his upper lip and chin. The four Russians laughed at him.

More punches slammed into Jack's ribs, hard enough to bruise but with not enough force to break—an outcome he suspected was more a product of sadistic calculation than a result of blind fortune. The beating went on for several minutes, during which all Jack could do was tune out and retreat into the fortress of his own mind. He knew they wouldn't kill him. If that was what they had come for, they'd have done so in the street and made a clean escape. No, this was them having fun at his expense. When it was over, they would make sure he was still breathing.

He vowed that leaving him alive was the last mistake any of them would ever make.

When the assault ended, Jack spied the dashboard clock. It was 3:20.

Every part of him hurt now. The Russians had pummeled his head and torso, and the men seated beside him had kicked his shins and stomped on his feet. Jack gasped for breath and concentrated on muting his awareness of his injuries. They weren't life threatening. His bleeding was superficial. He would suffer, but he would live. That made this pain irrelevant. He focused on drawing in breath and pushing it back out, until he had mastered his pain.

Now he owned it. He could ignore it, or he could harness it. It served *him* now.

He slowed his breathing. Lifted his head. Shot a murderous look at the man on his left. "You're the one in charge."

A predator's grin from the brute with the blond crew cut. "Major Danko. I'd say it's a pleasure to meet you, Mr. Bauer— but I think we're past polite lies, don't you?"

"I'm going to kill you, Major. With my bare hands, if I have to."

"I'm sure you'll daydream about it—all through your trial."
He noted the deepening of Jack's baleful stare. "Yes, you heard
me correctly. We've been ordered to bring you back to Moscow
so you can stand trial in public for your crimes." A contemptuous
roll of his eyes. "Absurd, I know. But that's politics for you. If it
were up to me, I'd stop this truck, march you into the desert, put
a bullet in your brain, and leave your corpse for the buzzards."

"What's stopping you?"

"My sense of duty as a soldier," Danko said. "Something
you apparently gave up when you went rogue and murdered
our consular officers in New York."

There were plenty of people in the world to whom Jack owed
apologies, but he didn't count the Russians among them. He
hardened his mask of defiance. "They got what they deserved.
My only regret is I didn't finish the job and kill Suvarov."

Danko's eyes narrowed; he took Jack's measure. "Regret, by
definition, comes too late, Mr. Bauer. A lesson you'll soon
learn—when I hand you over to my superiors."

• • •

The distance between the Citroën and the Hummer had shrunk.
According to the tracking data on Harper's phone, she now
lagged the H2 by just under three kilometers. She credited the
car's beast of a V6 for the reduced following distance.

She glanced at the tracker. At this speed, they were less than
an hour from Hargeisa. Worst-case scenarios crowded her
imagination. Just as Jack had feared that they would lose the
missiles if they had been loaded onto an aircraft, Harper knew
she would have no chance of rescuing Jack if the Russians got
him aboard their jet.

Ease off the gas, she reminded herself. She didn't want to get
too close. At just under three klicks, she had the advantage of
being hidden from the Russians' view by the cloud kicked up by
the Hummer, while still being able to see the road through the
partially dissipated and settled dust. It was vital she not get so
close that she lost the ability to see the road in front of her, or fall
so far behind that her car's dust trail became distinct from theirs.

Anxiety and impatience got the best of her. She dialed ASIS again. Gave her call sign, recited the color and word of the day, and asked for a secure line to Chu. Then she waited.

Ninety seconds later, he answered, sounding flustered. *"Harper? You okay?"*

"So far. Any progress on your end?"

She could almost hear him shrug. *"Kind of."*

"Crikey, Chu! What's going on in Hargeisa? Have we stalled that plane yet?"

"Not quite. We hit a few roadblocks."

"Such as?"

"Finding an asset who can get to the plane, for one."

Appalled, she let her jaw drop open. "You're telling me we don't even have an asset on-site yet? Why the hell not?"

"Airport security's tighter than ever these days. You know that."

"In *civilized* countries. This is *Somalia* we're talking about!"

"Technically, it's Somaliland, which considers itself politically separate from—"

"Not the point, Chu! They can call it whatever they want— their security still leaks like a sieve." She reined in her temper. "This doesn't have to be brain surgery, Jiro. I don't care if it's subtle. Have a sniper shoot out their tires, if that's what it takes."

"You want to stall them or send them into lockdown?"

"Yes or no, Chu: Can we ground the plane or not?"

"We'll try."

That wasn't a valid answer, but Harper was tired of the argument. She moved to the next item on her agenda. "Let's say that's a yes."

"I didn't say that."

"I know. I'm being optimistic."

"That's a change."

"Be quiet. Assuming we find a way to keep them from leaving with my asset, I'll need some gear and supplies once I reach Hargeisa. You ready to write this down?"

"I'm recording the call."

"I need ten magazines, fully loaded, for my F88. Three kilos of C-4 with a hundred yards of detcord, nine detonators, and a multichannel remote trigger. A pack of smoke grenades, and half a dozen tear gas canisters. I need a nine-millimeter sidearm with a suppressor. And throw in a suppressor for the F88. And a pair of gas masks. And body armor."

"Is that all? You sure you don't want an Aston Martin with twin rocket launchers? Or maybe a helicopter that turns into a submarine? Or a wristwatch with a laser in it?"

"Chu, I can put a bullet between a man's eyes at eighteen hundred meters, and I've been having a very bad day. You sure you want to mock me right now?"

"Harper, do you hear yourself? You sound like you're going to war. Is one Somali asset worth all that?"

"I never said he was Somali."

"What is he, then?"

"Important enough to save. Can you get me the gear I need?"

He sounded doubtful. *"If you really want explosives, I'll have to run it through channels. And I wasn't kidding when I said we've been red-flagged by HQ. People are asking questions. I wouldn't count on the brass approving your requisition."*

"Then don't ask. We must have a safe house or a weapons cache somewhere in Hargeisa. Find one and get back to me." Noting that the distance to the Russians was growing again, she sped up slightly to stay in their dust shadow. "And, Chu?"

"Yeah?"

"Keep that plane on the ground."

A put-upon sigh. *"I'll see what I can do."*

• • •

Eerie, hallowed stillness lay over the tomb-covered hills in the center of Saburtalo Cemetery. Situated a few kilometers west of downtown Tbilisi, its wooded environs were all but deserted except for the dead. A handful of paved roads snaked between steep slopes, which were packed with multiple tiers of mausoleums, drab and utilitarian concrete blocks that reminded Karl Rask of all the worst aspects of Soviet-era civil architecture.

He sat on a plain bench of carved, rough stone and squinted until a cloud passed in front of the afternoon sun. As if chasing the shade, the man he had come to meet arrived from behind him and sat down on his left. "Prompt, as ever, Mr. Rask."

Rask spoke to al-Qaeda's envoy without looking at him. "Mr. El-Jamal."

Uneasy silence followed. A cool breeze wafted over them, chilling Rask's bare hands. He considered tucking them inside his jacket pockets to keep them warm; then he thought better of it. Neither he nor el-Jamal had acknowledged aloud what both knew to be true: They were each squarely in the sights of the other's unseen sniper. One mistake, or one poorly chosen word, might be enough to end both their lives in the span of a breath.

Rask cleared his throat. "I'm not in the habit of giving refunds. But these are special circumstances. I've never lost an entire shipment before. Especially not one so valuable." He shifted his gaze to the bench, where a disposable phone he had brought lay between them. As soon as el-Jamal looked at the phone, Rask said, "Pick it up."

"Why?"

"It's a burner phone. Untraceable. When you switch it on, it'll launch a banking app that's been preset to transfer your refund. I'll wait while you do it."

"You could have sent the money back to me without this meeting."

"True. But it's not safe for us to talk on the phone, and there are things I want to say."

El-Jamal activated the burner phone. "Such as?"

"First, I apologize. My operation's never had a setback like this before. I regret that your time was wasted, and that you endured unnecessary exposure as a result."

"Anything else?" El-Jamal initiated the refund transfer.

"Just my assurance that nothing like this will ever happen again." As he'd expected, el-Jamal met his promise with a skeptical expression. Rask held up one hand. "You have my word, Mr. El-Jamal. Steps have been taken. And I hope you and your organization will see this refund as a gesture of good faith, so that we can continue to do business in the future."

The phone beeped as the transfer finished. "We see this as compensation. Nothing more." His phone emitted a soft chiming tone. He checked it and nodded. "The transfer is complete." He dropped the burner phone on the ground and crushed it under his heel. "As for our future, Mr. Rask . . . it remains to be seen if you have any place in it. If my employers should deign to work with you again, I will be in touch." He stood and smoothed the front of his trousers. "Good day."

In accordance with the terms agreed upon before the meeting, Rask remained seated while el-Jamal departed. He stood only when he heard the voice of his sniper through his earpiece tell him, *"They're gone. You're all clear."*

He rubbed his palms together to warm them as he followed the footpath down the hill to his town car. Standing outside it were his bodyguard, Olaf, and his driver, Georg. As always, Georg was dressed like an undertaker, while Olaf sported the attire of a gravedigger.

Olaf opened the rear passenger-side door for Rask as he drew near, then shut the door behind him after he was inside. Georg climbed into the driver's seat while Olaf circled around the back of the car to get in behind him. Once they were settled, Georg started the car, then looked up to regard Rask by way of the rearview mirror. "Where to, sir?"

"A very good question. I will be returning to my hotel. You, however, will not."

"Sir?"

Olaf clamped his left hand over Georg's mouth, and with his right sank a hunting knife into the driver's chest. Georg struggled, then twitched as his strength failed.

Rask watched without emotion as Georg's life ebbed away. "I know you're the one who tipped off the mercenaries, Georg. I even know why you did it. You love your wife, and fighting cancer costs money. I won't lie and say you could have asked me for the cash. I wouldn't have given it to you. But I wish you'd been smart enough to rob someone else." He got out of the car. From inside came the ugly music of struggle and surrender as Olaf made sure his work was done.

Olaf got out of the car, stripped off his blood-soaked leather gloves, and tossed them into the car beside Georg. With a wave he summoned another town car, whose driver wisely averted his eyes from the carnage in the other vehicle. Rask settled into the backseat of his replacement ride, while Olaf retrieved a bundle of incendiary charges from the first car's trunk. He set the timer on the charge, lobbed it into Georg's lap, then climbed into the new car next to Rask.

"Let's go," Rask told his new chauffeur. "The Radisson Blu Iveria."

"Yes, sir."

They wended their way through the cemetery's serene roads at a modest speed until they passed through the gate. Seconds after they pulled onto the main road that led back to downtown Tbilisi, a distant explosion sent a reddish-orange pillar of cloud into the afternoon sky. It was to the chauffeur's credit, Rask thought, that he never took his eyes off the road. "What's your name, driver?"

"Kristof, sir."

"Do you want to know the secret to a long and happy life, Kristof?"

"Of course, sir."

Rask admired the dissipating fireball in the distance.

"Loyalty, Kristof. It's all about loyalty."

• • •

Still half-sick from the sedatives the Russians had pumped into him, Jack knew he was in no condition to take on four Spetsnaz commandos by himself. But as the pristine façades of Hargeisa streaked past outside the speeding Hummer's windows, he knew he was running out of time to resurrect his ability to fight. The airport was dead ahead, which meant they were only minutes away from hauling him onto a jet intended to take him to his doom.

The man in the front passenger seat dialed a contact on his phone. Though he spoke in hushed Russian, Jack heard enough to translate the commando's side of the conversation: He had just instructed the jet's pilot to begin the preflight check and prepare for liftoff.

Not good.

Jack's nose throbbed with pain, and the blood on the front

of his face had dried into a brittle crust. It was hard for him to breathe through his nose, but respiring through his mouth had left it parched. All his ribs ached, and when he tried to clench his right hand, he found he had no sensation in his fingers, a lingering consequence of the untreated damage to his axillary nerve during the showdown with the mercs back in Burao.

Despite all that, he was sure he could wreak enough havoc to break free if only he could slip his hands out of the too-tight steel cuffs, or get his feet out of their short-chained shackles.

I just need one thing to go right. Just one.

He knew the Spetsnaz weren't likely to give him that chance. They were special ops professionals, trained just as well as he had been, and they had the additional advantages of being younger, stronger, and armed. *Plus, they outnumber me four to one.*

His sole advantage lay in the fact that he knew something they didn't.

Crammed into the center of the backseat, he had an unobstructed angle on the rearview mirror. More than an hour earlier, he had noticed the faintest shimmer of sunlight off the windshield of a car some distance behind them. He had been prepared to write it off as a coincidence—but half an hour later, he had spotted it again. Though it was irrational to pin his hopes on such a small shred of evidence, he wanted to believe Harper was following them.

To make sure the driver didn't make the same observation he had, Jack had done whatever had been necessary to fix his posture and sit tall. Even when he had wanted nothing more than to let his head droop and sink into the comfort of unconsciousness, he forced himself to stay awake and to keep his head up. The Russians had read his behavior as dumb pride. All he cared about was that he had blocked the driver's view of the road behind them.

They pulled up to the runway gate of Hargeisa International Airport. The driver's tinted window descended with a hum of electric motors. They were met by a guard with a wrinkled uniform on his back and a peashooter on his hip. Danko handed a bundled stack of ten thousand euros to the driver, who passed it like a relay baton to the guard. The stern-faced Somali thumbed through the brick of currency notes, then smiled and waved the Hummer through. His compatriots inside the guardhouse opened the double gates, and the driver wasted no time speeding out onto the tarmac.

They pulled up beside a Learjet whose immaculate white fuselage shone like a second sun. The only break in its reflective splendor was its open staircase hatch, beside which stood a trim man in his forties, sporting salt-and-pepper hair and a crisp, short-sleeved white pilot's uniform. His eyes were hidden behind amber-hued Ray-Bans, but his crow's-feet peeked out on either side of the aviator-style sunglasses.

Deployment from the Hummer proceeded with military speed and precision. The two men up front got out first and opened the rear doors. Both drew their sidearms and covered Jack while the men on either side of him got out. Danko reached back in and dragged Jack out. Even through his shoes, Jack sensed the heat of the black paved runway under his feet—and then he felt the muzzle of a Russian-made GSh-18 semiautomatic pistol in the small of his back.

Danko pulled Jack toward the jet. "Move."

"I'd move faster if you took the shackles off my legs."

"Shut up. Keep walking." Danko ushered him up the steps of the jet and snapped in Russian at the pilot, "Get us in the air—now."

The pilot followed them up the steps, arguing in Russian with the Spetsnaz commander. "We can't take off yet. We're still waiting on clearance from the tower."

"I don't give a damn about the tower. Once my men are on board, close that hatch and get us airborne. Because if you can't, I'll be happy to leave your body on the runway and have one of my men fly this thing home. Do I make myself clear?"

The lack of a retort from the pilot made it clear that he had.

Barely able to walk in whatever direction he was shoved, Jack stumbled down the center aisle until Danko pushed him into one of the jet's luxurious chairs. Two of the other Spetsnaz entered, each man hauling two large black duffels. They stowed their gear, and then found seats at the aft end of the cabin. The last member of their team pulled up the staircase hatch, folded it over, and secured it closed.

Danko sat beside Jack, grabbed him by the back of the neck, and grinned. "Take your last look at the sun, Bauer. Because once I get you to Moscow, you'll never see daylight again."

04:00 P.M. - 05:00 P.M.

One moment the Learjet resonated with the rising whine of its turbofans' increasing power; the next, their high-frequency shriek became a long, dwindling, downward sonic spiral. Mumbled profanities from the pilot and copilot were echoed by even harsher Russian vulgarities from the Spetsnaz in the back of the plane. Nothing seemed amiss outside the aircraft, which led Jack to wonder what had gone wrong.

Danko unfastened his seat belt and stalked forward to the cockpit. Jack turned his head and closed his eyes to eavesdrop more effectively on the Russians' argument, but his efforts proved unnecessary. The three men made no effort to keep their voices down, which made it easy for Jack to translate their conversation in his head.

"Why aren't we taking off?"

"An error in the fly-by-wire system," the pilot said.

"What kind of error?"

The copilot said, "The flaps and stabilizers aren't responding. We can't fly without them."

Their reports fueled Danko's fury. "Why wasn't this found during preflight?"

The pilot was flummoxed. "Everything was fine during preflight. But as soon as we powered up to taxi to the runway, our attitude controls went haywire."

"How long to fix it?"

"Without knowing the cause? Impossible to say."

"Contact the tower. Get every mechanic they have. I want this fixed *now*." Danko strode back into the passenger cabin and snapped at his men. "Get him up, and grab your gear. We need to get off this plane and go to ground."

Two of the Spetsnaz retrieved their bags from the aft storage lockers, but the third approached Danko and asked at a confidential volume, "Are you sure that's wise, sir? It might be a minor malfunction. They could have it fixed in a few minutes."

"A *minor* malfunction, Soltsin? *Now?* Do you really believe that?"

The second man moderated his tone to strip it of challenging notes. "I agree, sir. The timing is extremely suspect. But moving Bauer puts us at risk in transit."

"Standing still, inside the plane, is even more of a risk. Gear up. We're leaving."

"Yes, sir."

Danko handed his duffel to one of his men; then he unfastened Jack's seat belt and pulled him to his feet. "Enjoy this reprieve from justice, Mr. Bauer. It will be short, I promise."

The Spetsnaz commandos ushered him off the plane with the same caution they had displayed when bringing him aboard. Two of them left the plane ahead of him, and they stood with their sidearms aimed at him while he was marched down the extended hatch ladder to the runway. Though he had been aboard the jet for only a few minutes, he already missed its crisp, cool air-conditioning and shelter from the unforgiving African sun, which dipped now toward the western horizon.

As before, he was forced inside the backseat of the Hummer. Danko and the man he had called Soltsin sat on either side of him. The other two Spetsnaz loaded the team's bags into the back of the vehicle, then got into the front seats. The driver looked back at Danko. "Where to?"

"We have a safe house. Ten Abdihasan Street, just off Wadada Berlin. Plug it into the GPS." Danko cast suspicious looks around the vehicle while his wheel man entered the address into the navigation system. "And stay alert. Someone might be following us."

The driver nodded once, then shifted into gear. He swung through a U-turn and sped back to the security gate, where he paused just long enough to pass the guards another bundle of euros. "We're coming back, and when we do, we'll be in a hurry. Understand?" The sentries acknowledged his instruction with curt salutes, then opened the gates.

Jack regarded Danko with a sour grimace. "No hood this time?"

"Why bother? It doesn't matter anymore what *you* see or hear. After all—you won't live long enough to tell anyone about it."

• • •

Through the unsteady perspective of her binoculars, Harper watched the four crew-cut Russians escort Jack back out of the Learjet. The Hummer was parked beside the jet, on a feeder lane that led to the main runway, several dozen meters inside a four-meter-tall perimeter fence topped with barbed wire. She had spotted the H2 only moments earlier, and until she saw the Russians lead Jack off the plane, she had feared her arrival was too late to help him.

Her phone shrilled at her from the passenger seat. She tapped its screen to accept the call. "Chu, you magnificent bastard. You got someone past security."

"Better. I hacked the jet's remote command systems from here, by way of an unsecured hard line in the airport's control tower. Did it work?"

She continued to observe the Russians as they packed Jack back inside the truck. "Yup. They just took my man off the jet and put him back in the Hummer."

"Great. What are you going to do now?"

"No idea. But keeping him on the ground keeps him in play, and that's half the battle."

"Unfortunately, the other half of the battle is the one that'll get you killed."

She tracked the Russians as they sped toward the security gate, just off the Guleej Haji highway. "How long can you keep them grounded?"

"Hard to say. As long as the tower doesn't shut down its hard line, and the brass at HQ doesn't pull our plug, I should be able to keep them chasing virtual ghosts indefinitely."

Down the road, a pair of airport security officers opened the runway gates for the Hummer, which raced away from the airport. Harper shifted the Citroën into gear and merged back into traffic. "Jiro, tell me you still have eyes on the Russians."

"Heading north on Guleej Haji, into the center of town."

"Tell me where they go. They're probably spooked after the jet malfunction. Can't risk them seeing me on their tail." She turned right and followed the highway. As was typical in many desert cities, almost all the cars in Hargeisa were white and small. Her ivory Citroën was just another mote in that pale automotive tide, but the Russians' hulking beige Hummer was like a rolling hill, calling attention to itself even from three kilometers ahead.

A few minutes down the highway, it veered left. "Jiro, where are they going?"

"Still on the main road. It jogs left, then straightens out into the Waheen Highway."

"Is that a fancy name for another wide dirt road?"

"Yeah, pretty much. It's short, less than half a klick. The big question is what they'll do when they get to the end of it."

"Keep me posted. I'm too far back to see them right now." The traffic was slow and chaotic, metal cholesterol struggling through unpaved veins. Only the fact that it was serving as her camouflage made it tolerable to Harper, who was otherwise tempted to succumb to road rage.

"At the end of Waheen, turn right, onto Road Number One."

"Copy that." She obeyed the instructions, and within less than a minute of steering onto Road Number 1, as its English signage called it, she sighted the Russians far ahead of her. "Visual contact restored. Any signal traffic since they left the plane?"

"Nothing."

Through the shimmer of heat radiation rising off the cars between them, Harper saw the Hummer turn left, off the main road. She accelerated in pursuit. "Where are they?"

"Abdihasan Street." Clacks of typing on a computer's keyboard. *"They've stopped, in a lot between two buildings. I'm*

zooming in for a closer look. Check your phone for the video."

Traffic slowed to a crawl, then stopped just long enough for Harper to look at her phone's screen. The image was pixilated but easy enough to parse: the Russians dragged Jack from the armored truck and pulled him inside the building on the north side of the lot.

"What do we think? Safe house?"

"That's my bet. The Russians aren't known for improvising this sort of thing. In my experience, they prefer to have contingency plans for their contingency plans."

She weaved through traffic all the way to Abdihasan Street, then decelerated as she made the turn. "I'm gonna do a slow drive-by of the house, then find a place to park."

"Watch yourself out there, Harper."

Her first look at the run-down house in which the Russians had taken shelter didn't yield much. It looked like every other poorly made pile of crap in that part of the city. But something about it struck her as odd. Every other shop and residence she passed had its doors and windows wide open to keep from turning into sheet-metal solar ovens. But the shotgun shack the Russians were hiding in was closed up and locked down, like a pressure cooker.

She pulled off the road a short distance down the street. Carrying a carbine past the local pedestrians would be sure to spark a panic; she tucked the weapon onto the floor by the backseat. *This is a recon, not an assault.* She paired her earbud to her phone, which she unplugged from the car's lighter. "Jiro, can you still hear me?"

His reply felt strangely close inside her ear. *"Five by five."*

"I'm gonna take a look around. Stay on the line with me."

"Not going anywhere."

Harper got out of the car. All she took with her was her phone, hidden in her pants pocket, and her binoculars, which were small enough to be unobtrusive in one hand while she walked. "Heading south on Abdihasan."

"I see you. Still no activity around the house."

"What about heat signatures?"

"Hang on. . . . Nope. Must be shielded against infrared."

She examined the strange building as she ambled past it on the other side of the street. From the outside, it looked just like all the other cheap, poured-concrete structures in the area.

Its front door opened. Harper averted her eyes and kept walking. As far as she knew, the Russians hadn't seen her in Burao; there was no reason to think they would recognize her, or even be able to discern her from the numerous other locals drifting past on their way to or from the nearby market. She slipped behind a street cart laden with fruit and peered over the top of its withered produce to get a better look at the Russians' hideout.

One of the Russians jogged to the parked Hummer while one of his comrades guarded the open door. The front door itself was thick and heavy-looking. A metallic stripe down the middle of its edge suggested it had been reinforced against more than bullets—it had been made to withstand a serious explosion. Since it wouldn't make sense to harden the door but leave the rest of the structure vulnerable, Harper assumed the entire place had been made to fend off a siege.

She watched the lone Russian hurry back to the house, toting a pair of black duffels he had recovered from the truck. As soon as he was through the front door, his brother-in-arms slammed it shut.

Harper wandered up the street without looking back at the house. "Jiro, we've got a problem. This place is a fortress."

"*That bad?*"

"Remember when I asked for three kilos of C-4? That won't scratch the paint here." Frustration chipped away at her morale. "There's no way I can fight my way in to get my man. Not without a major upgrade in both firepower and manpower."

All at once, Chu turned cagey. "*What kind of upgrade?*"

"A full strike team, on the double. Maybe some air support for—" She was interrupted by a loud crack from the other end of the secure line. "Jiro! You okay?"

"*I'm fine. That was just me, smacking my palm into my forehead.*" He got angrier as he continued. "*Have you lost your mind, Harper? A strike team? Face it, this is a lost cause.*"

"No, it's not. Get me tac support and I can turn this around."

"How am I supposed to arrange that for an op that isn't supposed to exist?"

"The same way you re-tasked the satellite. Call it an anti-terrorism op."

"Not a chance. Swiping time on a milsat is one thing. Sending troops into combat to save an asset whose name you won't even tell me is something else entirely."

"I don't have time for excuses, Jiro." She detoured off the road when she reached the gas station at the corner. "There's got to be a way to get me tac support."

"Not without approval from the HQ brass."

She doubled back toward her car. "Then get approval."

"How am I supposed to do that?"

She felt as irritated as Chu sounded. "I don't know. But we're running out of time, so you'd better think of something fast." She tapped her earbud to end the call.

Walking past the Russians' safe house, she needed to believe there was a way to bring Jack out of there, alive and intact. But as she turned her gaze and her steps away from the nondescript bunker, she feared Chu might be right. The safe house was impregnable.

Saving Jack was starting to look hopeless.

No. Stop that. Harper rebelled against her despair. She got back into the Citroën, picked up her carbine, and sharpened her mind for battle.

There's always a way. And I'm gonna find it, no matter what it takes.

• • •

It didn't matter how many times some GRU field officer assured Danko that a safe house was secure. Even after he had confirmed that the glass in the windows was bulletproof, the doors and walls were blast hardened, and that the curtains were lined with Kevlar to block both bullets and shrapnel, he always wondered what detail he might be missing.

Never trust your fate to a castle you didn't build yourself.

He'd read that advice in some dusty tome of Russian history, though he'd long since forgotten who had said it. Some nineteenth-century tsar or other. Not that it mattered.

He peeked through the leaden curtains. Nothing on the street seemed amiss. Just hordes of Somalis drifting through their miserable, poverty-stricken lives, like sewage riding the tide.

There but for the grace of Mother Russia go I.

In the middle of the room, Soltsin and Yakunin secured Bauer to a solid aluminum chair. Soltsin had protested that it seemed like overkill to cocoon Bauer in duct tape, particularly since the man's wrists and ankles were still shackled, but Danko insisted they take no chances.

A tinny voice bleated from the phone in Danko's hand, reminding him he'd been on hold for ten minutes. He lifted it to hear General Markoff bluster, *"Speak up, damn you!"*

"General, this is Major Danko."

The general's mood brightened. *"Major! What's your ETA?"*

"Uncertain. The plane is suffering technical difficulties. Or so I'm told."

His news turned the general's tenor gruff. *"Where are you now?"*

"The GRU safe house, north of Road One." He continued to study the people drifting past on the street outside.

A grunt of acknowledgment. *"Any resistance?"*

"Not so far." Behind him, Yakunin injected the prisoner with a fresh dose of sedative. "And we have Bauer under control."

"Good."

"Not entirely. I think the mission's been compromised."

Skepticism colored Markoff's reply. *"Based on what evidence?"*

"The timing of our plane's malfunction. And reports that Bauer's been working with a partner. A black female operative from Australia."

"I've seen the report. Have you seen her in your vicinity?"

"Not yet." He turned away from the window and faced Bauer, who was slumped with his chin against his chest. "But if she's on to us, it might be a good idea to kill Bauer now and head to the backup exfil site in Ethiopia."

Markoff's voice turned to fire and iron. *"Absolutely not! Moscow wants that man delivered* alive, *Major. President Suvarov plans to make Bauer's trial last for months. It's to be the centerpiece of a political pageant that will humble America for decades to come. So let me make this perfectly clear: If Jack Bauer dies in your custody before we bring him to trial, I will use the full might of Russia's government and its military to ensure that the remainder of your days on this earth are short, excruciating, and drenched in shame."*

Danko knew it was not an idle threat. Still, he took it in stride.

"What if I deliver a video of Bauer's confession? If I can make him name his crimes against Russia and admit his guilt, would that be enough to satisfy President Suvarov?"

A long pause followed his proposal.

"That would depend on the quality of the confession. Tell me what you come up with, and I'll see what I can do." Markoff hung up.

Danko put away his phone and turned toward Bauer. His men looked back at him.

"Titov? Wake him up." He cracked his knuckles. "I need to talk to Mr. Bauer."

• • •

Minutes bled away. Alone in the Citroën, Harper monitored the Russians' safe house through her binoculars as the shadows lengthened and bands of violet tinted the sky on the eastern horizon. There had been no movement around the house. Only once had she noticed any shifting of the curtains inside, as if someone had moved from one window to the next, on the lookout for any sign of trouble from outside. The crowd on the street started to thin. Sundown was approaching, and the city's Muslims were preparing to answer the call to evening prayers.

Harper's phone buzzed on the passenger seat. The screen showed Chu's secure line as the source—the call she'd been waiting for. She answered it. "Tell me something good."

"I wish I could."

She couldn't mask her disgust. "Let me guess: no tac support."

"Worse. Someone at HQ got wise. You've been ordered to terminate your rogue op and proceed to your exfil point outside Berbera by nineteen-thirty hours."

Despite her best efforts to stay calm, she felt her hands close into fists against her will. The shortsightedness of the ASIS bureaucracy never failed to enrage her. "I can't just leave my asset to the Russians."

"HQ disagrees. They've already cut off my access to the satellite, and my system's being shut down remotely by some deputy director in Canberra. It's over, Harper."

"Not for me, it isn't." She wanted to rage, *It's not fair, damn it!* But no one in charge was listening, so she stabbed her self-pity in its heart and remembered how to think like a soldier. If she couldn't bring the fight to her enemies, she would make her enemies bring themselves—and Jack—to her. "Screw the tac team. I'm not that badly outnumbered. I just need to level the playing field. Any luck finding me a safe house or a weapons cache?"

"I thought you might ask me that. Lucky for you, HQ can't remotely erase the scrap of paper in my pocket. Ready to write this down?"

"Go."

"Twenty-nine Wadada Cali Banfas, about three blocks off Saleebaan Road."

She scribbled the address with a marker on the car's dash. "Got it. What is it?"

"An ASIS safe house, stocked with everything you need."

"How do I get in?"

"Passcode on the door is nine, seven, one, five, one, eight, pound sign."

She jotted the code below the address. "How do I explain myself to the housekeeper?"

"Move fast enough and you won't have to. I cleared him out with an emergency evac signal about ten minutes ago, just before HQ shut me down."

"Outstanding. Will my field code open the safe house's weapons locker?"

"It should. But again, be quick. If HQ finds out where you're going, they'll redline you."

She started the car and eased into traffic, careful not to draw attention as she drove by the Russians' hideout. "Jiro, are you still running the hack on the jet?"

"*Affirmative. I ran that off my laptop. I can't help you with tracking anymore, but I can still keep their plane on the ground—for a little while, at least.*"

"Right. Do your best. I'm on my way to the ASIS safe house to gear up."

"*Be careful, Harper.*"

"Chu, did I mention you're a god among men?"

"*Thank me by not getting killed.*"

"Can't think of anything I'd like better. Ping me if anything changes. Harper out."

She ended the call and hooked a right into the sclerotic traffic of Road Number 1. Leaning on the horn wouldn't make any difference. Drivers in Hargeisa had grown deaf to the constant honking on the main roads. Instead, Harper threaded the needle by forcing the Citroën through any openings she could find in the wall of cars. Metal howled in protest as it was gouged, dented, and bent by her brute-force solution to Hargeisa's traffic problem.

In her rearview mirror, all she saw were shaking fists and vulgar gestures from the drivers of cars she had nudged aside. Ahead of her, she saw only obstacles to be overcome.

Hargeisa was a small city. Even though the ASIS safe house was on the other side of town, it wouldn't take her more than ten or fifteen minutes to reach it. But without Chu and his illegal satellite feed to keep tabs on the Russians' hideout, any time spent without eyes on Jack's last known location came with the risk that he might not be there by the time she got back.

She bumped two more slowpokes out of her way as she barreled through a right turn onto the Saeed Highway and raced northward between lanes at 160 kilometers per hour.

The clock was ticking now, for both of them.

• • •

Awareness flooded back in a hot rush. Jack's pulse raced, and his breaths were fast and shallow. He knew this sensation— adrenaline, a heavy dose, to counteract the sedatives he had been given.

His heart slammed inside his chest so hard, he thought it might burst free. Shocked back to consciousness, he remained disoriented for several seconds until his mind caught up to his senses. He was on his back, lashed to a wooden bench, with his hands cuffed underneath it. He was in a small room, with no other furniture, and no lighting save a naked bulb dangling from a frayed wire in the middle of the ceiling. Danko stood in front of him. The other three Spetsnaz lurked at the windows, acting as lookouts.

Danko loomed over him. "You're awake. Good."

"I'm guessing this isn't Moscow."

"There's been a delay in our travel arrangements. As much as President Suvarov would prefer you stand trial in Russia, your confession is really all that matters. If I can obtain it on video, you can stay here."

Jack knew to pay attention not to what Danko said, but to what he left unsaid. "And would I be staying here *alive*?"

Dead eyes and a shark's grin. "You're quick, Bauer. I'll give you that."

"And what, exactly, am I supposed to confess?"

"That you murdered our foreign minister, Mikhail Novakovich."

"Is that all?"

"You also murdered several members of his diplomatic staff—"

"I think you mean his Spetsnaz bodyguards."

Danko continued, "And you conspired to assassinate our president."

"Last I checked, he was still alive."

The commando punched Jack in the groin. Nausea churned in Jack's guts. As he fought the urge to dry-heave, Danko squatted beside him. "No thanks to you, Mr. Bauer." He grabbed Jack's chin and turned his head to face him. "This is the only time I will ask you politely: Will you confess your crimes against the Russian Federation?"

"What happened to Novakovich was *justice*."

Danko reacted with feigned disappointment—an insincere frown and a slow shake of his head. "I should've known you wouldn't take the honorable way out. So be it." He stood and walked to his open duffel. From it he retrieved what looked like a miniature version of a doctor's traveling surgical kit, as well as a collapsible steel baton. He set them on the floor in front of Jack, just out of reach. "For later." He snapped his fingers.

Two of his men left the windows where they had been standing watch and exited to a back room. Seconds later, they returned. One carried an empty metal washing tub. The other dragged a garden hose with a nozzle and had a towel draped over his shoulder.

Jack noted the torture paraphernalia with contempt. "Waterboarding? Is that the best you've got? I expected a bit more imagination."

"I like to start with the classics. To set a baseline and gauge your resistance level." Danko moved to stand by Jack's feet while one of the commandos placed the tub under Jack's head. Jack drew a deep breath before the Spetsnaz trooper pressed the folded towel over his face.

Though he expected the deluge from the hose, there was only so much he could do to mitigate his body's natural fear response as water rushed into his mouth and fractured nose and cascaded over his head. He tried to exhale his stored breath in short bursts, to push some of the water out of his upper respiratory tract, but it was as hopeless as he had feared it would be.

He had been on the other side of this process and knew it was merciless. With his head tilted back, there was nothing to prevent water from penetrating his sinus passages and pharynx. He quickly ran out of breath, and every involuntary cough provoked by the sensation of choking drew a little more water up into his lungs. Primal terror clouded his thoughts, and his muscles thrashed in vain against their cold metal bonds.

The towel was lifted from his face, and the commando with the hose released his grip on the nozzle. Danko put down the bench, once again setting Jack's head level with his body. Hacking and spluttering, Jack turned his head and fought to push the water out of his mouth and airway. Even as air found its way back into his lungs, the dread of asphyxiation lingered.

Danko smirked. "Ready to talk yet, Mr. Bauer?"

He refused to let the Russians see him beg. "I'm a little thirsty. Got any water?"

The wet towel was pushed back onto his face. As Danko lifted the foot of the bench, Jack flashed back to his days as a Delta Force operator, and the mandatory SERE—Survival, Evasion, Resistance, Escape—training he had endured. Part of that experience had been intended to harden his will against techniques such as waterboarding. Despite that, the key lesson he had retained was that no one could hold out for long against this barbaric form of torture. Even the toughest, most willful men he had ever known succumbed to panic in fewer than twenty-six seconds. Being waterboarded felt like drowning without the release of death. For all intents and purposes, the technique was tantamount to subjecting a prisoner to a mock execution.

Water hit Jack's face through the towel. Again he fought his body's involuntary response, but it was too strong. His arms jerked beneath the bench, pulling with such force that he feared he might break his own bones. He kept expecting the Russians to relent, to let him gasp a few desperate breaths before going on, but the torrent seemed endless. Gagging and struggling in vain against the Russians, the water, and his own wild convulsions, his mind retreated into the past, to memories of his daughter, Kim, and her children, of better days free from the strife and grief that had come to define his life over the past sixteen years. . . .

Pain and light banished his hallucinations of the life he had left behind. One of the Spetsnaz pressed on Jack's diaphragm and expelled the water from his airway. Reflex took over then, and Jack's lungs burned as he gulped air like a landed fish.

Danko loomed over him again. "You can make this stop, Bauer. Just confess your crimes, and I promise you a swift and merciful death."

"My only crime was *not* killing Suvarov when I had the chance."

The Spetsnaz leader heaved a disgruntled sigh. "Your dossier said you were stubborn. It failed to note you're also foolish. No one is coming to save you, Bauer. And no one can survive this indefinitely—not even you. Mark my words: For you, this is the end of the road."

Jack took a deep breath. "Then shut up and get on with it. I hate long good-byes."

It was brave talk, a product of pride and fury. But as Danko lifted the bench to tilt Jack's head back, and the wet towel was pulled tight over his face, Jack knew Danko had told him the truth. No one could take this punishment forever. *Sooner or later, everyone breaks.*

Water filled Jack's nose and mouth, and he knew his breaking point was coming.

It was only a matter of time.

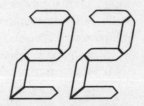

05:00 P.M. - 06:00 P.M.

Just as Chu had promised, Harper arrived at the ASIS safe house on Cali Banfas to find the large T-shaped dwelling ostensibly deserted. She saw no other vehicles near it as she parked behind the building, but she still took the precaution of peeking in some of the windows before she risked going inside. The few rooms she glimpsed looked unoccupied, so she returned to the front door, which was set back from the steps, on a covered porch.

A rusted black mailbox was mounted on the wall beside the door. She pushed it from the left, and it pivoted from the center of its top edge to reveal a digital keypad in a recessed nook. She keyed in the code Chu had given her. A muffled *thunk* signaled the retraction of the magnetic bolt that secured the door against intruders. She opened it and slipped inside.

On the other side, a narrow hallway. She did her best to tread lightly as she moved deeper inside. Behind her, the front door closed with a soft *click*, followed by the *clunk* of its magnetic security bolt snapping back into place. Her footfalls were swift but soft as she moved through the safe house, checking each room to verify it was empty. The last thing she needed now was an unwelcome surprise from a fellow ASIS field operative.

She reached the last room, the house keeper's command center, and entered her ASIS field agent code into its door's keypad. The door unlocked, and she stood to one side as she pushed it open. The room was unoccupied, like the others. Its bank of internal and external security cameras had been left on.

Harper shut off the house's cameras, then rewound the system's stored recordings, past the point of her arrival, to just before the house keeper's hasty exit half an hour earlier. She observed his movements, including his trip to the house's concealed weapons locker—a narrow walk-in, less than one and half meters wide, that was concealed between the walls of two of the bedrooms, and accessed through the back of one room's closet. She fast-forwarded to his departure from the house, then halted the playback and ordered the system to erase all material recorded after that point. *That ought to cover my ass.*

She swiveled her chair away from the security monitors, to the command center's row of laptop computers. There was no time to waste on subtlety. She logged in to the ASIS database in Canberra and called up its dossier about Jack Bauer. His résumé was impressive. He had earned a degree at UCLA before he joined the U.S. Army as an officer candidate. Before long he became a special forces operator. After returning to civilian life, he had remained in government service. First as a SWAT officer with the Los Angeles Police Department, and later with the renowned Counter Terrorist Unit. Then she saw the addendum to his dossier that documented his 270 confirmed kills in the line of duty, and her jaw went slack. *Two hundred seventy confirmed? I don't even want to know how many unconfirmed kills he has.*

Harper pushed past her surprise and focused on the information she needed: his photograph and his list of known aliases. There were more than she expected, even for a man who had done extensive undercover investigative work against the drug cartels. She uploaded his dossier photo into the passport-generating application on her laptop, and concocted biographical information to fit him. *Your new name is John Sullivan. You're Canadian, from Vancouver. Date of birth?* She knocked a few years off his true age, just to be kind. *May 10, 1969.* The rest of his vital statistics she copied from his dossier; then she sent the finished file to the passport printer.

Now to pack a bag for the trip.

The printer hummed and buzzed though its slow digital churn as Harper made her way to the bedroom across the hallway. The closet door was still open. She pushed past the clothes hanging on the rod to find the keypad for the hidden door. It accepted her code, and the door snapped ajar as its locks released. *Let's see what's on the menu, ASIS.*

As she'd hoped, the safe house's weapons locker was well stocked, at least partly because there had been little violence recently in Hargeisa. Harper moved down the narrow space, taking inventory as she went. By the time she reached the end, she had made up her mind.

First, she pulled a Kevlar-reinforced tactical carrier vest off the wall and put it on. Once its straps were comfortably secure, she strapped on a hip holster and filled it with an HK P30, complete with a steel suppressor. Then she tucked three full spare magazines of ammunition for the pistol into the lower left pockets of her vest. Next, she found spare magazines for her carbine. She put three in the lower right pockets of her vest and tossed half a dozen more into a black knapsack, along with an optical scope, three smoke grenades, and a canister of tear gas.

Then she treated herself to the big kids' toys: six bricks of C-4, a box of detonators, and four Claymore-style antipersonnel mines.

Her last stop before leaving the locker was the petty cash box. Her code didn't open it, but a short injection of liquid nitrogen from a canister taken off the safecrackers' shelf and a swift hit with the grip of her HK shattered its lock like crystal. Despite its name, the contents of the box were anything but small: four wads of paper currency totaling ten thousand euros, and a small muslin bag packed with a minor fortune in uncut gemstones.

For expenses, she told herself, stuffing the cash and the stones into her new knapsack.

By the time she returned to the command center, the bulky machine in the corner had finished producing the fake passport. Its photo had printed perfectly behind the holographic watermark; its interior travel stamps had been generated to match foreign customs records created in cooperation with those nations' intelligence services; and the data in its embedded RFID chip had been reprogrammed to match the new identity inside the document.

Good enough for government work. She tucked it inside the knapsack and pushed it to the bottom, beneath the ammo and explosives.

There was only one item left on Harper's mental to-do list. She logged back on to the laptop and erased its record of the creation of the new passport. No doubt her log-ins had set off alarms at ASIS HQ, and it was likely the house keeper was already on his way back with orders to investigate, and to detain her on sight.

Which makes this a good time for me to be someplace else.

Harper walked to her car, tossed the knapsack onto the floor in front of the passenger seat, and climbed in. *If ASIS learns I raided the safe house, I've just torched my career.*

She pushed that worry from her mind. That was a problem for tomorrow.

Today, she had a debt to repay—no matter the cost.

$$\bullet \ \bullet \ \bullet$$

Insubordination was the sort of offense that could be fatal to the cohesion of a small combat unit. Most elite soldiers rarely if ever found themselves in situations where they had to consider going over the heads of their immediate superiors. Of those who did, most chose the path of silence and least resistance. But as Soltsin listened to Danko waterboard the American prisoner in the next room, he was torn between loyalty and duty, between honor and self-preservation.

He didn't want to press the send button on the phone. Once he did, it would connect him to someone with whom the regulations said he shouldn't be speaking. It would be a grave breach of protocol, not just as a Spetsnaz commando but as an officer in the Russian Army, as well.

Maybe if I wait a little longer, it will be over.

The sounds of struggle and protest ceased for a few seconds—and then the splashing of water from the hose into the tub resumed, along with Bauer's muffled cries. Soltsin closed his eyes and wished he could see another way forward. He was no soft-heart. Waterboarding was a valuable aid to interrogation when used judiciously. In practice, it took only the smallest amounts of water to achieve the desired effect, to terrorize the subject into revealing his most guarded secrets in order to bring the induced panic to an end.

That wasn't what Danko was doing. He was using too much water, and applying it for far too long each time. No one Soltsin had ever met could stand even thirty seconds of the treatment. Anything longer than that was just slow murder, a gradual push of the subject's system into emesis so that he could choke on his own vomit.

After the first few minutes, he had become convinced that Danko had lost control—but no one in the unit would call him on it. Now twenty minutes had passed, and neither Titov nor Yakunin had shown any sign of refusing the major's sadistic orders.

Soltsin stared at the phone in his hand. If he didn't press SEND, the prisoner was going to die in their custody, and the entire team would have to answer for it.

He made the call.

While he waited for it to go through, he covered his free ear with one hand to block out the sounds of Bauer's gagging and gurgling.

A woman answered, speaking in a dour voice. *"Extension."*

"Rasputin Seven Two."

"Authorization."

"Midnight sun."

"Hold." It took a few seconds before his call was routed to its intended recipient. General Markoff picked up, sounding impatient and annoyed. *"Well? Did he break?"*

"No, General, he hasn't."

"Who is this?"

"Captain Soltsin, sir."

"Where is Major Danko?"

"Continuing the procedure, sir. But not in a manner I would deem effective."

His report gave the general pause. *"Explain."*

"The major has deviated from known and proven techniques of interrogation."

"*The line is secure, Captain. Speak plainly.*"

"Major Danko is waterboarding your prisoner to death, and unless you order me to stop him, there's nothing I can do."

"*I thought I made it clear to the major that Moscow wants Bauer delivered alive.*"

"That was my understanding, as well, sir." From the hideout's main room, he heard the hacking, desperate cough of Bauer being returned to level for a few moments between sessions. "However, Major Danko seems more interested in breaking Bauer, even if it means killing him."

"*Hrm.*" A long delay followed as the general considered the matter. "*I can't commend you for committing insubordination, Captain.*"

"I expect to face disciplinary proceedings for my actions, sir."

"*Yes. That said, is it possible you're being alarmist? Could the major's method work?*"

"In my professional opinion? No."

"*And you're sure he's breaking established protocols?*"

It was difficult for Soltsin to express his betrayal in such plain language, but it had to be done. "Yes, sir. Major Danko is using too much water for too long a time. Unless his procedure is halted, he will kill the subject without obtaining useful testimony."

"*That is not an acceptable outcome, Captain.*" Over the line, a tired groan. "*On my behalf, order Major Danko to cease and desist all enhanced interrogation of Jack Bauer. If he refuses to comply, I authorize you to relieve the major of command by any means necessary. Is that understood, Captain?*"

"Yes, sir."

"*Contact me as soon as you're in the air to Moscow.*"

"Yes, sir."

Markoff ended the call. Soltsin tucked away the phone and steeled himself to confront his commanding officer. For his own sake, and that of his men, he hoped he wasn't too late to save Bauer. Because if Bauer died by their hands, they were all going to wish they had died with him.

• • •

Delirium and desperation were all Jack had left. He thrashed beneath an endless surge of water, long past the point of fighting to stay calm. All hope had left him. He couldn't remember anything but the fear; his whole existence had been reduced to the struggle between his overtaxed body's desire for death's release, and his killer instinct's fierce will to live.

His spirit was an ember on the verge of being extinguished when the floodtide ceased and his feet were allowed to fall level.

The impact on the concrete floor jolted him enough to dispel the illusion of near drowning. He turned his head and fought to expel the water that had pooled in his sinuses and chest. Between ragged coughs, he listened to the Russians arguing above him.

"You need to stop," said Danko's subordinate. "You're killing him."

"So what if I am? You know who he is, what he did!"

With two whooping coughs that almost turned into dry heaves from his empty stomach, Jack forced out enough of the water to let himself breathe in again.

The subordinate put a hand to Danko's chest, only to have it swatted away. Undaunted, he went on challenging his superior. "If you kill him, we'll all pay for your mistake." An accusatory look at the other two Spetsnaz. "I don't want to die in Siberia. Do you?"

"Don't listen to him!" Danko pointed at Bauer. "That man's a criminal! He murdered members of our government on protected diplomatic soil. He deserves every second of this."

"Stand down," the second man said. "That's an order."

"Damn you, Soltsin! I'll have your head for this!"

"I don't think so, Major. I have orders from General Markoff to cease your—"

"What orders?" Danko's eyes grew as his anger bloomed. "Did you go over my head?"

"You gave me no choice." He looked at the others. "Titov, Yakunin, think before you act. I have orders from General Markoff to terminate this interrogation by any means necessary—up to and including removing Major Danko from command. Do you understand?"

"Yes, Captain," said the younger of the two junior men. His comrade nodded.

"Put away the hose. You're done here."

Danko drew his combat knife and lunged at Jack. "The hell we are!" He sat on top of Jack's legs and reached for the waistband of Jack's pants. "No more games! Confess and you can die like a man! Play hero, and I'll make sure you die in agony—and in pieces!" He turned his knife so that its blade was below his hand, edge forward, a classic knife fighter's grip.

The major leaned in to push the weapon toward Jack's groin. Soltsin seized Danko by his shoulders and pulled him up and back, off Jack, to the end of the bench. "Stop!"

"Let me go!"

Jack's hands were still cuffed under the bench, but his feet, though shackled together, were otherwise free—and the Russians' awkward grappling had just presented him with an opportunity. He lifted his feet and kicked at Danko's blade. Just as he'd hoped, the major tightened his grip by reflex to avoid losing hold of the weapon. Instead, the Spetsnaz commander's face contorted in horror and surprise as the blade sank into his gut.

The room froze for a fraction of a second as the Russians realized what had just happened. In their stunned hesitation, Jack landed one more kick with both feet and drove Danko's blade deeper in as well as upward, toward his heart.

Danko gurgled on his own aspirated saliva; then he gagged and went limp in Soltsin's grasp. His deadweight became too much for the captain to bear. The major's corpse slipped from Soltsin's hands and landed with a *smack*, facedown on the concrete floor.

The three Spetsnaz stared at Jack, who glowered back at them. "Who's next?"

His taunt snapped Soltsin into action. The captain pulled a Taser from Danko's belt and thrust its metal contacts into Jack's ribs. Thousands of volts shot through his soaking-wet body. He convulsed in agony as a charnel odor of burnt fabric and flesh filled the air. Then the edges of his vision closed in and converged, plunging him into the cold comfort of oblivion.

• • •

Amber light painted the sides of houses. Shadows stretched away from the setting sun, long and shapeless. The only people left on the streets of Hargeisa were the ones the Muslims called infidels and heathens, the ones for whom the muezzin's summons to prayer meant nothing. Carts stood folded closed and padlocked; cars were parked in haphazard fashion, several rows deep along some streets, abandoned in haste by those in a hurry to reach the nearest mosque.

Strangely deserted by comparison was Warsame Street, a short diagonal lane of cracked pavement that linked Abdihasan Street and its nearest parallel, Xaji Dalaayad Road. That was where Harper parked the Citroën, just around the angled corner from Abdihasan. A small copse of trees and shrubbery surrounding some compact buildings offered a modicum of cover for a retreat from the Russians' hideout, which was directly across the intersection.

Down on one knee in the foliage, Harper spied the Hummer through her binoculars. *Guess the Russians are still here. As long as Jack's alive, chalk one up for luck.*

She kept her knapsack close at hand while she pondered how to distribute its party favors. Several cars had been parked along the road's shoulders. Though it looked as if they had boxed in the H2, she knew the oversized SUV had more than enough power and mass to bash through that flimsy automotive barricade with ease. All the same, if she made a bid to pull Jack out of danger, the numerous empty cars now littering the area would provide good cover.

Overhead, the sky had shifted from blue to violet in the time it had taken Harper to assess the area. Daylight made a swift surrender to dusk. The sun's dying rays crept up the façade of the Russians' hideout with such alacrity that Harper could almost track them in real time.

She broke cover and crossed the street, taking full advantage of the deepening shadows all around her. Her objectives were simple and clear: predict where the Russians would be when they emerged from the hideout; deduce where they would move to seek cover when she opened fire; anticipate what means they would use to pursue her after she fled with Jack;

and then lay traps to thwart them at every turn.

The Hummer was parked in front of the sole entrance at the front of the building, making that the Russians' most likely point of egress. The areas surrounding the armored truck would need to be prioritized as kill zones. Harper also planned on taking out the Hummer itself—assuming she could get away with Jack before they got him inside the hulking thing.

She knew of several routes through side streets that would be easily passable for the Citroën but be too narrow for the H2. Those were her pocket aces, her paths to freedom. The only risk was that the Spetsnaz—who were known for their adaptability and ingenuity—would tactically acquire (or, in layman's terms, *steal*) one of the other nearby cars and give chase. Based on the slipshod manner in which they had been parked, Harper determined she would need to destroy only the eleven nearest cars to both obstruct pursuit and leave the Russians without immediate access to a new ride.

Another stand of small trees at the corner of the Russians' hideout concealed her sprint behind the house. She noted a large vehicle parked at the back door, hidden beneath a weathered tarp. She lifted it to see a beat-up old Land Rover.

Must be the safe house's backup transport.

Harper stabbed all its tires with her knife, then rolled under the high-clearance SUV to sever its fuel line with one deft swipe of her blade. Pungent fumes from spilling gasoline filled the air as she scrambled clear of the spreading mess.

She worked her way around the back of the house, moving like a ghost through its shadow, until she rounded the far side and reached the front corner facing Abdihasan Street. It was a good vantage point from which to lay down suppressing fire toward her sniping position across the road. She backpedaled fifteen paces, then found a thick knot of weeds—a perfect place to dig in the first of her Claymores, rigged with one of her remote triggers.

The next phase of her preparations demanded she travel light. She left her knapsack behind and took only the few components she needed. With her Austeyr strapped across her back, she crawled along the front of the house, past the steps to the front door. In the nook beside the steps she planted her next Claymore. Once its detonator was primed, she slithered over the dusty ground, to the other side of the truck, and planted another antipersonnel mine against the hideout's foundation, its front toward the Hummer's passenger side.

In a crouch, she jogged back to her knapsack and extracted the C-4 bricks. She broke each one in half and impaled it with one of the miniaturized radio-detonator sticks. It took only a few minutes to pair each to a unique channel on her remote control.

She took a hijab from the knapsack and wrapped it around her head and throat, leaving only the oval of her face exposed. Toting the knapsack over one shoulder, she slipped back into the street and paused by each parked car along her route just long enough to kick half a brick of primed C-4 beneath it. As she passed by the Hummer, she wadded its hunk of plastic explosive into a ball, lobbed it over the nearest parked car, and watched it roll beneath the armored truck.

Three years of varsity softball finally pays off.

Paranoid, she checked the hideout and other buildings along the street for any sign of spying eyes, but all appeared to be quiet. She cut across the intersection and sneaked wads of C-4 below a trio of vehicles parked along the oblique corner where Abdihasan and Warsame streets met. Then she ducked into the cluster of trees near the cars and resumed her somber vigil.

She woke her satellite phone and dialed Chu's direct line.

He answered on the first ring. *"Harper? You okay?"*

"Right as rain. I'm set to go. Release the hold on their jet."

"You sure? If I break off, I can't get back in."

"Trust me, Jiro. Whatever happens, I'm ready. Wipe your laptop and get clear of this. Come tonight, HQ's gonna cry bloody murder. So keep your head down, right?"

"Whatever you say. And Harper? Be careful."

"Always. Now, scat. I got work to do."

Harper ended the call, shut off her phone, and tucked it away. The last thing she needed was for it to ring when she needed stealth. She wasn't worried about missing any calls; the only people who had her number were Chu and her superiors in Canberra. The bosses would only call to shout at her. Chu wouldn't call back—he'd already done all he could.

The rest was up to her now.

She unslung her carbine and was momentarily annoyed the safe house's armory hadn't had a suppressor for it. The approaching fall of night would make her ambush more precarious—muzzle flash from the Austeyr would give away her position from the first shot.

Which means I'll have to make that shot count.

Stretched supine across the rocky soil, Harper had nothing more to do than wait for the Russians to emerge from hiding—and hope Jack was still alive and in a condition fit to be rescued. Otherwise, the night was about to take an ugly turn, for both of them.

• • •

A normal man would have stayed unconscious for up to an hour after receiving a shock like the one Soltsin had put into Bauer; the renegade American began to stir after only twenty minutes.

Despite the fact that Soltsin now wanted Bauer dead as payback for Danko's murder, he had ordered Yakunin and Titov to free him from the bench and prepare him for travel. They had objected but ultimately obeyed because they were loyal soldiers, just as he was—and, unlike their slain former commander, none of them were fanatics. The pair stood between Bauer and the door, while Soltsin stood on the other side of the prisoner and regarded him with contempt.

"Proud of yourself, Bauer?"

Lying on his side with his hands cuffed behind his back, Bauer struggled to sit up and pivot to face Soltsin. His hateful stare mirrored those of his captors. "I did what I had to do. And you'd have done the same."

It was true, of course. What infuriated Soltsin was the knowledge that he had made Bauer's revenge on Danko possible, by interfering and compromising the major's situational awareness. *If I hadn't blocked his view of Bauer, or tried to hold him back, he'd still be alive.* Reason reasserted itself and short-circuited his guilt. *And Bauer would be dead, in which case, you and the rest of the team would all be facing a firing squad or a slow death in a gulag.*

His curiosity nagged at him. He knew he would never have a better opportunity to satisfy it. He suppressed his bitterness before he spoke. "Let me ask you a question, Bauer. When you killed our foreign minister and his men . . . was it professional? Or personal?"

Bauer studied him through narrowed eyes, no doubt trying to deduce whether the question itself was a trap. "Personal."

It wasn't the answer Soltsin had expected. "How so?"

"Novakovich sent the man who murdered the woman I loved. In my home." Pain and hatred burned in his eyes as he looked up at Soltsin. "She died in my arms."

"So it wasn't about the business with your ex-presidents? Or the death of Omar Hassan?"

"I wanted justice for Hassan. But I *needed* revenge for Renee."

Soltsin nodded. Vengeance he understood. It transcended politics. Strange as it seemed to him, it defused his wrath to know that Bauer was a man driven by honor as well as by passion. Something about it just felt so very . . . *Russian.*

A phone's muffled ringing interrupted his musings. The three Spetsnaz commandos looked around the room in confusion until Soltsin remembered that Danko's satellite phone was still in a pocket on the leg of the major's pants. He marched over to the man's corpse, which Yakunin had draped with an old tablecloth from a closet in the back of the house, reached under the improvised shroud, and retrieved the phone.

The screen displayed a local number. He answered in gruff Arabic, "What is it?"

A man answered in halting Arabic. *"Your plane is ready."*

"You're sure?"

"Yes. Mechanic says it is good to fly now."

"We're on our way. Tell the guards at the runway gate to expect us."

"I will."

Soltsin hung up without wasting time on social pleasantries.

He stuffed Danko's phone into his pocket. "The jet's fixed. We're leaving."

He reached down, grabbed Bauer under his armpits, and hoisted him to his feet. "No more small talk, Bauer. This is the end."

The American spit in his face and flashed a predator's grin. "I'm just getting started."

A hard jab in Bauer's solar plexus doubled him over, and a solid punch at the bottom of his rib cage knocked loose a strangled yelp of pain. "I didn't save your life out of pity. I did it because my men and I will suffer if we don't bring you back to Russia alive." Titov opened the front door. Soltsin seized Bauer by his blond hair and yanked his head up, to force him to meet his gloating stare. "But make no mistake, Mr. Bauer. I look forward to *seeing you die*."

06:00 P.M. – 07:00 P.M.

The front door of the hideout opened. Harper slipped her index finger inside the trigger guard of her carbine and peered through the optical scope to line up her shot and choose her targets.

Her crosshairs landed on the first Russian out the door. A flat-nosed bruiser with a crew cut. Toting an AK-74 assault rifle and wearing a tactical vest whose bulkiness betrayed its Kevlar inserts. She shifted her aim past him and found a younger, thinner Spetsnaz prodding Jack outside with the muzzle of his own AK-74. Jack's nose was broken, his hands were cuffed behind him, and he shuffled in awkward half steps because of the short chain on his ankle shackles. A third Russian, a few years older and with aquiline features, trailed Jack and the others out of the hideout into the post-sundown twilight and closed the door behind him.

Sick anticipation churned in Harper's gut. Where was the last Russian? She was certain she had counted four of them leaving the jet and entering the truck at the airport. So why were only three escorting Jack out of the enemy safe house? Was one of them staying behind? She couldn't imagine why that would be the case, but one of the Russians was unaccounted for.

Maybe he's in back, checking the backup vehicle, she reasoned. *But why would they bother when they have a Hummer that's practically an armored car?* It made no sense. Either way, she was running out of time in which to act. If she let the Russians get inside the truck with Jack, she'd have almost no chance of stopping them without getting Jack killed, as well.

She targeted Flat-Nose as he crossed in front of the Hummer. *Do I wait or do I fire?*

Her finger closed on the trigger. The bang of the carbine echoed off every building for blocks around, and its muzzle flash lit up her position like a neon sign. Flat-Nose spun and rebounded off the front of the truck as her shot landed lower than expected, in the center of his vest. The Russian at the back of the group pulled Jack behind the truck, and the younger man charged forward, unloading on full auto in Harper's general direction.

She hit the ground. Bullets shredded the trunks of trees above her, raining splinters on her head. Pinned down, she snapped off a few rounds of suppressing fire, then watched for muzzle flares from the Russians' retaliatory barrage.

A yellow-white flash from the rear of the Hummer. Two more, from behind different cars parked across the street from her position. None of the Spetsnaz had moved where she'd expected. The only people at risk from her Claymores were Jack and his captor. Though she'd planted C-4 under the cars concealing the other two Russians, both vehicles were too close to her own position for her to detonate those charges without catching herself in the blasts.

Another brilliant plan down the tubes. Now what?

More harassing fire ripped up the ground on either side of her. It was clear she needed to attack, retreat, or find a better position. Now that she knew Jack was alive, she wasn't going to leave him, but a charge would be suicide. She shrugged off the knapsack, opened its top flap, and retrieved her smoke grenades. At best, they would give her a few seconds of concealment, nowhere near enough time to flank the Russians.

Another hail of bullets bit chunks out of the trees around her. Even falling back might get her killed if she stumbled into the wrong patch of open ground.

No more playing it safe.

Harper grabbed the smoke grenades, two in her left hand, one in her right. She pulled the pin on the lone grenade with her teeth, then hurled it with a sideways toss at the car across the street. A half juggle transferred another grenade to her right hand. A clamp of her teeth and a twist of her head dislodged another pin, and she chucked the live grenade at the other car.

As the first grenade detonated in a dense bloom of gray fog, she pulled the last one's pin and lobbed it into the street in front of her position. Then she lifted her carbine and pumped bullets through the windows of the Russians' cover cars, peppering the crouched Spetsnaz with shattered glass as the second grenade erupted, adding its murk to the scene.

When the third grenade exploded and completed the pea-soup curtain between Harper and the Russians, she sprang to her feet and started running.

She would get only one shot at this.

If it went wrong, she and Jack were both as good as dead.

• • •

Slumped against the Hummer's rear fender, Jack feigned shock and disorientation. Soltsin, the acting commander of the Spetsnaz team, was perched at the corner of the vehicle, snapping off controlled bursts with his Kalashnikov. His two comrades had charged forward to take cover behind cars parked along the road's shoulder. As gunfire scoured their truck and the front of the safe house, Jack closed his eyes until he identified the attacker's weapon by its unique sound: a Steyr AUG-style carbine. It was Harper.

Dull reports echoed in the street—the sound of smoke grenades. Jack tensed. *If she's popping smoke, she must be moving. Something's about to happen.*

Two more bursts from the Austeyr were answered by the bright music of breaking glass, followed by running footsteps. Soltsin scrambled past Jack toward the other end of the Hummer.

Twin explosions from the street buffeted everything in the lot with overlapping shock waves and crisscrossing storms of burning shrapnel.

A chaos of metal and smoldering debris bounded off the truck and launched Soltsin backwards against the safe house and knocked his rifle from his hands. He rebounded off the house, stunned but still conscious as he struck the ground. He blinked against the furnace-hot surge of air that trailed the blast front, then blindly pawed the ground in search of his weapon.

Jack dived at him.

His hands were still behind his back, his stride still curtailed by chains, but he used his weight to full effect, hurling himself at Soltsin. His shoulder crunched into the Russian's jaw and slammed it shut hard enough to break a few teeth. Jack's clumsy lunge knocked Soltsin on his back, with Jack on top of him. Before the commando could respond, Jack rammed his forehead into the man's nose, shattering its most fragile bone and cartilage, and pounding the back of the Russian's head against the hard ground. Blood poured from Soltsin's nostrils, and his eyes crossed beneath fluttering lids.

Jack rolled off Soltsin and put his back to him. He grabbed the ring of keys from Soltsin's belt and by touch found the ones that unlocked his handcuffs and shackles. He freed his hands first, then his feet, and pocketed the keys.

A blur at the edge of his vision was his only warning—Soltsin's knife plunged toward him. Lightning reflexes honed by years of close-quarter combat training took over. He pivoted into the attack rather than away from it, deflected Soltsin's arm, and thrust the L-shaped inner edge of his hand into the man's larynx. It felt like hitting a tree.

Soltsin lifted his knife for another attack. Jack snared the Russian's arm and kneed him in the groin. An extra tug of pressure bent Soltsin's elbow enough to break his grip on the knife. As it tumbled between their feet, Jack threw a trio of hard jabs into Soltsin's gut before hammering his face with a right cross. The commando stumbled half a step. Jack let go of his arm and put him on the ground with a swift kick to the solar plexus.

The Russian landed hard on his back—right next to his rifle.

There was no time for Jack to disarm the man; he'd be dead before he closed the distance. Going for the knife would be equally futile.

He ran.

A hard right turn put the Hummer between Jack and Soltsin.

Ten yards ahead of him, two bonfires raged. Each roared skyward from the bent, blackened wreckage of multiple cars. The narrow gap between them was choked with smoky fumes, and the blistering heat made him wince and miss a step as his resolve faltered. Passing between them would be a death sentence, but it was his only route to freedom.

He pushed past his fear and sprang forward—then a rifle shot split the air and sent a slug tearing across the side of his calf. It was a grazing wound, but the blaze of pain was enough to knock him off his feet. He landed facedown in the dirt, then twisted to look back.

Soltsin marched toward him, his rifle braced against his shoulder. His cold, merciless glare made it clear what would happen next.

Jack was about to die.

• • •

By the time the C-4 under the cars went up, Harper had been halfway down the road, running flat out. Even still, she'd only narrowly escaped the blasts' main area of effect. The shock wave had knocked her flat into the road's gravel shoulder and pelted her with red-hot chunks of metal.

She'd paid her injuries no heed. Back on her feet, she'd darted across the street under cover of smoke and then doubled back, vaulting and bounding over the parked cars in the south end of the lot before navigating the random labyrinth of smoldering debris between her and the Hummer. A ragged curtain of smoke drifted between her and the truck. When it broke apart, she saw someone sprint toward the burning cars. She raised her carbine—

—then held her fire when she saw it was Jack.

She drew a breath to call out to him.

A rifle shot, harsh and clear, cut her off. Jack stumbled and fell. She turned her head to see the last of the Spetsnaz emerge from cover behind the truck and advance on Jack, his weapon braced against his shoulder.

No time to aim. Harper trusted her instincts and fired, three fast shots in semiauto. One hit the Russian center of mass and knocked him sideways. The second tore through the edge of his shoulder. The last missed him and ricocheted off the truck behind him.

She kept firing and charged. Her running barrage was erratic but served its purpose: it harried the Russian back behind his vehicle. He fired a long burst in full auto as he retreated, forcing Harper to hit the dirt as rounds churned up the earth around her. She felt a jolt of impact and thought she was shot, but there was no pain. *Call that a lucky break.*

She returned fire to push the Russian the rest of the way back into hiding. Her carbine clacked empty. She ejected the spent magazine and loaded a new one as she scrambled to Jack, who lay on the ground, clutching his left calf. "C'mon, mate! We gotta move!"

He reached for her outstretched hand. "Little help?"

She pulled him up with her left hand while keeping her Austeyr pointed at the truck with her right. As soon as Jack was standing, she directed him southward with a sideways tilt of her head. "Fall back! I'll cover—"

The Kalashnikov rattled like a jackhammer on steroids as it sprayed the area with high-velocity rounds. Metal bit into metal as slugs danced through the maze of wreckage.

Jack and Harper ducked behind a quarter panel that had wedged itself into the ground edge-first, like a fallen blade. Another hail of bullets pealed against its scorched, dented surface. She rolled out to the right and returned fire. When the Russian fell back to the far side of the Hummer, she smirked. He'd retreated into the kill zone of one of her Claymores.

She handed her carbine to Jack. "Keep him there."

He took the Austeyr in his blood-covered hands and prairie-dogged over their sheltering hunk of scrap. Despite his injuries and haggard state, his aim was steady and sure. While he kept the Russian pinned under cover, Harper retrieved her remote detonator from her knapsack.

The device emerged in pieces, a broken spaghetti tangle of severed wires and shattered plastic. When she saw the misshapen slug wedged inside its main circuit board, she realized what she had felt hit her during the Russian's wild fusillade. The detonator had saved her life by stopping a round that would almost certainly have severed her spine. Unfortunately, that sacrifice now meant she had no way to make use of the traps she had laid.

She discarded the fragged detonator into a nearby scatter of rubble. "Time for Plan B."

Jack pumped a couple more shots at the Russian. "Do you have a Plan B?"

"Aside from making a run for it?"

More bullets screamed over their heads and tore patterns into the long stretch of empty ground behind them. Jack studied the terrain with a frown. "It's too far without cover. I won't make it." He turned a meaningful look at Harper. "But you can."

"Without you? Not a bloody chance, mate."

He fired off the last few rounds in the carbine's magazine, ejected it, then handed the weapon back to Harper. "We can't stay here." They both ducked lower as more automatic fire from the AK-74 eroded the few large pieces of vehicle scrap they needed for cover. Then Jack's countenance hardened and took on a fearsome quality. Harper knew he had an idea.

Jack dug a set of keys out of his pocket. "Give me your sidearm."

"What're the keys for?"

"The truck."

The prospect of running toward the Russian and his assault rifle twisted Harper's guts into knots. "Are you out of your mind?"

"There's no cover for a retreat, but there is for an attack." He stole another look at the vehicle. "Do you have any more smoke charges?"

"No, just a tear gas canister."

"Even better. Give me that, too."

She dug the canister from her knapsack, but she was still in denial. "This is crazy."

"I know," Jack said. "But it's our only chance." He ejected the full magazine from the HK P30, gave it a cursory check, then shoved it back in. "We need to alternate fire and cover each other when we reload. This only works if we keep him pinned down. Understand?"

A fretful nod. "Got it."

She handed him the tear gas and two magazines for the P30. He tucked the ammo into his waistband and the canister into his front pants pocket. Then they waited for the Russian to empty another magazine on futile suppressing fire.

As soon as his weapon went quiet, Jack rasped, "Go!"

She sprang from cover first and unleashed a halting, staccato rain of bullets around the Hummer. Jack moved a few paces behind her on the right. Just before her magazine ran dry, he took over the task of laying down suppressing fire with her P30. She reloaded on the move. They reached the next piece of cover as a flurry of return fire erupted from the front end of the H2. Sparks flew as bullets pierced the metal hood lying atop a smoking tire.

Jack tucked the pistol behind his back and threw a hopeful look at Harper. "Ready?"

"Set. On three." She hefted her carbine as Jack took out the tear gas canister and stuck his index finger through the ring of its pin. Harper pivoted and waited for the end of the Russian's latest salvo. When she was sure he had to be running low, she started her countdown. "Three." A few more shots pinged off the orphaned car hood above them. "Two." More tiny divots were ripped from the ground beside Jack. "One." But for the crackling of flames, silence. "Go!"

Harper leaped to her feet and unleashed a fully automatic barrage at the truck, whose bulletproof glass and armored side panels registered little more than scuffs as they deflected her attack. Jack pulled the pin on the tear gas canister, waited two seconds, then lobbed it in a high, graceful arc over the vehicle. His timing was perfect: it erupted as it hit the ground, spewing toxic white vapor in a fast-growing cloud.

This time there was no mad salvo of return fire from the other side of the oversized SUV. Just loud and painful-sounding retching and the wet spatter of vomitus hitting the ground.

Jack used the Hummer's electronic key to start its engine. "Go! I'll unlock the doors when we get there!" Together they broke from cover and dashed toward the idling truck.

The Russian staggered to the front of the truck. His eyes were bloodshot and awash in chemical tears, and the front of his black fatigues were flecked with vomit and spittle. Harper knew the man likely couldn't see anything more than the blurriest of shapes—but with a Kalashnikov, that would be more than sufficient to get the job done.

She and Jack dived for cover as the Spetsnaz loosed a wild burst over the hood.

One round slammed into the middle of her Kevlar-lined vest. It felt as if she'd been gored by a charging bull. Blunt force punched the air from her lungs, knocked her flat, and left her gasping and writhing on the rocky ground. The carbine tumbled from her hand, but all she could think about was the terror of not being able to breathe.

The Russian pushed forward around the truck, leading with his rifle.

Jack drew the pistol from behind his back and rolled under the Hummer.

Half-blind, choking, and dazed, the Russian took half a second too long to figure out where Jack had gone. As he turned toward the truck, Jack fired twice, parallel to the ground.

Blood and bone exploded from the Russian's savaged ankles. His finger squeezed reflexively on his trigger as he collapsed, emptying his magazine into the air. He struck the ground howling like an animal, hoarse and inchoate. Then Jack silenced the Russian's primal screams with a single mercy shot that scattered his brains behind his head.

Harper's diaphragm and lungs slowly relaxed enough to let her inhale. Jack rolled out from beneath the truck and crawled to her side. "You okay?"

She grinned. "Nothin' a week in Rome won't cure."

He held up the ball-shaped wad of C-4 she'd lobbed under the truck earlier. "Yours?"

"Used to be. You can keep it."

"Can't say you never gave me anything." He turned his head and listened as distant sirens grew louder. "The cops are coming." He helped her up, then unlocked the truck's doors with the press of a button on its electronic key fob. "We need to get out of here."

"Roger that." She pointed at his bleeding calf. "I'm driving."

"Whatever you say." He opened the rear driver's side door and climbed in. She got in the front. Once they were both inside, she locked the doors and fastened her seat belt. When she looked in the rearview mirror, she was pleased to see he had already strapped himself in, as well. "Good man. Now, hang on. This might get a bit bumpy."

She put the truck in gear and stomped on the gas. It lurched forward, a beast with more horses under its hood than she was used to, and the force of acceleration pinned her back against the seat. It bashed through the wall of burning car parts along the shoulder of the road and scattered even the largest pieces every which way.

As she skidded through the turn onto the busy Road Number 1, a quintet of Jeeps emblazoned with the logo of the Hargeisa Police Department swerved to avoid a head-on collision. Each Jeep was packed with cops decked out in riot gear and bearing assault weapons. It was clear they had come prepared to fight, but none of them seemed to know what to do as Harper barreled past, leaving the smoking ruins of Abdihasan Road in her wake.

In the backseat, Jack dug through the Russians' luggage and pulled out a first aid kit. "Keep it steady. It's hard to wrap a bandage with you running the Dakar Rally."

"Picky, picky." She checked her side mirrors. Flashing lights slalomed around slower cars in the deepening twilight. "The bronze don't mean to let us off easy."

He wrapped gauze around his bloodied calf, then looked over his shoulder. "Nope."

She dodged around a minivan. "Killing Russian special operators is one thing. But I won't fire on peace officers."

Jack frowned. "I'd rather not, if I can help it." He wound a long strip of medical tape around his bandaged leg. Then he pressed his palms to his swollen, bloodied nose and set the break in its bridge with a hard push and a wet snap that made Harper's eyes water just hearing it.

Determined to evade capture, she nudged the fender of a small hatchback to force it into a spin and create an accident that would slow their pursuers. It and a trio of cars crunched to a stop in the middle of the road without serious damage or casualties. "Looks like that did the trick."

Jack pointed forward. "Not quite."

She shifted her eyes from the mirror to the road ahead.

A wall of cars, two rows deep, stood with red-and-blue lights flashing, blocking the corner where Road Number 1 met the Waheen Highway, the only direct route back to the airport. Massed behind the automotive barricade were dozens of police in paramilitary gear, all of them readying assault weapons for action as they noted the H2's approach. Only then did Harper remember that the headquarters of the Hargeisa Police was located at that intersection.

"Remember what I said about it getting bumpy?" She lifted the hand brake and yanked the wheel to the left. The tires squealed in protest as she accelerated through the sudden turn, down a narrow alley whose corners clipped off both side mirrors in fountains of sparks. A high-pitched scream of stressed metal filled the truck's interior as Harper forced it through the too-narrow passage. She feared they were about to get stuck in the middle—but then they slipped out the far side, onto a dirt service road that paralleled Road Number 1, between the rear façades of two long rows of buildings.

The shortest route back to the Waheen Highway was to her right. No sooner had she made the turn than a half dozen police cars and a pair of HPD motorcycles swarmed onto the service road ahead of her. She stomped on the brakes. "So much for the easy way out."

She put the truck in reverse, floored the gas to build up speed, then twisted the wheel left as she lifted the hand brake again, forcing the massive truck through a bootlegger's reverse. As its momentum petered out, she shifted into drive and stepped on the accelerator, churning up dust behind her as she barreled down the service road.

Jack looked back as police bullets zinged off the rear window. "Now what?"

"Back to the highway." The words had just passed her lips when more flashing lights appeared at the far end of the service road. She turned right, down another dirt alley, this one webbed with laundry lines festooned with the evening's wash. "After a little detour."

Undergarments and bed linens flapped over the windshield and windows, as if the truck were passing through the world's most primitive car wash. Women young and old scampered out of the way as the Hummer raced past; then it broke free of the cotton jungle. The path ahead was occupied by wheeled wooden carts huddled beneath a forest of orange umbrellas.

Harper leaned on the horn and put pedal to metal. The engine roared; merchants and patrons scattered. The armored SUV went through the bazaar like a wrecking ball, reducing pushcarts to toothpicks and leaving nothing in its wake but gray exhaust and strangers' curses.

On the other side of the plaza, Harper swerved around more obstacles—minivans parked at oblique angles, tiny clumps of sad-looking parched trees—and then made a suspension-punishing high-speed right turn back onto cracked asphalt. A sign blurred past on her left: AHMED TAKHTUUR ROAD. "Good news," she said to Jack. "This leads back to the highway."

"Bad news." He hooked a thumb over his shoulder. "We still have company."

Whirling lights dominated her rearview mirror again. "Ideas?"

He squinted at the road, then reached for one of the Russians' bags. "Slow down."

"What?"

"Just a little. I need a few extra seconds." He moved fast, pulled something from the bag, and concentrated as he worked with his hands.

Behind them, the sirens grew louder and the lights drew closer. Jack looked up. "More speed! Now!"

She put the pedal down, and the H2 flew like a rocket.

As the lights in the mirror receded, Jack opened his door and dropped something out. Then he slammed his door and ducked. "Down!"

Harper lowered her head as far as she could without losing sight of the road.

Behind them, a flash brighter than the sun blinded her, and thunder split the air. A shock wave lifted the truck and pushed it forward down the left side of the fork in the road. Its bulletproof and blast-resistant rear window erupted inward, a fury of stinging shards that flayed Harper and Jack with tiny cuts.

Five seconds later, they were still alive and moving, and Harper almost didn't believe it. All she saw in the rearview mirror—after the glow faded—were empty overturned cars, buildings without a single window intact, and a fleet of police vehicles stranded at the edge of a deep and smoldering crater.

When Jack sat back up, she cocked an eyebrow at him. "Fancy."

A boyish grin. "*And* I still have my seat belt on."

At the end of the road she merged onto the Waheen Highway and resumed her death race through the city's nighttime traffic as the last hues of twilight faded to indigo.

He pointed at the road. "Don't let up—they still have radios. It won't take 'em long to figure out where we're going."

"What happens when we get to the airport?"

In the mirror, she spied the ghost of a wicked smile on his face.

"Trust me—the airport won't be a problem."

• • •

The floor beneath the backseat was littered with bloodstained gauze pads by the time Harper and Jack veered off the Guleej Haji onto the access road for the airport's runway. Jack dabbed another glass-shrapnel wound dry and dropped the bandage onto the floor with the others. Brief flashes of sapphire and crimson in the rearview mirror snared his attention. He looked over his shoulder at the trio of police vehicles that continued to hound them.

"I'll give them this much: They're persistent."

A nervous look from Harper. "We're coming up on the gate."

"Speed up."

Her face scrunched in disbelief. "What?"

"Trust me."

If she doubted him, she kept it to herself. Her hands tightened into a death grip on the steering wheel as the speedometer needle swung past 145 kilometers per hour and then past 150.

Jack leaned forward, worried his gambit was about to backfire. "Give 'em the horn!"

She forced her palm against the horn three times without slowing down.

Ahead of them, the guards scrambled to open the gate just in time to let the Hummer scream past at 165 kilometers per hour.

Harper was gobsmacked. "What just happened?"

"The Russians paid for an express lane."

Amused understanding. "And they think we're the Russians."

"Bingo. Hang a left. We're taking their jet."

He loaded fresh magazines into her carbine and the pistol as they cruised toward the waiting Learjet. Harper slowed and brought them to a halt a few meters from the plane. Jack used the electronic key to shut off the engine and unlock the doors. "Away we go."

He took the Russians' first aid kit with him as he left the truck. Harper grabbed her knapsack and followed him. As they approached the jet's stairs, he handed her the carbine and kept the pistol for himself. He led her up the steps. When a pilot in a dress white uniform appeared in the hatchway at the top, the man found himself staring down the muzzle of Jack's P30.

"Quiet," Jack said. "Back inside."

Harper cut in, "We don't need him." To the pilot: "Get out. Now."

The pilot wasted no time scrambling down the steps, past Jack and Harper, and then running for his life across the tarmac, toward the control tower.

Jack glared at Harper. "What're you doing?"

"I can fly this thing. Get inside."

They climbed the last few steps and pivoted into the cockpit, where the youthful copilot, who also sported a crisp white uniform with short sleeves and a gold-braided cap, looked up with an expression that made Jack think the kid was about to soil himself. He raised his hands and said in fear-stuttered Russian, "Don't shoot! I'm not armed!"

Jack answered in Russian, "Get off this plane if you want to live."

That was all the invitation the young aviator needed. He sprang from his chair and dashed out the hatchway, down the stairs, and across the tarmac, just as his partner had done.

Harper jumped into the pilot's seat and began checking the instruments of the idling luxury jet. "We're good to go. Close the hatch and strap in."

"Whatever you say." Jack left the cockpit. Through the open hatchway he heard the banshee wailing of sirens—the police were on the tarmac. He pulled up the staircase hatch and locked it down for flight. As he moved aft, he shouted to Harper, "The cops are right on us!"

Her reply brimmed with confidence. "Not for long."

The jet's turbofans pitched upward as Harper ramped up the power. Jack flumped into the nearest seat as the aircraft lurched into motion and pivoted away from the hangars, toward the feeder lane for the runway. Outside his window, he saw police vehicles race toward them. An officer wearing a visored helmet and tactical body armor stood in the back of an HPD Jeep. He tried to steady his assault rifle for a clear shot at the jet.

A left turn by the jet put the police directly behind them, out of Jack's view. Now on a main runway, the jet picked up speed— but so did the police, who took advantage of the broad straightaway to try to pull up alongside them.

Jack leaned into the aisle to holler a warning to Harper— and then he saw that she had bigger problems. They were taking off directly into the path of a 747 on a landing approach. Fear of dying in a head-on midair collision clenched Jack's guts in a knot.

Outside the windows, painted lines on the tarmac melted into a long yellow blur. The pulsing police lights receded as the jet slipped away from them. Then the nose lifted at a steep angle as Harper pushed the aircraft into an almost ballistic profile. The engines screamed in protest, and the combined pressure of takeoff and a banking turn crushed Jack against his seat and left him fighting to breathe for seconds that felt like forever.

A droning roar shook the frame of the Learjet. A white leviathan streaked past outside his window, between the jet and the ground, its quad jet turbines hammering them with deafening turbulence. Seconds later, it banked into open sky and climbed.

Down on the runway, the police vehicles swerved beneath the 747's wings, only to be blown away like tumbling dice by the passenger jet's exhaust. Sparks flew as their lights smashed and their roofs skidded across the tarmac.

Harper called back from the cockpit, "We're clear."

It was the first truly good news Jack had heard in a long time. He spent a few minutes treating the rest of the wounds he had absorbed over the past day, and then he changed the soiled, saturated dressing on his abdominal wound from the ricochet on the *Barataria*.

After he finished, a personal inventory confirmed what he suspected: He couldn't find a part of himself that wasn't exhausted, bleeding, or in pain. He leaned into the aisle.

"Harper? Anyone chasing us?"

"Not yet."

"Tell me if that changes." He reclined his seat until it stretched flat, then closed his eyes. "If we're done saving the world for today, I'd like to pass out for a while."

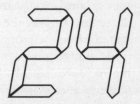

07:00 P.M. − 08:00 P.M.

A hard bump of turbulence woke Jack from a fitful slumber. He was groggy, and the sky outside had grown dark. There were few lights to see on the ground, but the jet was cruising and level, both good signs. When he reached for his seat's controls, he realized how stiff his limbs had become after even a short period of inertia. He would ache tomorrow.

He straightened his seat, rubbed the grit from his eyes, and stood. The compartment was tall enough that he didn't need to stoop, but when he lifted his arms to stretch, his palms pressed against the overhead. Using the leverage to his advantage, he arched his back, then twisted side to side in an effort to work out some of the kinks and tension the day had inflicted. A series of satisfying pops from his lower vertebrae, and he grunted in relief. *Much better.*

The engines' pitch deepened—they were slowing. Jack moved forward into the cockpit. Harper looked up as he entered. "How was your nap?"

"Fine." He sat in the copilot's seat. "How long was I out?"

"Half an hour, give or take." She held up a hand to forestall further conversation as voices crowed through the earphones of her headset. After a few seconds of focused attention, she lowered the headset's mic in front of her face. "Learjet Echo Papa Mike One Nine going to one two one point one." She reached down and adjusted the radio's frequency. "Ambouli approach, Learjet Echo Papa Mike One Nine, level fifteen thousand." More chatter in her ear. "Right to zero six zero, down to nine thousand, Learjet Echo Papa Mike One Nine."

She eased the aircraft into a gradual descent while steering into a gentle right turn. In the distance, on the curve of the horizon, twinkled the lights of a major airport. All at once, Jack's relaxed posture tensed. "Ambouli International? The U.S. naval base in Djibouti?"

A sidelong shift of Harper's gaze conveyed her disappointment. "After all we've been through today? Relax. I'm not giving you to the marines. A pal of mine's gonna meet us on the ground and drive us to the seaport. The Americans will never know you were there."

He wanted to trust her, but his entire life had taught him to expect betrayal. Even his closest friends, like Tony Almeida, had at times become his enemies. It was a hard history to overcome. Harper fixed him with a look that signaled she recognized his wariness. "Don't believe me?" She gestured with her chin to the knapsack on the floor behind his chair. "Open it."

He picked up the canvas backpack and opened its top flap. The bag was mostly empty, but the first thing his hand found alarmed him. He pulled out an unexploded Claymore.

Harper shook her head. "Not that. *Under* that."

Suspicious, he set aside the mine and reached back inside the knapsack. This time he came up with a thick wad of euro notes and a passport. He put down the sack and thumbed the corners of the paper currency. They were all 100-euro bills. A glance at the passport informed him he was now a Canadian named John Sullivan. "What's this?"

"Call it a going-away present."

He tucked the money and the passport back in the knapsack. "Mind if I keep the bag?"

"Suit yourself, mate."

Jack stared ahead into the night. Far below, streets lit by electric light marked the jet's transition from Somalia to Djibouti. Grids and constellations sprawled in glowing designs across the surface, signposts along the route back to the modern world. Gazing down, Jack could almost imagine himself on approach to Los Angeles or New York—

He banished those thoughts from his mind. There was no point torturing himself with memories of places to which he could never return. As it was, images of his family haunted him every time he closed his eyes. His daughter, Kim, his grandchildren . . . they would all grow up without him. To them, he would never again be anything more than a face in a photo album, a blurry figure in seldom-watched home videos.

This wasn't the life he'd wanted, but it was the one he'd had to accept. He refused to pity himself. Life was too short to waste any of it on regrets.

Harper exchanged another round of jargon with the air traffic controller, then resumed their descent to the seaside international airport. "Buckle up, mate. We're on final approach."

Jack strapped himself into the copilot's chair and tried to relax.

He had a fistful of cash and a new identity. Things were looking up.

Of course, he knew they wouldn't stay that way.

They never did.

• • •

Despite the assurances she'd made, Harper hadn't been certain her friend—if Saladin al-Hazred could truly be called a friend— would show up to drive her and Jack to the seaport. But there he'd been when they landed, his crooked teeth shining in the glow of halogen lights and his palm open and waiting for a bribe. Because the ride had been arranged for Jack's benefit, she hadn't felt bad about asking him to peel a few bills off his stack to pay their confidential chauffeur.

Perhaps more eager to disappear than she'd expected, Jack paid Saladin double to get them to the port as quickly as possible, and Saladin had enthusiastically complied.

Now she and Jack stood on a pier of the Djibouti Container Terminal, facing each other at the end of the gangplank to the Dutch container ship MV *Palawan*. Horns blared and deckhands shouted at one another in several languages as the ship prepared to cast off and set to sea.

Jack appraised the ship with a half smile and a nod. "It'll do." His eyes returned to Harper. "Another favor someone owed you?"

"Something like that. I hope you like hot weather. Her next stop is Cape Town."

"Sounds perfect." He adjusted his grip on the strap of the knapsack over his shoulder. "You sure you won't get your head handed to you for helping me?"

A roll of her eyes. "The brass'll be steamed. But thanks to you, I'm getting sole credit for helping the Yanks recover a pair of loose nukes. Something tells me I'll be fine."

He laughed. "If you get a medal, send me a picture."

"If you ever settle down, send me a postcard."

A nod. "Maybe I will." The container ship's horn blared, like the trumpeting roar of some titanic beast. Jack looked up the gangway at the men frantically waving him aboard.

He didn't move. Harper nudged his arm. "Better hurry. Your ride's leaving." He seemed spellbound, lost in thought. She kissed his cheek and broke his spell of distraction. "I don't know what you're looking for, Jack. But I know it's not here." A sad smile. "Time to go."

Moving with reluctance, Jack climbed the gangplank. Ten strides up, he stopped and looked back at Harper. "Have I thanked you?"

She thought it over. "No."

He cracked a weary smile. "I will."

Then he turned and trudged up the gangplank, which the crew pulled in behind him.

Stentorian notes erupted from the container ship's main stack as its propeller churned the water beneath its stern. Crawling at first, the massive vessel picked up speed as it slipped away from the dock and made its way toward open water.

Harper stood on the end of the pier and watched the *Palawan* vanish into darkness.

Contrary to what she'd told Jack, she knew to expect a major reprimand from her superiors when she got home to Australia. She was going to catch hell for letting the infamous Jack Bauer "escape" her custody. But that was a hell she could live with.

• • •

Jack stood on the bow of the *Palawan* and enjoyed the ocean breeze washing over him. It struck him as odd that twenty-four hours earlier he had stood on the forecastle of a different ship, bound for a different port. Now, after an insane series of detours, he found himself at sea again.

He looked forward to a decent night's rest in the ship's infirmary. Unlike the *Barataria,* the *Palawan* carried a number of civilian passengers, enough of them that international maritime law required the ship to employ a licensed physician. Jack chortled to himself. *I might be able to get patched up without having to run from the cops for a change.*

His next steps were a mystery to him. Before the pirates' attack had unraveled all his designs, he had been on the verge of finding a way inside the organization of international arms dealer Karl Rask. Now, all the bribes he'd paid to create his cover identity had been wasted, and all the months he had worked to position himself on the periphery of Rask's operation were squandered. He was back at square one.

The *Palawan* was heading to Cape Town, South Africa. That would be a good place to regroup, Jack decided. There was always no-questions-asked work in Cape Town. Fixers in need of skilled shooters, people in need of unofficial help. When he was ready, he could arrange off-the-books transportation back to Eastern Europe, where Rask did most of his business.

If I can make it back to Chechnya, there has to be someone there who could point me in the right direction, someone who still owes me a favor or two.

Sooner or later, Jack vowed, he would infiltrate Rask's inner circle. And once he did, he planned to sabotage it, one dirty deal at a time, until he burned down Rask's entire criminal empire and left the man himself lying dead in the ashes.

It wasn't the noblest thing to live for.

But for Jack . . . it was enough.

For now.

ACKNOWLEDGMENTS

Of all those who deserve my thanks, my wife, Kara, is at the front of the list, for continuing to give me her love and support during good times and bad.

I also offer my gratitude to my editor, Melissa Frain, and her dutiful assistant, Amy Stapp, for giving me a chance to write a tale of one of my favorite characters; my agent, Lucienne Diver, for negotiating the business details that make my eyes glaze over; my friend Marco Palmieri, for recommending me to Melissa for this gig; and to my friends and fellow *24* novelists, James Swallow and Dayton Ward, for understanding how much this gig means to me.

I also owe heartfelt thanks to my friend, former merchant marine Phillip Sandusky, for sharing his extensive experience and knowledge to help me get straight the technical details for those portions of this story set aboard the fictional cargo ship *Barataria*.

Lastly, thank you, vodka, for making this labor possible on a short deadline.

ABOUT THE AUTHOR

DAVID MACK has been extraordinarily rendered to an undisclosed location, where he currently is at work on his next novel. To learn more, visit his official website, **davidmack.pro,** follow him on Twitter **@DavidAlanMack,** or join his fan page at **facebook.com/TheDavidMack.**